I'LL
FIND YOU

I'LL FIND YOU

a novel of suspense by

CLAIR M. POULSON

Covenant Communications, Inc.

Covenant

Cover image © copyright 2001 PhotoDisc, Inc.

Cover design copyrighted 2001 by Covenant Communications, Inc.

Published by Covenant Communications, Inc.
American Fork, Utah

Printed in the United States of America
First Printing: February 2001

08 07 06 05 04 03 02 01   10 9 8 7 6 5

ISBN 1-57734-801-X

Library of Congress Cataloging-in-Publication Data

Poulson, Clair, 1946-
    I'll find you /Clair M. Poulson.
      p. cm.
    ISBN 1-57734-801-X
    1. Prisons--Officials and employees--Fiction. 2. Ex-prisoners--Fiction. 3. Kidnapping--Fiction.
I. Title
    PS3566.O812 I18 2001
    813'.54--dc21   2001028118
                          CIP

To my mother
for the inspiration she has always been to me.
My love of books came mostly from her.
Also, her devotion to my father, even though
he passed away many years ago,
has always been a great example to me
of true and eternal love.

PROLOGUE

Squeals of little children's laughter mingled with a warm summer breeze before floating cheerfully through the second-story window of Mindy Egan's home. She smiled and looked up from her cleaning. Through the large window of her son's bedroom, she caught sight of an older model green car moving very slowly down the street toward their house. Her eyes lingered longer than seemed reasonable to Mindy; and for reasons she could not fathom, she felt a sharp twist in the pit of her stomach.

Instinctively, she stepped closer to the window where she quickly spotted Rusty in the neighbor's front yard as he played with his constant playmate, Jeri Satch. Both almost six, both with tousled hair, both in blue shorts, and both barefoot, they squealed in delight as they chased a bright red ball across the lawn. Reassured, Mindy smiled and turned from the window as her infant daughter began to fuss in the room across the hall.

Mindy spoke softly to the baby and as she rocked the crib, she thought about how close Rusty and Jeri were as friends; yet they looked so different. Rusty was light-complexioned, with intensely blue eyes and sandy hair—and in spite of being constantly outside in the summer sunshine, he didn't tan easily. Jeri, on the other hand, had dark brown hair, and skin that seemed to tan instantly with the first appearance of the summer sun. Mindy sighed as she reached for the baby whose cries had intensified. But before her hands had touched her daughter, a terrifying scream from outside penetrated the house. Mindy whirled, and tore through the door, across the hall, and to the window of Rusty's room. Jeri was screaming, Rusty was nowhere to be seen, and an old green car was leaving a trail of blue smoke as it hurtled away from the curb.

"I'll find you!" Jeri screamed as Rusty's head popped up in the front seat of the old sedan and then was shoved roughly back down by the driver.

Mindy realized instantly what was happening, and fled in terror toward the stairs. She ran outside, stumbled, fell down the steps, picked herself up, and rushed across the lawn to where Jeri continued to scream and call Rusty's name.

"Mindy, what's happening?" Katherine Satch yelled from her porch.

"Call 911! He took Rusty!" she shouted.

"Who took . . . ?"

"Just call!" Mindy screamed.

Katherine dialed. Jeri cried. Mindy stared in horror as the green car carrying her son turned a corner two blocks away and disappeared. The mild breeze that only moments before had carried the laughter of children now dispersed the blue exhaust.

When the cops arrived minutes later, Mindy described the green car. She tried to describe the driver, but all she could recall was a black baseball cap.

Little Jeri finally calmed down enough to be of some help. "I told Rusty to stay away from the man in the car," she sobbed.

"What did he say to you kids when he stopped?" Officer Howard Green asked.

"He wanted to know where somebody lived."

"Where who lived?"

"I don't remember." Jeri started to cry again.

"Mrs. Egan says he was wearing a black hat. Can you think of anything else about the man that will help us recognize him when we find him?" the officer asked.

"You've got to find him. You've got to get Rusty back," Jeri sobbed. "He's my best friend ever."

"We will, Jeri, but we need your help," he assured her. "What else can you remember?"

Jeri was thoughtful for a moment. "His hands were dirty," she said at last.

"Like with dirt from the ground, or spilled food, or maybe grease?" the officer asked.

Her face brightened momentarily. "Yeah. Like when Dad works on the car," she agreed.

"Good," Officer Green said. "He must be a mechanic."

"He wasn't a mechanic," Mindy said firmly.

The officer looked at her. "Why do you say that?"

"His car smoked. Mechanics have cars that run well," she reasoned.

"Maybe," the officer said, "but not necessarily. What else can either of you recall about either the man or the car? Did it have Utah plates?"

Mindy thought hard. She had no idea. Neither did little Jeri, but she remembered something else. Brightening, Jeri said, "He smokes."

"He smokes," the officer repeated. "And how do you know that?"

"A cigarette fell out of his mouth when he grabbed Rusty," she revealed.

A look from Officer Green to his partner sent the other officer scurrying across the yard. "Marlboro," he said when he returned a minute later carrying the partially burned cigarette in a plastic bag.

More police came. Mindy was assured that the department was doing everything that could be done to locate the suspect's car. Thirty tense minutes passed. Mindy's husband, Patrick, rushed in. He embraced his wife who started crying again. The terrible story of the kidnapping of his son was recounted for his benefit.

Jeri, whose eyes were red, sat tentatively on her mother's lap. "I'll find you, Rusty," she said softly and then, before her mother realized what was happening, Jeri was off her lap and racing for the door.

"Come back here, Jeri!" her mother ordered.

Jeri paid no attention, and in a moment she was outside and running up the street in the direction where the green car had taken her best friend forty minutes earlier. Her mother caught her and carried her kicking and screaming back to the Egans' house.

"The police will find him," she assured her daughter, but Jeri was not buying it.

"It's my fault he's gone. I should have grabbed his hand," she agonized. "I've got to find him and tell him I'm sorry."

"It's not your fault," Officer Green said. "It's the bad man's fault, and we will find him."

They found his car.

They did not find the man with greasy hands who wore a black baseball cap and smoked Marlboro cigarettes, or the little sandy-haired, barefoot boy wearing a bright yellow shirt and blue shorts.

The car had been stolen from a garage in Salt Lake City several weeks earlier. The plates on it were Utah plates but belonged to a 1978 Buick. They too were stolen. The car was only about a mile from town, abandoned in a small grove of trees beside the road. Tire tracks indicated another car had been parked in the grove as well. It appeared that the abductor had left another car there for the very purpose of switching. Now the police had no description to work from.

Rusty Egan, a sweet boy, a well-behaved boy—Jeri Satch's best friend—was in serious trouble. Rusty Egan was gone.

CHAPTER 1

Seventeen Years Later

"I can't eat this hamburger. The grease is so thick it has drenched the entire bun," Jeri said in disgust as she shoved her meal away.

"The food's usually pretty good here, but not always," her roommate, Kate Duffy, said. "Mine must be better than yours though, because I intend to finish it. Then we can go someplace else and find something you like better."

"I'll wait while you eat," Jeri said. "But I don't need anything. I'm really not very hungry anyway."

Kate, a junior, was tall with short, blonde hair, and hazel-green eyes. A physics major at the University of Utah, she was very bright, and had almost perfect grades. Jeri, a year older at twenty-two, was a senior and just weeks away from a degree in accounting. She was good with numbers, but had worked harder than Kate to maintain a decent GPA. Not that she wasn't smart, for she was, but Kate was one of those extraordinarily intelligent students.

And she could see right through Jeri's loss of appetite. "It's all about Warren Tharp, not grease," she mumbled as she lifted her burger to her mouth. "You're worried about your date with him tonight."

A look of pain crossed Jeri's face. "Yeah," she moaned.

"He's a great-looking guy," Kate said after a moment of silence.

"I know." They had been through this conversation before.

"He's a great guy," Kate added.

"Yes, I know," Jeri admitted.

"He's committed to the Church."

Jeri nodded.

"He will succeed in life, and he will make a great husband and father."

"I'm sure he will, but is he for me?" Jeri asked, as much to herself as her friend.

"He's falling in love with you, Jeri."

Jeri flinched, pushed back her long, dark hair, which she always wore straight and parted in the center, and lifted her eyes from the greasy hamburger. The conversation had never gone this far before. "You don't know that," she said defensively.

Kate shook her head. "Everybody knows that. All you've got to do is look at his face when he's with you. He can't see anybody but you." Kate chuckled then added, "He's a smart guy, I'd say."

"He's never told me how he feels," Jeri responded.

Kate placed her half-eaten hamburger on the table and looked Jeri sternly in the eye. "May I be really candid with you, Jeri?" she asked.

"Are you ever not candid?" Jeri retorted, managing a grin.

With a shrug, Kate said, "He likes you a lot, girl, but he's afraid to tell you. You are as cold as a fish with him. He's falling in love with you but is scared to death of being rejected. Give him some time. And you warm up. Loosen up. Have fun. I know you have feelings for him. Let him see it. Don't throw him away, Jeri. He's a great catch."

Jeri looked up as the front door of the restaurant opened. A group of students surged in, laughing and shoving. Their happiness made her feel even more miserable. Yes, she liked Warren. And yes, it could be tough finding a better guy. But somehow, she had just never felt comfortable in his presence. She thought about that for a moment and then fitted her feelings into words for Kate. "Warren's too good for me," she said frankly.

"Too good!" Kate roared so loudly that the milling students at the door all looked her way.

"Yeah, he's a law student. And at BYU, no less. He's super-intelligent, like you. He hasn't seen a B since his mission. I seldom see an A." Jeri went on listing all Warren's great qualities while minimizing her own. Kate listened with growing impatience.

Finally, she had heard enough. "I can't believe you, Jeri! From the moment he first saw you he was struck with you." Kate grinned as she recalled that day. "Let's see, that was at the BYU-Utah football game last fall. And he had courage enough to approach you then, right here in enemy territory."

Jeri didn't need to be reminded. That day in Rice Eccles Stadium as the two rival teams were playing a tense, very close game, he had tapped her on the shoulder and said, "Hi, I'm Warren Tharp. I'm from BYU." A week later, she had gone out with him for the first time. That was nearly four months ago. He continued to be persistent, and she continued to resist. Tonight she intended to tell him she didn't want to go out with him again. And she was miserable.

"Let's not talk about this anymore," Jeri said glumly. "Finish your hamburger and let's get out of here."

Warren arrived at the appointed hour. Kate answered the door of their off-campus apartment. "I was almost late," he said with a grin to the tall blonde. "The freeway was awful."

"You're never late," Kate smiled. "But Jeri is. She'll be ready in a few minutes."

"Great," he said with his usual enthusiasm.

Not so great, Kate thought to herself as she considered Jeri's resolve to dump him tonight. "Yeah," she said to him, "great. Sit down, Warren. Can I get you something while you wait?"

He shook his head and smiled at her, and she felt her face redden. He did things to her that he apparently did not do to Jeri. Warren stood only an inch or so taller than Kate's five feet, ten inches. With his short, brown hair, hazel-brown eyes, and easy smile, he turned her head every time. And he was so easy to talk to. *If only . . .* she thought, but cut herself off sharply. He only had eyes for Jeri. Kate's embarrassment passed quickly, and she and Warren soon fell into easy conversation. When Jeri finally came out, she was determined to have a good time with Warren. She had resolved that at the end of the evening she would tell him this date was their last one. At Jeri's smile, Warren beamed, rose quickly to his feet, and reached for her hand.

Later, as Warren and Jeri left the apartment, Kate felt a twist of pain deep inside. It was partly for Jeri, for she really cared for her roommate, but it was also for Warren. He was going to be hurt tonight, and she hated the very thought.

Jeri and Warren laughed and talked in his car as they drove toward the city center. The date had begun very well. Then it happened. It had happened before. In fact, it happened often enough to keep Jeri from ever forgetting the past.

A young mother crossed the street as they waited at a red light. Holding tightly to her hand was a small boy. He had a tousled head of sandy hair and was wearing a pair of blue shorts! As he walked in front of the car, he looked right at Jeri. Their eyes locked for a moment. The little boy smiled, and Jeri felt a pain in her stomach that was so agonizing she was afraid she might throw up.

Seventeen years had not eased the anguish of that fateful day when Jeri had screamed and called Rusty's name as he was hauled away. Since then, not a day had gone by that Jeri had not recalled that horrifying incident. It had left a terrible scar on her life and on her very soul.

Of course, Warren could not possibly know how seeing a little boy who reminded her of her lost childhood friend would affect her. Nor could she explain. All she could say was, "Take me home, Warren. Please take me home."

He looked at her as he approached the next light and was shocked at how Jeri appeared to be shriveling before his eyes. Her long, dark hair fell across her face, concealing her anguish. Warren's heart went out to her. He had grown fond of this girl. He had to get her to talk about whatever it was that was hurting her before he could try to help her. That did not seem likely now. She had so quickly withdrawn inside herself and was sobbing pitifully, her face toward the passenger window.

Warren took her home. There was nothing else he could do. She wouldn't talk. She wouldn't look at him. She had withdrawn into a world of her own, one he could not penetrate. At her apartment, before he could get out to open the door for her, she did it for herself. As the door swung shut, he heard her say, "Please don't call me again, Warren."

"You did what?" Kate demanded angrily as Jeri tried to tell her why she was home so soon.

"I told him to take me home and not to call me again," she said meekly.

Kate shook her head in stunned disbelief. "Why? Jeri, that's crazy. You could at least let him down easy."

"I had to. I couldn't go on like this," Jeri answered.

"But there must be a reason. And I know you like him, so it must be something else," Kate said, still shaking her head. "You are not a cruel person, but what you did tonight was cruel."

Jeri sat on the sofa and held her head in her hands. She said nothing more, but quietly began to cry. Totally perplexed, Kate moved over, sat beside her, put an arm around her shoulder and said nothing for several minutes. Jeri sobbed, then dabbed at her eyes, comforted by her friend's gesture of concern.

Finally, Kate broke the long silence. "Let's talk about it, Jeri. I'm loud and obnoxious at times, but I can listen, too. Something is wrong. Spit it out. Maybe I can help."

Silence settled in again. Kate was patient. At last, Jeri lifted her head, absently tucking her hair behind her ears. "I like Warren, but I will never love him . . . Oh, you'll never understand," she said.

"Try me," Kate responded softly.

Jeri drew a deep breath, shrugged from beneath the arm of her roommate, and slowly stood. She paced for a moment, then faced Kate. "It happened a long time ago. And I have failed him," she said.

"What happened a long time ago? And who did you fail?"

Jeri turned away and spoke very softly. "Rusty Egan. He was kidnapped."

"An old flame?" Kate asked, stunned by her friend's words.

"He was my best friend. I promised I'd find him. I didn't." As she spoke the tears again began to trickle down her face.

"Let's take it from the top," Kate suggested reasonably, patting the sofa. Jeri sat down again, and for the first time in many years she vocally recounted the kidnapping of her childhood friend, Rusty Egan.

"Nothing was ever heard of him again?" Kate asked when Jeri had concluded her story.

"Nothing," Jeri confirmed.

"And Rusty is the reason you don't, or can't, let yourself develop a relationship with any other man?" Kate asked with new understanding.

"I guess," Jeri said with a shrug. "I've never really thought of it that way, but maybe that's it."

"What happened is terrible," Kate acknowledged. "It is one of the most terrible things I've ever heard, but there is really nothing you can do. You know that, don't you?"

"I guess," Jeri said again. "But I promised."

"Jeri, you were only five years old."

"Almost six," Jeri said.

"Okay, almost six, but it has been, what, seventeen years?"

"It will be seventeen years on June thirteenth."

"Okay, so what are the chances after all these years that Rusty will ever be found. Like you, he would be twenty-two now, right?"

"Yes, we are just weeks apart in age."

"You need to somehow put all this behind you, Jeri, and move on with your life. What you want to do is . . . "

"Kate! You don't understand," Jeri broke in. "I promised him! And . . . and . . . it was all my fault."

"Jeri, you aren't making sense. What was all your fault?"

"That he was kidnapped. I should have grabbed his hand or screamed louder, or thrown dirt in the guy's face. Something. Anything."

"You've thought about this a lot, haven't you?" Kate queried gently.

"Every day for seventeen years."

"Yeah, and you've thought of things you might have done. Jeri, you were just a little girl. Don't kid yourself. There is nothing you could have done. Quit blaming yourself and get on with your life . . . and Warren's."

Slowly Jeri's head began to move back and forth. She rose again from the sofa and said, "There is no future for me with Warren."

"There could be."

"He's out there somewhere, Kate. I just know it."

"Rusty?"

"Yeah."

"And if he is still alive, and I know it's cruel to say it, for he could be dead, but if he is still alive, then he will have grown up in a completely different world from you. You would never know him. If you ever actually saw him, which is extremely unlikely, you would never recognize him," Kate reasoned.

Jeri nodded her head, then she shook it. "I will never forget his eyes—they were such a deep blue. If I ever see his eyes, I will know him. Believe me, Kate, I will know him."

"But there would be nothing you could do for him now. His life will be set, and almost certainly it will not be at all like yours."

"But I promised," Jeri said stubbornly as the phone began to ring.

Kate picked it up. "Hello," she said. After a moment's silence, she went on, "Yes, she's here, but I don't think she wants to talk to anyone right now."

"Warren?" Jeri asked softly.

Kate nodded, and Jeri simply shook her head. Kate spoke into the phone again. "She'll be fine, Warren. Thanks for your call. I'll see you around."

After Kate hung up, an agitated Jeri opened the door, and with a forced smile at her friend and roommate said, "I'm going for a walk," and went quickly outside.

She walked for several minutes on the partially lighted streets, her mind in a turmoil. Kate was probably right. Rusty was gone forever. It was childish, even a little sick to think she might ever find him again. Instead, she had to find a way to put his memory away and go on with her life. Quietly, she prayed as she walked, asking for help, begging the Lord to help her forget, if it was His will.

But as the days and weeks passed, she did not forget.

CHAPTER 2

"Your qualifications are most satisfactory, Miss Satch. I do wonder, however, why you are seeking employment in California when Utah has a strong demand for good young accountants."

Jeri held eye contact with the balding, kindly man who had spent the past fifteen minutes interviewing her. He was the senior partner of a large accounting firm in Sacramento. James R. Akerman was a giant of a man with more hair on his eyebrows than on his head. She sat thoughtfully as she considered his latest question. He waited patiently.

Finally, she said, "I'm not sure. I just felt like this was where I needed to live."

"Needed?" James queried, lifting one massive eyebrow.

That shook her a little, for she could not explain to him about prayer and the whisperings of the Spirit and her long search for a little boy who was no longer a little boy. Sacramento was where she honestly felt she had been directed to move following graduation. And she was sure of the reason. Or at least she felt she was.

When she did not answer right away, he said with a smile, "Perhaps we needed you. Okay, we'll give you a try."

Jeri breathed a sigh of relief and offered a silent prayer of gratitude. The job hunt had been easy. If only the search for her childhood friend could be like this. She returned his smile. "Thank you, Mr. Akerman, for giving me a chance."

Not many weeks had passed before Mr. Akerman was thanking *her*. And that was a big deal, because Mr. Akerman was the head of the firm, and Jeri was the newest accountant. But her work was excellent and quickly came to the attention of her superiors. Mr. Akerman made a trip downstairs to personally commend her on the quality of her work.

As the weeks went by, the company began giving Jeri more and more large accounts to handle, one of which was for a large, private prison. The account was complicated and contained errors from the in-house bookkeepers that made it unusually difficult to keep things in balance. Eventually, Jeri's supervisor told her it might be necessary for her to visit the facility in person and work with the bookkeepers there. "Perhaps you can help them set things up differently and make both your work and theirs a whole lot easier," she suggested.

For some reason, the thought of going to a prison, even though she was assured that her work would be in the office area, gave her the creeps. She delayed as long as she could, but finally, out of fear of damaging the excellent reputation she had built in the office, she made arrangements to drive out of the city and visit the bookkeepers at the prison.

Intimidated was not a strong enough word to describe how she felt as she went through the various levels of security and finally arrived in the cubicle of the chief bookkeeper. Her stomach churned and her mind was in a whirl. She was not sure she could handle this. But as she began the work, the maze of numbers she dealt with soon had her feeling at home. Ms. Gray was a gentle woman with hair that matched her name. And she was easy to work with. She took copious notes as Jeri made suggestions that could improve their bookkeeping system. She promised to work closely with her subordinates, and apologized for making Jeri's work more difficult. She was gracious and sweet. By the time Jeri was ready to leave, she felt like Ms. Gray had been a friend for years. She had even progressed to a first name basis.

It was Emily Gray. "Call me Emily, please," she had been told, and it came easily.

"Emily," she said as she carefully placed her bundle of papers in her briefcase, "how do you get used to working in a place like this?" Her work done, Jeri had begun again to feel uneasy.

"It's like any other office," Emily smiled. "If I had to work back there," she went on, pointing toward the mysterious bowels of the huge complex, "I would probably seek employment elsewhere."

"Do you ever have to go back there?" Jeri asked.

"Not very often. My work is here. But the management wants all of us to be familiar with the facility, and periodically, we are asked to accompany tours just to keep ourselves *in touch,* as they say." She smiled, then her smile became something more of a grin with a hint of mischief included. "That reminds me," she said. The mischief had seeped into her voice.

"Of what?" Jeri asked, feeling just a little apprehensive.

"Of a group that will be going through the prison today. I haven't been on a tour for some time now, and I suspect that management wouldn't object if I went and took a guest," she suggested brightly.

"Oh, no! I don't think I could do that," Jeri objected.

"Sure you could. In fact, I think it would be most appropriate since you will be working with us."

"But I was told I would not have to go back there when I was given this assignment," she responded quickly.

Emily was taken aback. "I'm sorry, Jeri. Of course you don't have to, but believe me, it is safe back there. It's not like you are alone. We are escorted by officers every step of the way. But if you would rather not, that's surely okay with me."

Jeri's face burned. Why was she such a coward? she wondered. Then, taking a deep breath, she said, "I'll do it." No sooner were the words out than panic clutched her chest.

"If you're sure," Emily Gray said, no hint of mischief left, only a look of concern.

Jeri was far from sure, but she had embarrassed herself enough in front of her new friend. "I'd like that," she said as firmly as she could muster.

Thus it was that thirty minutes later, Jeri and Emily, along with a small group of men, were escorted into the rumbling interior of the prison. As doors rolled open and then closed behind them with cold finality, Jeri shivered. Emily noticed. "It's okay. It was the same for me the first time. It gets better. Just imagine how it must be for the men and women who are locked up in here."

"We are locked in here," Jeri said, trying to seem lighthearted and carefree. But her voice trembled and her hands shook.

So far, they had not seen any inmates, but that changed as they entered the intake area. Men dressed in solid-colored jumpsuits were escorted past them. The correctional officer who was escorting them told the group that different colored suits were used for different classifications of inmates, based upon the time they had left to serve, the violence of their offenses, their work status, and other criteria. Those in white were the more trusted inmates who helped with much of the physical labor in the facility.

Two or three of the men in white jumpsuits spoke a polite greeting to the visitors, and Jeri began to relax. She was not sure what she had expected, but these men seemed nice. She returned a friendly, "Hi." They went on about their business and she concentrated on the information the officer was giving.

Before long, Jeri was quite at ease as they were led from one section of the prison to another. She realized there really was nothing to be frightened about. However, when they finally entered the glass-lined corridor surrounding the prison cells, she again began to feel uneasy. Catcalls came her way and several men whistled. Emily grinned. "Those are for you. No one whistles at me and I'm quite certain they don't whistle at these guys."

"Am I supposed to be flattered?" Jeri asked lightly.

"You are a very attractive young woman," Emily said. "And that is the way these men let you know they notice you. Believe me, they don't see many as pretty as you in here."

Jeri was relieved when they finally left the cell blocks. Seeing men locked up like this did not give her any pleasure. In fact, it made her sad. And, despite being nervous herself, she felt embarrassed for them. It was like a zoo, like they were on display behind the large sheets of bullet-proof glass.

Next, they proceeded through the recreational area, where several men were engaged in a variety of physical activities. Some where playing handball, others ping-pong. A half-dozen were involved in a noisy game of basketball. Finally, they approached several men who were working out with weights in a well-equipped room. Here, no barriers separated the inmates from the visitors and Jeri felt her flesh crawl as they approached the men.

Bare from the waist up, this group was clearly in excellent physical condition. In fact, although she felt herself growing red from embarrassment again, Jeri could not help but admire the well-built young men. Bulging muscles moved smoothly and attractively, tan skin gleaming with perspiration. "These men spend several hours a day with the weights," the officer said. "I ought to do as much."

Then he turned to the inmates. "How's it going today, guys?" he said. One of the men, a tall, especially good-looking young man, was just getting off a bench after lifting what looked to Jeri like impossibly heavy weights. He stood and turned toward the visitors. "Doing as well as can be expected," he said with a grin that rocked Jeri to the very core as he looked directly at her with his deep blue eyes. He had a strong face with a prominent jawline and square chin. Jeri couldn't take her eyes off of him.

"Hello, Randy," Emily said. "It's good to see you."

"Same here," he said, his eyes only momentarily darting from Jeri's face before swinging back again. "Who's the chick?"

Jeri was paralyzed. All she could do was stare at the ruggedly handsome face of the sandy-haired young man. "This is Jeri," Emily said. "She's here to help with the prison accounts."

"Jeri?" the young man said, his face suddenly very serious. "Jeri who?"

He was still looking deep into Jeri's eyes, and she knew she should speak. She tried, but her voice wasn't functioning. Emily came to her rescue. "Jeri Satch."

The look on his face then matched her own. And the easygoing con was suddenly speechless. One of the other fellows chuckled. "Sorry, miss. We don't see gals who look like you in this place very often. And Randy here, he's kind of shy."

The correctional officer spoke to another of the men, and then he said. "Well, we better keep moving. You men take care."

With an effort, Jeri tore her gaze away from the young man with the deep blue eyes, sandy, shoulder-length hair, and massive muscles. She could scarcely breathe. The rest of the tour was a blur. Emily kept looking at her with concern and finally asked, "Jeri, are you all right?"

One of the men in the tour broke in with a chuckle. "She's just not used to seeing men with physiques like those weight lifters have."

"I'm fine," Jeri muttered. But she was not fine. She was very *not fine*. In fact, she was deeply shaken.

Back in the office area of the prison a few minutes later, Emily said, "I'm sorry, I shouldn't have taken you back there. I didn't know it would frighten you like that."

Jeri waved her off. "No, it's all right. I'm glad you did. There really wasn't any reason for me to be afraid."

"Something is wrong," Emily insisted.

"I'm fine."

"You're pale, your eyes have a wild look about them, and when you were in the weight room, I thought you were going to faint."

"I thought so, too," Jeri admitted.

"So what was it that upset you?" Emily asked softly. "Was it the strength of those inmates?"

"No. It was nothing. Really," Jeri insisted. "I'll be fine. It's just . . . just . . ."

"Just what?" Emily broke in.

"I don't know," Jeri said awkwardly. "I guess it was upsetting to me seeing those men locked up like that, their freedom gone. They seem so . . . so normal, I guess."

Emily chuckled. "They are, in a sense. They just made errors in judgement, committed criminal acts, and are being punished. One day each of them will again be out on the street and you would never know they had been in if you didn't know them. Hopefully, they will leave here better men, although a lot of them return time and again."

"It's too bad," Jeri said. "I'm sure many of them are basically good guys."

"That's true. On the other hand, some of them are basically bad guys," Emily said. "And don't ever forget that. There now, you're looking better. Sorry for the shock it gave you back there."

"I'm fine, really. Thanks for letting me see what it's like. It's not something I will soon forget."

An understatement, Jeri thought as she drove her car back toward the office a few minutes later. No, she would not soon forget. In fact, she would never forget. What she did not know was whether she would act upon the shocking fact she thought she had learned that day in the weight room of the prison, and if she did, how she would go about it.

For so many years she had been certain she would recognize Rusty's eyes if she ever saw them again. The strong young man in the weight room had those eyes! Of that she was sure. And that grin. It could have been on the face of her childhood friend and made a perfect fit. Finally, the look on his face when he saw her was almost confirmation in itself. Randy—that's what the handsome inmate was called. Of course, she had never expected that Rusty would keep the same name after he was kidnapped.

But was that man Rusty? Or was she wrong? How could she ever know? And considering where he was, did she even want to know? These and a hundred other questions haunted her as she drove back to the office.

It couldn't be, she kept telling herself, yet her heart told her it was. But why in prison, she thought with a heavy heart. And what horrible thing had he done to land himself in such a place? Her head buzzed. Her stomach rolled. Her hands were clammy. "Rusty, is it you?" she asked the bleak interior of her car.

She expected no answer. And in that, she was not disappointed.

CHAPTER 3

Randy Moore, Inmate #556770, sat on his bunk, slowly shaking his head. "What's the matter, Moore?" his cell mate, a hard, mousy little man of about forty asked. "You seem kind of glum."

Looking up, Randy said, "They brought this group of visitors through the prison today."

"Yeah, I know. I saw them," Chum said. "There was a gal with them. A real looker."

"That's what has me puzzled. She looked at me like she thought she knew me," Randy told him. "But there's no way. And it gets more weird. I swear there was something familiar about her. But I don't know what it is."

"Ah, you're just dreaming," Chum said with a grin. "You'd just like to know her, is my bet."

"Not really. She's way too classy for me. Anyway, I'll be in here for a while yet." Randy closed his eyes, his head down.

Chum watched his cell mate for a moment and then frowned, something he did a lot. "More to this than you're saying," he observed.

"Maybe it's her eyes," Randy said, keeping his own closed. "They were almost as dark brown as her hair. Only thing I can figure. She must have eyes like someone I used to know."

Chum continued to watch him. His face grew harder. He began to clench and unclench his fists. Randy looked up and saw the change in his cell mate. And he knew immediately what it was. Chum was thinking about *the money*. He always got like this when he was thinking about *the money*. Randy wished, as he had many times before, that he had never confided in Chum.

But he had. A half-million dollars taken in the robbery that put Randy in prison was hidden. Only Randy knew where it was. But he'd made a promise to Chum that bound the two of them together. Randy had claimed he lost the money when his car had careened into the river the night the cops caught him. But that was not true. Randy thought the cops doubted it, too, and that was what he had told Chum. The little convict was quick to point out that the cops would be watching him when he got out, and would follow him when he went to get the money.

Chum was also quick to come up with a solution. For a fourth of the loot, after both men were free, Chum would get the money for Randy. The deal was sealed with a handshake, and even though Chum was small, Randy had an uneasy feeling that to go back on the deal with his cell mate of nearly two years could well prove fatal. Chum was thoroughly mean. Randy had learned that after the first few weeks of their forced association, but not until after he had confided in him.

Chum addressed the subject of the money, as though he knew Randy was thinking about it. "Don't go getting no ideas about sharing the money with some gal," he hissed.

"Oh, come on, Chum," Randy said in as light a tone as he could muster. "That's crazy."

"Not so," Chum broke in. "You and me got a deal. Just don't forget it. And this gal nor none other ain't gonna get in the way of that deal."

"That's right," Randy confirmed. "But this gal, she's nobody. Why, good grief man, I don't even know who she is, and anyway, she's from a whole different world than me. I'll never see her again. I'm just puzzled why she looked at me like she did, that's all."

The hard look on Chum's face did not soften, and his eyes got that peculiar glint that made Randy's palms sweat. "Make sure you don't forget, that's all," Chum said in a voice that made Randy's insides churn.

"A deal is a deal," Randy agreed, hiding the uneasiness he felt. "And I won't forget. When me and you are both out of this joint, we'll have some spending to do."

Chum nodded his head. "That's right. Now forget that gal."

"What gal?" Randy asked with a grin.

Chum's face finally softened. "That's my boy," he said quietly. "You'll be all right yet."

But Randy did not forget her. As the days passed, the girl's face haunted him. And her eyes—those beautiful, sparkling, dark brown eyes—were frozen in his memory. And the more he thought of it the more he was convinced that he had seen her somewhere before. He searched his memory. There had to be something there. But no matter how much he pondered, nothing came of it. He was careful not to tell Chum about his fascination with those memorable eyes.

In turn, Chum sensed a difference in Randy. The young convict had become somewhat withdrawn and overly thoughtful. Suspicion, anger, and resentment burned inside the older inmate. Charles Chumbian, alias Chum, aged forty-something, was not a trusting man. In several shallow graves across the country, corpses moldered: morbid, undiscovered evidence of what became of those who gave even the appearance of betrayal to the suspicious eyes of Chum, and also of those who stood in his way of getting what he wanted.

Though serving time only for simple burglary, Chum was an undiscovered and extremely dangerous mass murderer. Not even to a cell mate he pretended to like did he divulge the sinister secrets of his past. Nor did he hint at the terrible fate in store for Randy Moore when Chum had his greedy hands on the stolen money, all of the money, none of which he would ever share.

***

Jeri Satch stared at the numbers in front of her. Despite the suggestions she had given Emily Gray at the prison, the figures were a mess. Several phone calls over the past two weeks had failed to bring about much improvement. Another trip to the penitentiary was necessary.

The thought made Jeri tremble. Although she had tried every way she could conceive of to convince herself that the inmate she knew only as Randy was not her childhood friend Rusty, she was afraid he really might be. The thought kept her awake at nights, and distracted her at work. It brought on repeated periods of choking tears, and frightened her more than she cared to admit. She was afraid of the prison, but felt compelled to return there and find some excuse for seeing him again, to look at him more closely, to study those captivating eyes, to speak to him, to get a feel for what or who he really was. What she *really* wanted was to see him and come away knowing that Randy was not Rusty, to end this nightmare so she could continue to hope and search for her lost friend.

She reached for the phone, intending to call Emily. Her hand trembled. She replaced the receiver and stared at the phone. Tomorrow, she thought. Perhaps I'll call her in the morning. It was late in the afternoon, anyway. She had another account that needed her attention. She turned to it and busied herself, trying to thrust away the uneasiness that had settled upon her.

Back in her apartment that evening, she was cooking a light dinner when the phone rang. The sound of the familiar voice she heard lifted her spirits instantly. "Kate!" she almost screamed and was surprised with herself when tears began to flow.

"Okay, Jeri, what gives?" Kate asked sternly.

"Nothing, it's just good to hear from you," Jeri said. "You can't believe how lonely it is here. I'm looking for a roommate, but right now I'm still living alone."

"Are you sure you're all right?"

"Of course I'm all right. I love my job, and we have a great ward here. This apartment is really nice. Lots better than where you're living, for sure."

For the next twenty minutes, the two friends chatted amiably. Just talking to Kate relieved much of the tension Jeri had been feeling the past few days. But Kate was perceptive and she finally brought the conversation around to the missing childhood friend. "So how goes the search for Rusty?" she asked unexpectedly.

"Huh?" Jeri asked, caught off guard.

"I guess I should ask, are you seeing any guys?"

"Not dating them," Jeri answered.

"Jeri, I wish you would. Rusty will probably never show up, and if he does, like I told you before, he'll probably . . ." Kate broke off abruptly as she heard a gasp on the line. She waited a moment and when Jeri said nothing, she asked, "Is there something you're not telling me? Remember, I'm a good listener."

Silence prevailed for several seconds. Finally, Jeri spoke in broken, hesitant phrases. "There is this guy . . . I'm sure it can't be Rusty . . . his eyes . . . and the way he looked at me . . . can't be Rusty."

"Okay, girl, let's back up and start over."

"Oh, it's nothing, I'm sure. This phone call is going to cost you a ton. You don't have time for my problems." Jeri wiped her eyes as she spoke.

"Jeri, are you crying?" Kate asked.

"A little," Jeri admitted.

"Okay, quit worrying about the cost of this call. Tell me about this guy you met."

"Well, I didn't really meet him. I just saw him," Jeri began.

"Where?" Kate asked.

"In . . . in . . ." she started, but cut herself off. She tried again. "I have an account I do some work for. They have terrible books. I went there to meet with their chief bookkeeper. I saw this guy there. His name is Randy."

"Where is there?" Kate asked firmly. "What kind of business does he work at?"

"He doesn't work. Actually, he was working out there, lifting weights," Jeri explained. She was having a very difficult time saying Randy was in prison.

"Oh, you do the accounting for a health club or something," Kate stated. When Jeri did not respond right away, she asked, "Not a health club? So what is it?"

"A prison," Jeri blurted.

It was Kate's turn to be silent. She was stunned. Finally, over the next few minutes, the story came out. Kate, practical as always, finally said, "You've got to find a way to see this guy again. You can't go on thinking it's Rusty when it almost certainly isn't."

"Yeah, right. I've got to go back anyway. They're still making a lot of mistakes on the books."

"Then you'll see him again?" Kate asked.

"Well, I don't know. You see, they have a normal office," Jeri told her. "The prisoners are not allowed there. And there are over two thousand of them."

"Then ask for another tour. Or better yet, ask to see this one guy.

You've got to clear this up and do it quickly. If you don't, you'll drive yourself crazy."

That was what Jeri needed to hear. She was grateful for the reinforcement Kate had just given her. "Okay, I'll do it," she replied firmly.

"Great," Kate said enthusiastically. "Let me know. Call as soon as you've seen this guy again. And, Jeri, I'll be praying for you. It can't be him. It just can't. A prisoner. That's even worse than I had imagined. Oh, and there is one more thing I've been going to tell you. It's what I really called about."

"Let me guess," Jeri said quickly. "You've met a guy."

"Well, yes, sort of," Kate admitted.

"Okay, so tell me about him. And he had better be great, or I won't let you go out with him," Jeri said with a chuckle.

"He's great, but . . . well, you know him already."

"From the ward there?" Jeri asked.

"No, from BYU," Kate revealed. She plunged on. "I've gone out with Warren a couple of times."

"Great!" Jeri squealed. "That's neat." And she really meant it.

"Not so great, Jeri," Kate countered glumly. "He's still crazy over you. I think he only asked me out so he could grill me about you."

"You like him, don't you?" Jeri asked.

"Yes, but I don't mean to interfere with . . ."

"Interfere!" Jeri interrupted. "How could you be interfering? He's not for me. I told you that. I told both of you that."

"I know, but he's still not convinced," Kate told her. "I think he'll be calling you."

"Tell him not to, then."

"You know Warren, Jeri. You don't tell guys like him what to do. He'll be calling you. And if you change your mind about him, I promise, I won't stand in the way."

***

To call the night sleepless seemed like an understatement to Jeri. Tumultuous would better describe it. In any case, she dragged herself into the office a minute late, determined to visit the prison that day and find a way to see the guy they called Randy. And despite the outcome of that encounter, she was also determined to cut Warren off sharply when he called, *if* he called.

Putting her other accounts aside, Jeri began working on the prison figures. As she hoped, she found a repeat of an old problem. She dialed Emily who agreed to meet with her that afternoon. Jeri put the prison account away and settled restlessly into other work. But her mind kept creeping forward to the afternoon. She skipped lunch and arrived at the prison early.

As badly as she had wanted to come, deep depression settled over Jeri as she was admitted beyond the first set of electronically controlled doors. Emily smiled when Jeri entered her office, then she frowned as she said, "I'm sorry that we keep causing you headaches. What have I done now?"

Jeri forced a smile and said, "Oh, it's not that big of a deal, but it is the same old thing again." She opened her briefcase and began to pull out papers. "Anyway, it's not you, it's one of your staff."

"That makes it me," Emily said firmly. "And I promise, I'll get things corrected."

For the next hour, the two women worked amiably, but as they finished and Jeri began to gather things up and put them back in her briefcase, Emily said quietly, "What's really bothering you, Jeri?"

"What?" Jeri responded, surprised.

"You look pale, Jeri. You look like something is eating on you." Emily smiled reassuringly and added, "I'm sure it's none of my business, but if you feel like talking, I'm a good listener."

Jeri hesitated. She had been wondering how she could go about getting another escorted trip into the cell block area of the prison, but how much did she want to tell this woman about her problems? Emily sat silently, waiting as Jeri considered what to do. Finally, she made up her mind and asked, "Can we talk in confidence?"

"Oh, absolutely," Emily assured her. "If there is anything I can do to help you, I'd love to. You are such a sweet girl."

Her motherly concern soothed Jeri's fears and she said, "Let me begin by telling you a story from my past." Emily listened attentively but did not interrupt as Jeri proceeded with the story of Rusty's abduction so many years before. When tears began to flow down Jeri's cheeks, Emily had to rub her own eyes. Jeri did not mention that she had promised Rusty that she'd find him but she did explain how his image had haunted her over the years.

When Jeri had concluded the story, she stopped, not sure how to mention the guy she saw in the prison and how she wanted to get another look at him. Emily helped out. "So why is it that you are suddenly so troubled now? It sounds like you've lived with this nightmare for a long time and it hasn't stopped you from getting your degree and a very good job. It's something more. Please, tell me about it."

Jeri knew she had to go on, but it was so difficult and embarrassing. She wiped her cheeks dry with the clean tissue Emily offered, then she said, "You remember how I was when we were touring the prison the other day, don't you?"

"Oh, yes, and I'm so sorry," Emily began.

"Don't be, please," Jeri begged. "Let me explain what really happened. I'm afraid I was less than honest with you. You see, it has to do with Rusty."

"Your lost childhood friend," Emily said softly.

"Yes. This is embarrassing. Stupid even. But . . . but . . ." she stammered.

"Go on," Emily urged.

"That guy that was lifting weights," she began.

"There were several," Emily reminded her. "But you must be referring to the tall, good-looking young one."

"Yes. They called him Randy. When he looked at me, he smiled." Jeri began to tremble. Emily placed a hand on hers and gave her a reassuring smile. "This is crazy, I know," she resumed. "But his eyes, his smile. They were . . . they were . . ."

"Rusty's?" Emily asked perceptively.

Jeri dropped her head and nodded, wiping at her eyes.

"And you want to see him again," the kindly woman said. "That can be arranged, but first, let me tell you something about him. Randy is one of the more popular prisoners back there, both among inmates and staff. He's courteous, which is not true of many of them, and he's intelligent. He always has a smile for visitors, like he did for you. But he is also a very bad man." Emily frowned deeply. "He has quite a long record, mostly burglaries, petty thefts, that kind of thing.

But the big one, the one that landed him in here, was an armed robbery. No one was hurt, thank goodness, but Randy got away with a half-million dollars. The money was never recovered. He claimed it was lost when the car he was driving, just before he was arrested, plunged into a rather large river. Rumor is that he had already hid it somewhere and intends to get it when he gets out. So despite his looks and demeanor, he is considered one who probably won't change, simply because he doesn't seem to have any remorse at all for his crime."

Jeri nodded. "I just need to know, that's all," Jeri said. "I'd really like to see him again, now that the shock has worn off. It's almost certainly not Rusty. But I would just feel better if I knew for sure . . . if that's even possible."

Emily nodded in understanding. "I'll see what can be arranged," she said as she pushed back from her desk and rose to her feet. "Wait here, I'll be right back."

"You won't tell anyone why . . ." Jeri began.

"Absolutely not. I'll make up a reason for your request to see him. Hang tight. I shouldn't be long."

Permission was granted, but rather than requiring Jeri to go back into the prison blocks, she was told she would be allowed to see him through the glass in the visiting area. "You may speak to him if you like," Emily told her. "But remember, he won't know why you have requested a visit or even who you are. Handle it like you want, but don't expect too much."

"Thank you," Jeri said with a sigh. "It's more than I could ever expect." As she spoke she held up one hand. It was trembling slightly.

"Are you okay?" Emily asked. "All you have to do is look at him if you want to. You don't have to say a word."

"I know. I'll see what happens, I guess. Thank you for giving me this chance."

***

"You have a visitor, huh?" Chum said after the intercom announced his name. "You never have visitors."

Randy just shrugged. "Probably a cop or something, wanting to know where the money is."

Chum's face grew dark. "You won't say anything." It was not a request. Randy was uneasy, and again, he wished he had never said anything to Chum about the money he had hidden.

Randy stood and stepped to the mirror. He ran a brush through his long, thick hair, and faced the steel door, uncomfortably conscious of Chum's eyes on him. When the door opened, and he stepped out of the cell, Chum said, "Careful what you say, Randy."

As if it was any of his business.

It took several minutes before Randy was finally ushered into the small visiting booth and the door shut behind him. There was no one on the other side, so he pulled out the chair and sat down. He examined the glass. There was no phone through which to speak, but he already knew that the sound of his voice, should he choose to use it, would carry through the area around the glass, a specially designed sound system that nothing physical, like paper or metal, could be passed through.

He sat patiently, wondering if a mistake had been made when the door on the far side of the glass opened, and the blood drained from Randy's face. It was the girl, the attractive brunette, who had left him so unsettled in the weight room a few days before. What could she be doing here? he wondered.

Jeri's eyes were down; she was not looking at him. She found her chair and sat down, her eyes still staring downward. Randy could not take his eyes off her face. Her skin was smooth and tan, and her lovely face with the soft, curving chin was framed by straight dark hair, very long and shiny, and parted in the middle. Randy guessed she was about five feet seven. Something about her seemed so familiar. And she wasn't just attractive—she was beautiful. He was mesmerized. Finally, she took a deep breath and then looked up and directly into his eyes. He stared back at her, neither of them attempting to divert their gaze, for several long moments. He knew those eyes! He knew this girl! He couldn't be wrong. But how? It was impossible. It was crazy.

The look on her face when she finally broke eye contact mirrored how he felt his must look. She said nothing, but she was trembling, and her eyes began to glisten. Finally, unable to stand the suspense any longer, Randy broke the silence. "Do I know you?" he asked.

She jerked when he spoke, and her eyes, which had been surveying him, met his again, briefly, then she looked down at her hands which she held folded delicately on her lap. If Randy was anything, he was not a coward, although his experience with members of the opposite sex was extremely limited. "Well, do you know me then?" he asked, a little more forcefully this time.

She opened her mouth as if to speak, then it snapped shut. She looked up, her eyes scanning his face. Randy waited, but his patience was wearing thin. Finally, she spoke. She said only one word, and that in the form of a question and in the voice of a little girl. "Rusty?"

He found himself swept back through the years of his life, before the pain, the heartache, the anger, the hatred, and other emotions that had helped to form who and what he now was. His mind went back to something he had forgotten, but which now struggled to make its way to the surface.

Rusty.

The word hammered at him, it made his head pound. He closed his eyes, putting his hands over his face, his head down. *Rusty.* What was it? Why did it sound so familiar? He had to hear it again. He mumbled, "Say that again."

"Rusty?" she repeated, in the same little-girl voice.

The fog in Randy's mind began to lift. He squeezed his eyes shut tightly. A face appeared. A young face. A little girl's face. Long dark hair. Smooth tan skin. Perfectly white teeth. Sparkling brown eyes. Like hers. Like the girl opposite him in this horrible place. A name. He needed a name.

The face faded. No name. No face. No memory.

He looked up. Jeri's face peered anxiously through the glass. She was leaning close to it. He leaned back, shaking his head gently. "Did you remember something?" she asked in a very mature, grown-lady voice. A very pretty voice.

"I . . . I don't know. I thought . . . no I don't know what you are talking about. Rusty. Is that supposed to be someone's name?" he asked.

The girl nodded, disappointment clouding her eyes, dejection on her face. "Sorry, but I guess I can't help," Randy said.

"Well, thanks anyway, Randy," she said in a voice that was clearly becoming choked with emotion.

He smiled at her. Despite his troubled life, Randy had always been able to smile. That was what had carried him through much of the pain and misery he had endured. And it had served him well when he wanted something from people who otherwise would not give him anything. "My name is Randy," he said, still smiling. "Would you mind telling me yours again?"

She hesitated, then rubbing at tear-filled brown eyes, she said, "I'm Jeri. Jeri Satch."

The smile dropped from his face like he had been slapped. Again, he felt his mind tumbling back through troubled years. And again he bowed his head, put his hands over his face, closed his eyes tightly and tried to remember. Remember what? There was nothing to remember. He didn't know this lady. He hardly knew any ladies. In his world, as far back as memory went, he knew only the man who called himself Uncle Bill and a succession of hard, angry women. Ladies like the one through the glass were not a part of his world.

And yet, there seemed to be something. Something beyond . . . beyond Uncle Bill . . . beyond the beatings, and the starvation, and the humiliations. But what? He could not grasp it.

Jeri. So familiar. *Rusty.* So familiar. So close. Yet so far away. Then there was nothing. He looked up. There was a hopeful look on her face again. Never in his miserable life had he wanted to fulfill someone's hopes like he did now. But why? He didn't even know this girl, and anyway, all his life he had been taught to take what he could get, not to help others!

No problem. He couldn't help anyway. He couldn't remember anything that would help her. He didn't know what was happening in his head, but whatever it was, he told himself, he didn't know this lady. He couldn't help this lady. She was very pretty, but there was no reasonable reason why he should help her. So he shook his head and said, "I don't know why you came here, but we obviously don't know each other. Sorry." He grinned and added, "Too bad, because you are one good-looking chick."

Her face colored, and her eyes misted again. Her whole body shook. She stood, unsteadily. She looked at him for a long moment, smiled a sad smile, then said, "Thank you for your time. I'm sorry I bothered you. I thought you might be someone I used to know."

"Sorry," he said. And in a way he actually was.

She stepped out of the visiting booth. His door opened and he too stepped out. It was like going back in time, back to an old world. His few moments with the girl who called herself Jeri had been like living in a different time and place. Despite her obvious sadness and disappointment at him not being who she thought he might be, she had been like a light to him. Someone refreshing and sweet, unlike anyone he had ever known. The thought that he would probably never see her again depressed him, put him in a dark mood.

Back in the cell block a few minutes later, Chum looked up from the book he was reading and asked, "So who was it?"

Randy's dark mood caused him to snap, "No one you'd know."

Chum came to his feet like a striking snake. "That wasn't what I asked. Who was it?"

Randy looked Chum in the eye and could see the hatred and anger there. He relented a little, but he was not about to tell Chum all about his recent visit. So he said, "It was someone who was looking for someone she used to know. Got the wrong name. It wasn't me she was after. She felt like a fool. So did I."

"Seriously? You didn't know this girl?" Chum queried, his eyes not quite so intense.

"Never seen her in my life," Randy lied. "Like I said, she thought I was someone else. Same name, but a long-lost brother. She apologized for wasting my time. Like I had anything better to do." He chuckled and was relieved when Chum dropped the matter and went back to his novel.

As Randy climbed onto his bunk and flopped down, all he could think about was the beautiful brunette, and wonder if sometime, somewhere, he had actually known her. But no, that wasn't possible. He tried to force her from his mind. Not an easy thing to do.

***

Jeri's mind was in a whirl as she returned to the prison offices. Seeing Randy again had only added to her confusion. She had hoped to be able to come away from this meeting with the certain knowledge that he was not Rusty Egan, her long-lost childhood friend. But looking in his eyes had only made it seem more likely that he was Rusty. And his strange reactions when she mentioned the name Rusty and then her own, were not what she had expected. Could he really be Rusty Egan?

She hoped not, for this guy was not what she would have wanted Rusty to have become, not that she knew what she expected. She had always wanted him to turn up dashing, debonair, and a good, honest person. That had been unlikely and very foolish.

"How did it go?" Emily greeted Jeri as she entered the book-keeper's office again.

"I don't know," Jeri said dejectedly.

"You mean you still don't know?"

"That's right. Listen, I better go now."

"You don't want to talk?"

"Not really. But thanks for everything, Emily," Jeri said, not wanting to be impolite, but also not wanting to spend another minute in that depressing building.

"Call me when you feel better," Emily offered. "If I can help, I'd like to."

"Thanks," Jeri said, picking up her briefcase and walking briskly from the office.

CHAPTER 4

Over the next few days, Jeri tried very hard not to think about Randy. She had prayed for help in forgetting about him and getting on with her life. She had not prayed for help in knowing if Randy was or was not Rusty. Somehow, despite all her doubts, she already knew. She had found Rusty.

Now she must forget him.

When invited to a multi-stake young singles dance, she forced herself to go. She danced with a dozen different guys, told herself she was having fun, and went home and cried herself to sleep. When one of them called and asked her out a couple of days later, she made up an excuse, then kicked herself for not accepting. How could she forget Randy/Rusty if she didn't begin to date? She promised herself that she would accept a date with the next guy who asked her out. She even noted her commitment in her journal, for that way she felt it would be dishonest to refuse.

The very next evening, the phone rang and Jeri picked it up, thinking about her commitment. If it was a guy, she would go out with him.

It was a guy.

It was Warren!

"Hi, Jeri," he said, sounding as if he were in the next room. He didn't have to tell her who it was. She knew his voice so well.

"Warren," she said. "What are you doing?"

"I'm missing you, Jeri," he said, and from the tone of his voice, she knew it was true. "How are you doing?"

"I'm doing fine," she said. "How is law school going?"

"It's going well, but I needed a break."

Jeri began to feel very uneasy. "A break?" she asked.

"Yes. Just a short one," Warren answered brightly. "I don't have any classes Thursday or Friday, so I decided to take a little trip."

"Warren, where are you?" Jeri asked nervously.

Warren chuckled. "California."

"California?"

"Yeah, you know, Sacramento. I was lucky and got an early flight. I'm at my hotel now. And since the evening is not too far gone, I wondered if you would mind if I came by."

Jeri's first impulse was to say "No," but she remembered her commitment to herself. It seemed more like a trap now, but what could she do? "Yeah, okay, that would be nice, Warren," she said.

Surprisingly, it was nice. She actually enjoyed his company, more than she ever had before. She found herself attracted to him in a way she had not been when they were dating. The only problem was Kate. She felt guilty, because she knew how Kate felt about him. But she remembered Kate's promise that if anything ever developed between her and Warren, she would not stand in the way.

They went out for ice cream and then visited a park where they simply strolled and talked. To Jeri's delight, thoughts of Randy caused very little interference. They talked about law school. She told him about her job and how much she enjoyed it. She told him about her ward and what a great bishop she had. And when he asked to see her after work the next day, she did not hesitate.

They spent the weekend together. She even took him to Church with her on Sunday. When it came time to catch a plane that afternoon, she found it hard to say good-bye. "I'll be back," he promised, and she did not discourage him.

That night, as she got ready for bed, she kept thinking about Warren and what a great four days they had enjoyed together. And for the first time she wondered if finally, after all these years, she could forget about Rusty and let a relationship build. She hoped.

The phone rang and she reached for it, looking at her watch, wondering if Warren was home already and calling to let her know.

But it was not Warren. "Jeri, it's Kate. How's it going?"

It was going fine. For the first time in a long time, things were good. But could she tell that to Kate, after having just spent four enjoyable days with Warren?

Kate made it easy. After some small talk and catching up, Kate asked, "So did you find Rusty or not?"

"Yeah, I think so," Jeri said.

"That prisoner?"

"Uh huh."

"How do you know?"

"I went to see him. I visited him in the prison."

"Same eyes?" Kate asked.

"I'm sure. And same face, only older, of course. And he's so tall now—must be six feet three at least."

"What did he do to get put in prison?" Kate asked. "If you don't mind my prying, that is."

"Of course not," Jeri told her. "You're my best friend. He is in for armed robbery."

"Oh, my!" Kate exclaimed.

"Yeah, my thoughts exactly," Jeri agreed. "He stole a half-million dollars. It's hidden and he plans to get it when he gets out of prison."

"He told you that?" Kate asked in astonishment.

"Oh, no. They told me that at the prison. They say he said it was lost in a river, but they don't believe that at all."

"That's awful," Kate moaned. "Does he remember you?"

"He claims he doesn't. We didn't talk much."

"What was your impression? Do you think he remembers you?" Kate asked.

"Well, sort of," Jeri responded. "I mean, you should have seen his face when I called him Rusty and then again when I told him my name. But he said I had the wrong guy. We left it at that."

"Not exactly your type anymore?" Kate asked gently.

"Not exactly. He's a criminal now. A bad one, I think."

"So how did it go with Warren?" Kate asked with a suddenness that took Jeri's breath away.

"How . . . how . . ." Jeri stammered.

"How did I know?" Kate asked with a chuckle. "He told me he was going down to surprise you. I was tempted to call and warn you, but I decided to let things take their own course. So how did it go?"

"Fine." What else could she say?

"Just, fine? Nothing more?"

"We had a good time." Jeri felt awful. "I'm sorry, Kate. I don't mean to hurt you."

"Jeri, I encouraged it, remember?" Kate said sternly.

"Yes, I know, but that was before you went out with him. It isn't fair of me."

"Jeri, I told you, I will not interfere. I think you had more than just a good time, didn't you? And I'm glad. Really I am. So go for it girl. It sounds like you finally have that old memory out of your system. So let it happen." Kate sounded sincere. Jeri hoped so, and for all she knew, maybe this time something *would* happen. Time alone would tell.

"Thanks Kate," Jeri said. "You're the greatest."

"So is Warren."

Yes. So is Warren.

***

Randy Moore, Inmate #556770, was having a hard time sleeping nights. Between thoughts of the girl in the visiting booth and the ever-increasing animosity of his cell mate, Randy was tighter than a drum. Chum was convinced that someone else was after the money. Nothing Randy could say seemed to dispel the notion from the mousy little inmate's greedy mind. If it wasn't for the threat of extended prison time, Randy would beat the little pest to a pulp. It was tempting. And it was frustrating that he couldn't do it—but he couldn't.

And that girl, Jeri. Her face, her eyes and her voice all seemed to assail him each time he closed his eyes. He couldn't quit thinking of her. And it kept him awake a lot of the time. But finally, late on Sunday night, he fell asleep. He dreamed. The dream woke him with a start.

Drenched in sweat, he thought about the dream, and then he remembered. In the dream, a little girl had shouted at him not to talk to a man in an old green car. But he had done it anyway, and the man had grabbed him and shoved him in the car. The little girl had screamed, "I'll find you!"

The man was Uncle Bill. The little girl had long, dark hair, beautiful brown eyes, and was wearing blue shorts. But it was her voice, as he thought about it, that finally triggered his memory. "Rusty," the girl in the visiting booth had said. And it was the same voice as the little girl in blue shorts. And now her name, Jeri Satch, came back to him with such clarity that he wondered how he had ever forgotten.

For the rest of that long night, Randy lay awake remembering. He recalled the events of the day Uncle Bill had snatched him from in front of the house where he had lived with a loving family. He couldn't recall their faces, but he remembered the feelings of security and love he had felt there. He had never experienced those feelings since.

As he replayed his childhood in his mind, he became increasingly angry. He had always hated Uncle Bill. But his former feelings paled in comparison to the hatred that seethed within him now. How could he have forgotten how he came to live with Uncle Bill? Then he began to recall the terrible things Uncle Bill had done to him, things he had not wanted to remember, and it began to make sense. He had forced himself to forget. But now it was all back. And all because of a little girl who had made a promise, and had kept that promise.

He had to see her again. He had to talk to her.

Randy didn't fool himself. He and Jeri were worlds apart, but at least she could help him learn more about who he really was, and he would like that. Not that it would change who he had become, but somehow he wanted to know. Maybe someday he could look up his real family. And maybe not, for he knew he was very different from them now. But he really wanted to know.

Then, when he got out, after he got his half million, he would find the man he had always known as Uncle Bill. And he would even the score!

***

Shortly after Kate and Jeri concluded their phone conversation, Warren called to say he had made it safely home. They talked for well over an hour. Jeri mentioned Kate's call but she did not give him a lot of details. After she finally hung up, she felt lonely, depressed. She found herself missing Warren terribly.

As Kate must be.

Jeri dropped her head into her hands and cried.

The very next day, she got a call from Emily at the prison. "I've tried to make the changes you recommended," she told Jeri.

"Oh, it's great," Jeri said. "I shouldn't have to make another trip out there if your staff keeps doing the kind of work they are now."

Emily cleared her throat and Jeri shivered. "Actually," the book-keeper said, "I'm really calling to ask you to come. But not to see me."

Jeri groaned. "Is it about Randy Moore?"

"Yes, it is."

"Who wants to see me about him?"

The answer she got was not one she wanted to hear—especially after Warren's visit. Randy wanted to talk to her. "The warden said it's very important to Randy that you come. The warden himself asked me to see if I could get you here."

Jeri quickly thought of a way out of it. "I can't. It's not work related, so I better not drive all the way out there."

Emily chuckled. "I'm sorry to do this to you, but the warden anticipated that. He said you are welcome to come in the evening."

Jeri swallowed hard. She remembered again the little boy getting in the old green car and despite what he had become, she knew she had to go. "When?" she asked.

"Tonight, if possible," Emily responded.

***

It was a sober Randy Moore that greeted Jeri through the glass that evening. "Hi," he said. "Thanks for coming."

She studied his face for a moment before answering. He looked very tired, like he hadn't slept well for some time. His long hair was neatly brushed, and his teeth gleamed. It looked like he had just shaved; there was no dark shadow on his face. The muscles of his arms, his chest, and his shoulders bulged attractively against the white prison garb.

"So what can I do for you?" she asked, a little more sharply than she had intended.

"I'm sorry if I'm putting you out," he said. "But you are the reason I can't sleep nights. I just need a few questions answered, if you will do that for me."

"I'll try," she said. This time she was more contrite. The look on his face and in his eyes was not only one of fatigue, but of pain. She couldn't help but wonder what terrible things he might have suffered over the years.

"Thanks, Jeri. First, what does Rusty stand for?" he asked. "I mean, that was just a nickname, wasn't it? Because of the color of my hair?"

"You remember?" she asked, astonished after their last meeting.

"Yes, I remember. I haven't slept well since you were here the other day. Much of it has come back to me. I'm who you thought I was. So, what is my name?"

"Rusty Egan," she told him. "And Rusty is your actual name."

"I see." He leaned forward, his face very near the glass that separated them. "Are my parents still alive?"

"Yes. Your mother writes to mine every Christmas. They have moved a lot over the years. Losing you was very hard on them."

"They probably hate me, don't they?" It was more of a statement than a question.

"Hate you? Rusty, they could never hate you. Why do you say that?"

"Because it was my fault. You warned me. That is, if you were the little girl that was my friend. You told me not to go with him, not to get in that old green car. But I let him grab me. They must hate me for that," he explained.

"You were five, Randy."

"Rusty. Please call me Rusty. I'm not Randy Moore. That's the name Uncle Bill gave me. I never knew that before, but now I do. I hate the name. I hate him!" His words were hurled in anger from his mouth. His face became red as he spoke.

"Who is Uncle Bill?" Jeri asked, hoping Rusty would not lose control of his temper. There was so much she wanted to know, and so much he needed to know. And this would probably be the last time she would ever see him.

"He's the guy that took me. I lived with him until I ran away when I was fifteen. I hated him then, and I hate him worse now. But he will pay for what he has done. I'll make sure of that."

"Randy . . . I mean, Rusty, you mustn't talk like that. Please."

His face darkened, "And who are you to tell me who to like and who to hate?" he asked angrily.

Tears sprang to Jeri's eyes, and Rusty's face softened. "I'm sorry, Jeri," he said in subdued tones. "It's just that you have no idea what my life has been like. Look at you. Pretty, well-dressed, educated, a good job. But me, I'm a criminal. Always will be. And he made me this way. I can't change now."

Jeri shook her head. "But you can. Anyone can." She wiped her eyes. He looked at her, his eyes so full of pain and anger that it tore at her heart. "Rusty, you told me the other day that you were not who I was looking for. Now you say you are. What happened? Why did you change your mind?"

"I didn't. But you made me think. And I . . . I . . ." he stammered and then stopped.

She broke in. "You what, Rusty? Tell me."

"It's stupid. Crazy, even," he insisted.

"Please, Rusty," she pleaded.

"Well, okay," he said, lowering his eyes. "I had a dream last night. But you know how dreams are. They get things all mixed up and that. But it was enough to make me remember, that's all."

"What did you dream about?" she insisted. "It must have really been dramatic to make you remember something you had forgotten. And how did you forget?" she asked. "How could you ever forget something like what happened to you?"

"You don't want to know," Rusty said, lifting his head. There was anger in his eyes again, and a look so intense that it frightened her. "I think I made myself forget. I had to."

Jeri left that alone but asked him again to tell her about the dream.

"It was screwy, I think," he admitted, his face softening and some of the anger fading from his intense blue eyes. "Let me just ask you a few questions. How were you dressed that day?"

"The same as you," she answered.

"Blue shorts?" he asked.

"Yes! We both wore blue shorts. Was that in your dream or do you just remember it?"

"Both, I guess." He smiled, and a mischievous look appeared on his ever-changing face. "You were cute in blue shorts. I'll bet you'd really look good in blue shorts now."

Jeri blushed. "Probably not," she said uncomfortably. "What else did you want to know?"

"Sorry," he said, "I didn't mean to embarrass you, but you are a very pretty gal."

"Thank you," she said, not sure she liked getting compliments from a criminal, even if that criminal was Rusty. He was not the same Rusty she had known—far from it, she reminded herself.

"The car Uncle Bill took me in was green, wasn't it?" he asked, the smile gone, the anger reappearing.

"Yes, and it was old and beat up. The cops found it not too far away. He must have switched cars," she told him. She was amazed at the speed with which his emotions changed. She wondered about his mental stability.

Rusty put both hands over his eyes for a few moments, deep in thought. When he looked at Jeri again, he said, "I remember now. He had another car in a bunch of trees. He said something about how the cops would never find us so I just as well quit crying. I didn't, and he hit me in the face with the back of his hand." As the memory of that came back, his eyes grew even more angry. "He'll pay for that and a lot more," he vowed.

Jeri found herself sympathizing with him. How could the man do that to a little boy? It seemed so horrible. She could see why he was so angry. And she wondered what other awful things Rusty had suffered at the hands of the man he knew as Uncle Bill.

"Did I have a little brother or sister or something?" Rusty asked.

"Yes, your mother was tending to your baby sister when you were kidnapped. Was that in your dream, too?"

"No," he said slowly. "I just seem to remember that." He looked at his lap again for a moment, then looked up and asked, "Did you shout, 'I'll find you,' as Uncle Bill drove off with me?"

Jeri nodded.

"But it was just an accident that you ran into me here, wasn't it? You haven't really been looking for me all these years?" he asked with a sheepish grin.

She wasn't sure how to answer that. A man like him, a criminal, a bad man, would never understand about prayer. Finally, she simply said, "I never stopped looking."

"But why?" he asked, leaning close to the glass again. "Why did you look for me? You were just a little girl then."

"You were my best friend," she said simply. "And it was my fault he took you. I never stopped looking."

"Your fault!" he said with a hard laugh. "It was my own. You tried to stop me. I can remember that now."

"I should have grabbed you," she said, "but I didn't."

A smile creased his face again. "You're forgiven," he said.

She found herself smiling at him. "Thank you."

"Time's up, Moore," a correctional officer said as the door opened behind Randy.

"Just a few more minutes, please?" Rusty asked.

"Nope, time's up. Say good-bye to the chick," he ordered.

Rusty turned back to Jeri. "Thanks for coming. You've been a lot of help. But I didn't get half my questions asked. Will you come back?" he asked.

"I . . . I . . . don't know," she stammered.

"Please. I just need to learn more about who I am, or at least who I was," he pleaded. "I know we can never be friends, and I'd never even ask that. But you found me; please, help me learn a little about myself."

"We'll see," she said as she felt her resistance fading.

"Thanks," he said, and he was gone . . . again.

It almost felt to her like that other time, many years ago, when he was jerked out of her life. But this was different now. He was a hardened criminal. She was a faithful Mormon girl. Their worlds were different.

And there was Warren.

CHAPTER 5

The phone was ringing as Jeri fumbled with the key at her apartment door. She had stopped by the store on the way home and her arms were full of groceries. By the time she hurriedly placed the groceries on the table and reached for the phone, it had stopped ringing. She glanced at the caller ID. As she suspected, it was Warren, and she saw that he had attempted to call her a half dozen times during the evening. She checked her voice mail, and sure enough, he had left her not one, but three messages.

"I'll keep calling," he said each time, "until I reach you."

"You won't need to," she said aloud as she began to dial.

"Where have you been?" Warren asked as soon as she identified herself to him. "I've been trying to reach you all night. I thought you said you'd be home tonight."

She did not feel like telling him about Rusty. There was no need, and anyway, Rusty was nothing to her now. She had found him. She had answered his questions—at least all he'd had time to ask. And her heart was racing at the sound of Warren's concerned voice. There was no need to upset him now with something that was over. A phase in her life that had already served to nearly ruin her relationship with Warren once before was best left in the past.

"Sorry, I've been shopping," she said as lightly as she could. "I usually do that on Saturday, but, well, you know, last Saturday was kind of busy."

He laughed. "And a good day it was," he said, and he did not press her further for an explanation of her evening.

An hour later, he said, "I guess I better go. If I keep making calls this long, I'll have to drop out of law school."

"I made this one," she reminded him with a chuckle. "And I'll spend my money how I like. Other than a couple of student loans and my rent and car payment, I have nothing essential to buy."

"Except groceries," he reminded her. "As long as it took you tonight, that must amount to quite a bit."

"Are you saying I'm fat?" she asked.

"Oh, no! Not at all. You are beautiful," he told her. "And I'm sorry about your phone bill. It was me calling you, so I should pay it."

"Forget it, pal," she said. "It was worth every penny. I've missed you."

***

That night, it was not Warren who entered her dreams; it was Rusty. "Tell me who I am," he kept saying to her, and she awoke with those words on her mind. Twice more during the week, she dreamed similar dreams, and each time she awoke when he begged, "Tell me who I am." The last time was Saturday night, and for an hour after that, she lay awake. When she left the prison Monday night after her visit with him, she had no intention of going back. But the recurring dream and his repeated plea left her feeling guilty. She had to go back. But she could not let him or his questions of the past interfere with her newfound relationship with Warren. For some reason, she felt that if Warren knew about Rusty and her interest in him, even though it was not anything like her interest in Warren, he would disapprove strongly.

All through Church that morning, Jeri's thoughts jumped from Warren to Rusty and from Rusty to Warren—different kinds of thoughts, but all very intense and unsettling. Finally, after Church, as she was preparing some dinner, she decided that she had to either see Rusty again or forget about him altogether.

But after eating, she had been unable to decide for sure what to do. Finally she knelt beside her sofa and prayed. "What should I do?" she asked the Lord. "Please help me."

For several minutes she discussed her plight with the Lord, then she finally arose, and the first thing she saw was her scriptures on the end table where she had left them after Church. She picked them up, and opened them at random. She found herself staring at the twenty-fifth chapter of Matthew. She had underlined several verses in that favorite chapter in the past, and as her eyes rested on verse thirty-four, she began to read. A few moments later, she was reading verse thirty-six, and she was stunned. Why, she asked herself, had she selected this particular scripture? She read the last phrase of verse thirty-six again. It said, ". . . I was in prison, and ye came unto me."

She read it half a dozen more times before going on to the next few verses. She stopped on verse thirty-nine and read it again. There the Savior was saying, "When saw we thee sick, or in prison, and came unto thee?" She was trembling by now, but she pressed on to verse forty. There Jesus was answering the question from verse thirty-nine. ". . . . Verily I say unto you, Inasmuch as ye have done it unto the least of these my brethren, ye have done it unto me."

Slowly, Jeri closed the book and slid off the sofa and to her knees. She had received an answer. She thanked the Lord. She now knew she had to see Rusty again, for he was truly her brother, and he was in prison. And furthermore, she had caused him to remember the past. Now maybe she could help him in some way. Surely she could. Else why was she directed to those particular verses of scripture?

Glancing at her watch, she knew there was plenty of time to get to the prison while visiting hours were still going on.

***

"You still haven't told me why you got your hair cut," Chum said to Randy. His eyes were hard, distrusting. "There's something you aren't telling me. Who was it you saw Monday night in the visiting room? Was it that same girl again? Come clean, Moore, if you know what's good for you. You and I are partners now. There are no secrets."

"We are partners over the half million," Randy agreed. "But that's where it ends. If I choose to visit someone, and someone chooses to visit me, it's nobody's business but mine."

Chum came angrily to his feet. "How do I know you aren't working out a deal with someone to get the money for you before you get out?" he demanded.

Randy looked at his cell mate with contempt. "I guess you don't. You have only my word, and I'll give it to you again. No one else will be told where the money is. I will work with no one else in recovering it when I get out of this hole. Now, you're going to have to be content with that."

An uneasy silence prevailed. Randy's thoughts went immediately back to Jeri. Why hadn't she come? Was she not coming again? She had to. He had too many unanswered questions. He had to see her at least one more time. He had even cut his hair so he would look more like the kind of guys she must go with in an effort to minimize some of the differences in their lifestyles. He wanted her to trust him enough to talk to him some more. That was all he wanted. Her trust was enough. He had sacrificed his long locks for her. Now, if only it was not in vain.

Just then the intercom came to life. "Inmate Randy Moore, you have a visitor."

Chum came to his feet swearing. Randy ignored him and left the cell. Someday, he told himself, he would have to deal firmly with Chum. But that would have to wait, like dealing with Uncle Bill would have to wait. For now, he had a visitor, and that could only be Jeri. He felt an elation he had not felt in a long time.

***

For a second, Jeri did not recognize the man in the white jumpsuit on the other side of the glass. Then she realized it was Rusty, but with his hair short. He had gotten rid of all those long locks of hair. She was surprised at how good he looked. He was downright cute. But she quickly pushed those thoughts aside. She was here because she had been directed by the Spirit to come.

Rusty was smiling as he sat down opposite her. "Hi, Jeri," he said. "Thanks for coming again. I sure hoped you would."

She smiled back at him. He really looked good. She felt more at ease. Maybe she had already helped him. A little more help, if she could give it, would be great. "So how are you doing, Rusty?" she asked.

"Better than I have for a long time. I've missed you, though."

That's not what she needed to hear, because she was not so sure she had missed him. She missed Warren. "I'm sorry it took me so long to get back. I'm kind of busy, you know."

"I'm sure," he said pleasantly.

Jeri smiled. Maybe she had missed him a little. Slightly shaken, she asked, "What questions can I answer for you today?"

He had a lot. He began with questions about his parents and his brothers and sisters. She filled him in as much as she could—his father's occupation, what he looked like, what his mother was like, what his brother and sister were doing.

Finally, she asked, "You won't be in here forever will you?"

"Oh, no," he agreed quickly. "It looks like I might be getting paroled in just a few months."

"That's great," she said. "Then I'll see if I can find out your folks's address and you could go meet them."

For the first time in their visit, his face dropped. "Oh, I don't know about that. I'm sure they won't want to know what I've become."

"Your parents are great, just like mine. They have never quit loving you, I'm sure. Please, promise me you'll look them up when you get out."

Rusty slowly shook his head. "I don't think I can do that. But I do appreciate you telling me about them. They are radically different from the people I was raised around." He paused, looking thoughtful, so Jeri said nothing. Finally he spoke again. "There is something else. I remember going to church with them. I don't remember anything about it. Are they religious fanatics or anything?"

Jeri took a deep breath. "No more than I am," she said. "We are members of The Church of Jesus Christ of Latter-day Saints."

Rusty rocked back on his chair. He looked stricken. "Mormon!?" he exclaimed.

"Yes, your family is an active Mormon family, just like mine," she said defensively. "Does that bother you?"

"Oh, no," he said after a moment. "I'm just surprised, that's all. Let me guess, they're from Utah, aren't they?"

"So am I. They might still live somewhere in Utah. Like I told you before, they've moved a lot. I'll send you their address. I'm sure my mother has it."

"I don't think so. I was quite sure before you ever told me about this Mormon business that they would never want to see me. Now I know it," he said. "Forget it. I'm glad just to know about them, but I'm not interested in meeting them. We live worlds apart now. Nothing can change that."

"It could," she said timidly, "but only if you would let it."

"Well, I'm not going to let it," he said angrily. "Can we talk about something else?"

"Sure," Jeri agreed. But she was sick at heart. She had hoped that by coming here again she might say something that would steer him onto a different path. It didn't seem now like that was likely to happen. The rest of the visit, though cordial, was more strained, and she was relieved when the officer came to end the visit.

"It's been good talking to you," Rusty said. "Will you come again?"

Jeri shook her head. "I don't think that's such a good idea."

"But we've barely begun. There is so much you can tell me," he protested.

"I don't think you really want to hear it . You sure don't seem happy about what I've told you today," she said.

"I'm sorry," he responded meekly. "You have to understand, this isn't very easy for me. Uncle Bill raised me to hate Mormons. It's hard to just shake off something like that."

"Even after all he did to you, whatever that was besides kidnapping you? Come on, Rusty, you know you shouldn't let him affect how you feel about your real family."

Rusty nodded, "I'm sure you're right. Please come again. You don't know how hard it is in here."

She relented, remembering the scripture that had sent her here on this Sabbath day. "Maybe I might consider it if you'll tell me about life in here, about you, that sort of thing."

"If you come, Jeri, maybe I will."

"Agreed," she said decisively. "Next Sunday afternoon okay?"

"Sooner would be better," he said wistfully.

"No, Sunday. See you then."

Jeri had thought about calling her parents to tell them she had found Rusty, but she didn't because she simply didn't know how to tell them. But now she knew she had to. If she was going to see Rusty again, she had to have something to give him: an address, maybe a picture or two, or even some memento from their childhood.

When she got home, there was a message on her machine from Warren. "I'll call again at eight," his voice informed her. Smiling, she looked at her watch. An hour. She had time to talk to her mother. She began to dial.

"Jeri, it's so good to hear from you," her father said when he answered the phone. "We haven't heard from you for a while," he said.

"I'm sorry Dad, I've been rather busy," she answered lamely.

"Too busy to let the ones you love know how you're doing?" he chided gently.

"No. You're right. And that's why I'm calling now. Is Mom home?"

"Yes, she's here. But I want to talk to you for a minute before I surrender the phone to her," he said. "Tell me about how your job is going."

She did, and she talked about the ward, and she told him that her car was running fine and she was feeling very well, thank you. Finally, she said, "Dad, could you get Mom on the phone with you? There's something I've got to tell both of you."

"Ah," her father murmured. "So you have been busy."

"Oh, Dad," she said with a laugh. "It's not like that."

"Like what?" he asked.

"Just get Mom."

"I'm already here, Jeri. It's good to hear your voice. What is it you have to tell us that's so important?" her mother asked.

"Well, two things," she said. A moment before it had only been one, but her father's reaction had inspired her to tell them about Warren first, so she did.

"Are you telling us there is a serious romance in motion?" her father asked.

"I don't know, but we had a great time when he was down here."

Her mother spoke up, "But I thought you had broken it off with him. It seemed that every time a boy got interested in you, you let old memories get in the way."

"That's true Mom," she admitted, "and that's the other reason I'm calling."

"You mean you have finally quit worrying about your promise to Rusty to find him?" her father asked. He sounded hopeful. Neither of her parents had ever understood how she felt. Time, they always told her, should have eased the hurt and the need to look for someone who might not even be alive anymore.

She smiled with satisfaction as she prepared to tell them the big news. "Actually, you're right, Dad. I'm not looking for Rusty anymore."

"Thank goodness!" her parents said in unison.

"Not that I don't care anymore," she said. "I've quit looking. I have found him."

There were two gasps on the other end of the line, then there was silence. She waited. It was her father who finally gave in and broke the silence. "You're not serious," he said. That was all.

"Oh, quite serious, Dad. I found him. I've seen him. I've talked to him. He is very much alive and well," she announced.

"My," her mother sighed. "I've got to sit down."

"I already am," her father said. "Are you sure it's him?"

"Positive," she told them. "It's Rusty all right. I always told you I'd know him when I saw him. And I did. Oh, I admit, I wasn't sure for a while, but now I am. He remembers, too."

It took an hour to explain it all to them. Jeri was sure they were in shock by the time she had finished. She left nothing out. She even told them about the missing money and his haircut and the scripture from the twenty-fifth chapter of Matthew. They were both excited and saddened.

"The poor boy," her mother lamented. "And his poor mother. It might have been better if he had been dead. A criminal. How terrible."

"Jeri, a word of caution," her father said.

"I know, don't get involved," she said. "I had no intention of going back after that second visit. I thought it was enough that he knew who he was. I'd done what I promised. I'd found him. But something kept nagging at me. I prayed and then I read that scripture. I've got to see him again. And that's where I need your help."

It turned out that her mother had several pictures that had come the past Christmas from Rusty's mother. "I'll send them," she said.

"That would be great," Jeri responded. "And please send their address. I don't know that he'll ever make contact with them, but I think he should have the chance."

"You're right, dear," her father admitted. "But remember who and what he is now and be careful."

"Dad, I know. Anyway, there's Warren now. And . . ." She glanced at her watch. "Oh, I've got to get off the line. Warren's calling at eight, and that's in just a couple of minutes."

"Great," her father said. "But before you go, there is one more thing. Someone's got to let his folks know. It's only fair."

"Not yet, Dad. Please," she pleaded. "Let me try to get him to do it before one of us does. Now, gotta go. I love you both."

She hadn't been off the phone for a minute before it rang.

CHAPTER 6

"Your phone's been busy," Warren said the moment Jeri answered.

"It wasn't eight yet," she chided with a chuckle. "I was talking to my parents."

"Great. How are they doing?" he asked.

"Fine.

"Where were you earlier? I tried to call late this afternoon," he said.

"Oh, I was visiting someone. We had a great sacrament meeting today," she said, attempting to change the subject.

It didn't work. "So did we," Warren answered. "But who were you visiting? Was it someone I met when I was there?"

"No, it was just someone I'm trying to help," she said, wishing desperately he would drop it.

"A member of your ward?" he asked stubbornly.

"No, a nonmember. There are a lot of those here you know. It's not like at BYU," she said, feeling a touch of annoyance at his persistence.

"Hey, don't get mad," he said. "I was just wondering. Why can't you tell me about her? You know I'm interested in everything about you."

"I know," she said.

"It *is* a 'her,' isn't it?"

"Who?"

"Oh, come on, Jeri. You know what I'm talking about. Who is the woman you visited?" he persisted.

Jeri was angry now. She liked Warren. She liked him a lot. But she had the feeling he would not understand about her visiting someone in prison. Especially *the someone* she was visiting. He would ask her to leave it alone. But she couldn't. Not yet, at least. Maybe after one more visit she could.

Jeri didn't realize it, but she had been lost in thought and hadn't answered Warren's question. When he finally spoke again, it was in a very annoyed tone of voice. "What gives, Jeri? Who is the woman? Or is it a man?"

Her anger at his persistence overruled her better judgement, and she shot back at him, "It is a man, and he's in prison, and I'm just trying to help him find his past."

That terse admission brought silence to the line. She instantly wished she could recall her words, but she could not. Now she would have to tell him the story of Rusty and all she could do was pray that he would somehow understand.

His next words, when they finally came, did not make it seem likely that he would understand. "Jeri, are you crazy? A prisoner? A criminal? You visited a man who is in prison? I can't believe this. My goal in studying law is to become a prosecutor, to lock the bad guys up and you want to get them out!" he shouted.

"Warren, I never said anything about getting him out!" she shouted back. "I am only trying to help him. And no one but me can do it. You'll never understand. That's why I didn't want to tell you about it. I was afraid you would react this way."

"What other way should I react? The woman I love is seeing a convicted criminal. And I'll bet he's not an old man. And I'll bet he's good-looking. Jeri, how could you?"

Jeri was crying so hard she could barely talk. She had to get off the line with Warren. Maybe a little time would make it easier for her to make him understand. She so desperately needed for him to see how she felt and why. She said, "I'm going to hang up, Warren. Read Matthew chapter twenty-five." She sniffled and wiped her eyes. "And when you are calm and ready to let me explain without exploding again, then you may call me back." Before he could respond, she hung up.

Jeri hugged her knees to her chest and cried. She cried like she had not done since the day Rusty was taken. She had lost her best friend back then, and now she had probably lost another guy, one who had begun to mean a lot to her, more than she had realized.

She did not want to lose Warren, but he would probably not call her back.

She waited by the phone, just in case, hoping and praying. Nine o'clock came and went. Ten o'clock came and went. Eleven. No call. She went to bed. She didn't sleep. About three o'clock, she got up, read the scriptures for a while, prayed some more, ate a huge dish of ice cream and a half-dozen cookies. That ought to be good for my figure, she thought. Not that anyone cared!

She went back to bed at four-thirty, and finally drifted off to sleep.

The ringing of the phone wakened her. Startled, she looked at the clock. It was six o'clock. Trying not to get her hopes up, she reached for the phone.

"Jeri, I'm so sorry."

Jeri's heart leaped. "Warren, I was afraid you wouldn't call."

"I wasn't sure, either," he admitted. "It has been a long night."

"For me, too. I feel like I've been run over by a truck."

"You have, a dumb truck named Warren," he told her.

"You are not dumb," she said. "I'm glad you called, but we don't have a lot of time to talk now. I'll have to be getting ready for work soon."

"And me for school. It's been the longest night of my life," he said. "Well, one of the two longest. I think you know when the last one was. I love you, Jeri, and I thought I had lost you forever that night," he said.

"After that night, I never intended to go out with you again, Warren, but the problem was not you. The problem is with me. And I think that problem is solved now," she said.

"I hope so. If we can just get past this prisoner thing."

"I hope we can. But you've got to let me explain, and that will take longer than either of us has this morning. Did you read the scripture I told you about?"

Warren chuckled, but it sounded suspiciously like a forced chuckle. "I read the whole chapter. It wasn't hard to figure out which verses you were thinking about. But Jeri, that scripture was referring to people who are unjustly imprisoned, like the Prophet Joseph. You have to realize that."

"Warren, it does not. It does not say that!" She was getting angry again. How could she ever get him to understand? He was being so blind.

When he spoke again, his voice was condescending, patient. It was like he was speaking to a small child. "It really is, but I know you meant well. It would be best if you didn't visit this guy again, whoever he is."

Tears erupted. She could not find her voice. So she simply hung up. Not five minutes had passed before the phone rang again. She did not pick it up. She had to cool down. She had to think of a way to get Warren to listen. It would be so much easier in person. Maybe she should fly to Utah. She would have to think about it.

Jeri showered and was getting dressed when the phone again began to ring. She looked at her caller ID. It was Warren. She answered. "Hi, Warren. I'm sorry. We need to talk later. I've got to go now. Please keep an open mind," and before he could say a single word, she hung up again.

***

Jeri and Warren were not the only ones who had spent a long and restless night. So had the other component in this difficult equation. Rusty had tossed and turned all night, much to the annoyance of his cell mate. When they finally climbed out of their bunks for roll call, Chum had a look in his eye that frightened Rusty, despite the difference in their size. Rusty was much larger and stronger. And he could be mean when it struck him to be, but that was not very often. Chum, however, looked like he could kill—and right now, Rusty could be the victim.

"Randy, you will not visit the next time someone comes to see you," Chum said from the side of his mouth after the officer who was doing the count had passed their cell.

Rusty looked at him, watched the burning eyes and the hatred that lurked in their dangerous depths. "Why shouldn't I?" he asked as calmly as he could after the guard was out of earshot.

"I didn't say you shouldn't. I said you wouldn't," Chum hissed.

Randy's temperature began to rise. "And since when was it up to you who I visited?"

"Since we became partners."

"Who I visit has nothing to do with the money, Chum. One fourth of it is yours. That's our bargain, and I intend to keep my part of it."

Chum wasn't buying it. "You are uptight, pal. And the only thing it could be is the visitor you've had again. It was the same girl, wasn't it?"

Deciding it might be better to stay close to the truth, Rusty nodded. "Yes, it is, but it's not like you think."

Chum swore. "You are a liar, Randy. Whoever she is, forget her. You are not going to visit again."

"Maybe not. I'm not sure she's coming back again, anyway," he said, trying his best to keep from grabbing the man around the throat and strangling him.

"So it is the girl?"

"Yes, it is, but she is only trying to help me learn who I am."

"Oh, how sweet!" Chum snapped sarcastically.

Randy nodded. "It's a long story."

"And it's about to get shorter. So she is someone you know?" Chum asked. "Or is she someone you used to know?"

"Used to know. A long time ago."

Chum swore again. "And you expect me to believe she is not getting the money for you?"

Randy decided this was a good time to mix a lie with the truth. "She is my sister, Chum. She is the girl who came in here that day that you asked me about. She seemed familiar. That was why. We are brother and sister. She's helping me learn about my past, and what I've learned stinks," he said with venom.

More vile language erupted from Chum. "You're a liar—you look nothing alike. And even if she is, do you really expect me to believe she isn't going after some of the money? Let me make it clear to you, Randy. We . . ."

Rusty interrupted. "My name is Rusty! Don't ever call me Randy again." That was a stupid thing to say. He didn't know why he had said it. Anger, he supposed.

"Randy," Chum said defiantly, his fists clenched. "When I make a deal with someone, it is permanent. Anyone crosses me, even you, and the result is death! Is that clear?"

"I'm not crossing you," Rusty insisted.

"I'll kill you, and your sister, too, if you do anything with that money other than what we have agreed on," he threatened.

There was no doubt in Rusty's mind that Chum would do just what he said, and despite how angry it made him and how angry Chum was, he knew one thing for sure, Chum would not kill him now, for he wanted that money desperately. But once he had it, well . . . who knew? As for Jeri, as different as they were, he had discovered a long-buried affection for her and no one, if he could help it, would hurt Jeri. She was so good, so clean, so beautiful. No one would hurt her, and especially not Chum. And he didn't intend to be killed himself. So maybe, just maybe, Chum would have to go.

Those were dark thoughts, dangerous thoughts, but Rusty was angry. He had been beaten and abused much of his life, and from the day he had fled the home of Uncle Bill, he had sworn it would not happen again. More than one man had felt the pounding of his fists, and Chum would feel worse than that one day. But not in here, for that would delay his release. And he desperately wanted his freedom.

Both prisoners let the matter drop, each hating and distrusting the other, but neither in a position to do anything about it now. Later that day, as he feverishly worked the weights, Rusty kept thinking of Jeri, hoping she would come back. Not just because of what she could teach him of his past, but because she was so different from anyone else he knew. She was so refreshing. And yet, he knew, they were so different. She would not come many more times if she came at all, and that thought was hard to bear.

Randy also promised himself that he would never let her know about the hidden loot. He had to protect her from Chum at any cost. Maybe the way to do that for now was to make Chum think that he really didn't like his "sister," or what he had learned about his past. And while this was certainly true about his past, his family, and their Mormon connection, he would need to take it a step further than that. The right thing would be to refuse to see Jeri again if she came, but that was more than he could bear. She was his past, or at least his only connection to it, and it was hard to sever that. He had been so lucky after all these years to learn who he really was. He was confused. He shouldn't feel this way. What did the past matter anyway? He pumped the weights harder, frustrated and angry and depressed.

***

Jeri was so tired that she fell asleep on her bed as soon as she got home from work. She slept so soundly that even the ringing of the phone did not awaken her. In fact, she did not wake up until after midnight. She then got ready for bed, ate a few bites of aged salad that she found in her refrigerator, and headed for her bed again. But she stopped short and checked her caller ID. Warren had called. She couldn't believe she had slept through the ringing of the phone. That was evidence of how fatigued and tired she had become.

She went back to bed and fell asleep shortly. She was almost ready to leave for work the next morning when the phone rang. She glanced at the caller ID, expecting the call to be from Warren. But it was Kate's number. She picked up immediately.

"Hi, Kate," she said, trying to sound upbeat.

"Jeri, what is going on?" Kate asked with uncharacteristic sharpness.

"What do you mean?" she asked in surprise.

"Why won't you talk to Warren?" Kate asked. "He's going crazy. He just called and said you are not answering your phone."

"Didn't he tell you what's going on?" she said defensively.

"Only that he's been trying to talk to you and that something is wrong," Kate responded.

"Oh, Kate," Jeri moaned. "It's so complicated. I haven't got time to explain right now. But it's not like it seems. Please, Kate, don't you be angry, too. I'll call after work, if that's okay, and I'll explain. I don't know what to do."

Kate's voice was softer, more understanding when she spoke again. "Is it about Rusty?"

"How did you know?" Jeri asked.

"History repeats itself. Call at six o'clock. I'll be here."

Emily called Jeri that afternoon. She was kind but firm. "Jeri, I don't think it is wise that you keep visiting inmate Moore."

"I know, you are probably right, but he wants to know about his past," she told him.

"You mean he remembers?" Emily asked.

"Yes, he does now."

"I see. Well, my advice still goes. It would be best if you forgot the past," Emily said.

"I'm trying, honest I am," Jeri told her, "but he wants to know more about who he was. Ever since he was kidnapped, his life has been a nightmare."

"I'm sure it has, but you can't let yourself get emotionally involved. I'm glad you found him and that he now knows who he is, but Jeri, for your sake, leave it alone from now on."

"I can't . . ." Jeri began.

Emily interrupted. "I wish I had never helped you. You must, please, for it can only end in heartache. I've seen girls before who fell in love with inmates, and it never works. Believe me. Never!"

Jeri smiled to herself. "I appreciate your concern, Emily. You are such a dear. But you don't understand. I am not falling for him. I am only helping him find his past. My mother is sending some pictures for me to give him. Then I don't intend to see him again. By the way, how did you know about my last visit to him?"

"The warden talked to me. He's concerned, too."

"Oh, Emily, I'm sorry if I got you in trouble. But believe me, it's not like you think. Haven't I told you about Warren?"

"I guess not. Who's Warren?"

"My boyfriend," Jeri said boldly.

The sigh from Emily was evident even over the phone. "I didn't know you had a boyfriend."

"Yes, he's a really neat guy. He's a law student. And get this, he plans to be a prosecutor," Jeri told her even as she wondered if she had lost Warren for good. She hoped not. With Kate's help, maybe she could still salvage the relationship.

"I'm glad to hear that," Emily said. "I'll let the warden know. He'll be relieved."

"Thanks, Emily," she said.

"Quite all right. You are a special girl, and I just wouldn't want anything to happen to you. Randy is a popular inmate, but he has had some history of violence in his past, and there is the matter of a half-million dollars. The warden is certain Randy knows where it is and that he intends to get it when he gets out. I'm glad you are about through with him."

"Me too," Jeri said, and she wondered if that was really the truth. She was so terribly confused right now.

"When are you bringing the pictures to him?" Emily asked.

"As soon as I can after they come," she told her friend.

"Then don't see him again after that. Is it a deal?" Emily pressed.

Jeri thought about it for a moment. It would be best. It would help with Warren. "It's a deal," she said firmly, and she was pretty sure she meant it.

CHAPTER 7

It was raining and cold as Jeri hurried from her office to the parking lot to retrieve her car. She was anxious to get home and call Kate. Now that she had committed to only see Rusty one more time, she was confident that Kate would understand and that she could also patch things up with Warren.

The rain came down harder as she drove toward her apartment. A block from home she sat impatiently at a red light. Distracted by thoughts of the call she had to make to Kate, and wondering how best to handle it, she failed to see a small gray car that was coming from her right too fast to stop as the lights changed. She started out, then, too late, caught the flash of gray, screamed and slammed on her brakes.

The gray car struck the front fender on the right side of her car and spun her around on the rain-slick road right into the path of another car that had started through the intersection from the other side. The second impact caught the front left fender and her air-bag exploded. She was vaguely aware of her car continuing to slide, the second car bouncing against her door, and then of her car finally coming to rest. Then she blacked out.

When Jeri came to, she could hear the scream of sirens, and it frightened her. She tried to look around but found that she was strapped to a stretcher, and it gradually dawned on her that she was in an ambulance and that the sirens were coming from it. She struggled, and a firm hand restrained her.

"It's okay now, young lady. You'll be all right," someone clad in white said. "We'll have you to a hospital soon."

"Was I in a wreck?" she asked stupidly.

"Yes, but you'll be okay," she was told.

"What about my car?" she asked.

"I think someone's insurance company will be buying you a new one," the kind voice said. "Now, relax. It'll all be fine."

She did more than relax; she blacked out again.

The next thing she remembered, she was in a hospital bed with tubes running out of both arms and pain coming from everywhere. "Oh," she moaned. "I hurt."

"She's coming around," a voice said, and an instant later a nurse appeared above her. "You've had a nasty bump," she was told. "But you will be all right."

A doctor arrived. "So, you've decided to quit sleeping?" he said with a chuckle. "Here, let me have a look at your eyes."

He opened them one at a time, shining a light in each one. "That's looking better," he said after he had finished. "You have a small concussion, but you are progressing nicely."

"My shoulder hurts," she complained.

"It's okay now. It was dislocated, but it snapped right back into place. It'll be sore for a while, but believe me, you will be just fine," he assured her.

"It hurts," she reminded him.

"Of course it does," he said gently. "And so do your other cuts and bruises, but I have given you some painkillers and you will sleep quite a bit for a while. You'll soon feel a lot better."

She drifted off again, assured that she was going to heal.

***

"Kate, have you talked to Jeri yet?" Warren asked the moment Kate answered the phone. "I've been calling all night, and she isn't answering."

"I talked to her this morning, and she promised she would call me back at six tonight," Kate said. "But she didn't. And I've been trying to call ever since. I'm getting the same results as you."

"She's probably visiting that prison," he said bitterly. "Do you know about that?"

"Well, I think so, but . . ."

"She's visiting some guy there," he cut in. "A prisoner. She wouldn't admit it at first, but I finally got it out of her. Kate, I don't know what's going on, but I don't like it."

Kate didn't know what to say. She realized that Jeri must have gone back to see the prisoner she had seen lifting weights, the one she thought was Rusty. But could it really be him? How could Jeri know for sure? Maybe that was what Jeri was going to tell her tonight. So why hadn't she called?

"Do you know anything about this guy?" Warren asked when she didn't respond.

"Maybe a little," she said, hedging. "I'm not sure. But Warren, I am sure of one thing—you can trust Jeri. You need to give her a little time, I think."

"I can't, Kate. I'm going crazy," he said.

Kate longed to see Warren, to take him in her arms and soothe him, but she couldn't interfere with the thing he and Jeri had going. Her heart ached. It ached for Warren, it ached for Jeri, and it ached for herself.

"Why did I have to fall in love with such a complicated woman?" Warren asked.

His words pierced Kate to the soul. She wondered much the same thing. But she could not give voice to her feelings. "Warren, there are things in Jeri's past you need to have her tell you about. She's not really so complicated; she just needs to sort out some extremely painful memories." She wondered if she had said too much. She hoped not, because it was Jeri's place to tell Warren about Rusty, not hers.

"What kind of memories, Kate?" he asked.

"I can't tell you. She must do that herself. All I can tell you is to be patient, please."

"I'll try, but it's hard," he said. "I better go now. I want to try calling her again."

A half hour later Kate also tried, but the phone just rang. She kept trying until well after eleven o'clock that night. By then she was getting very worried. This was not like Jeri. She would have called if she could.

Warren called Kate back at 11:30. "I'm going out there," he announced. "She might be mad enough at me to ignore my calls, but she would not ignore yours. Something is wrong, and it has to do with that criminal she's been seeing. I'm almost certain of it."

"Warren, you can't do that," Kate warned him. "You have classes. You can't afford to mess up your second year in law school. You can't cut classes."

"But I've got to know that Jeri is all right."

"Let me find out," Kate said firmly. "You met her bishop, didn't you? Give me his name and the name of her ward. I think she told me that, but I can't remember it. Anyway, I'll find her bishop and he can find out what, if anything, is going on."

"Thanks Kate," Warren said. He told her the bishop's name and the ward.

"Good, I'll call him in the morning," she promised. "For now, you get some sleep."

Kate was up early. She dialed Jeri's number. As she feared, there was no answer. So she called information and got the numbers for Jeri's ward and her bishop. She got no answer at either place. In desperation, she looked up Jeri's parents's number. She was glad she still had it. Surely they would know what was happening.

Jeri's father was at work already, but her mother answered the phone. "I've been trying to call Jeri since last evening," Kate told Sister Satch. "I really need to talk to her. But she isn't answering. Have you heard from her lately?"

"Oh yes. She called Sunday night," Kate was assured.

"Good. Did she tell you about what's been happening?" Kate asked.

"Well, yes." Sister Satch seemed hesitant.

"I know about Rusty and what happened when he and Jeri were children," Kate told her. "Did she call you about that?"

Kate had guessed right. "Yes, she's found him," Jeri's mother told her. "She also has a boyfriend."

"She told me a few days ago that she saw a guy that looked like it might be Rusty, but she didn't call after that," Kate said, hoping for more information.

To her immense relief, she got it. After Jeri's mother had explained what she knew, Kate talked to her about Warren. "He was very upset about her visiting a prisoner and got sort of angry before Jeri could tell him the whole story. He's been trying to call her but is getting no answer. I've also been trying with the same result. We are both worried."

"So am I, now," Jeri's mother said. "Maybe I should try to call her bishop."

"I tried that, but I got no answer. Do you know the number of the firm she works for?" Kate asked hopefully.

"Yes, I have it here somewhere. Just a moment," she said. "It might take me a minute to find it. Hold on, please."

Kate waited, then after several minutes, Sister Satch came back on the line and read her the number. "I can call," she said.

"Let me," Kate insisted. "I'll let you know as soon as I find her."

There was a message giving the firm's office hours and inviting Kate to leave a message. She hung up, looked at her watch, and decided to call back after her first class. It was mid-morning before she was able to get home and call again. A receptionist answered this time and informed Kate that Jeri had not come in for work that morning. They had called her home but got no answer. "Are you a friend?" the young lady asked. "She has never done anything like this before."

Kate assured her that she was a friend and it was not like Jeri to just not show up for work. She was really worried now. "Something has happened to her or she would be there," Kate said, almost in a panic.

"Would you hold please, I have another call coming in," Kate was told. She didn't want to hold. She was worried, but she had no choice.

When the receptionist came on the line after a couple of long minutes, she said, "You won't believe this. That was a call about Jeri on the other line."

"About her? Is something wrong?" Kate asked in alarm.

"Yes. It seems she was in an accident after she left work yesterday, and she's in the hospital. She has been unconscious most of the time and just barely was able to ask a nurse to call us."

"How badly is she hurt?" Kate asked.

"They didn't give me any details, only that she would be off work for a while," she said. "I've got the number of the hospital. You can call it yourself."

Kate did and was told that Jeri was still heavily sedated and she couldn't talk on the phone. They did tell her that Jeri would recover fully. Now all she could do was call Jeri's mother and then, when he was out of classes, call Warren. Then they would simply have to wait.

***

Jeri was in the hospital for two days. Other than some bad cuts and a concussion that turned out to be more serious than the doctor had first thought, she was not hurt too badly. But her face looked awful. It had taken a beating and she didn't want to be seen by anyone, least of all Warren. She talked to Kate several times but asked her to tell Warren she needed some time and for him not to come. She wanted to see him, but not the way she looked now. Kate told her that Warren wasn't happy with that, but he would try to be patient.

Jeri's parents flew in from Utah, and worked on the matter of the loss of her car. It was a complete write-off, and the other insurance company had agreed to replace it. Her father was able to purchase another car, and her folks were there to take Jeri back to her apartment when she was released from the hospital. They stayed the next day, making sure she was settled and comfortable, then returned to Utah and Jeri's younger siblings.

The pictures Jeri's mother had mailed came while her parents were with her. Her father offered to deliver them to the prison and save her having to go there again, but she insisted that she would take them when she felt better and when she looked better. She owed that to Rusty, she explained.

By Monday, Jeri was back at work, even though she was still bruised and sore. She thought about going to see Rusty that night, but since this was to be her last visit with him, she wanted to wait until her face was back to normal.

Warren called that night, and she finally told him about Rusty. She had wanted to do that in person and he had offered to come to Sacramento. But she didn't want him to see her bruised up, and there was no way she could go back to Utah for a while, so she settled for the phone, inadequate as it was.

He took it much better than she had expected. "I wish you had told me this a long time ago," he said.

"You wouldn't have understood," she told him. "Nobody did. I know it seemed like something that would never happen, but somehow I felt like I had to keep looking. Now that I've found him, I can let it go at last. I'm sorry, but I really didn't think you would understand, so I didn't say anything."

"It's okay. You won't be seeing him anymore then, will you?" he asked.

"Just once. I have . . ." she began.

"Jeri!" Warren interrupted. "You can't do that. Leave well enough alone. Please," he begged.

"Just once more," she repeated. "I'm taking him some . . ."

Warren interrupted again. "Send him whatever it is. Seeing him will do no one any good."

"You really don't get it, do you?" she retorted angrily. "I have lived with this nightmare for so long that it has become a part of me. Getting rid of it isn't that easy. I owe him one more visit. I'm taking some pictures of his family to him, and giving him their address. Then it's up to him what he does."

"Well, I hope so," Warren said, a little more contrite now. "I still wish you wouldn't go again. But if you must, please promise me this will be the last time."

"It will be," she assured him.

"Good, so when are you going?"

"As soon as my face looks better."

"For crying out loud," Warren exploded. "I can see you wanting to look good for me, but for him, a criminal? Give me a break."

She gave him a slammed phone instead. He could be so infuriating, and for no good reason.

But a little voice in her head seemed to say, "Is it really for no good reason? Put yourself in his shoes." But she deliberately shut the little voice out.

***

Rusty was depressed. He had expected Jeri to come back on Sunday. She hadn't, and now he wondered if she ever would. As each day passed, more fragments of childhood memories came back to him, and he wanted to talk to her about them. And Chum was becoming increasingly unbearable. He gloated when there was no visitation call for Rusty, and constantly reminded him that even if that should happen, Randy was to refuse it. And he insisted on calling him Randy, which, for some reason, infuriated Rusty more all the time. But Chum didn't seem to care about that.

The week dragged on, and Chum kept up his taunting and nagging. Finally, when Rusty's patience snapped, he did what he had promised himself he would never do. He knocked out Chum's two front teeth.

That got him locked down for a month, which meant, among other things, no visitors. That hurt. And it also could affect his parole date. But despite those things, he felt good about it. Although he knew he had made an enemy for life. It also left him without a concrete plan on how to recover his half-million dollars. He and Chum would definitely not be cell mates again, but he would still have to use him. Rusty knew this was dangerous, but he had no other choice. He would just have to deal with that once he was out of prison—whenever that was.

***

It took two weeks for Jeri's face to heal to the point that makeup would cover most of the remaining bruises. During that time, she had several civil—even nice—phone conversations with Warren. He apologized and then did not bring up Rusty's name again. Things seemed to be back on track.

In fact, Jeri found she was dreading seeing Rusty again. But she felt she had to, so on a Thursday evening, two and a half weeks after her accident, she presented herself at the jail. And she was told she could not see Rusty for another two weeks. When she asked why, she was told he had assaulted another inmate and was locked down as punishment.

Reality hit her squarely in the face. Rusty was an inmate, a criminal, a violent one, it seemed. Perhaps she shouldn't see him again. She thought about mailing the pictures and a letter and leaving it at that. But as the next week went by, she kept putting off that simple task. Deep down, she really wanted to see him again despite everything that indicated it was a bad idea. She could not decide why she wanted to see him. Something just tugged at her conscience. She kept reminding herself that he was a criminal, he was violent, and that he was not the same Rusty she had known as a child. The smart thing was to just forget him and mail the pictures and address.

It was not that simple. She stewed, she worried, she cried. She tried to put him out of her mind. She put the pictures in an envelope. The next day she addressed it. She even put a stamp on the envelope and sealed it. She finally carried it to the mail. She had only to drop it in the box and then forget about Rusty forever.

She could not do it.

CHAPTER 8

The meeting Warden Jones was late for on this cool December morning was an unusual one. Not that he was not frequently called to testify at parole hearings, because inmates' prison histories were often the deciding factor on parole dates. Inmate Randy Moore had been a model prisoner up until he was placed in lockdown for assaulting his cell mate. No new charges had been filed, because it seemed obvious that inmate Chumbian might have incited the assault. None of that was particularly unusual. What made this hearing unusual was that pressure was being brought to have Moore placed on parole as quickly as possible, and the source of that pressure was unusual indeed. Something like this had never happened before, at least not in this facility.

What was even more unusual was who was behind the source of the pressure to get him paroled. It came from a most unlikely place: the bank he had robbed, whose money was still missing, was placing great pressure on the Sacramento Police Department to intervene in Randy's behalf. It presented a most intriguing mystery to the warden.

The Chief of Police himself had already arrived at the prison, and had it not been for a delay just as he was leaving his office, the warden would have preceded him to the hearing room. But there was a disturbance in the prison, and Warden Jones had been detained by a phone call.

Warden Jones apologized as he slipped into the room, and he had no sooner seated himself than the chairman rapped his gavel and called the hearing to order. Rusty had watched as the warden came in, trying to judge from his face what his testimony would be like. He was stone-faced, and seemed slightly out of breath. Rusty interpreted that as a bad sign. Of course, what could he expect? He had only been released from solitary confinement the preceding evening. It was almost certain that his parole was going to be denied and a new hearing scheduled two or three years down the road.

In fact, he had resigned himself to that as he whiled away the long days in solitary confinement. He should never have allowed Chum to push him as far as he did. Now Chum would almost certainly be getting out first, and he would be waiting for him. That was not a pretty thought.

The chairman spoke. "Inmate Randy Moore, would you please stand?"

Rusty rose to his feet and faced the parole board. He considered himself Rusty now. He was not Randy, and that name only served to irritate him now that he knew who he really was. He wanted to tell the chairman to address him by his real name, but he wisely chose to remain silent on that issue. He forced a smile.

"You are here today for a hearing to determine if a date should be set for your parole, do you understand, that?" the chairman asked.

"I do, sir. Thank you sir," Rusty said smoothly.

"Have you called anyone to testify in your behalf today?"

"There is no one sir," he replied.

"Very well, you may be seated and we will begin," the chairman said.

"Thank you sir," Rusty said as he sat down.

The chairman then read aloud the criminal record of inmate Randy Moore, frowning as he did so. Rusty looked around the room. There were two men in dark suits whom he had never seen before. Beside them was an older police officer who had more brass and gold on his uniform than Rusty had ever seen. He was sure he was here to represent the police in insisting that he be kept in prison for the maximum of his term.

The chairman read on, finishing with, "The inmate has now served two years of a sentence of five to fifteen years. That is not very long considering the nature of the offense he committed. Warden Jones, perhaps we could begin with you. Please describe the behavior of this inmate during the past two years."

Warden Jones gave a flowery account of Rusty's prison record. The members of the board were smiling. Then the smiles disappeared as he said, "Unfortunately, he did get involved in an incident a few weeks ago that has blemished his record."

"And what was that?" the chairman inquired, leaning forward as if he were eager to hear the negative report.

"He got in a fight with his cell mate," Warden Jones began.

"Did he start the fight?" one of the board members asked before the warden could finish.

Rusty knew what lay ahead. They'd just as well end the hearing and send him back. He had struck Chum first, and he had never denied that.

"Well, let me explain what happened; then perhaps inmate Moore could clarify if need be," the warden said. "You see, it appears that he did take the first swing, but it was provoked."

The chairman turned to Rusty. "Is that true, inmate Moore?"

"Yes, sir," he answered, hoping they would not ask for clarification, because he would have to lie if they did. There was no way he could tell them the fight was over the stolen money and their deal for recovering it when they were both out of prison.

"Tell us about it," the chairman ordered.

Rusty had not anticipated this and he had not fabricated a story, so he had to think fast and do the best he could. He was inspired as his mind raced ahead. He replied, "It was over a girl." That much was sort of true. "I had a girl coming to visit me and Chum didn't like it."

"What difference would that make to another inmate?" one of the board members asked.

Thinking quickly, and having no idea how close to the real truth he was, Rusty said, "He hates women. I hadn't had any visitors before and then this girl came, a girl I used to know. He said girls were trouble and not to see her again. I told him he couldn't tell me who to see, and it just got worse from there. He finally made me so mad I hit him. I know I shouldn't have, but I did."

He stopped right there, pleased that he hadn't veered too far from the truth. "Warden, have you verified any of this?" the chairman asked.

"As a matter of fact," the warden said, and he was actually smiling a little, "a young lady showed up at the prison recently. She is an accountant and does much of the work for this facility."

Rusty listened with interest. This was all new to him. He had never been told why Jeri had come to the prison in the first place.

"She is very bright, and pretty too, I might add," the warden continued. "She came to meet with our bookkeeping staff to help them make some changes. While here, she was given a tour of the facility. She saw Inmate Moore and thought she remembered him from the past. She asked to see him again, and I allowed it. It turns out she knew him as a child. It's all as simple as that."

Rusty couldn't help but sigh in relief. It was not as simple as that, but it would do.

"Thank you, Warden, is there anything else?"

The warden said there was not. The chairman then said, "Chief Harriman, we'd like to hear from you next."

Rusty had begun to feel good about the proceedings. That changed radically when the man in the decorated uniform was identified. Rusty knew the name, but he had never even seen the police chief before. This could not be good. He was certain the Chief of Police of a city the size of Sacramento did not have idle time to waste on an inmate like himself. Two or three more years began to look like ten or twelve.

"We'll get to you men from the bank shortly," the chairman continued, nodding at the two men in dark suits.

Or a lifetime, Randy thought at that stunning disclosure. He was sunk. He would spend the maximum fifteen years.

He was soon surprised.

Amazed.

Suspicious.

Chief Harriman recited that the theft had been committed with the use of a toy gun. That was true, but very different from the story told in his sentencing about how it looked identical to the real thing. That is what surprised Rusty. The chief made no mention of the chase that ended up with a car in a river and the money gone. That was amazing. But when Chief Harriman stated that the police department had every reason to believe Inmate Moore would be a model citizen after being paroled, he grew very suspicious.

Then he sat and listened to one of the men who was identified as George W. Smith, President of Sacramento Bank of the West, and he knew he was being set up. Mr. Smith stated that the insurance carrier had paid them off for their loss, so they were only out the few hundred dollars a year that their premiums were raised. He said, "This young man testified at his sentencing that the money was lost in the river where his car ended up shortly before he was arrested. We are convinced he was telling the truth."

That was a lie. Rusty knew they didn't believe the money was really gone. He had avoided a trial by entering a plea to a lesser charge than was first brought against him because they did not have an airtight case against him, according to his attorney. And they had not been allowed to question him extensively on it at the sentencing. But he had it hidden, safely hidden. And they surely suspected that.

That was where Chum was to have come in. And still might, although the thought was a grim one.

The President of the bank was still talking. "We would recommend to the board that the inmate be released on one condition," he said.

Rusty thought, and that would be that I return the money. No way!

"And what would that condition be?" the chairman asked.

"That he pay back what it has cost us in increased insurance premiums," was the response.

"And how would he do that?" the chairman asked. "He certainly has no income."

"We will work with him in finding a job, and then we would take part of his wages until it is paid," Mr. Smith proposed.

"Sounds more than fair to me," the chairman said. "Inmate Moore, they are making available a great opportunity for you upon your parole. A job and a chance to pay them back what they are out is all they ask. What do you think? If we give you an early parole, and that is by no means certain, we will have to meet and discuss it when this hearing is over and make a decision. But if it does happen, are you agreeable to signing an agreement along the lines of what President Smith just proposed?"

Rusty was not an idiot, and he wanted out of this place. He agreed, and parole was set for the eighteenth day of December. That was just two weeks away! Amazing! But he would have to be really careful, because he was certain the bank and the police had another agenda. Surely they wanted his half million.

Rusty was to spend his remaining days in the prison completely separate from Chum. But he knew he had not heard the last from him, and maybe, if he was very, very cautious, he could still use Chum to help him recover the money, after the other inmate was also released.

Rusty was not surprised when, the following evening, a note was slipped to him from another inmate. Word of his pending parole had reached Chum, and Chum was responding. The note, neatly hand-written, read:

December 12

Randy,

I will be out very close behind you. I will look forward to seeing you then. Don't worry about finding me. I will find you. We'll have a great time. Life is too short to do otherwise. Sorry to hear that your girl friend gave you the boot. And sorry about the misunderstanding.

Your pal, Chum.

The note, if it fell into the wrong hands, was certainly harmless enough. But there was no doubt in Rusty's mind, as Chum had intended, that it was a threat. Chum would find him. They would get the money, and unless he cooperated, Chum would cut his life short. And he was not to ever see or talk to Jeri again.

Clear as a bell.

With that depressing thought on his mind, Rusty settled down to watch television for the evening. He was surprised when his name was called on the intercom to go at once to the visiting area. And his heart beat a little faster. It would be Jeri. It was the only person it could be.

***

Jeri was apprehensive as she was escorted to the visiting booth. She carried the stamped envelope she had not mailed. She couldn't get out of her mind the fact that Rusty had been violent in prison. It was frightening, but despite that, she had been unable to force herself to send the letter. Finally, she had compromised. She decided to leave the letter at the prison and let the prison officials give it to Rusty. A quick check with Emily confirmed that it could be done and would be, but then she decided she would take just a minute and show them to him through the glass.

She would have come on Monday evening but was invited to a singles family home evening, so she found herself at the prison on Tuesday. She was trembling as she sat down and watched for him to appear on the other side of the glass.

CHAPTER 9

Jeri could not control the tingling sensation that ran from her head to her toes as Rusty walked into the room, a wide grin on his handsome face. His muscular frame filled the shapeless white prison jumpsuit, and the muscles of his arms rippled below the white sleeves. He moved her in a way that no one ever had.

Not even Warren.

The thought that this was to be her last visit brought unwelcome pain to her heart, but she sat up straight and clenched her fists in her lap in firm resolve. This would be it. She had promised. She would never visit Rusty in this place again. When this visit was over, Warren would fill her thoughts and desires.

She hoped.

"Hi," Rusty said as he sat down, and she couldn't help but remember the beautiful, innocent little boy he used to be. How she wished that he was still that innocent, instead of the wicked, violent, worldly man he had become.

"Hi," she said as these thoughts rushed through her head. "It's good to see you."

"Not nearly as good as it is to see you," he countered. Not once had the grin left his face. For a man who had been locked in solitary confinement for several weeks, he was certainly happy. She couldn't understand why. He leaned toward the glass and his grin was replaced with a look of concern. "What happened to you?" he asked. "You've been hurt."

"Oh, it was nothing. I'm fine," she said, surprised.

She thought she had managed to cover the remnants of the bruising on her face effectively with makeup. Apparently she hadn't.

"What was nothing?" he insisted.

Jeri could not resist the pleading in his eyes, those beautiful blue eyes she had never forgotten. She told him about her accident.

"Oh, Jeri, I'm sorry," he said. "Did it ruin your car?"

"Yes, but I have another one now. My parents came from Utah, and Dad helped me with the insurance and all. It could have been a lot worse."

"Well, I'm glad it wasn't," he said, and somehow she felt that he really meant it. Him a criminal and all. That came as a bit of a surprise to her. Was he really all that wicked? she allowed herself to wonder.

"That's why I didn't get back to see you like I promised. And then, when I finally was able to come, they said you were in solitary confinement and couldn't have visitors," she ventured. She wanted him to know that she knew he had been in trouble, even though she was not sure why.

"Yeah, sorry about that," he said sheepishly. "I lost my temper and I shouldn't have."

Suddenly becoming more judgmental than she had intended, she said, "I guess you must do that sort of thing a lot."

He did not hesitate in his reply. "Not really. I've done some stupid things, but I don't lose my temper very often." He hesitated, as if scanning his past, and then he added, "But when I do, I guess I can get really ugly."

"The poor guy you hit . . ." she began but stopped when she didn't know how to finish.

"Yeah, the little mutt," he said, and the grin he had carried into the room earlier returned. "I'm a lot bigger than him. He didn't stand a chance."

"Why, Rusty? Why did you hit someone?" She was actually hoping he had a good reason, if such a thing were possible.

"The someone was my cell mate, and it was because he had it coming."

Rusty seemed rather smug to Jeri. Let down, she felt a touch of anger. "That's no excuse," she scolded.

"My oh my," Rusty said, sudden anger flashing in his blue eyes. "You seem to know a lot about what I should and shouldn't do. Is that why you came today, so you could tell me how no good I am? Well, go ahead—you won't be telling me anything I don't already know."

Jeri felt her eyes begin to fill. She hadn't meant to get on him like this. Whatever in the world had gotten into her? She hastened to repair the damage. "I'm sorry, Rusty. I didn't mean to say those things. I'm sure if someone did to me whatever he did to you, I would have lost my temper, too. I certainly lose it enough. Let's forget this and get on to something else, like these," she said, lifting the envelope of pictures from her lap.

"Not just yet," Rusty said. "I know I'm a common criminal. But I think you ought to know what Chum did to . . ."

"Chum?" Jeri interrupted. "What a strange name. Who is he?"

"He was my cell mate. Be glad you don't know him. I may be a thief, and I may get angry and thump people at times, but he is just plain mean. Not very big, he isn't, but I'd bet he's killed before," Rusty told her.

"Oh, Rusty!" she moaned.

"Yes, and who knows what else," he went on. "Believe me, it has not been easy living in the same cell with a guy like him month after month."

"Did they make you go back with him?" Jeri asked. "You know, after you got out of wherever you were?"

"Solitary. I was in solitary confinement. But no, they're afraid he might make me mad again, and he probably would have done so. He would sure be angry if he knew what I was doing right now," he told her.

"Why?" she asked, surprised. "What business of his is it if you have a visitor?"

"I think he hates women."

"So he thinks you have to as well?" she asked.

"It's more than that," Rusty explained. "I won't get into it all, but he told me I was not to visit you again. I said I'd do as I pleased, and he got really mouthy with me. What he said would shock a good little Mormon girl like you. Anyway, I lost it." He began to grin again. "And he lost his front teeth."

"He deserved it," she hissed. "He had no right."

"There, you see? Maybe we aren't so different after all," Rusty quipped.

"Oh, you!" Jeri said, but she found herself smiling. "Here, I brought some pictures. They said I could show them to you, then they will give them to you to keep if you want them. This is your mom and dad." She held the picture up to the glass.

"They're Mormons, you say," he said as he leaned close to the glass to see them better.

"Is that really so bad?" she asked.

"That's what I've always heard," he replied. "Nice looking people, anyway. Are you sure they are my folks?" he asked doubtfully.

"Positive," she said. "I know it's hard to see from a picture, but you have your mother's eyes and your father's chin."

"Really," he said very solemnly. "And here I always thought they were mine."

Jeri laughed. Rusty may be a criminal, but he did have a sense of humor. She held up a picture of his sister and explained that she was the one who was a baby when he was kidnapped. Rusty stared at it in awe, then he said, "Wow! She's a knockout."

"Yeah, isn't she though?" Jeri agreed. "I haven't seen her for several years, but she is very pretty. Like your mother," she added.

Rusty studied the picture for a long time. When he looked up, his deep blue eyes locked on Jeri's and she felt that tingle again. She had to look away to get rid of it. He was not the same boy she had known as a child, she reminded herself sternly. She fumbled in the envelope and pulled out a picture of his little brother. When she lifted it to the glass and looked up, his eyes were still on her face, and the way he was looking made her uncomfortable. His words made her more so, "She's pretty, my sister, but so are you," he said. There was no grin. His face was solemn.

Becoming increasingly uncomfortable, she said, "You have a little brother." She waved the photograph in front of the glass.

"Jeri, please," he said, his eyes not leaving her face even yet. "Don't get me wrong. You are the most beautiful girl . . . woman . . . lady, I have ever met. But I know my place. We are from different worlds. You don't have to worry about me ever bothering you."

"Thank you," she said curtly. But she was struggling with her own feelings.

If only things had been different!

But things were as they were. She said, "You have a good family, Rusty. I hope someday you can get to know them."

"They won't want to meet me," he said harshly. "Like you, they are from a different world than me."

Jeri offered no reply. "Their address is on this envelope, Rusty. If you change your mind, I'm sure they'd love to hear from you."

He shook his head. "I don't think so. Keep the pictures. I appreciate you showing them to me, but now I've seen them, that's good enough."

"Rusty," Jeri protested.

"I mean it," he said. "I would only make their lives miserable. I'm not a good person. They are, I suppose. Keep them."

Jeri nodded. "Whatever you say, Rusty."

The door behind him opened. "Time's up," the officer said.

It had gone by so quickly. "It's been good to talk to you," Jeri said. "And I guess this is good-bye."

"What! No more visits?" he said. "Oh, come on, you're just giving in to Chum." He was smiling, but only with his mouth. There was hurt in his eyes.

She looked down. "No more," she repeated. "But I'm glad I found you."

"I guess I am, too," he agreed. "One thing's for sure, though."

"What's that?"

"I will never go by Randy again. I like Rusty better." With that, he smiled at her again, and she felt a pain deep inside. She smiled back, but hot tears began to flow. "Oh, and one more thing, Jeri. Please don't tell my family about me." The officer opened the door, beckoned, and Rusty was gone.

Forever, she thought. Now he really is gone.

Jeri wiped her eyes and left the building as quickly as she could. Once she was back in her car, she laid the rejected envelope of pictures on the seat and gave in to her emotions. She cried long and hard. When at last there were no more tears, Jeri hoped she could finally put to rest the little lost boy from her childhood. She had to get on with her life.

Jeri stopped at a restaurant on her way home. She was emotionally drained, and there was no way she was up to cooking for herself that night.

Her waitress asked her if she was all right. "I will be," she said.

"A man?" the woman asked knowingly.

Jeri nodded. "They can be awful sometimes," the woman said. "But again, what would we girls do without them? If one gets too hard to handle, there's always another." She smiled ruefully. "That's my philosophy."

Jeri nodded again, irritated. It was not her philosophy, and she had better get on with the business of getting to know Warren better. Tomorrow she would call him. Tonight she had to rid herself of old feelings and memories.

It was late by the time Jeri got home. She was a little irritated when she saw that Warren had been calling all evening long, and had left three messages on her machine. She went to bed without listening to them. Tomorrow, she promised herself. Tomorrow would mark the start of a new life for Jeri Satch.

Tonight would mark the end of an old one.

***

Rusty Egan, alias Randy Moore, Inmate #556770 was having a hard night. He was elated that he would be released in just a few days, but despite his best intentions, Jeri Satch had gotten to him. He knew they had practically nothing in common, but he couldn't get her off his mind. The thought that he would never see her again was an unwelcome one.

He drifted into a restless sleep that night and dreamed of freedom, lots of money, and Jeri Satch. He also dreamed of Chum, and he awoke with an uneasy feeling that he would regret ever meeting that mousy little man. The uneasy feeling was centered around the dream where Chum and Jeri had met beyond the walls of the prison. Most of the dream was fuzzy, and he had no idea what Chum had done to Jeri in the dream, but the one thing that stood out in his mind was his own words, the ones that awoke him. He clearly recalled shouting at Jeri, "I'll find you, Jeri! I'll find you!"

"Who will you find?" his disgruntled cell mate asked.

Embarrassed, he pretended he didn't have any idea what the man was talking about. His cell mate was soon peacefully snoring again, and Rusty struggled through what was left of the troubled night. The remainder of his dreaming centered around Chum, Jeri, and a half-million stolen dollars.

***

The phone wakened Jeri shortly before her alarm was set to ring. She picked it up and answered groggily, in an almost unintelligible slur. "Hello."

"Jeri! Where were you last night?" Warren demanded. "I was worried sick. You weren't in another wreck were you?"

Jeri came fully awake at the sound of Warren's voice. "Warren, why are you calling so early?" she asked.

"Because I have an early class today and I couldn't go through the day wondering if you were all right," he answered.

"Of course I'm all right," she said a little sharply.

"No more wrecks or anything?" he asked in a calmer voice.

"No more wrecks," she agreed, struggling to get her legs free of the sheets so she could swing them over the edge of the bed.

"Good, I was worried sick," he told her. "Where were you last night? I called a dozen times."

"You did?" she said.

"Why didn't you return my call when you came in?" he asked softly. "I hardly slept all night."

"I'm sorry Warren. It was so late when I came in that I went straight to bed." Feigning ignorance of his messages, she added, "Did you leave a message for me?"

"Yes. Didn't you check?"

"I told you, I went straight to bed," she answered. "What class do you have that is so early?" she asked him, trying to deflect his demands about where she had been the previous evening.

It didn't work. He did not even mention what the class was. "Please, Jeri, where were you?" he asked in a less demanding tone.

"I ate out," she said. "I didn't feel like cooking, so I went to a restaurant."

"Not all night," he said. "Were you visiting that Rusty guy at the prison?"

It was the first time Rusty's name had come up between them in a long time. "I hope you weren't, because you promised."

Jeri brushed her tangled hair back and pulled her nightgown down over her knees before she answered. She had hoped he wouldn't ask. But since he had, she guessed she just as well get the issue out of the way once and for all. "Warren, I didn't make it there when I had planned because of my wreck."

"I know," Warren replied. "The last time we talked of it, you hung up on me. When you didn't mention it again, I assumed it was done."

"Oh, really," she said, heating up. "Then why did you think that was where I had been? Didn't you think I'd keep my word?"

"Oh, no, Jeri, it's not that," he protested.

"But it is that," she shot back. "Well, let me tell you this. I went last night because they wouldn't let me see him until then because he got in a fight and got himself locked in solitary confinement."

"Oh, great!" Warren broke in.

"Let me talk, Warren, or I'll slam the phone again," she said. When he didn't say anything more she knew he believed her. She said, "I went last night and I showed him the pictures Mom sent me. He said he didn't want them. I told him I wouldn't be back to see him again, and I left. It's finished, Warren. Now instead of arguing, let's just talk. I haven't got very long."

They talked. And again that night they talked. And to Jeri's delight, there was no argument at all. If they could just keep it like that. They talked about Christmas, and Warren asked if she was planning to come to Utah. She said she couldn't; a new account that she would be working on would not allow her enough time off.

"Then I'll be coming down there," he announced. "I'll stay in a cheap motel and visit you every minute when you are not otherwise occupied."

She was glad.

She thought so, at least. If she could just quit thinking about Rusty, alone and miserable in that cold, stuffy old prison.

CHAPTER 10

The prison grapevine being what it was, it was no surprise that Rusty learned of the impending release of Chum. He too had received a parole hearing and had been granted a release date. The word that filtered through the prison to Rusty was that his former cell mate would be released early in March. Rusty had known that such a thing was likely to happen but had hoped he would have more time to see if he could figure out a safe way to recover his money and disappear before Chum got out.

As it was, he would either have to get the money some other way, and he knew that would not be easy. Or else he would have to wait and let Chum help and hope the little creep didn't get away with it all.

There was one other choice. It did not appeal to Rusty, but it did occur to him. He could wait for Chum to get out, stalk him and do what he had to do to keep the man from either getting the money or becoming a threat to Rusty's own life. He drew short of thinking murder, because that was not part of Rusty's makeup. But disabling the creep, he rationalized, was not only a good way to protect himself, but also would, he was convinced, save the lives of others.

As his release date drew closer, Rusty became more apprehensive about Chum. He received two more notes from the older inmate. Each was full of veiled threats. Rusty had to admit that the man would not be easy to outwit. He was indeed a lethal foe.

True to her word, Jeri did not visit again before Rusty's release. Of course, he had not told her that he was getting out before Christmas, so he supposed she might give in and try after he was gone. But frankly, he doubted it. Anyway, it was silly of him to even think of her. They had nothing in common.

Except their early childhood. And his family. Rusty began to regret not taking the family pictures that Jeri had brought for him. And that regret planted a seed. It was only the beginning of an idea, and not a good one, he supposed, but he let it grow nonetheless. By the time he was released on the eighteenth day of December, it had blossomed into a full-blown idea.

He would get the pictures of his family. He would get their address. He would get to see Jeri again. And finally, he just might be able to recover the stolen money. All he had to do was find out where Jeri lived, and he knew that could be done, even though it might take a little time. But it had to be done before the first of March.

Rusty tried not to think about the police and the bank officials. He was certain they had their reasons for helping him get an early parole, and he was equally certain those reasons all had to do with a certain half-million dollars that were missing. But he did not worry too much about it. He would take his time and outsmart them.

What Rusty did not expect was for a representative of the bank to be waiting for him the very day he was released. He didn't know the man, but he literally met him at the door and took his bag of belongings. "You are riding with me," the fellow said curtly.

"And who might you be?" Rusty asked.

"I work for a bank you know quite well," the man responded. He clearly found the idea of giving a ride to the man who had robbed his employer very distasteful.

"I see, and where are we going, Mr. . . ." Rusty waited for a name.

"Hampton," the bank's man replied curtly.

"Mr. Hampton, where are we going?" Rusty repeated.

"To your apartment."

"But I don't have one. That's what I need to be doing today—finding a place to live."

"Oh, you have one all right," Mr. Hampton grumbled. "But you will have to repay the bank for the rent."

"What if it isn't what I like or is more than I can afford?" Rusty pressed. As they talked they were walking into the parking lot.

"It isn't," the man said shortly.

"I don't have a job yet," Rusty replied reasonably.

"You do, and you start tomorrow," he was informed.

"I see. And where will that be at?" Rusty asked. He tried to stay outwardly calm, but his insides were churning. The bank definitely had a plan and he would have to be extra careful not to let them carry it out.

"You will be at Pink's Auto Body," Mr. Hampton said. "Not the best job . . . but better than you deserve."

"You don't like me very well," Rusty said with a grin.

"I can't think of a reason why I should," Mr. Hampton retorted sharply. "Here is the car."

It was a black limousine. A uniformed chauffeur opened the trunk, dropped in Rusty's bag, and gently shut the lid. Then he opened the door of the car and waited while Mr. Hampton entered and seated himself in the plush seat. Rusty stood there uncomfortably. The chauffeur gestured for him to join the bank man, which he did.

Rusty had never ridden in such luxury, but he would, he promised himself. As soon as he had recovered his half million. The ride took thirty minutes. Not a word passed between Rusty and Mr. Hampton the entire trip. When they finally stopped, it was in one of the older sections of Sacramento, in front of an old but sturdy apartment building.

After showing him to his room and giving him the key, Mr. Hampton turned to him and held out a paper. "Mr. Moore," he said, "this is the address of your employer, Pink's Auto Body. Be there at eight A.M. sharp tomorrow."

"How am I supposed to get there?" Rusty asked.

"Walk, call a taxi, I don't care. Just be there," he was told curtly. "Your payments to the bank for both your rent and your restitution will be withheld from your check. Arrangements have been made. And don't forget your first appointment with your parole officer. I am told you already know when and where."

Rusty nodded. He had already met the man and he knew what he had to do. "That will be all then," Mr. Hampton said, and turned away, clearly glad to be rid of Rusty.

No more glad than Rusty was.

The apartment was liveable but small and old. It consisted of three rooms, a bedroom, a bathroom, and a combination living room and kitchen. It contained only the barest furnishings: an ancient white electric range, a small yellow refrigerator, a badly worn sofa and matching chair, an old wooden table with two scarred wooden chairs, a twin bed with one set of bedding, a much-used chest of drawers, a radio alarm clock, and a mirror. That was it. There was no television, no microwave—only the bare essentials.

Rusty took his time putting his clothes and few other belongings away. They didn't take up much space. He counted out the money he had been given upon release. He had two hundred dollars to live on until he got a paycheck, and he didn't imagine there would be much left of that by the time the bank took their cut. He allowed himself a smile. It could be worse. At least he had a place to stay, and before the day was over he would have some food in the house and something to wear to work. He decided that he really was lucky after all.

That night, he sat eating a pizza he had cooked for himself and thought about his future. That was not something Rusty had done a lot of in his life. Now there was a reason to. He was a free man again, and when he found a safe way to retrieve his stolen loot, he would be a rich man. And he knew who he was. He no longer had an Uncle Bill, and one day he would settle the score with the man who had claimed to be. But that could wait. What couldn't wait very long was finding out where Jeri lived. He wanted the pictures and address of his family.

He wanted to see her, too, stupid as the thought was.

Actually, what he mostly wanted was to see her.

***

It had been two weeks since she had seen Rusty for the last time. The envelope containing the pictures and address sat on the dresser. She wished he had taken them. She couldn't get herself to throw them away. She didn't even want to put them out of sight in a drawer, and yet they tormented her, for they reminded her of Rusty. They were also her last link with him, and despite all her best intentions, she simply could not part with that link.

Warren had called at least a half dozen times in the past few weeks and they had not argued once. Nor had Rusty's name come up again. But somehow, there seemed to be a little tension. It even showed up in the letters he wrote almost daily. Rusty was the problem. Warren, she was certain, was jealous. That was ridiculous of him. Rusty was nothing to her but a memory.

Or was he?

The turmoil continued, and it intensified as Christmas approached. Warren would be here Saturday morning. He was going to rent a car and come straight to her place, even though he had a motel room reserved through the week. He had to return to Utah the following Saturday, December twenty-ninth. His pending visit both excited and disturbed her. She did not love him, but she supposed that would come. She did enjoy his company, and a week with him in town would be a real test for their relationship—their romance—if that was what it was.

She looked at her watch. It was nearly ten. She turned on the television to watch the news. Warren would not be calling that night, but she had talked to him for a half hour last night. She thought of Rusty in his dingy prison cell and felt very sad. Life could be so unfair.

For the hundredth time in the past two weeks she thought of Rusty's parents. He had asked her not to tell them about him, but she wanted to. Maybe, she told herself, as she had done so many times, talking to them might help bring closure to that part of her life. Nothing else had brought it. And she wanted that to happen. It had to happen.

Impulsively, Jeri switched off the television and reached for the phone. It was so easy. In less than a minute she had the number for Brother and Sister Egan in Flagstaff, Arizona. They had lived there, Jeri's mother had told her, for nearly three years now. It would be so simple to dial, and maybe, just maybe, that was what she needed to do. After all, she had searched for Rusty for most of her life. Who was he to tell her she couldn't tell them where he was. She had talked to her parents about it. They said it was up to her, but she could not forget what her mother had said. "Jeri, only you can decide. But if it had been you who was kidnapped, and someone had found you, I would want to know."

But Rusty didn't want her to tell his parents. Jeri looked at her watch, then reached for the phone. It still wasn't quite ten o'clock. She should do it.

She shouldn't do it.

Why shouldn't she?

She did.

"Hello," said a voice Jeri recognized as that of Mindy Egan.

"Hello," Jeri said hesitantly. "Is this Mrs. Egan?" She felt foolish. She knew it was. She was only buying time. Maybe she should just hang up.

Her mother's words kept her from doing that. Rusty's words kept her stalling. "Is your husband at home?"

"Yes, but he's gone to bed already," Mindy said. "He has to leave early in the morning on a business trip. Could I give him a message?"

Boy, could you, Jeri thought. "I guess I can tell you, but this is rather important. I know it's a bad time, nearly ten and all."

"It's nearly eleven," Mindy corrected her. Jeri had not thought about the difference in time zones and she almost hung up. "Who is this, anyway?" Mindy asked impatiently. Jeri continued to clutch the phone. "What do you want?"

Jeri wondered if she should just hang up, as her mother's words battled with Rusty's, but her mother's advice won.

"Are you still there? Who is this? I'm going to hang up," Mindy Egan was saying angrily.

"Oh, please don't, Mrs. Egan," she said urgently, her mind finally fully made up. "This is Jeri Satch."

"Jeri!" Mrs. Egan sounded alarmed. "I haven't heard your voice in years." There was a short pause. "Why are you calling, Jeri? Has something happened to your mother?"

"Oh, no. She's fine," Jeri quickly assured her. "I'm calling about something else. I'm sorry it is so late. There is something I want to tell you, and I was sitting here trying to decide if I should or not, and I finally decided I could not wait any longer. I forgot all about the time difference."

"That's right, you are in California, aren't you? I just received a card from your mother. She wrote a long note with it. She said you were in Sacramento, that you had a really good job, a nice boyfriend who is going to be a lawyer, and that you had been in an accident but that you were okay now."

Jeri couldn't help but smile. "She said all that?" she asked.

"Oh, yes, and more. I just answered her today," Mindy said, "but it won't go out in the mail until tomorrow. Your mother has been such a good friend over the years. But I am just going on and on. I'm not even giving you a chance to tell me what you called about. I'm sorry."

"Yeah, well, this is kind of hard. I wish I hadn't called so late, so I could tell you both at once," Jeri said.

"Is it really important?" Mindy asked doubtfully.

"Actually, yes. My timing's just bad."

"Is it something I can tell him in the morning?" Mindy pressed. "Patrick has a hard time getting back to sleep when something wakes him up at night."

"Well," Jeri said, "I guess, but I think you'll wake him tonight after you hear what I have to say."

"Let me be the judge of that, Jeri. Go ahead. I can't take much more suspense," Mindy said with a chuckle.

"I . . . I . . . don't know how to say this. I . . ." Jeri found herself overcome with emotion and she started to cry. She couldn't help it and she couldn't stop.

"Jeri, what is it?" Mindy was alarmed now. "Whatever is the matter?"

Jeri fought to compose herself, finally did, and when she could put words together, she said simply, "I found Rusty."

There was an audible gasp on the other end of the line. And then there was silence. Then Mindy spoke, and she sounded angry. "Jeri, is this some kind of joke?"

"No, really, I found him. I would never joke about this. He was my best friend," she said, and again her emotions stopped the flow of words.

Silence prevailed for what must have been a minute. Then Mindy Egan asked, "Are you absolutely sure?"

"Yes," Jeri managed to answer. "It's him, all right."

"Patrick!" Mindy yelled so loudly Jeri jerked the phone from her ear.

There was no sound except what was probably Mindy sobbing. Then she heard her husband, Patrick. "What's the matter with you?" he called from somewhere else in the house.

"Come . . . fast . . ." Mindy pleaded.

Jeri heard running steps. Then again the sound of Rusty's father's voice. "What is going on, Mindy? You scared me to death. Who's on the phone?"

"Jeri Satch."

"What is she doing calling and upsetting you in the middle of the night?" Jeri heard him say.

"She found Rusty."

"What?" he exclaimed. "Give me that phone!"

Jeri braced herself.

"Jeri Satch, is it?" he demanded.

"Yes."

"What kind of ridiculous thing is this you are telling Mindy?" he demanded in anger.

His anger was just what she needed. It brought her out of her tears and restored her voice. "I told her I found Rusty. It's the truth, Mr. Egan. I really did."

"That's impossible. We gave him up for dead years ago," he retorted.

"But I didn't," she shot back. Then words spilled from her. "I've seen him. I've talked to him. He remembers me. He remembers you. But he had forgotten. It's a long story. I'm sorry I upset you, and he would be really angry if he knew I was calling you. But I had to."

"Jeri, stop!" Patrick Egan ordered. "Let me think." He was silent a moment, perhaps getting his composure. Mindy was crying in the background. At last, he said, "You are serious, Jeri?"

"I am," she responded.

"I'm sorry," he said in a soft, gentle voice. "This is such a shock."

"I know," she answered. "It was to me, too."

"You are absolutely certain?" he asked, and now there was a hopeful, almost pleading sound to his voice.

"Positive. Absolutely," she said.

Jeri heard another click on the line and Mindy said, "I'm on another phone. Tell us, Jeri, where is he?"

She told them. They cried. She cried. They thanked her. They asked how they could see him and when. She told them it might not be possible, that he might not let them. "He doesn't like Mormons," she said.

"But he is our son. We must see him," Patrick countered. There was not a trace of anger left in his voice, just immeasurable sadness mixed with shock and joy. He sounded just like what he was, a father who had found a long lost son, one whom he had continued to love and to grieve for. "We must see him," he repeated.

CHAPTER 11

Whistling was not something Rusty had done much of in his life. He had never known very much happiness. He considered himself good-natured, and people generally seemed to like him. But he had been raised in an extremely abusive environment until he had finally fled, and even then, he found himself in miserable circumstances most of the time. So for him to be whistling at a little past seven o'clock in the morning as he strode quickly down the street was most unusual.

He felt good. The sun was not yet up, but the sky was clear, promising a sunny day. It was cool and a soft breeze was blowing from the west, and that added to his feeling of euphoria. He was a free man. He had wealth stored away. He had a job, one he thought he might even enjoy. He had a few dollars in his pocket. He had a new name, and that, in a way, made him a new man. Life didn't get much better than this, he decided.

He wasn't even bothered by the fact that someone in a blue Ford sedan seemed to always be somewhere behind him. The cops or someone hired by the bank, he was sure, but there was no way he was leading them to his money. As long as he didn't break any laws, they couldn't bother him. He felt great.

It was a half hour's brisk walk from Rusty's apartment to Pink's Auto Body. He arrived there fifteen minutes early. The shop was a fairly large one, and the front door to the office was open. He stepped in and looked around. The place seemed to be deserted, but after just a short wait, a large, beefy man with a round, pink face entered from the door that led to the shop itself.

"What can I do for you, sir?" the man asked.

"Are you the boss?" Rusty asked, a smile on his face.

"Sure am. Pink's the name," the big fellow said. "Do you need an estimate or something?"

"No, Mr. Pink . . ." Rusty began.

The owner cut him off with the wave of a huge arm and chuckle. "No 'mister,'" he said. "Folks just call me Pink. Real name's Sam Crawford. Always went by Pink. Couldn't help my color." He laughed as if pleased with himself, then he went on, "So what do you need, sir?"

Rusty extended a hand. "My name is Rusty . . . well, Randy Moore, but I prefer to be called Rusty. That's my real name. I was told to be here this morning."

The fat pink face of Mr. Crawford underwent a radical change. The pink turned an ugly violet and his eyes narrowed. His mouth pinched shut. He glowered at Rusty for a moment, and after he did not accept Rusty's offered hand, Rusty awkwardly withdrew it. "Moore, huh?" he said at length. "Well, at least you look decent, even though we both know you're not."

Rusty felt the color creep into his face, but he held his tongue. This was not going to be easy, he decided. "I'm here, ready to work," he said, still trying to smile and stay positive.

"And that's what you will do or you'll be out of here so fast you'll think your backside is your front," he was rudely informed. "Let's get one thing straight right now. There is one reason and one reason only that I agreed to give you a job. I owe the bank you robbed a favor. I told them I'd give you a chance, but one screwup and I'll fire you. So you just do as your told, don't take nothing that ain't yours, and don't pick no fights with the working men here, and the bank'll get their money."

Rusty nodded his head. "I'll do the best I can, sir," he answered meekly.

"You better. I never hired no cons before, and like I said, I wouldn't have done so now, but I got pressured. I need to fill out some forms, then you can get to work."

The forms listed Rusty as Randy Moore. He recalled Jeri as she tried to get to him take the address of his parents. He regretted refusing that. Not that he had any intentions of ever trying to get to know them, but it would be helpful to get a birth certificate so he could establish himself as Rusty Egan rather than the name Uncle Bill had given him. Well, he would see to that when he found her, if he did, and this was just added incentive to do so.

A half dozen other workers filtered in, punched the clock, and entered the shop. Rusty soon heard the shop come to life with the sound of hammering, grinding, and cursing, laughing men. The euphoria of the morning was gone. Depression hung heavy on his heart.

"Sign here," Pink said, pointing with a huge finger to a space at the bottom of one sheet of paper. Rusty signed as Randy since he could see that forcing the name issue would lead to confrontation, and he didn't need that in his life right now. "And here." He signed again. "One more," Pink told him. That done, he said, "Okay, let's get to work."

Rusty had no idea how much he would be making, and that seemed like something he should know, so he drummed up his courage and asked, as politely as he could, "Sir, how much will I be making?"

"More than you're worth," Pink said. "This is a union shop. You get union scale."

That was it. The amount was not disclosed, but if it was union scale, it would be all right. He let the matter drop. Rusty followed Pink into the shop. "Everybody listen up," the big man shouted. It took a moment, but the shop became very quiet as tools were shut down and hammers dropped. It seemed that everyone knew who the boss was in this place.

"This here's the convict I told you about," Pink began. "Whatever you don't want to do, he will. He'll keep the place clean. And he'll stay busy or you will let me know. Got that?"

Everyone seemed to have gotten it. Pink swung around and walked out. All six men stared at Rusty until finally, the oldest of the group said, "You have a name?"

"Rusty," he replied, hoping that would not cause him problems with the boss later.

"Rusty, I'm Jim," the older man said extending a hand. Rusty shook it, surprised. Maybe he could stand it after all. "I'm foreman here." Then he introduced the rest of the men, and each one stepped over to him and shook hands. "Pink says you'll do what we need, cleaning and such, but he doesn't come in here much. You will want to keep things clean, but have you had any experience at body work or mechanics in general?"

Rusty had. Uncle Bill tinkered with cars, and as much as he hated the man, Rusty had learned a lot from him. And every job he had held from the day he ran away at age fifteen was with cars. He had worked both as a mechanic and in body shops. He explained that.

"Good, clean things up here for a few hours and then we'll see how you do on one of these wrecks," Jim said, waving a greasy hand toward cars currently being worked on.

Things were looking up. Rusty felt himself letting out a sigh of relief. His depression lifted. He started with a broom and he worked hard until noon. All six men trekked across the street together to a hamburger joint for lunch. "You have any cash?" Jim asked thoughtfully. "I know you just got out of prison. If you're broke, I'll lend you some until Friday. We get paid on Friday."

"Thanks, I have a little," Rusty said.

That was the only reference any of his coworkers made to his prison sentence. He helped one man grind a fender for a little while, spent some time in the paint shop when one of the men had to leave for a doctor's appointment, skillfully hammered out a bad dent, and did other odd jobs during the afternoon. He knew what he was doing, and the other men could see it. He even lifted the front end of a Cavalier by himself when he was asked to jack it up so they could block it. That drew a chorus of hearty cheers. By the time five o'clock rolled around, Rusty felt like he had earned the respect of all of them. He hoped so. As they all filed into the office and punched out, Pink appeared. "The con work, Jim?" he asked.

Rusty gritted his teeth. Jim smiled and said, "Worked hard, boss. He knows what he's doing. Strong as an ox, too."

Rusty wasn't bothered by the car that shadowed him as he walked home. He found himself whistling again. Pink was a jerk, but the guys were all right. Maybe this job would work out for as long as he needed it.

***

Friday night it was raining again. Some of Jeri's friends from the ward had invited her to go to a ball game with them that night, but she declined. Her apartment was a bit of a mess and she wanted it to be just right when Warren came tomorrow. She cleaned until late, then finally settled down with a book. The light winter rain was soothing as it dropped from the eaves outside her living-room window. She was tired, and the book slipped to the floor as she drifted off to sleep.

She woke up to the ringing of her doorbell. She picked up her book, ran her fingers through her hair, and glanced at her watch. It was after nine. Who would be calling on her at this time of day? Especially on the Friday night before Christmas. It wouldn't be her home or visiting teachers. They had been here already. She hurried to the door and peered through the peephole. Amazed, she swung the door wide, "Brother and Sister Egan," she cried. "It is so good to see you. Please, come in."

"Hello, Jeri," Mindy said. Her face was drawn and her eyes were red. Patrick's face was also very sober.

"Please, sit down," she offered, gesturing to the sofa.

"We won't stay long," Mindy said, but she and her husband sat down wearily.

They were clearly not happy. There could only be one reason why they were in Sacramento, and there seemed to be no doubt that they had met Rusty and it had not gone well. That did not surprise her.

She was wrong. The visit had not gone badly; it simply had not occurred. What they told her left her in shock. It was totally unexpected. "We have been to the prison, Jeri," Patrick Egan said. "Why didn't you tell us Rusty was being released?"

"Released?" she asked in surprise. "I don't understand. I just talked to him two weeks ago, and he didn't say anything about being released. There must be some mistake."

"There is no mistake," he said sternly. "They told us he had been released on parole Monday. They refused to give us any details because they didn't believe it when we told them we were his parents. Even though we gave them the name you said he was going by, they were firm in their refusal."

"We didn't know where else to go," Mindy added. "We hoped maybe you knew where we could find him."

Jeri was shaking her head. "I have no idea. I can't believe he's really out. And I have no idea where he would go. He didn't tell me much about himself. All he wanted was to hear what I could tell him about his past. Honestly, I don't even know if he would stay in Sacramento."

"He hasn't made contact with you?" Patrick asked hopefully.

"No. He doesn't know where I live and my phone is unlisted," she said. "I'm so sorry."

"It is not your fault," Mindy said quickly. "We are grateful to you for all you have done. We had hoped to see him, no matter the outcome, but at least we know he is alive. That is more than we've even dared to hope for in years."

"Would you let us know if you hear anything, or if you can learn anything?" Patrick asked.

"You know I will," she replied. "Tuesday morning, I'll call Emily, the woman who is in charge of bookkeeping at the prison. Maybe she can tell me where he went."

"Only if they lied to us tonight," Patrick said. "They told us they didn't have an address. That they simply sent him out the door. They wouldn't have given it to us if they had known it, but they claim they don't."

"I promise, I'll call Emily. Maybe she can help," Jeri said. "I just can't believe he's out. He never let on to me at all."

The Egans planned to fly back to Flagstaff in the morning. Jeri offered them a room for the night. She had a spare bedroom and bed, but they had already arranged for a hotel. They left even more despondent than when they came.

Jeri was depressed herself. Not that she was not glad to hear that Rusty was out of prison. She hated that place. But what would he do now? Where would he go? Would he get in more trouble? She shuddered and wept. What a miserable life he must have.

She sat up late, worrying endlessly about the guy she was supposed to have forgotten. She slept little, and was tired and cranky when Warren arrived at the door the next morning, a big smile on his face and a beautiful, red long-stemmed rose in his hand.

He handed her the rose. She thanked him and allowed him to give her a quick kiss on the cheek, and welcomed him halfheartedly into her apartment. She found a vase and put the rose in water and set it on her kitchen table. Then she made small talk while she fixed him a mid-morning snack. She was so tired after the long, restless night, that she knew she was horrible company, but he seemed so glad to be with her that it didn't appear to bother him at all.

They spent the afternoon at the zoo, then Warren took her to dinner at one of the nicest restaurants in town, and after that, to a concert. He was well prepared for their time together. He had made reservations in advance at the restaurant, and he had the tickets in hand when they arrived at the concert hall. "I purchased them on the Internet," he told her proudly.

Dinner was filling and very good. The concert was great. But she was sleepy and drifted off several times, her head leaning comfortably on Warren's shoulder. If it bothered him, he didn't give any indication of it. He sought for and held her hand during most of the concert. They had dessert at a small ice-cream shop afterwards. Then they went back to her apartment where they sat close together on the sofa and talked until after midnight.

She kept yawning. He finally noticed. "You are tired," he said. "So am I, actually. I better be going." He stood and pulled her gently to her feet.

They strolled slowly across the living room to the door, hand in hand. He turned toward her, one hand resting on the doorknob, the other still holding hers. "Thank you for a super day . . . and evening," he said with a smile.

"Thank *you*," she said. "You made the plans. I am impressed. I can't wait to see what else is in store."

"Secrets," he said. His head came slowly down toward hers. She had the impulse to turn her cheek to him again, but she resisted, and his lips touched hers. She expected a quick peck, but it didn't work that way at all.

His arms came around her waist and he pulled her gently to him. Their lips pressed together firmly. Slowly, she found her arms coming around him and he responded with a still tighter embrace. Finally, he released her. Their eyes met, and he murmured, "You are beautiful, Jeri."

And he was quite handsome, but she said nothing, because images of Rusty came unbidden to her mind, breaking the spell Warren had so skillfully woven. "I'll see you in the morning," he said. "I'll pick you up for Church at eight-thirty."

"I'll be ready," she promised.

After Warren had left, Jeri threw a private little tantrum. "Leave me alone," she said aloud. "Get out of my mind. How can I ever be happy if you keep popping in there?"

She was referring, of course, to Rusty. She wanted to fall in love. She wanted to feel what Warren was feeling, and Rusty was interfering. She went to bed in tears.

CHAPTER 12

Sunday morning, two days before Christmas, arrived clear and cool. Jeri awoke early despite having gone to bed late. She and Warren attended Church together and spent a leisurely afternoon in her apartment. Later, after fixing dinner for Warren, Jeri took him to an activity with a few other young single adults from her ward for the evening. They played table games until quite late after having spent a couple of hours singing Christmas carols around the ward. Warren had a strong, clear tenor voice, and it blended nicely with Jeri's alto. They had a really good time, but Jeri could see that Warren was getting impatient. She knew that he wanted her alone again. She was not sure that was such a good idea.

He finally convinced her that they should leave the others and go back to her apartment. There they snacked, listened to Christmas music, and talked well into the morning. Warren expected and got a lingering kiss at the door. He murmured words of endearment. She thought some, but did not voice them. She found herself wondering if this relationship was right for her. She wanted it to be, but she needed time and he was pushing too hard. It made her feel uncomfortable.

After Warren had gone, Jeri reflected on the evening, and she had to admit she had enjoyed herself. Warren had been fun when they were with the group. It was only when they were alone that she felt uneasy. But her evening had been marred with thoughts of Rusty. She wondered where he would spend his Christmas Eve, and if he would even think of the Savior. She doubted it. There had been no religion in his life since that fateful day so many years ago when he was stolen from his family.

Would Rusty be alone somewhere, doing nothing and feeling depressed, or would he commit some heinous crime? Jeri even wondered if he would spend his Christmas Eve in a bar getting drunk.

She remembered the unrecovered stolen money that Emily had told her about—the money the authorities thought was stashed somewhere. Jeri wondered then if he had retrieved it, and if so, was he now far away from here, spending the money and making a new life for himself, such as that might be.

Jeri's heart ached for Rusty. He was still her friend after all these years. She had tried to forget him, but she had failed. She had found him and had lost him. These thoughts depressed her, and she spent a half hour before retiring to her bed, reading the Christmas story from the scriptures and trying her best to get him out of her mind. As she read, a feeling of peace settled over her and she finally laid her scriptures beside the bed. Her last thoughts before she went to sleep were of Warren and how they would spend Christmas Eve together.

***

Uncle Bill was a drunk. He was also a thief and a coward. He preyed on those weaker than himself. That had included Rusty until Rusty had finally gotten big enough to fight back when he was abused. He had learned to hate the smell of alcohol on a man's breath because that was always the time when things had been at their worst with Uncle Bill.

Rusty had rejected most things about Uncle Bill in his own life. But at the top of the list was the use of alcohol. He had tasted it a number of times, but he had chosen not to drink. The one thing he had learned from Uncle Bill that became part of his life, besides how to work on cars, was that the most productive way to make a living was to steal. Uncle Bill had been good at that and had never been caught. Rusty had not been so lucky, but once he got his hands on the money he had already stolen and done time for, he would be set for many years to come.

***

Rusty walked to a bar and grill on Christmas Eve, just because he was lonely. He needed human companionship. He had money in his pocket from the small paycheck Pink had reluctantly given him at the end of his shift on Friday. He spent some of it on dinner. After finishing his meal, he moved to the bar and ordered a coke. That got him some strange looks, but no one said anything. He sat and sipped for a few minutes, surrounded by people, but all alone.

"Hi, stranger. You must be new around here. Could you use a little company?" a sweet voice asked. He looked up from his drink to find an attractive woman standing at his elbow. She was painted and dolled up and smelled of alcohol, but Rusty was lonely.

"Sure, I'm Rusty," he said with an encouraging smile.

"People call me Candy," she said as she laid a soft hand on his arm and swung herself gracefully onto the bar stool at his side. She didn't need much encouragement. "They call me that because I'm so sweet," she added.

"Nice to meet you, Candy," Rusty said nervously. He took a sip of his coke, not sure what else he should say to her.

Candy didn't have that problem. "What ya drinking?" she asked. "I'm dry. I could use one too."

Rusty raised his hand and the bartender moved toward him. "Another coke for the lady," he said.

"Coke!" she said in disgust. "I gotta have something stronger than that."

Rusty felt the blood rush to his head, but he said to the bartender, "Whatever she wants, then. Just set her up."

"Coke and rum," she said with a giggle and the bartender brought it to her.

"Sorry," she said to Rusty. "Don't you drink?"

"Sure, Coke," he said, "and an occasional Sprite."

"Oh, well, I guess that's okay," Candy said. She squinted thoughtfully for a moment, took a generous drink of her rum and Coke, and then looked at Rusty again. "What did you say your name was?"

"Rusty."

"You're a cute guy, Rusty. First time in here?" she asked.

"Yeah," he mumbled.

"Hope it's not the last," she said as she laid a hand on his arm again and leaned toward him. "I'm in here most every night. You and I can get to be good friends."

Her breath hit him square in the face, reminding him of Uncle Bill. He was repulsed, and drew back a few inches. But Candy only leaned farther toward him. She moved her free hand from his arm to his shoulder, and then slid it around his neck until she was nearly hanging on him.

He looked at her eyes. They were so glazed he could not make out the color. Blue, he supposed; and when she was sober, they might be very pretty. The same was true of her face. It was painted far too much for his taste, but she could be very pretty. He had thought, when he first saw her, that she was. He was not so sure now.

Candy burped, blowing more alcohol-infused breath into his face. "'Scuse me," she said as he leaned away again. "Rum makes me burp."

Rusty was uncomfortable and getting a little ill. He slid from the bar stool, and stood up. She staggered, hanging tightly around his neck. Her drink spilled down the front of her lacy red blouse. He tried not to stare, because the blouse didn't cover much and it embarrassed him.

"Want to go to a table, do you?" she asked with a grin. "Lead the way."

Short of shoving her away from him and causing a scene, a table seemed like a good idea. At least he would have that between them.

Or so he thought. The table was not very big when he found one, and once they were seated across from each other, she leaned over so far that her sagging blouse rubbed the table and her mouth was directly over his coke. She shouted when she talked, because they were right next to the dance floor and the music was loud. He slid his glass from beneath her leering face and leaned back, almost gagging from the noxious smell of her breath. It was hard not to look at her without being embarrassed, so he glanced about the room. Everyone else seemed to be having a good time. Candy was certainly not the only girl in there with glazed eyes, a ton of paint, and a low-cut, revealing blouse. But he was the only guy who seemed ill at ease. The men had their hands all over the girls and the girls had their hands all over the men.

Rusty thought of Jeri. Compared to the girls in this bar, she was an angel. She was beautiful in a natural sort of way. She wore modest clothes and only light makeup, and though he had only spoken to her through glass after that first encounter in the weight room, he could imagine how sweet her breath must smell. He longed to see her again.

His eyes came back to the face of Candy. He tried not to look below her face for there was far too much to see there right now. She smiled and brought a cigarette from her purse and put it between her too-red lips and lit it. She sat back and blew cigarette smoke at him. It killed the odor of alcohol, and for a few minutes he was able to sit there without the urge to flee. But when she had finished her cigarette, she downed the last of her drink and leaned across the table again. Thoroughly repulsed, Rusty made a plan to escape. It was a simple one. He would stand up and walk out of the bar. He let her smoke most of another cigarette, saying nothing as she shouted words at him that he could barely hear through the din of the bar. Finally, when he could take no more, he made his move.

And Candy made hers.

Rusty simply pushed back from the table and took a step toward the door. He had planned to keep walking, but Candy's move stopped him. She lurched quickly to her feet and was in front of him before he knew it. "Sure, I'd love to dance," she said and draped her arms around his neck and brazenly pressed herself against him. She swayed, and to keep her from falling and dragging him to the floor with her, he put his arms around her waist.

Candy giggled. Rusty gagged. And they danced, or at least they moved together around the floor. The more they danced, the more she sagged, until his strong neck and shoulders ached from her weight. The music ended, and he directed her back to their table, determined to get out of there. She finally made it easy for him. "You sit right there and order me another rum and Coke," she instructed. "I need to visit the little girls room for a minute, love."

He nodded and watched gratefully as she staggered away. He could not believe he had thought her pretty at first. He turned and headed for the door. A dark-complexioned man with long, unkempt hair blocked his departure. "Hey, how'd you luck out and get Candy tonight?" the man asked.

"Just my lucky day," Rusty said in disgust. "Now it's yours. She's yours for the rest of the evening."

"Gee, really?" the drunk said with wide eyes.

"Really. You sit right there and wait for her. She'll be back in a minute or two."

With that, Rusty finally hurried out of the bar where he drank in the cold, clear air in large gulps, purging his lungs of Candy. Then he began to walk, and for the rest of the evening he played hide and seek with the man assigned to tail him.

He found that it was not impossible to lose the guy, but he intentionally let him find him after a few minutes each time he had managed to shake him. But his success at losing his tail did not give him total confidence in his ability to retrieve his half-million dollars by himself. He could never be absolutely sure there were not others watching him as well, ones he somehow failed to see. At any rate, it made for an entertaining evening since he had nothing better to do.

Finally, a little after one o'clock on Christmas morning, he drifted back to his apartment. As he approached the entrance to the building, he smelled cigarette smoke, but could not see anyone lurking nearby. His nose was very sensitive to the smell of burning cigarettes. He had smoked heavily before going to prison. Once in prison, however, he had quit, gone to lifting weights, and found that, after a few months, he didn't crave tobacco anymore. And he knew he was more healthy and fit.

Rusty prided himself in his physical prowess. He was strong and well built, and as soon as he could, he would have weights in his apartment, or else he would find a club where he could work out. He stood at the bottom of the steps to the old apartment building, wishing he could lift weights right then. It would help to relieve the loneliness he was experiencing. The cigarette smoke drifted by again, and he began to be nervous. Someone was close by, watching him and smoking.

There were bushes, tall and dense, that grew on either side of the stairway that led to the entrance of the building where he lived. Other buildings filled the street, spaced closely together with narrow alleys running between them, dark, and choked with weeds and bushes. The smoker was either lurking in the bushes beside the entrance or was in one of the closest alleys. Rusty drifted to his left, sniffing the air. The cigarette smoke grew more faint. He then drifted to the right where it was more pronounced.

He couldn't help but smile to himself. Whoever was hiding and watching him was probably becoming nervous, suspicious at least that Rusty knew he was there. He was bored and in no hurry, and the street was deserted and mostly quiet, so Rusty decided to keep narrowing it down. Maybe he would get a glimpse of the man.

For a time the smell faded away. Then after ten minutes or so of patient waiting, standing where he had smelled the smoke the strongest, Rusty was rewarded. The smoker's craving became stronger than his good sense. He lit a match, and Rusty caught the faint sound on the air. Turning his head slightly, he saw the momentary flare coming from within the bushes to the right of the entrance.

A car came down the street, and Rusty waited until it had passed. Then he moved as if he were going to enter the building. He even started up the steps. When he was nearly at the top, he stopped and looked into the bushes to his right. They seemed to sway slightly. Turning, he walked down the stairs and back onto the sidewalk. He stood there for a moment, then his annoyance turned to anger, and he darted around the bushes. A figure bolted out, bumping into Rusty and nearly knocking him down.

Like a cat, Rusty recovered, snaked an arm around the man's neck, and threw him to the ground. He went down with him, punching the man once in the face. His stalker struggled to free himself, but Rusty's months of lifting weights paid off, and he had very little trouble restraining the stranger.

Finally, when it was clear that he could not get loose, the man shouted, "What do you think you're doing? You could be arrested for assault."

"You struck me first," Rusty said angrily. "You nearly knocked me down. I was only defending myself."

"I accidentally bumped into you," the man protested.

"Here, let's get you to your feet," Rusty suggested, pulling the man up as he stood himself. The lights of a car came on from a block or so away. Rusty realized his error and quickly pulled his captive into the nearest alley and clamped his left hand over the man's mouth. With his right hand he held the man's arms bent tightly behind his back. "Not a sound, or I'll break your arms," he threatened. Resistance faded.

Rusty feared that the headlights belonged to the car that had been tailing him all night long. He cursed himself for his carelessness. The car would be here in a moment. Even if it drove on by, he knew it would be back, or at least the driver would. He had to hurry.

The car moved by slowly, and as soon as it was out of sight, Rusty pulled his captive deeper into the alley. Suddenly, the man got one hand free and it went inside his coat. Rusty doubled up his fist and struck a hard blow to the man's face. He went down. Then, making no attempt to be gentle, Rusty tore the man's coat open and pulled a small revolver from a shoulder holster. He quickly searched the man from head to foot, taking a knife from a sheath inside his waistband. The man, dazed at first from the punch, began to struggle again. Rusty swiftly pulled the man's belt from his pants, rolled him onto his stomach and tied his hands behind his back as securely as he could. Then he ejected the bullets from the cylinder of the gun, dropped the bullets into his pocket and flung the gun upward as hard as he could. He heard it land with a thud four stories up, on the roof of the building Rusty lived in.

"Hey, you can't . . ." the struggling man on the ground said.

"Shut up!" Rusty ordered. He leaned down, turned the man onto his back where he squealed in pain, and sat him up. "Who are you and why are you following me?" Rusty demanded.

"I'm not . . ."

Rusty felt his anger growing. "Tell whoever hired you that I don't have the money. It's gone, washed away in the river. And don't let me see you around here again." He shoved him back to the ground and ran from the alley. He had barely started up the entrance steps to his apartment building when he heard footsteps coming from up the street. He waited, his hand on the door. Probably his hide-and-seek friend, Rusty thought as the running figure appeared. He shouted, "Your partner's back in the alley. He lost his gun. Both of you had better steer clear of me if you know what's good for you."

The man skidded to a stop. "You better not have hurt him," the man threatened.

Rusty laughed. "Or what?" he asked, the man's threat nothing more than an admission of what Rusty suspected. "I am minding my own business," he added. "You best mind yours. And tell whoever is paying you to lay off." With that, Rusty backed into the building, knowing that if one of the men was armed, the other would be as well.

Back in his apartment with the door safely locked, Rusty leaned on his kitchen counter and breathed deeply. What he had just done was foolish. Yes, the bank would soon know that he knew that they were paying for him to be tailed. And yes, they would know he was still denying any knowledge of the half-million dollars. But on the other hand, they would be more careful now. And he would have to be as well.

Rusty also knew that whoever these men were, they carried guns. For him to do so was a violation of his parole. That gave them a huge advantage, and a dangerous one. Of course, to assault someone was also a violation of his parole, but he was quite certain they would not be telling his parole officer about that. The bank was behind this, and they wanted the money back. They also wanted him back in prison. But not, Rusty decided, until they had their money.

Deep in thought, Rusty suddenly remembered the bullets in his pocket and the knife in his waistband. He had forgotten all about them. He had to get rid of them. He stuck the knife in his dresser drawer, wiped the bullets clean of fingerprints, then folded them into a wad of toilet paper and shoved them back in his pocket. He pulled his shoes off and left them beside his bed and, in stocking feet, eased his apartment door open, peering into the hallway. It was empty. He slipped out, making sure he had his key and that the door was locked behind him.

Rusty knew that a stairway went all the way to the top of the building. He entered the stairwell and began to climb silently. Finally, he pushed open the door at the top and stepped onto the roof. Dropping to his knees, he began to crawl cautiously. He felt about him, determined to find the gun he had thrown up there. What little light there was came from a partial moon and the reflection of street lights. Finding the gun would not be an easy task, but he had all night, if he needed it.

Unless . . .

It hadn't occurred to him until just that moment that the owner of the gun, and maybe his partner, too, might come looking for it.

With his ears trained toward the stairwell where he had left the door hanging open, he hastened his search.

Luck was with him and his hand closed at last on the revolver. Now what to do with it was his dilemma. He shoved it in his pocket for now and had started back across the roof when he heard something creak.

The stairs! Someone was coming up the stairs. He eased himself slowly and quietly toward the stairway. The footsteps were soft, but they were definitely coming this way. He stood behind the open door and waited, his ears tuned to the approaching footsteps. There was only one man, of that he was quite certain. Rusty held his breath as he listened to the man's labored panting. The man was not in good condition, and when he finally stepped through the open door, he was almost stumbling. In the faint light, Rusty could see him silhouetted against the dark sky, one arm thrust slightly ahead of him, holding a pistol.

Rusty waited until the man was a half step beyond the open door. Then, moving swiftly, he snaked his right arm around the man's neck, while he drove a powerful punch into his kidney with his left. The man struggled only briefly before the effect of the kidney punch and lack of oxygen caused him to lose consciousness. Then Rusty lowered the man and searched him until he found his wallet, which he shoved into his own pocket. He didn't even look for the gun the man had been holding. But he did retrieve the revolver and the toilet-paper-wad of bullets from his pocket. He wiped the revolver off with his handkerchief and then slipped it, along with the bullets, into the man's coat.

Listening for the other stalker, and hearing nothing, Rusty hurried down the stairs as silently as he could. Seeing no one in the hallway, he slipped to his own door, inserted the key, and let himself in, locking the door and securing the dead bolt behind him.

He sank to the floor beside the door and listened. It was close to ten minutes, according to his alarm clock, before Rusty heard footsteps hurrying down the hall and out the door. What had started out as a welcome parole from prison was suddenly getting very complicated for Rusty. The need to get his money and leave the area was becoming more urgent.

He thought of Jeri, the one person in the whole world who might be considered a friend, and he shivered despite the warmth of his apartment. She could help him, if he could find her, but she could not know what she was helping him do. It was complicated, and it was not fair to her . . . But then, life had not been fair to him. He needed his half million, and he needed it soon.

I'm sorry, Jeri, he thought to himself, but I've got to find you.

CHAPTER 13

Christmas morning brought relative quiet to the usually bustling city of Sacramento. Only essential workers were on the job: police, medical personnel, firemen, service station attendants, and a smattering of other workers across the city. Most businesses that were open were only lightly manned. Traffic was light and there were very few pedestrians, mostly homeless men and women who trudged slowly around the city in search of a free meal. Jeri awoke to the screaming of a siren penetrating the peacefulness of the morning as it passed her apartment building

It's Christmas, she thought as she jerked awake. Warren would be there for breakfast and they would open presents together. There were not many. Most of his were at his parents' home in Sandy. Hers were piled beneath the small artificial tree she had bought.

First things first, she decided after she had showered and dried her hair. This was the first Christmas she had spent anywhere other than with her family. She called them and was still on the phone, talking while she applied makeup, when the doorbell rang.

She looked at her watch. "Oh, it's almost nine," she said to her mother. "That must be Warren at the door. I better go."

"Jeri," her mother said with a twinkle in her voice. "Is it getting serious, this thing with Warren?"

Jeri tried to laugh and make it sound natural. "He thinks," she said.

"What about you?" her mother pressed, much more serious now. Jeri knew her mother could see right through her.

"I don't know, Mom," she said honestly. "I need to take it slow. I better go now. Love you and Merry Christmas."

Jeri scrambled for the door as the bell rang again, longer this time. Warren was getting impatient. Let him, she thought as she slowed her pace, and slowly opened the door.

"Merry Christmas, sweetheart!" Warren said as he practically lunged in and took her possessively in his arms.

Sweetheart? Don't push it, Warren, she thought.

But he was pushing it. He kissed her, and she found herself responding. It felt good to be loved, she realized. But how would it feel to love in return? That was the big question. In time, if he gave her time, she would probably know. They clung together for a long moment, as though they hadn't seen each other for weeks instead of just hours. Finally, he let her go and she stepped back, dizzy. Yes, he was pushing it.

Maybe she needed to be pushed. She didn't know. She was honestly confused. He had managed to create a tingle, but was a tingle enough? Maybe she should let him push and then maybe, just maybe, she could respond to his love.

"What, no breakfast?" he asked, laughing. "Slept in, didn't you? My fault. I kept you up too late."

"I've been on the phone with my family," she said, "for over an hour."

"Oh, what did you talk about, us?" he asked confidently.

She smiled. "That and other things." She wasn't about to tell him that most of her conversation with her mother and dad were about Rusty's release from prison and his family's disappointment at not getting to meet him. That was not something Warren would be interested in.

"Great," he said, obviously not really interested in what she had talked to her family about. "We can fix breakfast together."

There was something about Warren that make Jeri skittish this morning. He was, if anything, overexuberant. Like he had something up his sleeve. He kept touching her as they worked, and held her hand whenever there was an idle moment. She could hardly get away from him, get some space. He was pushing way too hard. She didn't like it, but tried not to let it show, telling herself again, as she had so many times, to give her feelings a chance to soften toward him, to blossom, as it were. Surely it would happen.

After breakfast, they cleared the dishes and sat down with their presents. Most, she realized, were her presents. "I'm sorry," she said after they had finished. "I kind of hogged things here."

"Not to worry, my love," he said. "Just being with you is the best present I could ever have."

My love? Slow down, Warren. A little pushing, maybe, but don't overdo it.

Those were her thoughts as he reached and pulled her into his arms. She tried to relax, to melt, but she was stiff, and only when he kissed her again, did she feel herself responding to him at all. Then it was not what it should be, or could be, she feared. He seemed not to notice. Did he not realize she was not in love? She didn't believe he had any idea. If only he would give her time, then maybe, just maybe . . .

Later in the day, they went for a walk. It was nice outside, and the exercise felt good. He used his credit card to call his family in the early evening, then together they fixed dinner. Warren liked to cook, and he was really good at it. He would even be better, she thought, if he could keep his hands off her.

They ate by candlelight, a traditional romantic setting. After they cleared up and washed the dishes together, they again found themselves sitting closely on the sofa. He took her hand in his and looked at her longingly and lovingly. "I really do love you, Jeri," he said.

She cleared her throat, not sure how to respond. *I like you* would sound corny, but that was how she felt. Even, *I like you a lot*, would be truthful. Nothing more.

He leaned close and kissed her. She accepted the kiss gratefully. It prevented the necessity of responding verbally. She clung to him, so he wouldn't say it again, so he wouldn't force her to respond. *Then again*, she thought as they kissed and hugged and were way too familiar for her comfort, *I may be giving him the wrong idea altogether.*

What he said a few minutes later confirmed that, and made it impossible not to tell him how she felt. "Jeri," he began, "I can hardly bear the thought of leaving you here alone on Friday. I will miss you terribly."

"I'll manage," she said. "And I would only be a distraction for you and your schooling if I were closer."

"Maybe," he said, "but I wish you would come back to Utah. You could get a job there."

"I like it here," she said. "I would need a real good reason to leave this job. It's a good one, and I am making good money. I am getting a decent raise next week. 'A New Year's present,' my supervisor said."

"I'll give you a good reason, Jeri. I've been wanting to ask you this all weekend. I guess there is no time like the present."

Oh no, she thought. *He wouldn't. Not yet.*

He did.

"Will you marry me, Jeri?" he asked.

Oh boy, how should she respond to that? Honesty, she knew was best. There was no other way. She cleared her throat. "Warren, I am flattered," she began.

"Is that a yes?" he broke in.

"I am flattered," she repeated. "I like you a lot."

"Like?" he asked, not attempting to mask his disappointment.

"Yes, like. But I'm not ready for the kind of commitment you are asking for," she said.

"So it's no?" he asked, his face showing the terrible disappointment she had just thrust on him. "I would be the best husband a girl could ever have. Please, don't say no." He was pleading, and it made her just a little angry.

"It is not yes and it is not no," she said, and when he started to speak again, she touched his lips with her finger. "Let me talk," she said.

He nodded, and she looked him squarely in the eye. She was hurting him. She didn't want to do that. But she did not weaken. "Warren, I have enjoyed our time together. I hope there is a lot more, but I am not prepared to commit to marriage right now. That is a big step, the biggest a person will ever make. I must be sure, and I'm not, yet."

"I can give you a few days to think it over," he said hopefully.

That was the wrong thing to say. "You will have to ask again sometime," she replied bluntly. "I'm sorry. I have wanted to tell you to quit pushing so hard, to let us take our time. There is no hurry. I've let you think I was more ready for commitment than I am."

"I thought you felt the way I do. I've told you I love you," he said, just a touch of anger filtering in with the hurt.

"But I've said no such thing," she responded. "That doesn't mean I can't grow to love you, but I'm not there yet. Please, give me time, Warren. Don't give up on me now. That isn't what I want either. I just need some time."

Warren's face grew hard. "It's that prisoner, isn't it?" he said in anger.

"No, it is not," she said truthfully, for Rusty was no longer a prisoner. Of course, Warren didn't know that and she saw no reason to tell him. But as she thought about it, she knew he was on the right track. She had not been able to purge herself of a friendship that had existed only in her heart for many years. Somehow, she had to, if possible. She just had to.

"I don't think I believe you," Warren went on. "You've been seeing him in that prison, haven't you?"

Jeri stood up and began to pace. She was more hurt than angry. "I have not seen him since the one time I told you about. I promised you, and I kept that promise, Warren."

"I hope that's true," he hissed, getting to his feet with clenched fists at his side.

"It is true, Warren. And I can't believe you don't believe me. I would never lie to you."

"Oh, Jeri, I'm sorry. I didn't mean it," he said and attempted to gather her in his arms.

She spun away from him. "Don't touch me," she spat. "I don't want you to touch me right now."

"Or ever?" he said. He was angry, but he was hurting, too. She felt terrible.

"I didn't say that, Warren," she argued softly. And that was not what she was asking. "Let me tell you about Rusty," she said. "I went to the prison like I told you I was going to do. And I took the pictures and showed them to him. He asked a few questions about his family, remarked about how pretty his little sister is, but when I told him I was leaving them for him, he wouldn't take them."

"Why?" Warren asked, obviously barely in control of his emotions.

"He wants to put the past behind him. He is not the little boy his parents knew and loved," she explained.

"Or the little boy you knew and loved," Warren inserted with a jab that hurt.

"No, not that little boy either," she said evenly and began to dab at her eyes.

"You love him, don't you?" Warren demanded.

"No, not in the way you are implying," she argued. "He was my childhood friend. We scarcely knew the difference between boy and girl. We were just best friends. And he was taken away, and I couldn't stand it. I promised to find him." She was saying more than she had intended to, but it kept the tears in check, so she continued. "And I found him, but he is not the same person anymore. I tried to help him find his family, but he doesn't want them."

"He's a criminal, Jeri," Warren reminded her.

"That's right. I know that, Warren, and it hurts, because it's not his fault."

"We all have to make our own decisions," Warren told her. "And though he was taken and put in a different environment, he made his. He chose to be a criminal."

"That is not true!"

"It is true, but you can't accept it. Until you do, I guess I don't stand much of a chance in your life." Warren picked up his jacket. "I think I better go now."

"Warren, please, don't leave while you're still angry."

"I'm not angry, just hurt. I thought I meant something to you."

"You do," she insisted, and now the tears started to flow.

"Sure, you *like* me," he said. "Well, I *love* you. And the way you kissed and held me, I thought you loved me too. What a stupid man I am."

"Warren, quit it. You are not stupid. You are a great person. I like you a lot, and I will probably come to love you. Please give me time."

"You've got it," he said. "There is nothing more than that for me to give now."

"Thank you," she said. "Please come back over tomorrow night. I'll be off work at four tomorrow. Please," she begged.

"Just one more thing," Warren said.

"What's that?"

"Did he kiss you?"

"What!? Who?" she cried.

"You know who. Rusty." His voice had become cold and hard.

"No, Warren."

"But he touched you, and you liked it."

"He did not touch me. There was glass between us. He couldn't have if he'd wanted to, and I'm sure he didn't."

Or was she sure?

"I'll be back," he promised, and he opened the door and left.

Jeri was not sure he would be back. She wasn't even sure she wanted him to come back. But she did not want it to end this way. Why couldn't he have seen that she just needed to let things move more slowly?

At work the next day, she was not herself. Her coworkers noticed it, and one of the women in the office said to her, "Did it not go well with your boyfriend this weekend?"

"It did not go well," she conceded, but she didn't expound, although everyone seemed to want to know.

From her cubicle, she dialed the prison and asked for Emily. They discussed accounts very briefly, then Emily said, "Are you all right? You sound kind of down."

"I've had a rough weekend," Jeri admitted. "I need some help from you if you can give it."

"I'll do it if I can," Emily agreed. "What is it you need?"

Jeri then explained about calling Rusty's parents and how they came from Arizona to see him only to find he'd been released. "I wondered if there was any way you could help me find where he went when he got out, so I can tell them. They really want to see him."

"I'll do what I can. But don't get your hopes up."

Emily called her back late in the afternoon. "He was paroled early," she told Jeri. "Officials of the bank he robbed and the police chief spoke in his behalf. Let me tell you, that came as a surprise to the warden. Anyway, parole was granted, and the bank promised to find him a job. That's all we know here except the name of his parole agent."

"Would he tell me how to get hold of Rusty?" Jeri asked hopefully.

"Maybe. If he thought it would help Randy . . ."

"Rusty," Jeri corrected.

"Yes, Rusty," Emily conceded. "If he thought it would help for his family to make contact, he might. It's worth a try." She then gave Jeri the officer's name and number. "Good luck," she said as they hung up.

"Thanks," Jeri replied.

Jeri was apprehensive when she drove home that evening. She had tried to call the parole officer and had almost left her number, but then, half hoping that Warren would come by that evening and not wanting to have to explain to him if the officer called while he was there, she decided to call back the next day.

Warren was standing at her door when she arrived. His face was long and his eyes were red. It wrenched her heart. Jeri surprised herself by kissing him lightly on the lips. "Thanks for being here," she said as she opened the door and invited him in.

CHAPTER 14

That evening was the nicest Jeri had spent with Warren. He did not push. He kept his hands mostly to himself. He was polite and gentle. For the first time in their relationship, he seemed to understand that her feelings were important. Warren might not have realized it, but the way he treated Jeri that night moved her closer to love than anything he could have done.

When they parted at her door after a late dinner out, it was Jeri who initiated a kiss. It was also Jeri who broke it off after just a moment. And she was grateful to him when he did not try to extend it. That night, her feelings toward him were positive. She liked him a lot more.

She still did not love him, but more than ever before she felt it might happen for her. And she was entertaining fond thoughts of him when she fell asleep that evening. She had successfully kept thoughts of Rusty in the background, and Jeri began to hope she might be able to put him there permanently. First, however, she had to find him one more time so she could try again to let his family meet him. She didn't need to see him or even talk to him; all she needed was his address so she could give it to his parents. As sweet as Warren had been today, that seemed like a sensible plan.

She called Rusty's parole officer from work and left a number there for him to return a call. She did not want him calling her at home, because Warren would be back, and she wanted nothing to interfere with the third chance their tumultuous relationship had been given.

It was late in the afternoon before the call came in, just a few minutes before she was to leave. But when she answered her extension, a very stern sounding male voice said, "This is Michael Ferrani. You left a message for me to call."

"Oh, thank you, yes, Officer Ferrani," she said quickly as the pace of her heart quickened.

"They usually call us Agent," he said flatly. "What can I do for you?"

"You have a prisoner . . ." she began.

"A parolee," he corrected abruptly.

"Yes, a Rusty . . . I mean, Randy Moore," she stammered.

"And?"

"Well, do you have one by that name?" she asked.

"What is your interest?" he inquired.

This was not going well.

"He is a friend of mine," she began. "I have been visiting him in prison. And I had some information about his family that I wanted to give him."

"His family?" the agent asked skeptically. "I don't show him as having any family, or a girlfriend, either, for that matter. I'm afraid I can't help you."

"Oh, please, let me explain," she said quickly, fearing that he was about to cut her off. "He and I were friends when we were little. He was kidnapped and I . . ."

Agent Ferrani broke in. "You must have your information wrong. Randy Moore is not the man you are talking about. He was never kidnapped. He has no family. He is a dangerous felon. Whoever you are, I would suggest that despite his good looks, you not let yourself fall for him."

"Please," she begged.

"Good day," he said and there was a click and a buzz.

"Ooh!" she fumed. The man wouldn't even listen. Angry, she dialed his number again, but instead of punching in his extension, she waited for a receptionist to come on the line and asked for his supervisor. She got right through and, as nicely as she could, tried once again to explain.

This time she was listened to, although it appeared that this man was skeptical of her as well. Finally, she said, "I am telling the truth. I am not romantically involved with Randy; I just want to let him meet his family, if he wants to. Please, if I could just have his address I will tell his parents and they can contact him there. Then what he does is up to him."

"This seems like a rather far-fetched story," the supervising agent said. "It might be well if we could know a little about you to help us determine if we should divulge that kind of information."

"Fine, call the prison. He was just paroled from there a few days ago. Ask for Emily at bookkeeping. She'll tell you who I am."

"Will you be at that number for a few minutes?" he asked.

"I will stay late if I need to," she answered, thinking about Warren and wondering how she would explain to him why she was late getting back to her apartment.

It was nearly an hour before she finally got a call back from the supervising agent. Warren would be at her apartment by now and was probably getting upset. She tried to keep the tension from her voice when she answered the phone. "I spoke to Emily," Agent Ferrani's supervisor told her. "It seems that she believes your story. And it sounds like you have a good job. You are certainly not the type we usually have chasing our parolees. However, I discussed this matter with Randy's parole officer, Agent Ferrani, and we both feel that it would be counterproductive at this point to bring up his past. He has a good job, he has an apartment, and we don't want anything to happen that will in any way jeopardize his successful completion of parole."

"But you don't understand," Jeri begged. "He comes from a good family. They want to meet him. It might be the best thing for him."

"I think your feelings for this convict run far too deep for your own good," she was counseled.

"I don't plan to look him up myself," she protested. "I only want to give his parents his address."

"You have my answer. We are not going to release information to you on his whereabouts, for your sake as well as his."

"Then let me give you the address of his family and you can contact them yourselves. Maybe they could convince you."

"Give it to me," he agreed. "But I make no promises." She had to be content with that. She would call Rusty's parents in a few days and give them the number and address of the agents if they had not made contact. With that determined, she headed for home, nearly an hour late. She was angry, both because of the agents's stubbornness and because they had made her late for her date with Warren. He was waiting at her door, and from the set of his jaw, she could see he was clearly upset, but all Warren said when she arrived was, "Where have you been? I have made plans for this evening and we are really going to have to hurry."

"I'm so sorry. I had to stay late at the office," she said lamely. It was the truth, she convinced herself. He asked for no details, and she was grateful to give none. She changed clothes in record time, freshened up, and was soon ready to go out.

Warren had been busy that day and he had a great evening planned. It went nearly as well as the night before. The only thing that marred it for Jeri was her concern over whether Rusty's folks would be contacted. As the evening came to a close, it was Jeri who found herself clinging to Warren, but he was smart enough not to push things. The tingling she felt when he held her in his arms was stronger, and she began to wonder if she was falling in love.

"Let's eat right here tomorrow night," she urged after a rather long and passionate kiss at the door. "We could fix it together."

Warren, his face flushed and covered with a big smile was quick to agree. It was to be their last evening together for quite a while, and they both wanted it to be a memorable one. They wanted it to be the best.

***

Coincidences play a larger part in the lives of people than many are willing to admit. Many who are religious question whether they are really coincidences at all, or the hand of God at work. Others might argue that perhaps some coincidences are caused by a greater power, but some just happen. And of course, there were those who would argue that they mean nothing at all.

Whatever the case, one was about to happen. Rusty, whom most of the men in the shop had grown to like and respect, was approached by Jim shortly after arriving at work Friday morning. "Rusty," Jim began. The men called him Rusty as he had requested, and they could see no reason to antagonize him, both because of the respect he had earned from them and because he was strong enough that it seemed unwise to cross him. "I would like you to run an errand for the boss, if you have a drivers license, that is."

Randy still had one. It had not been taken away when he was arrested, and it had not expired while he was in prison. "I have one, but is it you who needs me to run the errand, not Pink?" Rusty asked with a grin. Pink rarely spoke to Rusty.

"Well, we all do this for him from time to time, when he doesn't have time himself. This morning he asked me to have someone take care of it, and we are short two men right now as they are taking the day off." Jim dangled a set of keys from his fingers. "These are to my car," he said. "Why don't you take it?"

"The Camaro?" Rusty asked with awe. Jim's old Camaro was worth a fortune. He had spent a year restoring it on his own time in the shop and he had done an outstanding job. It was a beautiful, classy car. He couldn't believe Jim would trust him with it. It was a vote of confidence that made him feel really good.

After taking the keys, he asked, "Where am I going?"

Jim picked up a large envelope. "This needs to be taken to Pink's accountants. The address is on the front. He wants it taken directly to an accountant by the name of Howard. The receptionist can direct you to his office when you find the building. Be sure not to leave it with her, whatever you do. She has a tendency to be airheaded at times."

Rusty studied the address for a moment. Akerman, Burrows , and Smith was the name of the firm. The address was not a difficult one to find. "I've been in that part of the city before," Rusty said. "It won't take me long to deliver this."

"Good. Be on your way then."

Rusty started toward the door. Jim called after him, "Rusty."

Rusty stopped and turned around. Jim grinned. "Be careful with my car."

Chuckling, Rusty left. As he opened the car door and started to climb in, he looked around. His shadows were still there, he was sure of that, but they were more discreet since his encounter with them the other night. He wondered what they would think of him driving away from the shop in this classic Camaro.

It took just fifteen minutes to find the building that housed Akerman, Burrows, and Smith. Rusty had successfully spotted his tail by the time he got there. Two men driving a fairly new Buick were behind him too much of the time for it not to be them. When they parked less than a block from the parking lot where Rusty parked the Camaro, he was positive.

Ignoring the temptation to walk down the street and confront them, he entered the modern, largely glass office complex. He rode the elevator to the fourth floor and found the suite he was looking for. Despite his working clothes, the receptionist, a pretty girl dressed in a short green skirt and tight blouse that rode up her flat stomach, exposing bare, tanned skin, smiled broadly at him. "May I help you?" she asked.

Rusty grinned at her. "I hope so," he said.

"So do I," she countered. She had been filing something in a file cabinet that stood near her desk. She turned with a flair and sat down. She was a flirt. He knew the type, and they had always scared him away. Now he found himself holding his ground very well. "I'm Rusty," he said, and instead of stating his business, he waited expectantly. She did not repulse him the way the woman in the bar had done.

"I'm Allison," she purred. "It's nice to meet you." Then remembering her duties, she said, "What can I do for you?"

"I need to drop this off with one of your accountants. Howard, I believe it is."

"Oh, yes. You must be from Pink's," she said. "Are you new there?"

He nodded and she said, "I thought so. I thought I had met all the guys that worked there. Pink is too cheap to use a courier service. He always brings his stuff himself or sends one of his employees." She paused, looking Rusty over with more than casual interest. "You are . . ." She hesitated, her face turning slightly red as if what she had been about to say was improper.

"I'm what?" he asked, leaning toward her.

"Oh, never mind," she said.

He shrugged, and for some reason that seemed to get her talking again. "I mean, you know, most of the guys from there are greasy and have long hair and . . . and you . . . you are different," she finished lamely.

"Thank you," Rusty said, flashing her another smile. "Could you direct me to Howard's office? I was told to give this to him personally."

"Yes, well, that won't be possible," she said. "Howard's father died last night, and he will be gone for a week. I was told to take that to the accountant who will be covering for him until he gets back."

"I was told to deliver it personally," Rusty said. He could see that this girl, though pretty, was likely to forget all about the packet as soon as another man entered the reception area. "If you will direct me there, I'll take it to the guy who needs it."

"Girl, actually," Allison said. She told him where to go and then said. "Her name is on her door. Jeri. That's J . . .e . . .r . . . i."

Rusty froze. Could it be? He remembered Jeri telling him that she was at the prison doing something related to her job as an accountant.

"Are you all right?" Allison asked, standing up and stepping around her desk.

"Yes. I'm fine," Rusty said.

Allison laid a well-manicured hand on his arm and said, "Are you sure? You look rather ill."

"Would that be Jeri Satch?" Rusty asked, gazing at the girl whose hand still lay on his arm.

"Why yes, do you know her?" Allison asked, quickly withdrawing her hand.

"I do," Rusty said. "Thank you. I'll just take this to her then."

He wasn't positive, but he was quite sure Allison said, "That lucky Jeri," as he moved down the hall.

Rusty couldn't help but grin, for he was the lucky one. In fact, he couldn't believe his luck. He had tried to locate Jeri by calling information, but her phone was unlisted. The power and gas companies had also been of no help. He had made up his mind that she was the key to his half-million dollars, and somehow he had to find her. So far he had failed, and then, out of the blue, she had dropped right into his pocket.

He couldn't wait to see the look on Jeri's face when he popped in on her. And yet in a way, he was nervous. He already knew what his approach would be. He had rehearsed it a hundred times the past few days. He had planned to tell her, when he found her, that he had decided to contact his family. That wasn't true, but it was a good ruse. And then he was going to ask her for the pictures and the address. That would be the opening; his plan from there was sketchy.

Now his approach could be more spontaneous. She would have no reason to be suspicious of his motives. He grinned and quickened his pace, trying to outwalk the nervousness. He quickly found her office but was disappointed to find the door closed. He could see through the large window that she was not there.

"Jeri went home early," a man's voice said from behind him. Rusty whipped around. "You just missed her," he was told.

"Allison, the girl up front, didn't say anything about her leaving," Rusty said.

"Allison doesn't know everything," the fellow responded. "She only notices when the men leave." He chuckled at himself. "She was probably powdering her nose when Jeri went out. Did you have something for her?"

"These were for Howard, but Allison said Jeri was covering for him for a few days," Rusty explained. "Maybe I could just leave them on her desk." He was more disappointed than he liked to admit, for reasons that seemed vague and yet unrelated to the half-million dollars.

"Sure, just open the door and set them on her desk. She'll get to it first thing on Monday. Are they the papers from Pink's?"

"Yes."

"Sure, then just set them on the desk. They'll be safe," the man assured Rusty.

He opened Jeri's office door. The other man stepped back into his office, out of sight. Rusty dropped the envelope on the desk. He was attracted immediately to a framed picture of Jeri and her family. He stared at it for a moment, unable to deny what a beautiful girl she was. He glanced around the office, then noticed a small envelope on the floor by the door. She must have dropped it as she was leaving.

He picked it up, noticing that it was addressed to her and that it was unopened. The address on it was not this office. It had to be where she lived. Impulsively he stuffed it in his pocket and hurried out. His luck today was great. He had missed her here, but now he had her home address. He could deliver the letter to her. He would tell her that he found it on the ground outside the building and decided to take it to her himself.

Allison looked up as he entered the reception area. She had a smile for him again. "Did you find Jeri all right?" she asked. She was jealous of Jeri, Rusty decided. Maybe because she wasn't the prettiest girl in the building. Jeri was.

"She was gone, but I left the packet for her," he told her.

"Oh, I didn't see her leave," she said. "I'm sorry you missed her."

She didn't sound very sorry, and he grinned to himself as he left.

The men in the Buick were still parked up the street when he pulled out of the parking lot. He looked their way slowly as he passed them. They both ducked their heads as he drove by, but he got a good enough look that he was certain one of them was the one he had tangled with the other night beside his building. The one he had fought on the roof he had never seen closely. Impulsively, he swung the Camaro to the curb and jumped out. Not wanting to be recognized, they had not looked back. It gave Rusty time to dart across the street before they saw him. The Buick's engine started as he jerked the passenger door open and shouted, "You guys don't learn very well, do you?"

They learned better than he thought. The driver shoved the car in gear and floored it, roaring away. Rusty was thrown to the ground as the door was jerked from his hands. Tires screeched and a car narrowly missed him as it came from the rear.

It did not miss the Buick.

Rusty was back in the Camaro and on his way before the dust from the crash had settled. So much for the tail today, he thought to himself with a grin. As he drove back to the body shop, he began to rehearse his approach to Jeri. He checked to make sure the letter was secure in his pocket. After work he could take it to her. Well, it could wait until after he went home, showered, and changed clothes. He would have to take a taxi, but that was okay. He had money in his pocket.

CHAPTER 15

"If you'll grate the cheese, I'll get these peas on the stove," Jeri said as she pulled a package from the freezer compartment of the refrigerator.

"What do you grate it with?" Warren asked.

Jeri laid the package of peas on the counter and opened a drawer. "Here," she said, "and you can grate it into a large bowl. Try that cupboard over there."

They worked quietly for a moment, then Jeri said, "I can't believe I lost that letter from Kate. I was sure I put it in my purse. But when I got home it was not there. I hadn't even read it."

"You took it to the office with you?"

"Yes, my mail comes early, and I was in a hurry this morning. So instead of leaving it in the apartment, I took it with me. I thought I'd get a chance to read it at work. But I got so busy today I just didn't have time. It was crazy there. One of the guys had a death in his family and they asked me to take several of his accounts for a few days."

"As if you didn't have enough to do already," Warren said.

"Yeah, and I had planned to leave early so I could stop by the store for a few things for dinner tonight. And I did leave early." She stopped, her hands becoming idle as she thought back. "Oh, no."

"What?"

"I'll bet that letter fell out of my purse at the store. Oh, I'll never find it," she moaned.

Warren made a sympathetic sound and Jeri said, "If it doesn't turn up, I'll have to give her a call and explain what happened."

"She will understand," Warren said. "She's really a great girl. You are lucky to have such a good friend."

Jeri looked up at him. He was gazing toward the wall, seemingly in deep thought. He had spoken of Kate with more feeling than she would have expected. A moment later, he went back to work and Jeri sneaked another suspicious look at Warren. His back was to her, and she watched him for a moment as he grated the cheese. She wondered if he had more than a passing interest in Kate. Strangely, she felt a small, uncomfortable twinge of jealousy. She didn't like the feeling, but she couldn't quite shake it.

Jeri had planned quite an elaborate meal. It was another hour before everything was cooked, mixed, poured, and set on the table. "Ah, candlelight," Warren said with a smile as Jeri produced two tall white candles for the table and lit them. When all was ready, they sat down to eat. Warren offered the prayer, and they both began to fill their plates.

The doorbell rang.

"Who in the world could that be?" Jeri asked, puzzled. "Home teachers? No, they always call for an appointment, and they never come before seven." She glanced at her watch. It was not quite six yet.

"Probably an old boyfriend," Warren kidded with a chuckle.

"Yeah, like I have a lot of them around," Jeri shot back with a giggle as she got up and headed for the door.

She opened it and her jaw dropped. "Rusty!" she said in more than minor astonishment. He was grinning at her and her heart leaped involuntarily.

"Hi, Jeri, hope I'm not intruding," he said.

"You are!" Warren spoke up angrily from the table. He was already pushing back his chair and standing up. "Jeri and I were just beginning to eat."

"Warren!" Jeri exclaimed, and then was sorry she had spoken so sharply as she recalled her own jealousy that had been eating at her for over an hour now.

"Oh, I'm sorry," Rusty said, his face crimson. "Here, I just brought you this," he said, holding out the envelope to Jeri. "I found it on the ground outside your office building. Your address was on it, so I thought I'd bring it by. I'll be going now."

Jeri took the letter and looked at it, amazed. "Oh, Rusty, thanks! It's the one from Kate! I wondered where I'd lost it. He found Kate's letter, Warren," she said. "Isn't that great?"

"Sure," Warren mumbled, and somehow, the tone of his voice implied that he believed something fishy was going on. "What a coincidence," he went on, his tone giving evidence of how he felt about coincidences and this sudden appearance of Rusty.

Rusty was backing out the door. Jeri didn't want him to go, not just yet, anyway. But she wondered what she could do to ease the tension. Awkwardly, she said, "Just a minute, let me introduce you two. Warren, this is Rusty. Rusty, Warren."

"Good to meet you," Rusty offered, but Warren was not nearly as gracious. He mumbled something Jeri could not understand.

She turned back to Rusty, who had backed all the way out the door. "Thanks again, Rusty," she said. "I was just telling Warren about losing this letter." She touched the return address that was only an address, no name written above it. "It's from Kate, my former roommate and really good friend."

"Glad I found it," Rusty said, turning to leave. All his well-rehearsed lines had vanished in the confusion. Part of it came back and he said without really thinking, "I wondered, too, do you still have those pictures of my family?"

"Changed your mind?" she said with a grin at her childhood friend.

"Yeah, I'd like the pictures, and the address too, if you still have it."

"Of course I do. Come in and I'll find them for you," she invited.

"I don't mean to be a bother," Rusty said as he slipped nervously back through the door. "If you'll get it for me, I'll just be on my way," he said as Jeri shut the door behind him.

"Give me just a minute," Jeri said. "I think they're in my dresser." She disappeared into her bedroom.

Rusty glanced at Warren who was glaring at him. "Old home week, huh?" Warren said sourly.

"I just thought maybe I should contact my family," Rusty told him lamely. "I told Jeri when she brought the pictures to me at the prison that I didn't want them. After I got out, I got to thinking differently." That was not true, but what else could he tell Jeri's boyfriend who was so clearly upset over his appearance here.

"Sure," Warren said.

"It's hard," Rusty said awkwardly, trying to keep a conversation going while he waited for Jeri to return. He could hardly wait to get out of here. "I never knew I had a family until Jeri told me. Came as a bit of a shock."

"Probably a shock for your family, too," Warren said coldly. "I don't imagine it would be easy learning your son is a convict." He spit the last word out like it had a nasty taste to it.

Jeri entered the room just in time to hear him say his last sentence. "Warren, I can't believe you said that."

"And I can't believe you've been seeing this guy and lying to me about it." He was really angry now.

Rusty was getting worked up himself. Who did this guy think he was, anyway? "I don't know what you're talking about," he said, his deep blue eyes flashing. "I haven't seen her or talked to her since before I got out of prison. I'm here because I found her letter by her office. I thought after all she'd done for me that the least I could do was return it."

"Sure," Warren said again, disbelief etched into his stony face.

"Here, I'll take those and go," Rusty said, reaching for the envelope. "I'm sorry I bothered you, Jeri."

"Not so fast, mister," Warren said in a threatening tone. "There are some things I want to get clear here. Somebody's not being totally honest, and I want to know why."

"I don't know what you're talking about," Rusty said, as he realized it was him that was not being totally honest. Jeri, on the other hand was being totally truthful. He resented the insinuation that she would be anything other than honest. He felt like knocking the guy flat, and his hands clenched at the thought.

Warren didn't miss it. "Hit me if you feel like it," he said. "Then you can fast track it right on back to prison where you belong."

Warren was right, and that thought helped save the man from getting punched. Rusty had taken all he cared to, but he held his tongue and unclenched his fists at the thought of returning to prison. He turned to Jeri who was standing with her mouth clamped tightly shut, tears streaming down her beautiful face, her long, dark hair touching her cheeks as she bowed her head in shame and pain. The sight nearly broke Rusty's heart. Something about this girl touched a soft spot in him he didn't know existed.

"I'll go now, Jeri," he said softly.

She nodded wordlessly.

Warren spoke up again. "As soon as I learn how it is that if you two haven't been seeing each other, and that you just happened to find her mail on the ground at her office. Explain that, mister con man."

"I don't need to explain anything. It was a coincidence, that's all." Rusty had the door open by then with every intention of stepping through and leaving Jeri to deal with her jerk of a boyfriend.

It was her speaking up just then that stopped him short. "Don't go yet, Rusty," she said, her voice choked with emotion and pain. "Warren is right. This needs to be cleared up."

Rusty glanced at Warren who nodded smugly. "All right. I found the letter at her place of business," Rusty said formally.

Before he could go on, Warren jumped in. "You've told us that," he said. "The question is, what were you doing there? That seems awfully suspicious, considering all the denials I'm hearing about you two not having seen or spoken to one another since you conned your way out of prison."

"It was a coincidence," Rusty said, his anger building again.

"I don't happen to believe in coincidences," Warren said. "You've got to do better than that."

"I don't have to explain anything to you," Rusty said again.

Jeri could see the tension building once more, and she broke in. "Rusty, please, for my sake, tell us what you were doing there and how you knew where I worked." She looked pleadingly at Rusty with those dark brown eyes that were so full of hurt that he could hardly stand it. He had never known many good people in his life. But she was one. In fact, she was without a doubt the best he had ever known. She was so good he couldn't believe he actually knew her.

"I'll tell *you*," he said. "I don't owe your boyfriend an explanation."

Warren started to speak and Jeri said, "Not now, Warren, please. Let Rusty talk." She meant it, and finally, Warren clamped his mouth shut.

"I work for an auto body repair place called Pink's, Jeri," Rusty said, firmly addressing himself to her. "My foreman sent me to deliver some papers, accounts of some kind, to a guy by the name of Howard who works for Akerman, Burrows, and Smith."

"The firm I work for," she said.

"Yeah, but I had no way of knowing that."

"I know you didn't."

"Anyway, when I got there some chick, named Allison . . ." Rusty began again.

"The firm's professional flirt," Jeri broke in.

"Yeah, that's her. She said Howard's father had died and that he was going to be gone for a while and that an accountant named Jeri would be handling this account for him until he got back. I was surprised, then I remembered that you were an accountant, and that was the reason you had come to the prison and, through pure coincidence, saw me and recognized me," he said with malice and a quick glance at Warren. "I asked Allison if it was Jeri Satch. She said it was and offered to take the papers, but Jim, my foreman, had been firm about my not leaving them with the receptionist."

"She loses things," Jeri said with as much of a smile as she could muster. "She's an airhead."

"That was easy to see, so I said I'd take them directly to you, which I tried to do. But you were not in your office and some guy from across the hall said to leave them on your desk. I did that."

"Thank you, Rusty," Jeri said, and she impulsively stepped next to him and gave him a quick kiss on the cheek.

Guilt, something that Rusty had not felt much of in his life, flooded through him as the thrill of her sisterly kiss sent tingles down his spine. "There is one other thing I need to say, and then I'll leave," he said, his mind suddenly made up. "I did lie to you about one thing tonight."

"Yeah, here we go," Warren chimed.

Jeri shot him a dark glance and turned back to Rusty expectantly. "What was it Rusty?"

"The letter, the one I brought you from your friend," he said awkwardly.

"Yes," Jeri prodded.

"I didn't find it outside like I said. It was on the floor by the door in your office. I picked it up with the intent of putting it on your desk. Then I saw your address and I pocketed it. It gave me an excuse to look you up." He almost told her that it was for the purpose of getting his family's address, but he was finding it very hard to lie to this girl, one whom he recalled more and more about from their childhood friendship.

She made it easy for him. "So it gave you an excuse to come get the address of your folks," she said.

He neither confirmed nor denied it. He simply said, "I'm sorry. I'll be going now."

"Thank you, Rusty," she said. "I wrote your parents' phone number on the envelope below their address. Call them, please."

He nodded and stepped through the door and closed it. His taxi was gone. He had meant to call another one from her house, but with all the anger and confusion, that had turned out to be a bad idea. So he began to walk. His shadow was back. They hadn't taken long in finding another car after the accident in the Buick. The hair stood up on his neck. They knew about Jeri; they would learn more about her, he was sure. But now, after the past few minutes, Rusty was not at all sure he could involve her in the recovery of his money. He would have to come up with another way.

He thought about the fellow called Warren. He was obviously Jeri's boyfriend. And he was clearly very possessive of her. Rusty did not like him at all. He stopped walking, stood where he could see the entrance to her apartment building, and watched. His tail stopped a block away. Let them, he thought. They can wonder what is up if they want. He leaned against a palm tree and waited. He was not sure what for. One thing he felt sure of—Jeri and Warren were not made for each other. He could not see what someone as sweet as Jeri could possibly see in Warren, whoever he was.

Back in the apartment, Jeri was wondering the very same thing. She knew Warren had spoken and acted out of jealousy, but what shocked her was how judgmental he had been and how quick to jump to conclusions, not only about Rusty and his past, but about her relationship with Rusty.

As soon as Rusty left, she had invited Warren to finish the meal they had not even begun, but she was relieved when he said, "I don't think I'm hungry anymore. You eat and I'll help you clear up."

"I'm not hungry either," she said.

"Jeri, I was a fool," he admitted after they had stood awkwardly looking at each other for a moment. "I'm sorry. But you can see how it looked."

"Not really," she said coldly. "It was all innocent and pure coincidence," she said, intentionally using the latter word after what he had said about not believing in coincidences.

"I can see that now," he agreed. "Let's go to a movie or something. We can heat this up when we get back. Maybe by then we'll be hungry again."

But Jeri had a different outlook than she had an hour ago. This thing with Warren was leading to only one end, and that end was marriage. And she was not at all sure that was a good idea. If they disagreed this much now, she could hardly imagine what it would be like to be married to him. She did not love him, and right now, she didn't even like him very much.

"I think you'd better go, Warren," she said, putting her thoughts into action.

"Not on this note," he pleaded.

"It won't get any better tonight," she told him. "I really don't like you very much right now."

"Jeri, that isn't true," he said. "I'm sorry. What more can I say? You've got to forgive me. People make mistakes."

"Even people like you?" she asked.

"Yes, even people like me."

"But that's okay?"

"It has to be. None of us are perfect."

"True," she said. "But it is not okay for someone like Rusty to make some mistakes?" she asked pointedly.

"That's different," he explained. "He is a criminal."

"Yes, he is. He was also a little boy who was stolen from his loving and righteous LDS family and shoved cruelly into a dark and violent environment and was raised in that environment, Warren. Is it his fault he turned out the way he did?"

"Probably not, but he's still a criminal," Warren insisted stubbornly. "You feel sorry for him, and I don't blame you. But he could never be anything but trouble for you. I hope someday you wake up, Jeri."

"I do feel sorry for him," she agreed. "He was my best friend. I loved him like a brother."

"And you still do," Warren said sadly.

"Yes, and I still do," she agreed. "But *only* like a brother."

"Sure," he said quietly.

Jeri walked to the door and held it open. "Be careful going home," she said.

Warren looked lost and forlorn all of a sudden.

"Just like this, Jeri?" he wailed.

"Just like this. Go back to Kate, Warren. She loves you."

"But I don't . . . she . . . I mean, I love *you*, Jeri."

"On second thought, don't go back to Kate," Jeri said sadly. "I don't want her going through what you've put me through."

"I'll be back, Jeri," Warren said as he finally stepped to the open door.

"I don't think that's a good idea."

"You'll think differently. I can feel it. I'll be patient, and I'll be back."

He left, and up the street, Rusty watched him go. After his car was out of sight, Rusty walked slowly back to the apartment. He hesitated momentarily at her door, then he pushed the doorbell.

He waited for a couple of minutes, then pushed it again. He finally heard footsteps inside. Then he knew Jeri was looking though the peephole in the door. Then it swung wide. "Rusty, you're back. I thought it was Warren," the sweetest voice Rusty had ever heard said.

"I just wanted to tell you how sorry I am," he said, looking deep into the dark brown eyes so rimmed with red from the shedding of bitter tears.

"Don't be. It wasn't your fault."

"No, really, I'm sorry," he insisted. "I didn't mean to interfere with . . ."

"Warren and me," she completed for him.

Rusty shook his head and said, "I really didn't mean to ruin your evening. I'm sorry." Then he smiled at her. "I'm without a ride, Jeri. Could I use your phone to call a cab?"

"No," she said as a smile crossed the face that had just been so creased with pain it had nearly broken his heart. "But if you'll help me eat all this food in here, I'll give you a ride home. After all, it is the least I can do for my long-lost brother."

"Thanks, sister," he said, and the door closed behind him as he entered the apartment of the girl who had once been his best friend in the entire world.

CHAPTER 16

When the light turned green, Jeri started up again with a sideways glance at her handsome passenger. He was bent slightly forward, studying the passenger side rearview mirror. He had done that several times on the drive to his apartment. She glanced in the mirror herself, as she had also done several times, and saw headlights some distance back. The traffic was light this time of night, but there was always a car back there. She thought of Warren and impulsively slowed down and swung an illegal U-turn right in the middle of the block.

She gunned the engine and her car shot forward. "What are you doing?" Rusty asked in amazement.

"I think we're being followed. And I think it might be Warren," she said.

"Oh, would he do that?"

"What do you think?"

"Maybe. I can't say I'd blame him," Rusty responded.

The other car passed and Jeri was surprised to see it was not Warren's rental car. It was dark blue and quite new with two men in it.

"Was it?" Rusty asked.

Jeri was grinning sheepishly. "No. Sorry about that, but I'd swear that car has been behind us since we left my place, and I think you have noticed it, too."

He admitted it, but he said, "It is probably just a coincidence."

"And what is your stand on coincidences?" she asked. "Warren certainly doesn't believe in them."

"Sometimes I do," Rusty said. "And sometimes I don't. This time it's nothing, but you are going the wrong way to get to my apartment."

"Sorry, I'll turn, but I better do it legally this time."

"It would be easiest just to turn right at the next intersection and follow the next street," Rusty suggested, fighting the urge to lean forward so he could see in the mirror again. He knew who was following them, and he was quite sure they wouldn't want to be shaken right now.

"That'll work," Jeri agreed.

As they turned, Rusty glanced back up the street. Sure enough, there was a car back there. Jeri didn't seem to notice, but before they turned right again a block later, she glanced in her mirror and said, "Oh, no, Rusty. There's a car back there again."

"Probably not the same one," he said easily, but he was sure that was not the case.

When Jeri turned at the next intersection, he glanced back. The car was keeping pace with them. They were both watching now, and as expected, it turned right a few moments after Jeri made another right turn. "This is ridiculous," Jeri said, but from the quiver in her voice Rusty realized she was frightened. For some reason, that made him angry.

He knew who was back there and he was pretty sure he knew why. And he understood it. The bank wanted the half million back. But that didn't involve Jeri, and after the past few hours, he had resolved, despite his earlier thoughts to the contrary, that it never would. Jeri turned right once more and then left at the street they were originally on. The car kept coming.

"Rusty, I'm scared," Jeri admitted a minute later.

"Don't be; I think I've figured out who it is," he said.

"Oh, and who would it be?" she asked.

"I don't know for sure, of course," he said, trying to keep from telling her a direct lie. "But it could be my parole officer."

"Really?" she asked as she remembered her less-than-satisfactory contact with him, and with his boss.

"But there were two of them," she said.

"Could be," Rusty agreed easily. "They sometimes work in pairs; this is one time it might make sense."

"Oh," Jeri said, looking back once more. "And why is that?"

"Think about it, Jeri. I don't exactly have a good reputation and there are certain things I am required to do and other things I am not allowed to do. And there are still other things that might look suspicious to them."

She glanced at his profile in the dim interior of the car. "And what have you done tonight that might look suspicious?" she asked doubtfully.

"Well," he said, and she saw a grin on his shadowed face.

"Well, what?" she insisted.

"It may seem a little out of place for me to be visiting the apartment of a beautiful girl in a good neighborhood and going for a ride with her in her brand-new car."

Jeri shook her head and laughed. "Of course. I guess that makes sense, except that there are no beautiful girls here."

"Oh, but there is," said Rusty, admiring her long, dark hair and shadowed profile in the dim light. "And it does make sense because I am out of my element with someone as good and beautiful as you."

Jeri felt herself blush and was glad it was dark so Rusty could not see the effect his compliment had on her. "It could be your element, Rusty," she said after a few moments of silence. "You came from the same kind of family I did, you know."

"I know, but I was raised differently, too differently to ever change."

"Don't say that, Rusty. You have a good heart," she said with feeling. "And you are basically a good person."

"Who just happens to rob and kick people around," he said bitterly.

"And with whom I happen to feel just as safe as I did when we were five," she added. "You would never do anything to hurt me."

He hoped that was true. But was it? It hadn't been a little while ago. He had almost involved her in a sinister plot to recover a lot of money that was not his. That could have gotten her hurt. And right now he was endangering her by even being with her. The men the bank hired to shadow him day and night were not men who could be trusted. They were basically bad men. It was as simple as that. He had learned that the other evening, and he was not about to forget it. The thought of them following Jeri's car, and a quick check told him they still were, made him feel guilty.

She noticed them, too, and said, "They are still there."

"Pull over," he said impulsively. "There's a pay phone."

She did as he instructed, but she asked "Who do you need to call?"

"No one," he said as he began to open the door. "But this is not fair to you, Jeri. I'll just get out here. It isn't too far for me to walk from here."

She gunned the car back into the street, and for a moment his door swung open, but Rusty shut it with a couple of words she was not used to hearing. "Just what," he added to the profanity after the door was closed again, "do you think you're doing?"

"You are like a brother to me, Rusty," she said. "And I would never let my brother get out there. We don't know who is in that car, do we?"

"Jeri, you could get hurt," he said. "Please, I shouldn't be with you, brother or not."

"But you are with me," she said, "and I'm taking you to your apartment. I let someone hurt you once before, and it haunted me for seventeen years. I won't do it again."

"Jeri, that was not your fault, it was mine. And whoever is back there is following me, not you."

"All the same, I'll let you out at your apartment," she said.

"You are one stubborn lady," Rusty said. He was trying to sound disgusted, but Jeri only smiled.

"Seventeen years. I guess I am. How much farther?"

"About four blocks," he said. "Turn left at the second intersection ahead."

She slowed down as the light turned yellow, then with a glance in her mirror, she gunned her car and sped through the light. The car behind, which had been following much more closely for the past few blocks, had to stop. "Next intersection?" she said with a grin.

"Yes," he said. He could not disguise his admiration. But again the light was turning yellow and this time it was red when she got there. She pulled to a stop. He opened the door and jumped out with a shouted, "Thanks," as he did so.

The door slammed and Rusty ran in front of her car and sped to the sidewalk where he kept running, disappearing a moment later between some houses. "Darn you!" she shouted after he was out of sight.

She sat there fuming. Why couldn't he let her take him all the way home? Suddenly, she was aware of lights coming fast behind her. The traffic light changed to green, and the other car cut to the inside, its tires screeching on the pavement. A car coming the other direction slammed on its brakes, narrowly missing a collision. Stunned by the action, Jeri sat watching the blue sedan careen down the street. After a short distance, it slowed down and one of the occupants leaped from the car and ran into the shadows near where she figured Rusty would be if he kept running in the direction he was when she last saw him.

Parole officer?

Not likely, she thought. There was something else going on here, and she had no idea what. Unless . . . the missing money! Someone wanted the missing money. That had to be it, and there was no way Rusty would ever talk to her about that. A horn honked. There were lights behind her again. She looked up at the light as she started to push on the gas. It was yellow. The car behind her passed to the right and rushed through the light. It turned red and Jeri just sat there, her eyes filling with tears.

"I'll find you," she said aloud. "Well, Rusty Egan, I found you, but did I really?" He was a lost soul, and her heart grieved for him. There was nothing more she could do right now, so she drove slowly toward home. She had not gone far before her anger at Rusty leaving so abruptly abated. She began to worry about him. Something was wrong and he didn't want to get her involved. Rusty needed help.

Jeri swung the car around, her second illegal U-turn of the night.

***

Rusty finally entered his apartment and threw the door shut, locking it behind him. He panted in exhaustion. The run home had been a desperate game of hide and seek. Twice the men who pursued him nearly boxed him in, but each time he had managed to escape. He took a minute to get his breath, then he grabbed a small wooden chair and rammed it beneath the door handle. These men were more than just tailing him tonight. They wanted him for some reason.

Revenge?

Not likely. The bank wouldn't stand for anything messing up the recovery of the half-million dollars.

Then what?

Something crashed against his door. Then it came harder. Rusty looked around the room in desperation. The chair wouldn't hold for long. The door shook violently when it was struck the third time. One of the chair's legs splintered, another one was cracked. Rusty glanced at the window. Then, decisively, he opened it and leaped out.

Almost instantly he was struck with something from behind and he felt himself falling. Someone grabbed him roughly and turned him over, plunging a fist into his unprotected face. "Where is it?" a voice demanded.

Rusty shook his head and it began to clear.

"I said where is it?" He got punched again.

"I got nothing," Rusty said as the taste of blood smothered his tongue.

"Liar," the man said. "You got it. The girl had it, didn't she, and now you got it."

"I don't know what you're talking about," Rusty said.

His energy was returning. His muscles tightened. A siren sounded in the distance. A second face appeared in the gloom above him. "Cops," one of them said.

The men were running their hands all over him, searching thoroughly. "It must be in the apartment," one said.

"It's not. I looked. Maybe it's still in hers. I don't think he had anything big enough to contain a half-million bucks when he jumped from her car."

"Then it's still in her car," the first one concluded.

"If they brought it out of her apartment," the second one added. "You were supposed to be watching. If you'd seen them come out before they were in the car, you would have known. It has to be in something pretty big, like a suitcase or something."

"We'll go back there," one of them decided.

At that moment, Rusty exploded, every muscle in his body working. The men were thrown back like rag dolls. He punched one in the stomach and kicked the other in the leg. Sirens were getting closer. Tires screeched on the pavement. Headlights shone in the street. "Leave him alone!" someone screamed.

Jeri! Rusty recognized her voice.

The men ran. Sirens were very close now. Flashing red and blue light reflected off windows and leaves. "Get out of here," Rusty cried. "Leave now, please!"

Jeri was crushed. She wanted to help Rusty, but he didn't want her help. She rolled her window up as Rusty leaped for the open window to his apartment and scrambled through. She put the car in gear but couldn't move it. The cops had closed in, one car in front and one behind. She wondered what to tell the officers who were getting out.

One tapped on her window. "You all right, miss?" he asked.

She rolled her window down. "I'm fine, but . . ." She stopped herself. She had almost mentioned Rusty. She didn't know why, but she felt she should not do that.

"Someone called in, said a break-in was occurring in this building," he said.

"Two men ran that way," she said, pointing to the alley between Rusty's apartment building and the one next to it.

Two officers headed up the alley. "Take the car, cut them off," the officer at her window shouted to the one other officer at the scene. "On my way, Sarge," he said, leaping into the patrol car and speeding away.

"What were they doing?" the officer at the window asked.

"I don't know. Someone screamed." She didn't tell him it was her. "I pulled over to see what was going on. I saw two men run up the alley."

"You could get hurt, Miss," he told her. "You better clear out of here."

"Stupid of me," she said. "I guess I wasn't thinking."

The officer headed up the alley and Jeri drove off, her head spinning. Was Rusty all right? she wondered. She wanted to check, but she didn't dare. She drove around for an hour, finally returning to the dilapidated apartment building. All was quiet. Her body trembled, her knees shook. Even her teeth were rattling. Was Rusty all right? She had to know.

She was scared to death.

She remembered another time she had been scared. She had let Rusty be taken. She couldn't let him down again. She got out of the car and hurried into the building. The window he had climbed in was the third from the entrance. She would knock on the third door.

It was broken, hanging crazily on just one hinge. The lights were on inside. She stepped in, her heart racing. There was no one there. A quick look around told her it was Rusty's apartment. The envelope with his family's address and pictures was on the floor by the window. She picked it up, put it in her purse and left.

There was nothing to do but drive home, so she did just that. She entered her apartment a few minutes later. She had barely closed the door and locked it when there was a knock. Terrified, her heart began racing again. She grabbed a knife from the kitchen and approached the door. Peering through the peephole, she was relieved beyond words to see Rusty standing there.

She swung the door open, he stepped in, and she shut it behind him. "Rusty, are you okay?"

"I'm fine, but I need a place to stay," he said. What he didn't say was that she needed protection. He needed to get her out of here before they came back. They were convinced that she had somehow helped him recover the money, and they were determined to find it. "Somebody broke into my apartment," he added.

"So I saw," she said, so relieved that he was all right that it made her cry.

"Jeri, you didn't go in there?" he asked in alarm.

"I did," she answered.

"That was dangerous and foolish. And put that knife away before you hurt someone," he said as a grin began to cross his face.

Jeri looked at the knife like she had never seen it before. "I'm sorry," she said. "And how did you get here?"

"Same way as before," he said. "A taxi. Here I'll take the knife. You don't seem to know what to do with it."

She handed it to him sheepishly, just as another knock sounded on the door.

CHAPTER 17

Jeri looked at Rusty, fear in her eyes. "I'll get it," he said with a calmness that served only to add to her terror.

"The peephole," she stammered.

He nodded. "Get in the bedroom."

She backed away. "Let's call the cops," she said as the phone appeared at her side.

He shook his head and peeped out. "It is the cops," he said. She almost fainted with relief. But Rusty was not relieved. "I'll go in the bedroom. You talk to them," he suggested.

"Rusty, what do they want?"

"Answer the door and then you'll know," he told her.

Rusty disappeared into the spare bedroom and Jeri answered the door. "Can I help you?" she said, her voice squeaking.

One of the officers held a search warrant. "We need to search your house," he said.

"What!" she exclaimed. "You can't do that. I haven't done anything wrong."

"We think otherwise," he said, and the two pushed past her. "There'll be more officers here in a moment. You sit right over there while we work." He pointed at the sofa.

"You can't do that," she repeated. "I want to call a lawyer." She thought of Warren. He'd know what to do. But he'd probably say it was what she got for letting a convict in the house. She sat down on the sofa.

"Where is Randy?" the other officer asked.

"What are you looking for?" she asked.

"It's all right in here," he answered, waving the search warrant in her direction.

The door stood open, and a car squealed up outside. A moment later two more officers, both in plainclothes, hustled in. "Have you started?" one of them asked.

"Not yet. Moore is here somewhere. We need to find him first." The officer pulled his pistol. "Cover me. I'll check in here."

Jeri came to her feet as the others pulled their pistols. "I'll get him," she said.

"No you won't, sister," one of the plainclothes officers said.

"What are you going to do, shoot me?" she asked as she flung open the door to the spare bedroom and stepped in. "You better come out, Rusty," she said. She couldn't see him, but she knew he was there.

"Come out, both of you, with your hands where we can see them," an officer ordered.

Rusty stood up from where he had been hiding on the far side of the bed. He still carried the kitchen knife. Alertly, Jeri pointed at the floor and he dropped it softly. Together, they stepped from the darkness of the bedroom into the living room. The officers grabbed Rusty and frisked him.

"He's clean," one said. Then to Rusty, he said, "Okay Randy, you and the girl sit on the sofa. We have a little search to conduct."

As they sat, Jeri said, "Rusty, what is going on?"

"You'll have to ask them," he said.

"I did, but it didn't help."

"He knows," the only officer still in the room said. He was one of the uniformed policemen. It was apparently his job to guard the suspects while the others searched.

They weren't long. As the four of them assembled again a few minutes later, the second uniformed officer said, "All I found was this," and he waved the knife in the air. "What did you plan to do with this, Moore?"

"I gave it to him," Jeri said. "We had no way of knowing who was at the door, and I'd been followed all night. And someone beat him up," she said, pointing to the bruises on his face. Rusty hadn't said a word about that to her, hadn't had a chance, but she knew.

One of the plainclothes officers pointed a finger at Randy. "Okay, where is it?"

"Where's what?" Rusty asked defiantly.

"You know what," the officer hissed. He turned to one of the other officers and said, "Try her car." He turned to Jeri and held out his hands. "The keys."

She started to get up. "Stay put. Where are they?" he said.

"My purse. It's on the floor by the door. Bring it to me and I'll get them."

"Or your gun," he said with a laugh. "I'll find them myself."

"I am a law-abiding citizen and I don't own a gun."

"That may be," he said as he handed the keys he had pulled from the purse to another policeman. "Check it out," he said. He turned back to Jeri. "For a law-abiding citizen, you sure aren't choosy about the company you keep."

Jeri was seething. "You think you are so smart. You don't know anything about him. His name is not Randy Moore. This is Rusty Egan."

"Never mind," Rusty said. "They don't care."

Ignoring him, she said, "He was kidnapped when he was five. What kind of a life do you think he's had since then?"

"Never mind," Rusty repeated.

"No, they need to know. They can't treat you like this."

"They can. I've done some bad things, as you well know."

"And you went to prison for it," she said. "You paid your debt to society."

"He'll pay more before we are through with him," the older officer said.

"Car's clean, too, Lieutenant," the officer who went to search it said as he came back in.

The lieutenant glowered at Rusty. "All right. Come clean. Where is it?"

"I don't know what you're talking about. You've searched and you didn't find anything. Now get out!" Rusty said.

The officer turned and signaled to the others to head for the door. "We'll be back, I'm sure." They left, slamming the door behind them.

For a moment, neither Jeri nor Rusty spoke. Finally, she stood up from the sofa and faced him. "Okay, Rusty, what was that all about?"

He looked guilty but just shook his head. He didn't want to lie to this girl who had been his best friend when they were little. He didn't know what to say. Finally he stood up, too, and said, "I can't tell you. I'm not absolutely sure. It would be better if you didn't know. I will tell you this much, though. I have made enemies, and some of them want to find an excuse, any excuse to put me back in prison."

Jeri shrugged. "Okay, I won't press you, Rusty. But please, be careful."

"I will," he promised. "But it is you I am worried about. I'm sorry I got you into this mess. Now I've got to see that you don't get hurt."

"I can take care of myself," she insisted bravely.

"Sure you can," he said, "but I will feel better if we take some precautions."

"Okay," she said, suddenly feeling the exhaustion hit her. "First I want to see what they did to my house."

They looked together. A few things were out of place, but it wasn't what she expected. It wasn't what she had seen so many times on television. She straightened things, then said, "You better stay here tonight. You can sleep in the spare bedroom."

"That will be good for your reputation," he said facetiously.

"It's not my reputation I'm worried about," she said. "It's those guys who attacked you at your apartment. Why didn't the cops say anything about them?" she asked. "I don't understand at all what is going on here."

"It's best that way. Lock your doors. I'm leaving," he told her. "I'm pretty sure you'll be safe now." In the back of his mind he was resolved that he would not really leave her alone, just in case. He would wait outside all night. He could sleep during the day. He cursed himself for getting her involved in his troubles.

"You can't . . ." she began.

He simply turned and opened the door. "Thanks, Jeri, and I'm sorry. Be careful. Keep your door locked." And he was gone.

***

The police station was busy for a Saturday afternoon. A half dozen officers and two unscrupulous private investigators had their heads together. "I tell you, they have got it. She got it for him and stashed it somewhere, Lieutenant." The speaker sported a serious black eye where Rusty's head had butted him when he was making his escape the night before, outside his apartment.

"No, Arnie, I don't think so," the lieutenant said.

The argument had been raging for close to an hour. Lt. Ron Arthur, the older officer from the previous evening's search, was gruff, but he was also fair. He had been embarrassed by a search which, in his opinion, should never have been conducted. He said so now. "Your information was bad," he told Arnie and Joe, the private investigators. "You two are an embarrassment. You could be charged for breaking into Randy Moore's apartment. The chief is livid. He went to bat with the Parole Board to get Moore out of prison so the stolen money could be recovered. We tipped our hand on your say so, and I dare say we jumped the gun. It's going to be much more difficult from here on out."

Arnie grumbled. "The girl has it, I tell you."

Joe agreed. "No doubt about it. You guys just missed it."

"We did not miss it. It was not in the apartment or the car," Lieutenant Arthur said firmly. "And that brings me to the girl. We've done some checking this morning. She is Jeri Satch, a topflight accountant for one of the most reputable firms in Sacramento. She is from Utah, a Mormon, and one they term as active. She goes to church every Sunday, that sort of thing. Randy belongs to a family from Flagstaff, Arizona. His real name is Rusty Egan, just like she told us last night. He was kidnapped just a few days before he turned six. The Satch girl saw it happen and has lived with the horror of it ever since."

"How did they come to know each other now?" one of the patrol officers from the search asked.

Lieutenant Arthur explained. "It was a coincidence. She does accounting for the prison where he was being held. It's a private prison, as you know. She was given a tour the first day she went there, saw him, and recognized him."

Arnie shook his head. "A bunch of baloney if you ask me."

"Seems to be true, all right."

"Then what is she doing hanging around with him now if she is such a good girl?"

"I spoke with her this morning, Arnie. She was still upset, but she leveled with me." He went on to explain about the delivery by Rusty to the accounting firm, of the letter he found, and how he delivered it. "Her boyfriend, a law student from Utah, was there and Rusty's showing up didn't do her romance any good," he said. "The boyfriend left, angry, and Jeri gave Randy, or Rusty, a ride to his apartment. The rest we all know."

"She's part of it," Arnie insisted sullenly.

"She's clean as a whistle," Lieutenant Arthur insisted. "Leave her alone. She's out of this. Now we've simply got to keep watch and see what moves he makes to recover the money. She won't help him. She knows about it, because I told her a little while ago. I sort of doubt she will be seeing him again."

"So how will he get the money? He knows we're watching him," the lieutenant's partner, Detective Les Bering, asked.

"That remains to be seen. Arnie and Joe, I've spoken with the bank. You are both off the case. I want to make it very clear that you are not to interfere. We will man the surveillance ourselves, as we have since we left the apartment last night. That is, we will do it until the bank sends us a better team than you. You are dismissed now."

The two left grumbling. After they were gone, Lt. Ron Arthur turned to his colleagues. "They bear watching. I don't know what the bank was thinking. Assigning them to this case was like letting the fox guard the henhouse. I think they want a piece of the loot."

"Who knows, they wouldn't be beyond joining up with Moore," Detective Bering suggested.

Lieutenant Arthur shook his head. "I don't think that will happen. He knows them now, and he doesn't like them. No, he'll do something else. He's smart. We've just got to be smarter."

CHAPTER 18

The sun shone brightly as Jeri walked briskly toward her apartment. She had gone out shortly after Lt. Ron Arthur left. Her conversation with him had been enlightening. He trusted her, and she was happy about that. The night before, he and the others had given her the impression that she was somehow a suspect in something. Lieutenant Arthur let her understand she was not.

The two private investigators, he had explained, were unsavory characters hired by the bank Rusty had robbed. They were off the case, or would be before the day was over. But she knew there would be others and why. The police and the bank believed that Rusty had hidden the money and that he intended to recover it for himself. "If you have any influence over him at all, you might try to persuade him to turn the money over," he had told her. "He can go straight. He is a smart and talented young man. But if he turns up with the money, his parole will be revoked and he will be in prison again."

Then he told her the thing that shocked her the most. "We kept a surveillance here all night. We worried about Arnie and Joe. I guess Rusty did too." She was surprised that he used Rusty instead of Randy. It added to her faith in the detective. He went on. "Rusty watched your place all night long. He didn't leave until well after the sun rose. I'm sure he wanted to make sure you were okay."

That had given her a lot to think about. She didn't attempt to fool herself. Rusty was a convict. He had a criminal mind. And yet, she knew that hidden somewhere within him was a soft and gentle heart. She knew what he used to be and she desperately wanted to find that sweet soul who had been taken. Rusty's watching out for her through the long, cold night was evidence of gentleness and concern. She wanted desperately to uncover the real Rusty Egan and bury forever the fake Randy Moore.

She also knew that she must always keep him in mind as a brother, nothing more. They had been as close as brother and sister as children. She could help him if he would let her and they could continue to be like a brother and sister. There was no substitute for a temple marriage, and she would stay single all her life before she settled for less. That was a commitment she had made years before, and it was as deeply ingrained in the person she was as were other things such as avoiding tobacco, coffee, tea, and alcohol, and paying tithing.

It was too bad that Warren was so shallow in his thinking that he could not see that. But he had destroyed any hope of ever receiving her love. She didn't care if she never talked to him or saw him again. She was almost sure of that.

Almost!

Okay, so she wasn't sure.

She walked faster. Had Warren become more important to her than she thought? The terrible things she had experienced the night before had only reinforced the fact that he was a good man, just a little shallow. Or was that even fair? After all, he cared for her. And Rusty was a convicted criminal. But then, look at Rusty's past, she reminded herself. That was what Warren refused to do.

Oh, she didn't know what to think. Maybe it was time to go out with some of the guys here who seemed interested. She knew that some wanted to ask her out. But Jeri had built a shield around herself and they had never attempted to penetrate it. Maybe it was time to tear down that shield.

A horn honked and she looked around. Warren's rental car pulled to the curb. Warren looked awful. His short dark hair was mussed, and his eyes had dark circles around them, and they were red. Had he been crying? she wondered. Was he as miserable and confused as she was? She stopped walking and he rolled down the passenger window and called out to her. "Care for a lift?"

She hesitated. She had been so angry at him last night, and yet, seeing him like this was almost more than she could stand. He tried an awkward, embarrassed grin on her and that did it. Jeri had a soft heart and a tender place in it for him. "Where to?" she asked as she stepped closer and reached for the door handle.

"Anywhere your heart desires," she was told.

She climbed in and allowed Warren to take her hand and squeeze it gently. "You are looking at the most miserable, wretched man in this gray world," he admitted. "Saying I'm sorry is not enough. I know that, so I won't even try. But I couldn't leave Sacramento without seeing you again."

Jeri was touched. It was true that an apology would never be enough to bring things back to where they had been before Rusty knocked at the door last night. And Warren was clearly miserable. It touched her in a way that just moments before she didn't think she could be touched. His look was worth more than a thousand apologies. "I'm glad you found me," she said. "I was feeling terrible that you were leaving with us so angry at one another."

Warren nodded and pulled the car away from the curb. "Could I buy you some lunch? I haven't eaten yet today."

"Neither have I," Jeri admitted. Eating had been the farthest thing from her mind this morning. But it was early afternoon now, and her stomach was protesting. "That would be nice," she added.

They found a quiet café and went in together. The meal was adequate, but the mood was melancholy. Conversation was sporadic. Neither seemed to quite know what to say to the other. Rusty's name had not come up so far, and Jeri was most grateful to Warren for that. Kate's name did come up, and Jeri wondered again if maybe there was a place in his heart for her.

She did not know how she felt about that. Somehow, he didn't seem her type. Too shallow? Kate was not shallow, that was for sure. But people could change. She had tried to point that out to Warren about Rusty. Wasn't the same true of Warren? Couldn't he change? She thought about that as she watched him slowly eat, occasionally glancing up and catching her eye.

Her heart twisted miserably at the sadness she saw in his face. It made her want to reach out and take him in her arms and comfort him. But she did not. He would read too much into it. But still, his pain made her feel just terrible. She didn't eat much. She couldn't. He ate a lot, but then he always did. He finally finished and wiped his mouth with his napkin. "I couldn't have done that without you here," he told her, glancing at his empty plate. "Thanks for seeing me."

She nodded. "Thanks for lunch."

"I ruined everything," he said sadly.

"Not everything," she said. "At least we can part friends."

"So is this the end then?" he asked.

"Maybe," she said. Maybe? An hour ago it would have been probably. But he was different now.

"Maybe?" He asked the same thing she had asked herself. There was hope on his face.

"You hurt me, Warren," she said. "I was angry. More angry than I have ever been. Well, almost."

"Since you were five?" he asked.

"Yes, since then." Rusty had come up. Maybe that was good. Maybe that was bad.

"I was so insensitive," he said with downcast eyes. "I never knew, maybe didn't want to know, how much what happened back then hurt you."

"Nobody can ever know, Warren."

"I see that now. He was like a brother, wasn't he?"

"Yes. We did everything together. We even had our own playhouse in his backyard. His dad and me and him, we built it together."

"You were five, is that right?"

"Yes. Almost six, actually. Our birthdays are three weeks apart. I am older by three weeks. I turned six less than a month after he was kidnapped. But I was always older and maybe that's why I felt so responsible when it happened," she said, and her eyes began to fill with tears.

"It still hurts," he said.

"Maybe it always will," she agreed.

Warren leaned forward, pushing his empty plate aside, glancing at his watch as he did so. "I have time before I have to catch my flight. I'd like it to hear about it."

Jeri was more than a little surprised. "About . . ." she began and hesitated.

"About what happened. About you and Rusty. You must have been almost like twins."

Was this really Warren? Could he be this perceptive? Had he changed into a different man overnight? Whatever the case, she wanted to talk. It felt good to talk. "Yes, I think that about sums it up. We were like twins. And you really want to hear about it?"

"Please, Jeri."

She searched his eyes. She could still see the hurt, and it was deep, But there was also sincerity there. She would tell him. If this was the last thing she ever talked to him about, it would leave her with a good memory instead of a bad one. So she began. And he listened.

The waitress cleared the table. She brought some pie. She refilled their water glasses.

Jeri talked, she cried, she even smiled a little. Warren just continued to listen. He did not say a word. She went on for over an hour. She shared her feelings in a way that she had only done with Kate. He did not interrupt.

Warren nodded. He shook his head. He dropped his head. He even dabbed at his eyes. In a small way he thought maybe he could feel just a little of what she had been feeling for seventeen long years. He couldn't believe he had not asked her to tell him this story a long time ago. Things could have been so different.

She neared the end of her story. "So this was why, Warren, whenever I saw a little boy with sandy hair it brought the nightmare back."

"I had no idea," he said. Those were the first words he had uttered since she began to recite the bitter tale.

"Yes, so you see, that time in Salt Lake when you were taking me out and I suddenly fell to pieces, that was why," she said. "A little boy with sandy hair crossed the street in front of us, and he was wearing blue shorts. His mother was holding tightly to his hand. I couldn't stand it."

"So you had me take you home?"

"Yes. And I went on looking." Jeri studied the depth of Warren's green eyes. She saw understanding there, and she found that she still liked Warren. "So you see, I had to keep looking. I couldn't *not* look. I prayed about it. I fasted about it. And I came here for this job. You see, I think the Lord wanted me to find him. His only chance in life might be his . . . his . . . *twin sister*," she stammered.

Warren nodded in understanding. "What a fool I've been. I thought I knew you. I didn't know you at all."

"I know."

Warren looked at his watch, then he dropped his hand and grasped hers where it lay on the table. He squeezed gently. She smiled at him. "I have a plane to catch," he said.

"I'll see you off," she offered.

"I'd like that, but . . ." he stopped.

"But what?" she pressed.

"There are too many cars," he said with a laugh.

"I'll ride with you. I can get a taxi home."

He looked relieved. "Only if you let me give you the money for the fare," he said.

"It's a deal."

His plane was late. They spent an hour more than they planned. They walked around the terminal as they waited. At his coaxing, she told him about how she first saw Rusty in the prison and what had happened after that. Not once did he say anything negative. He was a changed man. Finally, as time ran out, he said to her, "Jeri, you woke me up last night when you asked me to leave your apartment. I was so mad at you that I swore I would never speak to you again. Then I began to think about me. Maybe that was the Lord's way of helping me see some of my shortcomings. I went through torture all night long. And it wasn't just because I might have thrown away what was happening between the two of us. It was really more about me and what I admitted to myself about how I am. It was not pretty. I went through a period last night when I found I did not like myself. I could see why you didn't love me, and it hurt, because it was my fault."

Jeri took his hand. His flight was called. She looked deep into his eyes. She didn't tell him what kind of a night that she had experienced. That wouldn't fit. She was just glad for what appeared to be a genuine change in him. She eased closer.

"So, this is it then, I guess?" he said.

"Maybe," she heard herself say.

His head bent down. Hers tilted up. She leaned in. He stepped in. Slowly their faces came together. Their lips met, and for a long time they clung to each other. Finally, as the second call was made for his flight they pulled apart. "Thank you, Jeri."

"And thank you, Warren."

"Good-bye," he said.

"For now," she answered.

She watched him as he grabbed his carry-on bag and rushed to the door and disappeared. Her eyes were filled with tears. Did she miss him already? Or was she glad he was gone? Either way, they were still friends. And either way, she could get on with the business of trying to save her *twin.*

Was that all she wanted?

Jeri had no idea. But at least as she turned and started back up the concourse, she felt good. She was happy, even content. She had made peace with Warren and that brought peace to herself. Somehow, she felt that even if she failed with Rusty, the world would not seem quite so bleak. Perhaps this day would be a turning point for her as it seemed to be for Warren. She would let life go on and just see what happened. Warren really was a pretty good guy.

If Warren called, she would talk to him. If he didn't she would try not to grieve. What had happened in the past that was ugly in their lives was just that, it was in the past. So were the things that had happened to Rusty. But she was still as resolved as ever to try to make it better. After all, he was her *brother.*

Or so she tried to tell herself.

***

The days passed quickly after New Years. Warren called twice. Kate called three times. The two had been together. "He still loves you," Kate told her one evening.

"And you love him," Jeri said perceptively.

"I don't know about that," Kate said with a laugh. "I do know this, he is a better person than he was. He told me a little about what happened to you guys down there. I'm glad he finally listened to your story, or that you finally were willing to tell him about it."

"It was a little of both," Jeri admitted.

"Jeri, I still won't stand in the way of you two," she said.

"Nor me in the way of you two," Jeri countered.

"It's you he loves," Kate said. "And I don't blame him."

Rusty did not call or come by. Jeri was tempted to look him up, but two weeks passed following New Year's day, and she had still not seen him. Lieutenant Arthur came by on the fifteenth of January. She panicked when she first saw him at the door that evening, but she felt better once he told her that Rusty was doing fine. He was working hard and nothing had happened as far as the money was concerned. "It might be well if you went to see him. He is a little withdrawn and lonely, according to his parole officer," he told her.

What he was really saying was that they needed to resolve this thing with the money; the bank wanted it back. She would not use Rusty, but somehow, if she could help and encourage him in the right way, it would be great.

Later that same night, after she had returned from a young singles activity, Rusty's mother called. "We got a letter last night."

CHAPTER 19

"It was kind of an awkward letter," Mindy Egan reported to Jeri. "Rusty said he had learned that he was our son and that he wanted to thank us for what we had done for him as a child."

"I'm so glad he finally wrote," Jeri said. "I gave him your address over two weeks ago. I finally located him again, or rather, he located me."

"He looked you up?" Mindy asked. She sounded surprised.

Jeri explained about the letter from Kate and the delivery of papers from the place he worked. "He looks good and seems to like his job," she said. She avoided discussion of any of the unpleasant things that had occurred that night. "So what else did he tell you?"

"He said he was sorry we missed him when we were there, and that he would like to meet us before he moves," she said.

"Moves?" Jeri's felt a painful hollowness develop in her heart. That did not sound good at all. Was he planning on grabbing the money and running? she wondered.

"Did he say where he was moving to and when?" Jeri asked uneasily.

"Somewhere in California, I suppose, but certainly not right away. He said he couldn't leave the state, so we would have to come there to see him," Mindy reported. "He also said that it would be wise to give him a few days notice so he could let his parole officer know. The tone of the letter was okay, like he wants to meet us, but it also gave us the impression that once he meets us, that is the end. It's like it would satisfy our curiosity, or maybe his," she said.

Jeri's mind was working quickly. She had to see him soon if there was any chance at all that she could somehow convince him to turn the money over. Once his folks had been here, she had a feeling he would do whatever he was planning to do to get the money back, and then he would probably just disappear. "So when are you coming?" Jeri asked as these thoughts ran through her mind.

"Probably this weekend. We thought we would try to fly in on Friday night. That's the nineteenth. Then we'll just have to see what happens. If we end up staying until Sunday, maybe we could go to Church with you."

"That would be great," Jeri said. And wouldn't it really be something if they could somehow persuade Rusty to go as well? That's a fantasy, she told herself. But the thought made her more cheerful and eased the worry in her mind.

"One more thing, Jeri," Mindy began. "If we mailed him a letter tomorrow, by the time it got to him it might not give him enough time to make the arrangements with his parole officers."

"Would you like me to talk to him and call you back?" Jeri volunteered.

"That was what I was about to ask, Jeri. And please, call collect."

"I'll try to talk to him tomorrow," Jeri promised.

"Oh, thank you so much. You don't know how much all this means to us."

But Jeri had a pretty good idea. She refrained from saying so.

Mindy went on. "He said some nice things about you. He said you even fixed dinner for him."

It wasn't quite like that. But he did eat the nice dinner she and Warren had fixed for themselves. She said, "Yeah, we had a good talk that night."

After the phone call was over, Jeri sat and pondered. She had the excuse she needed to see Rusty. Now she needed to find a way to convince him that he needed to go straight, and that meant returning the money. That would not be easy. He might resent the fact that the cops had been talking to her about the money, and he would wonder how else she could have known if she didn't admit to hearing it from them.

Jeri was restless that night. A lot of thoughts crossed her mind, but no great ideas impressed her. She finally admitted she would simply have to wing it and pray for last-minute inspiration on how to approach Rusty. She worked late the next day. It was after six when she finally left the building. She decided to find him before she went home, since he would most likely be off work.

There was no answer when she knocked at his door, so she went to Pink's. She knew the address after working on Pink's accounts for several days while Howard was out of the office. She parked and entered by the door marked "Customers." A large man with a pink face was leaning on the counter inside. He looked up and smiled when he saw her. "Wreck your car, young lady?" he asked.

"Not recently," she said. "I'm looking for a man who works here."

Before she could say who it was, the big man said, "Lucky guy. My name's Pink. I own the joint. Which one is it you're looking for?"

"Rusty Egan."

Pink frowned. "His name is Randy Moore, and you'd be well advised to steer clear of him and his kind."

"Oh," she said, mildly annoyed. "And what kind would that be?"

"Criminal types. He's an ex-con, or did you already know that?"

"I knew," she said shortly.

"Well, he's still working, and I'm not paying him to visit," he said tersely.

"I'll wait, then," Jeri said.

"I'll tell him you're here," he offered. That surprised her.

"Thank you," she said.

"I'll need a name."

"Jeri Satch."

Pink seemed to freeze for a moment. "Satch," he said almost as if speaking to himself. "You wouldn't be an accountant, would you?" he asked her.

"Yes."

"You worked on my accounts while Howard was gone." It was not a question. But Jeri answered as though it were.

"Yes, that was me."

"You do very good work," he admitted. "In fact, I was thinking about asking to have you assigned permanently. You did better than Howard. But if you have connections with Randy . . ."

"Rusty," she interjected.

He acted as if he had not heard her. ". . . then I think maybe I won't do that."

"Whatever makes you happy," she said. She didn't like his attitude. It was guys like him that made it hard for guys like Rusty to go straight. But he had employed him and paid him well. She knew that, having worked with the payroll. That puzzled her and so she asked, "If you think he's such a bad guy, why did you hire him?"

Pink opened his mouth as if to answer and then he snapped it shut. "Can't say?" she asked as an idea entered her head. She was so sure that she had figured it out that she said, "It's about the money he stole, isn't it?"

"You know about that?" he asked, confirming what she had just figured out.

"Of course I do. Lt. Ron Arthur is a friend of mine," she said and smiled at the surprise *that* put on his face.

"Are you working with Arthur, too?" he asked as if he had just discovered a co-conspirator. She nodded, and he asked, "So what are you here to see Randy about?"

"Rusty," she corrected.

"Why do you insist on calling him Rusty?" he asked.

"Because that is who he really is. How long is he going to be?" she asked. She could hear what sounded like grinding and hammering going on in the back, and the smell of fresh paint was making her slightly nauseated.

"Another thirty minutes," she was told.

"I see." Then she answered Pink's question and told him she was here to try to persuade Rusty to give up the money. Jeri paused for a moment and then asked, "What kind of work does he do? I mean, is it good or bad or mediocre? What?"

"Excellent," Pink admitted grudgingly. "But I am not comfortable having him here because of what he did."

"Do you have a few minutes? I'd like to tell you a story. Then you can tell him I'm waiting for him."

Pink nodded, and Jeri told again the heartbreaking story of Rusty's abduction. She tried not to cry, but that was impossible, and the crusty shop owner was genuinely moved.

"So he really is Rusty?"

"He really is."

"Tough break he had."

"The worst."

"I'm sorry. I didn't know. I'm indebted to you for telling me. And I think I'll request you do my accounts from now on."

"Oh, that won't be necessary," she said.

"I have a reputation here for turning out good work. I expect the same when people work for me. Howard's okay, but you are better. I'll ask anyway."

Jeri let it drop. She didn't need more accounts, but it was no use arguing with Pink. "I'll tell Rusty you're here. Maybe he can knock off now," he said.

Jeri was amazed at how the truth about Rusty's past could change attitudes. Pink opened the door and shouted, "Rusty! Someone here to see you."

Jeri's ears rang. The big man had an even bigger voice. The grinding stopped. Rusty had apparently heard him over his work. Not that she was surprised. Pink let the door swing shut. "He's coming," he said. "And good luck in making him see sense. I could use him permanently, and with more money to boot, if he would come clean."

"Thank you, I'll do my best," Jeri said cheerfully.

Rusty came out. Jeri could hardly recognize him for the dust and grease on his clothes and skin. He grinned when he saw her. He held out a hand and then drew it back. "I'm filthy. My parents call you?"

"Yes," she said.

"Great. Can you believe that, Pink?" he asked. Pink nodded. "I'm going to meet my family. Never used to know I had one."

"Jeri told me," Pink said, his face growing red. "Sorry about the way I treated you. Quite a history you have."

Rusty said, "Colorful, I guess you could say."

"Leave that car until morning," Pink told him.

"Are you sure? You said . . ."

"Don't matter what I said," Pink said gruffly. "Young lady wants to talk to you. Don't keep the likes of her waiting, you hear?"

Rusty grinned. "You're the boss," he said. He turned to Jeri. "Give me five minutes while I clean up."

When he reappeared, his clothes were still dirty, but his face and hands were scrubbed and his hair was combed. "This is the best I can do on short notice," he told her.

"You look great," she answered. And she was disturbed at how good he really did look.

Better than a brother.

Good thing she had standards.

Also good Warren was still in the picture.

"Are you in a hurry?" Rusty said when they had reached her car a minute later.

"I have all evening," she told him.

"Good," Rusty said. "You drive and I'll buy dinner. But first take me to my apartment. I can't be seen in public with a pretty lady like you without a shower and a change of clothes."

While she waited in his apartment for him to clean up, she looked around. He had a few things now. He had bought a small TV and an equally small stereo. She was pleased to see the pictures of his family propped up on the kitchen counter. She was also pleasantly surprised to see how neat and clean his tiny apartment was. She had not expected that. It was even neater than Warren's had been the one time she had been in it a year or so ago.

She shook her head. She shouldn't be comparing anything about Rusty with Warren. It wasn't right. Why not? she asked herself. After all, she and Rusty were more like brother and sister, she reminded herself.

When Rusty reappeared, she had to steady herself against the kitchen counter. For a brother, he sure did things to her. He looked so good. She hated to think how that grinning face might change when she mentioned the money. It would be even more difficult than she had thought.

As they were driving to the restaurant Rusty had suggested, she told him about his parents's plan. "They said you had to have enough time to let your parole officer know," she said, glancing his way as she spoke. The guilty look she saw on his face, though he tried to hide it, was alarming. He had other reasons for needing time. She knew it now, and it broke her heart. What she had to talk to him about later was really going to be tough. "They are so anxious to meet you, Rusty," she went on, trying to pretend that she had not noticed his reaction.

He seemed relieved. "I know it sounds corny," he said. "But I really do want to get to know them. Although I'm not kidding myself. They won't like what they see, and I know I could never be like them. Don't even want to be," he admitted.

"They are nice people," was all she could say. Oh how she wished he'd change.

The restaurant Rusty had chosen was quiet, clean, and very nice. The food was excellent. Palm trees graced the front walk, and a fountain spilled water cheerfully from the mouth of a coiled snake into a sparkling green pool filled with pennies beside the entrance. A young couple stood arm in arm flipping pennies into the water and giggling as Rusty and Jeri walked by.

It seemed to set the atmosphere for a meal that seemed a whole lot more romantic than brotherly. If only things were different with Rusty, Jeri thought to herself. But she had her standards, and even with thoughts and feelings that kept straying and had to be tucked back in place, she knew that she would never lose her goals. They were part of her.

So was Rusty. Seventeen years of waiting and looking and aching were hard to erase. And telling him what she had to tell him this night was getting harder and harder to face.

After the meal, Jeri ate cheesecake while Rusty drank a cup of coffee. Watching him, Jeri knew she had never wanted anyone to change so badly. Never had she cared this much.

As a sister.

Just a sister.

They finished and sat there, looking at each other. Neither seemed to want to leave. Classical music played softly in the background, and Rusty smiled. "It will probably surprise you when I tell you that I like classical music."

Surprise her? How about shock her?

It must have shown on her face, for he said, "It used to make Uncle Bill so angry. He would always play this hard rock stuff . . . drug music, I guess it was. And I would come home with something classical. He would beat me at first and throw it away, using the excuse that the cops would get me. He knew I'd stolen it. I didn't have any money. I got smarter, and I learned to hide it from him and play it only when he was out on a drunk somewhere or with one of his female friends." Rusty shuddered and his face grew dark. "I'll even the score someday."

"Rusty," Jeri said, frightened at the look on her friend's face. "What good will that do?"

"It will make me feel better!" Rusty exploded. "If it wasn't for him . . ." He stopped mid-sentence.

"What?" she urged, trying not to cower from his anger.

"Nothing. It doesn't matter now. It's too late for me anyway." The anger had faded and he seemed despondent. "Maybe it isn't such a good idea, me seeing my parents and all."

Jeri reached over and touched his hand. His mood lifted. "I'm sorry about all that's happened to you, Rusty."

She sniffled and he held out a clean napkin. She took it, dried her eyes, and blew her nose. "I'm sorry," she said.

"It's okay," he said. "I didn't mean to ruin the evening." He paused, looking deep into her eyes. His glistened a little as he said, "So tell me what you have to say."

"What do you mean?" she stammered.

"Jeri, you aren't fooling me. You have something on your mind. It may have been a long time since we were, what did you say, twins?"

She nodded.

"But I remember more all the time. I could always read your mind. Or at least I could tell when you were thinking something and surprise you with it. That is true, isn't it?"

It was true. She remembered, too. So she prepared to tell him what she had dreaded to say the entire evening. She asked him not to get angry. He promised. She told him about the money and Lieutenant Arthur.

He broke his promise.

He exploded. Now she knew the money really did exist. She tried to calm him. "Rusty, you have a good job now. You don't need the half million. Give it back and put the past behind you."

"You don't understand!" he shouted. Rusty lunged to his feet, picked up the check and said angrily, "I'll find my own way home. And tell my family I've changed my mind."

CHAPTER 20

Jeri was devastated. She had really messed things up. She berated herself all the way back to her apartment for handling such a delicate thing so badly. Not that she had any idea how she might have approached Rusty differently over the issue of the stolen money. She felt that it was her fault that he had taken it so badly.

Now she had to call and deliver the bad news to his family. How could she ever explain to them what had happened to cause him to change his mind? The truth, maybe? She had bungled it? She had offended him by bringing up what he had done to get him sent to prison? Or, he still had the fruits of his crime and was not willing to give it up? All were true. The first two would hurt only her, the last would hurt his family. And yet, despite how she had handled, or mishandled it, with Rusty the root of the problem was his unwillingness to part with something he had no right to.

She couldn't tell his family that. They had been hurt enough. It was better that they be angry at her than lose any respect they might have for their son. Resolving to follow this course, she arrived home, and went into the apartment, determined to make the call. She had to do it immediately for fear she might lose her courage.

Her phone rang as she reached for the receiver to make her call. "You're home, Jeri. Were you able to talk to Rusty and get things scheduled?" It was Rusty's mother. She was too excited to wait for Jeri to call. How angry would she be when she learned that Jeri had messed up their plans to finally meet the son they hadn't seen for over seventeen years?

As it turned out, she was very angry.

"He won't see us? You shouldn't have done that, Jeri!" Mrs. Egan exploded when Jeri mentioned bringing up Rusty's past to him.

"I'm sorry. I was only trying to . . ." Jeri started.

"Sorry won't help," Rusty's mother said. "You have no idea how we feel. He is our son. Why couldn't you leave well enough alone?"

There was clearly nothing she could do to calm the distraught woman. And she did not blame her for her anger. But she did have some idea how they felt. After all, it was she who had looked for Rusty for those many years. It was she who had refused to give up. Mindy Egan was still talking, but Jeri was absent from the conversation. That is until Mindy said, "So maybe we will just come anyway. But please don't try to help anymore."

That hurt. That really hurt badly. "I won't," Jeri said lamely. "I wish you luck." Quietly she hung up the phone, buried her head in her hands and cried bitter tears of recrimination.

She had scarcely regained her composure when the phone rang again. Having not moved, she had merely to reach for the receiver. She did so, then hesitated. What if it were Rusty's mother again? She couldn't take further recriminations right now. She withdrew her hand and looked to see who was calling. She was relieved when she saw Warren's number displayed.

It didn't take him long to realize something was wrong. As was his nature, he inquired. The relationship between Warren and her was very fragile, and she was determined to not be the reason if it disintegrated again. Mentioning Rusty was not the best thing for them. But he was the reason she was upset, and if anything was to ever come of her relationship with Warren, it would have to be despite Rusty Egan. Not that she was sure anything would, or even if she was sure it should. She was barely back to where she could honestly say she liked Warren again, and anything beyond that was mere speculation at this point.

At any rate, he asked, he pressed when an answer was not forthcoming, and she decided to risk it. "I just got off the phone with Rusty Egan's mother and she is very angry with me."

The ice that developed in the phone was instantaneous. "What were you talking to her about?" the voice that put the ice there asked.

"I was just telling her that Rusty did not want to see them," she said. She rushed on before Warren could interrupt. "He wrote to them, said he wanted to see them. They called me and asked if I would arrange it."

"They have no right to ask you to do that," Warren said.

"I wish they hadn't," she responded with a sincerity that Warren could feel.

"What happened?" he asked.

"I looked him up and tried to set up their meeting. However, I messed it up really bad." She paused for Warren's response. Surprisingly, there was none, so she went on, omitting details she knew would upset him, such as dinner with Rusty. "He seemed sincere about wanting to meet them, but there was something I felt like I should say to him, and I did and it made him angry."

Now he responded. "What did you say?"

"I told him that I had heard he had a half-million stolen dollars hidden somewhere and that I thought he should give it back," she said.

"Jeri," Warren said with a depth of feeling that melted the ice in the line. "You don't know how proud that makes me. You did the right thing, and if that made him angry, which it must have, then he clearly is not ready to give up a life of crime."

She resented his words a little, but she had to admit they were true. It was nice to hear him say she had done the right thing. She needed to hear that. She needed to hear more, so she asked, "How could I have handled it better, Warren? Should I have waited until after they had met him to mention the money?"

"Oh, no. You did exactly what needed to be done," he said, giving her the reinforcement her conscience called for. He should have left it at that, but he went on, "His parents must accept what and who he is now. And his attitude toward the money he stole clearly defines it. By the way, how did you know he had money hidden?"

"I didn't know it for sure until I asked him about it. The cops suspected it and asked me, if I could, to try to get him to give it back. If they catch him with it, he will go back to prison."

"And well he should. I'm glad you had the courage to try to help them."

She wished he wasn't so quick to agree. She didn't want to be angry with Warren right now. She was angry with Rusty and that was about more than she could take for one night. Warren was right, of course, but she didn't like to hear him gloat, and that was what it was starting to sound like. She tried to steer their conversation in another direction. It worked, and for the next few minutes they had a good talk. By the time she hung up the phone, she found herself wishing Warren was with her. She longed for comfort. Right now she could use his loving arms around her. He really wasn't such a bad guy.

An hour later, Jeri was getting ready for bed when she got another call. "Jeri, I am so sorry. I had no right to strike out at you the way I did. It was childish and inexcusable. Please forgive me."

Jeri took a deep breath. Of course she would forgive Rusty's mother. She would probably have done the same thing if their roles were reversed. She told her so, and Mrs. Egan went on, "It is such a disappointment."

"I knew it would be," Jeri said. "I wish things had gone differently. I should never have mentioned what I did."

"And what was that, Jeri?" Mindy asked, throwing Jeri into a panic. She couldn't tell her about the money. She had made up her mind not to.

She said, "Oh, I mentioned the robbery that he went to prison for. I shouldn't have. I regret it."

That was not enough to satisfy Rusty's mother. It was like she knew there was more to it than that. She pressed. "Jeri, I know that you would never have intentionally tried to hurt Rusty or us. So I'm certain that whatever you said needed to be said. Rusty's father and I have been talking ever since you and I spoke earlier. I just feel horrible about what I said to you. And we're both certain there is more that we need to hear."

"I don't think it would be a good idea," Jeri said.

"Please, Jeri." It was Rusty's father. Jeri hadn't heard him come on the line. "You don't want us to be hurt more, is that it?"

That was it, and she admitted as much.

"It is not his fault. We love him. He is our son. We lost him and that was not our fault or his. We have come to accept that. So please, whatever it was that upset him, share it with us."

What else could she do? So, despite her earlier resolve, Jeri told them about the money and Rusty's reaction.

They were upset, of course, but they accepted it better than she had. After talking it over for several minutes, Mr. Egan announced that they were going to come to Sacramento anyway. "You can show us where he lives and we'll take it from there. It is our only chance, and it may be his, too. Would that be okay with you?"

What could she say? It couldn't make matters any worse than they were. So it was decided. They would fly in on Friday afternoon and meet her at her apartment at about five. She would take them directly to Rusty's apartment. They would take it from there.

***

The Egans were not the only ones making plans to see Rusty. Actually, another person was also going to be looking for Randy Moore, his former cell mate. This was to be the last night in prison for the undiscovered serial killer, Charles Chumbian, better known as Chum. And all he could think about as he lay for the last time on his hard cot in a stuffy prison cell was what he could do with a half-million dollars.

That was what he intended to get. He had never for one moment entertained the idea of letting Randy Moore keep three-fourths of the money or even any of it. Now, though, he would not only take all the money, but he would take special pleasure in killing the young convict. He thought long and hard about how he would do it once the location of the money was revealed to him. He could scarcely wait for the next day. He intended to waste no time.

Then it occurred to him that Randy may have already gotten to the money. He hadn't heard rumors of his arrest, and that would almost certainly have reached the prison grapevine if it had happened. That meant that if he had recovered the money, he had done so without getting caught. And for that to have happened he would have needed help. And help would have most likely come from one source.

The girl.

The one Randy had called his sister. Never for a moment had Chum believed that. And she was also dispensable. Even if she turned out not to be involved, she was still dispensable. After all, she was the one who caused the rift between Randy and him that was making it more difficult to obtain his money. And Chum considered that money as already being his. He had from the very first day Randy Moore had mentioned it to him. Yes, the girl named Jeri had interfered with well-laid plans. She would pay for that and he would enjoy giving payment. And her beautiful body would join the others that lay all across the country in shallow, undiscovered graves.

Chum rubbed his hands together, relishing his morbid thoughts. He would get what he wanted, and others would be removed. He fell asleep with a smile on his face.

***

Jeri called Warren the following evening and told him of her call from the Egans. "I just wanted you to know," she told him. This was the first time she had called him, although he had called her several times since returning to Utah. Besides calling her, he had e-mailed her a number of letters. She had responded to his e-mails, and had found him increasingly easier to talk to each time he called. But she had not, until that night, been the one to initiate the contact.

"I am glad you told me," he responded warmly. "I hope they aren't too badly disappointed. And thank you for telling me," he added, inferring, to her way of thinking at least, that she was being more honest and up front about Rusty.

They didn't talk long, but it was a good visit. She did not have one moment of anger, and that was good, since Rusty had been part of the conversation. That had never happened before. Warren made her promise to call as soon as there was anything to report on the Egans's visit.

Kate called her later that night, and she asked how it was going with Warren. "Fine, I guess," Jeri said.

As always, their talks were warm and intimate. They were indeed best of friends. But Jeri was certain she detected an undercurrent of pain, perhaps even a touch of jealousy. Kate had it bad for Warren, and Jeri wondered if he would always be a source of friction in an otherwise perfect friendship. Time alone held the answer to that question.

Kate surprised Jeri when she announced that she would be

coming to Sacramento that weekend. "How did you ever arrange that?" Jeri asked with delight.

"I have a friend who is from Oakland. Her grandfather died and his funeral is Saturday. She has to drive home Friday. She would have been alone and I offered to keep her company if she would swing through Sacramento and drop me off at your place, if that is okay, of course."

"Okay? It's great. I can't wait to see you." Jeri was ecstatic. "When do you have to go back?"

"Sunday. It will make our visit short, but I'm still in school, and you know how that is."

Jeri knew, but already she was planning what they would do. She explained about Rusty's folks coming that same day and said, "It will make it a lot easier on me having you here. I am so happy."

Jeri slept well that night. Thursday she was so excited that her workday literally flew by. She wasn't even upset when her supervisor came in and announced that she would be taking over the account of Pink's Auto Body. She didn't even notice how Howard glared at her every time their paths crossed that morning and early afternoon. She had no way of knowing how angered he was. Being shown up by a woman was not something that Howard's ego could handle well, and to make matters worse, they didn't even give him one of her accounts to compensate.

***

Bad men have runs of good luck. Even very bad men have lucky days. Chum was having one. Wednesday was not one, but Thursday was turning out a whole lot better. He had devoted almost every waking minute since leaving the prison to finding Randy Moore. He had failed completely. His parole officer had refused to say anything. "Against policy," was all he would say.

But late Thursday morning, he got a break. Another former inmate who had known Randy crossed paths with Chum in a bar where he was taking a short break from his search. "Heard how Moore is doing?" Chum asked with a friendly grin.

The other fellow was afraid of Chum. He knew there was more to the dark side of that man than was publicly known. Inmates had talked about him outside of his presence. None liked Chum. Most knew he was a good one to avoid and certainly not one to offend. With that in mind, this former inmate tried to be helpful. "I hear he has a good-looking woman," he revealed.

Chum was instantly interested. "Oh yeah, how did you hear that?" he asked.

"Word's out, that's all. She's an accountant. Smart as well as good-looking," the man revealed.

"Does Randy's girlfriend work here in Sacramento?" Chum asked after ordering the man a beer.

"That's what I hear."

"Where?"

The other man stiffened. The tone of Chum's voice had undergone a distinct change. He was no longer asking friendly questions. This was a demand. He looked at Chum before answering. The man's eyes told him all he needed to know. He better have an answer and it better be a good one. Unfortunately, he did not, and within the hour, the Parole Office in Sacramento had one less parolee to keep track of. In Chum's mind, the man knew more than he was saying, and no amount of protest would change that. He died for trying to stay on the good side of a man who had no good side.

For Chum, the hunt for Randy was narrowed. There could only be so many accounting firms in the city. It was a process of elimination. And it was a lucky day for him. By mid-afternoon, he had visited several of them. An inquiry here and a question there eliminated the first five as the employers of the young lady Randy Moore had called Jeri.

At the sixth firm, a man who said his name was Howard was just leaving the building that fit the address in the phone book. "I'm looking for a young woman who handled some accounting for a friend of mine," he told the man. "I was told she could help me. I only know the first name. Jeri, I was told."

Chum did not miss the darkening of Howard's face, or the look of anger that filled his eyes. "She works here, all right," Howard hissed. "But she's the worst accountant in the firm." He seemed delighted to find himself in a position to do damage to her reputation. Chum was certain he had found an ally.

"Maybe I'll look for someone else. Just in case I change my mind though, could you tell me where she lives?" Chum asked. He was taking a chance, but he had a feeling Howard would give him the information he sought.

For his part, Howard was so angry with Jeri, and so jealous, that he was quick to respond. He did not miss the look of evil delight that was in the little man's eyes, but he was not in the mood to care. Jeri had done his reputation harm, taken advantage of him while he was gone for his father's funeral. That was low. If this man wanted her address, he didn't care. He would give it to him. He had to go inside and look it up, but within a few minutes, Chum was armed with the information he had sought. In finding Jeri, he had essentially found Randy. And in finding Randy, he was about to become a very rich man.

Yes indeed, even very evil people get lucky breaks.

And very good people get bad breaks.

CHAPTER 21

It was difficult to commit crime without transportation. But when one had just been released from prison and had just enough money in his pocket to eat for a few days, it required crime to obtain transportation. Since Chum intended to commit some very serious crimes in Sacramento, he decided that he would spend a few of his dollars and take a bus toward the coast and get himself outfitted in Oakland or San Francisco.

Now that locating Randy was within Chum's grasp, the urgency left him. He had always planned carefully, taken his time, stalked his victims long enough so that he knew their habits by heart before he struck. That seemed the logical thing to do now. So he boarded a bus an hour after his talk with Howard. When he came back to Sacramento, he would have a car, and money in his pocket. He had only slipped up once and that had been on a burglary here in Sacramento—and that error had cost him dearly. He had no intention of ever going to prison again. He would exercise extreme care, take his time, and in the end, he would be rich and Randy and Jeri would be buried.

***

Rusty walked home from work that Thursday night deep in thought. He was angry with himself for losing his temper and walking out on Jeri. She didn't deserve that. Several times last night he had been jarred awake by childhood memories of Jeri, of her pure innocence. It haunted him for reasons he could not understand. It made his day at work miserable, and he had even been short with a couple of his coworkers. He had apologized and cleared the air before leaving Pink's, but he didn't feel right as he walked slowly toward his apartment.

Torn as he was, Rusty tried to sort out his feelings. Jeri was special. Of that there was no doubt. Oh, she was out of his league and he knew it. She referred to them as twins, but whenever he looked at her gorgeous face and peered into her deep brown eyes, he saw more. Whenever he looked in the mirror and into his own eyes, he saw a crook, a criminal, a convict. He saw a man who took what did not belong to him and did so without remorse. Yes, he and Jeri Satch belonged in different worlds.

She did not understand what it was like to go without. She had probably never gone to bed hungry or had to dress in clothes that were tattered, torn, and badly soiled. She had never had to lie awake at night in fear of the man in the next room, wondering when he would come in and hurt you again, and make you want to kill him. She had not been forced to live alone at fifteen—wanted by no one, accepted by no one, looked down upon by everyone.

In Rusty's world, money made all the difference in how you were treated, how you were viewed, how you were able to live. He had money now, and he had paid a price to get it. Giving that up seemed unthinkable. But Jeri couldn't understand that. She had no experience in life that would help her relate to that kind of need for money. So he knew he had been wrong in treating her so badly when she suggested he should give it back.

Yet even while admitting he had wronged her, he refused to admit that she might be right. He made up his mind to apologize to her, but after that, he needed to quit seeing her. He needed to find a way to safely recover the money without involving or endangering her in any way.

His troubled mind turned to the other thing that was disturbing him so badly. He wanted to meet his family. It was a need that was growing more urgent, something he could not seem to rid himself of. He did not understand this strange longing that had developed within him. He knew they could never accept him as he was, and he certainly had no intentions of being like them, whatever that was.

Mormons. That was one thing they were, and his prejudices in that regard were deep-seated and strong. He had been taught that "Mormon" was a dirty word. Mormons were people to be shunned; they looked down on others. He believed what he had been taught.

By whom?

Uncle Bill, of course.

That thought brought him to an abrupt standstill. He hated Uncle Bill. He intended to find and repay that man's cruelty in a way that would make him regret ever having kidnapped and molested a little boy who had done nothing to him. So why would anything that Uncle Bill taught him about Mormons seem true? Why would he believe him, of all people?

Good grief. He pounded his head with his hand as he resumed walking. Uncle Bill was a cheat and a liar. Why should he be believed when it came to what he said about Mormons? Jeri was a Mormon. And Rusty had to admit that she was the embodiment of everything he could think of that was good. But despite the conflicting evidence, it was not easy to rid his mind of the prejudice he felt toward Mormons.

His parents were Mormons, but he was a part of them. Was it just curiosity that drove him to seek them out? Partly at least. Yet somehow it seemed important. It seemed like he simply had to know them, to talk with them, to spend some time with them. It was like now that he knew they existed, there was some power that drew him to them. And that thought in itself was frightening. Rusty didn't want anyone to have power over him ever again. Uncle Bill had misused that power, and he hated him for it. He didn't want to hate these parents he barely remembered, and whose faces, without the pictures Jeri had given him, he would not even recognize.

The apartment building loomed dark and foreboding as he approached. It was a lonely place. It represented his inability to provide a nice, comfortable place for himself to live in and his failure to ever forge a lasting friendship with anyone. But with the half million, he could change all that. Surely money was the answer to his loneliness, his low self-esteem, his lack of friends and comfortable surroundings. He could not give it up. That was too much to ask.

He also could not go on knowing he had hurt Jeri, and do nothing to rectify it. He could not do what she wanted, but at least he could apologize for how he had treated her, and maybe even try to explain how he felt. She would never understand, but it would make him feel better. And maybe, just maybe, she would not hate him. Somehow it seemed terribly important that Jeri Satch not hate him.

Rusty did not leave his apartment that night. He sat and thought of the money, and he tried to think of ways to get it without being caught. He was still being watched. He knew that. The watchers were just more discreet, more skilled, more patient. He also thought about Jeri, and his conscience continued to bother him. Finally, he made up his mind. He would come here right after work tomorrow and clean up. Then he would call a taxi. He would talk to her, he would thank her, he would tell her he was sorry. Then he might feel better.

***

Excitement met depression. It did not go well. They didn't like one another. They contended fiercely. Depression won.

Jeri could hardly wait to see Kate. She needed someone to talk to who would listen and understand, and Kate was that someone. But Rusty's folks were coming here, and he didn't want to see them. And it was her fault. Worse still, Rusty hated her. He didn't want to see her again. She had once again lost the friend, the brother, she had loved, and it hurt as deeply now as it did the day the man he called Uncle Bill had dragged him from love and security and thrust him into something that must have been so awful that Jeri could not even begin to visualize it, could never understand.

The things that had happened to Rusty in those dark ten years with Uncle Bill were beyond her capacity to even guess intelligently. What he had suffered, what he had endured, what he had fought to escape from must have been more terrible than anything she could ever imagine. She had lived a secure life, a sheltered existence, one where love and peace abounded. There was nothing in Jeri's experience that could in any way make it possible for her to know what Rusty might have suffered and endured.

Who was she to tell him what to do? She had no right to mention the half-million dollars. Oh, how she wished she hadn't. But Kate was coming, and she would listen. She might understand at least a little of how she was feeling; however, that thought didn't help much. The battle was over. Depression had won. Jeri was miserable to the very core. She cried herself to sleep.

Now that was something she understood. At least, it was familiar. She had done it enough.

When she awoke, she knew that she had shed an unusually large number of tears during the night, because her eyes were still red, and they felt as dry as the desert.

Eyedrops, a warm shower, more eyedrops, more makeup than usual, a light, tasteless breakfast, and a long, earnest prayer had her feeling a little better and looking as well as could be expected as she left the apartment to go to the office. She was still depressed, but it was under control. She had made up her mind to make the best of things. Kate was coming, and she wanted their time together to be fun. Rusty's family would be here that evening as well, and she was determined to be positive with them. They had enough heartache without her making it worse with tears and a long face.

Howard just happened to be approaching the door at the same time she did that morning. Jeri said, "Good morning, Howard." The look he cast her in response to her greeting jolted her. It was full of hatred. What had she done to him? He reached the door to their building a half step ahead of her. He held the door for her like it pained him, and he refused to meet her eye. He strode past her without a word of greeting and strode quickly toward the elevator. The door started to close, but she sprinted and thrust her hand in, halting its progress. Jeri stepped in and it shut, leaving her to ride up alone with Howard.

Elevators are uncomfortable places. It's like there is an unwritten rule that one person should never speak to another when behind those closed doors. A friendly smile or even the nod of a head seems inappropriate. None of that was true of course, and Jeri knew it. The past few months of riding this one every day had made it easier for her to speak to people while in motion in the little box. But with Howard, the silly, unspoken taboos seemed more than appropriate. And neither spoke or looked at the other until the door opened. Then, as they stepped out, Jeri grabbed his arm and said, "What did I do to you to be treated like this?"

Howard looked surprised. "Treat you like what?" he asked curtly.

"Like I'm poison or something."

He stopped and faced her. His face was hard, and she shivered, let go of his arm and stepped back. "Aren't you?" he asked, and he moved away quickly.

That made her angry. She couldn't imagine what the problem was. She got along well with everyone in the office. "What are you talking about?" she demanded as they entered the reception area.

"You took one of his accounts," Allison the receptionist said with a smirk.

Jeri turned on Howard. "Is that what this is about? You think I stole the Pink's account?"

"You did," he said.

"I did not. It was forced on me," she protested.

"Sure," Howard said, disbelief written all over him. He again strode off, and she let him go this time. She was stunned.

"Pink said you did better work," Allison revealed. "You shouldn't have. Howard can make your life miserable around here." She seemed to be enjoying herself. "I would watch my back if I were you."

Jeri said nothing. She was so angry she could have screamed, but that would not have helped. Instead she left Allison standing, still smirking, and walked briskly to her office. What had seemed such a pleasant place to work had taken on a gloomy air. All she had done was put in extra time to help Howard out and she was repaid in this way. She could have done sloppy work; she had learned in that week that Howard often did. It appeared in Pink's accounts. But she would never do that. It was not her nature. She hadn't intended to get assigned the account. She hadn't wanted it even on a temporary basis. She had only done it to help Howard out, and this wasn't fair.

But lately, she was learning at every turn that there were a lot of things in life that were not fair. She would just have to buck up and make the best of it. That proved hard to do that day, because it became clear that Howard was doing more just than glaring at her with hatred, as he had that morning. He was talking all over the firm.

He was telling little lies, she was sure, because some of her coworkers avoided her. She ate lunch alone. She worked without the pleasure of occasional chitchat. She had no idea what he was saying, but it seemed clear that whatever it was, it was being accepted as truth. Before the day was over, she wondered how long she would have a job. As she left that afternoon, Allison was still smirking. "What did I tell you?" she chanted as Jeri walked by. "You should always be nice to Howard and never try to show him up."

Wow! It was unbelievable. She had done nothing wrong. She had only done what she had been asked to do, and it felt like the whole office was against her. Jeri wished she knew what Howard was saying. Not that it would help. She was still the newest accountant on the staff, and he had been here for years. She had formed light friendships in the office, but no close ones. Howard, it seemed, had many friends. And to think she still had to meet Rusty's parents tonight and show them where he lived. She could hardly face the drive home.

What Jeri needed was a friendly face, and Kate couldn't have timed her arrival better. She was waiting at Jeri's door when she got home, her suitcase at her side. Jeri dropped her purse and her keys and threw her arms around Kate and began to cry. Thirty minutes later, she felt better. She had unburdened herself to her friend. Kate didn't have any answers to her problems, but she listened, she cried with her, and most of all, she cared. That was what Jeri needed most right now.

"What time do you expect Rusty's family to arrive?" Kate asked as Jeri stirred up some cold lemonade a few minutes later.

"I'm not sure. But I think it will be soon." She glanced at her watch. "Oh, my, it's after six. It could be any minute now."

The doorbell rang.

"That's probably them," Jeri said with alarm. "Do I look all right? My eyes must be terribly red."

"They're not bad," Kate reassured her. "The eyedrops did wonders. You look great."

"I wish I felt great," Jeri moaned. "But at least I'm in one piece, thanks to you."

"That's what friends are for," Kate smiled. "I'm just glad I could be here." The doorbell rang again. "Hey, you better get that. I'll stay in the kitchen for now."

Jeri smiled at her friend. She was so grateful for her presence. Somehow, not having to face this evening alone was, in itself, a great relief. She brushed at her long dark hair with her hand as she hurried to the door, getting her thoughts in order as she went.

As Jeri opened the door, her thoughts vanished and she stood, mouth gaping. After a moment, when she had not been able to form any words, Rusty said, "I know you're angry with me, and you have every right to be. But could I come in for just a few minutes?"

Jeri nodded, searched hard for her tongue, found it, and said, "Of course, Rusty. It's good to see you." Rusty smiled, but it was a pathetic smile. She was not the only one having a bad day. So was he. She could see it, she could feel it, and she felt just awful. "Kate," she called trying to disguise her unease. "There is someone here I'd like you to meet."

"Oh, I've come at a bad time," Rusty said. "I seem to have a knack for that. I'll leave and come back another time. I do need to talk to you."

Jeri wanted to talk to him, too. And with his folks due this evening, now was a good time. Kate entered the room from the kitchen. Jeri waved a hand in her direction. "Rusty, this is my really good friend, Kate. Kate, this is Rusty."

Kate's short, blonde hair bounced as she approached Rusty with a broad smile and an outstretched hand. "It is such a pleasure to meet you," she said with a friendliness that was infectious. "Jeri has told me so much about you."

Despite himself, Rusty smiled. "There's not much good to tell, so I guess you know some of the sordid stuff, too," he remarked.

Kate laughed. "But of course; you wouldn't want people getting a tainted picture would you?"

"Of course not," he agreed, relaxing under the glow of her smile. Rusty glanced at Jeri. She too was smiling, but it was uneasy, tentative. "I hurt people," he said as he saw deep in those beautiful eyes the pain that he had inflicted. Of course, he had no way of knowing that not all of the pain involved him.

Kate saw the change that came over him and she said lightly, "Hey, Rusty, get one thing straight."

He swung his eyes to her, not sure what to expect. "What's that?" he asked uneasily.

"People can change. I don't care about what they used to be—just what they are. Jeri and I are alike in that regard, aren't we, Jeri?"

"I know that," Rusty said as Jeri nodded her assent. "Jeri has taught me that. That's why I'm here."

"I just made some lemonade, Rusty," Jeri said. "Kate and I have been talking and we're thirsty. Why don't you join us in the kitchen?"

He agreed, but Kate said, "Maybe I could stay in here. I know Rusty wants to talk to you. I don't mean to interfere."

Before Jeri could answer, Rusty said, "No, you don't need to do that." Somehow, talking to Jeri with this pretty, intelligent, and friendly girl present made it seem easier. "What I have to say can be said in front of you. You are her friend, aren't you?"

Kate grinned. "The best. Almost. Seems though, that ever since we met and became friends, I've always had to take a back seat to some little guy she could never forget. So, if you're both sure . . ." Her voice trailed off.

Jeri looked at her with undisguised gratitude. "Please, let's all go in the kitchen."

The lemonade was just right, but Rusty barely sipped his. He seemed like he was anxious to talk. Jeri was hesitant, so Kate took control. "What did you want to talk to Jeri about?" she asked.

Rusty took a bigger sip, then placed his glass on the table. "I came to apologize," he said to Kate. Then, turning to Jeri, he said, "I'm sorry, Jeri. I was a real jerk. I know we have practically nothing in common but some very old memories, which, if it were not for you I wouldn't have. But I had no right to get angry with you. Will you forgive your *brother*?" he asked awkwardly.

Jeri nodded, her eyes glistening. "You know I will," she said softly. He's going to give up the money, she thought, and the idea brightened her day.

"Thank you," he said. Then he proceeded to darken her day again. "It doesn't mean I agree with you, Jeri. You have no idea what I have been through. Life owes me something."

Jeri bit her tongue. He had no intention of giving up what he had taken. It was all she could do to keep from shouting her frustration. But a warning look from her friend helped her hold her peace. Kate spoke up, "That's right, Rusty," she said. "Jeri has often remarked how awful your life has been, haven't you Jeri?"

Kate asked the question in a way that left Jeri with nothing to do but agree. She did so with a nod of the head, but Rusty saw it, and

Kate went on. "Why don't you tell us about it. I'd like to learn more about what you went through. And I know Jeri would, too."

Jeri wasn't at all sure she wanted to hear anything except that Rusty was willing to give back the money and straighten out his life. She was, however, grateful that Kate was here and that her mind, unlike Jeri's, was not cluttered with emotion. Jeri let the calmer head prevail. "Please, Rusty," she said, "I'd like to hear more about you."

"And that's why I'm here," he said aggressively. "It isn't pretty, but maybe after you hear a little of what I've gone through, you will understand why I can't just go handing the money back."

Jeri was sure she wouldn't understand at all, but another look from Kate had her nodding her head. "Where did the guy you called Uncle Bill take you that day?" she asked.

Rusty told her as much as he could recall. "You need to understand that I was scared to death," he told the girls. "And so I can't remember everything clearly. But he drove for several hours in the stolen car we were in. Of course, I didn't know it was a stolen car, but later, maybe even years later, I figured it out. He tied me up in the back seat and we slept in the car that night. We drove for at least another day. I didn't know where we had gone for a long time. It didn't matter to me then. All I wanted was to get away from him and go home. I can remember that much." Rusty looked at Kate. "I suppose Jeri's told you that I didn't remember anything about that night or my life before then until she helped me remember?"

"She told me."

Rusty went on. "We lived in a dirty, run-down house in Oklahoma City. It was in the worst part of the city. That's were I grew up. Years later, I learned that Uncle Bill . . ." he stopped and frowned thoughtfully for a moment. "I hate calling him that," he began again. "He is not my uncle and never will be. But I don't know what else to call him."

"Then that will have to do," Kate said easily.

Rusty glanced at Jeri and she nodded.

"Anyway," he said, "it was a long time before I figured out that Uncle Bill had intended to sell me to some people in Oklahoma. But while he was gone to Utah, they had been killed in a car wreck. So somehow he just ended up keeping me." He shuddered.

"That wasn't pleasant, was it?" Kate suggested.

Rusty shook his head. "It was horrible," he agreed.

Jeri forced herself to speak. "Tell us about it," she urged in an unsteady voice.

"I can't tell you everything," he said. "It's too . . ." He stopped and looked at his hands that were tightly gripping the almost full glass of lemonade. Jeri and Kate said nothing. Finally, his grip relaxed, and he looked up. "He did things to me," he said. "I can't talk about it."

Jeri's heart filled with ice. He had said enough. She knew that what had happened must have been more than just horrible. Rusty looked down again, and he said, almost as if talking to himself, "It's not that he didn't have women. That should have been enough." And then Jeri knew what she had feared most was what had happened to Rusty. He had been molested. She could not stem the flood of tears. She glanced at Kate. She too was softly crying. Rusty did not look up. "If there is a God, he'll get Uncle Bill for what he did. But I doubt there is a God. How could God let him do that to me? I was just a little boy. He said he'd kill me if I ever told a teacher or a neighbor or anyone. And he would have, too."

There was nothing Jeri could think of to say. Even Kate seemed at a loss. Big, tough, handsome Rusty Egan wiped his eyes dry. He stood and turned his back on the girls, embarrassed by his tears. He clenched his fists. "If there is a God, he better hurry, because if I get to Uncle Bill first, there won't be much left for God to deal with."

The ice in Jeri's heart grew colder. She watched the back of the man who had been the little boy next door, the little boy she had loved. The doorbell interrupted the prayer that was in her heart.

Before she could even comment on the doorbell, Rusty turned and, looking straight at Jeri, he said, "I'm sorry. I won't kill him. That much I promise you, Jeri."

Jeri nodded her thanks, stepped around the table, touched his arm, and tried to smile at him. Then she stood on her toes and lightly kissed his cheek. "Thank you, Rusty," she said with a depth of feeling that puzzled her. "I better see who is at the door."

CHAPTER 22

Jeri knew who would be on the other side of the door without checking the peephole. Of course, she had been sure a few minutes ago, had not checked, and had been wrong. She didn't want to be surprised again, so she peeked. She was not wrong this time. She glanced behind her to see Kate and Rusty entering the room. This was going to be awkward, but there was only one thing she could do.

She opened the door with a greeting on her lips. "Hello," she said. "It's good to see all of you. Please, come in."

She heard a gasp and looked around. Rusty's eyes were wide with surprise. He had studied the pictures Jeri had given him enough to know his parents when he saw them. After a quick hug from Rusty's mother and his little sister, Sandy, who was sixteen, Jeri shook hands briefly with his father and ten-year-old brother, Ryan. Sandy and Ryan had eyes only for the tall, good-looking young man who stood staring at them from across the room.

If anyone had doubted that Rusty was really Rusty, those doubts would have been erased in the frozen moment when the lost son came face-to-face with his family. The little brother who had come along several years after the kidnapping, was a younger, but otherwise carbon copy version of Rusty. Rusty's parents had not expected to see him, and his presence here came as a shock. Jeri's introductions a moment later were not really necessary, except for Kate, of course.

Rusty was big and strong and had spent most of his life watching out for himself. As a boy he had experienced more fear than most people would be subject to in a lifetime. He had grown up mostly on his own and had learned to deal with fear by using his physical strength and keen mind. But as he stood that evening in the presence of his family, he was afraid. They were his family; there was no doubt. Except for long hair and ragged clothes, he had looked very much like Ryan at that age. He didn't know what to say to them. He was afraid to speak to them.

His confusion turned to anger at Jeri. When the introductions were finished, he turned to her and said, "I thought you said you would tell them not to come."

Everyone stood awkwardly, wondering what to do, what to say, except Jeri, for she was not caught by surprise. She had been when Rusty showed up earlier, but since that moment, as Rusty told his sad story, she had been thinking about this moment, knowing it would come. She hesitated only a moment, looking the others over quickly before saying, "I kept my promise, Rusty. I have always kept my promises to you. They chose to come anyway."

"What were you going to do, bring them by the house tonight?" he asked, his anger tempered by what she had just said. She always did keep her promises.

"No, I was simply going to show them where you lived and leave it up to them. If you will recall, you left me with the impression that you didn't ever want to see me again. I'm sorry if my presence is making this worse for you, or for them," she said, nodding at the four Egans who stood frozen in place.

Kate stood beside Rusty, saying nothing, but she laid a hand on his arm in support. It seemed to help him. Jeri's words cut deep. He knew that he had no right to be angry at her. He could still feel the gentle kiss she had placed so impulsively and yet so tenderly on his cheek just a few moments ago. This was not her fault. Anyway, he had wanted to meet these people. He shouldn't be angry that they were here. And the last thing he wanted to do was hurt Jeri.

Rusty stepped toward her and Kate removed her hand as he moved. When he was but a step away, he looked deep into Jeri's eyes. They were brimming with tears, not an unusual thing whenever he and his big mouth were around. Then, as his fear subsided and his anger left, he said, "I'm sorry, Jeri. I should be thanking you, not getting angry."

She smiled, and he did something that surprised himself as much as it did her. He took that one more step and gathered her into his strong arms. She did not resist, and he crushed her gently to his chest. He did not speak another word as he did so, nor did Jeri say anything. But his embrace did not feel at all like that of a *brother*, she realized, as her heart raced and her whole body tingled. The embrace was not long, and he seemed embarrassed as he pulled away.

He turned to the man who stood with tearful eyes just to Jeri's left. "She tells me you are my father," he said, and Patrick Egan reacted by reaching for his son, his long-lost son, and crushing him with an embrace as firm as the one Rusty had just given to Jeri. "Welcome back to the family," the older man said with a broken voice.

A moment later, Mindy Egan stepped across the threshold of years from the horrible day she watched from an upstairs window as her son was cruelly whisked away, and gathered him in her arms as though he were still that same little boy. She cried as she held him, and with a voice strained with emotions she said something to Rusty that not one single person had said to him since the morning of that tragic day. "I love you, Rusty," were the words she whispered.

The scent of his mother's skin and the soft sound of her voice brought the years cascading together. From somewhere deep within his memory, Rusty recognized the feel and the smell and the sound of the woman who held him so tightly. It came rushing back as if her hug that long ago morning, just before he ran outside to play with Jeri, had been but minutes ago. He had loved her then, felt secure in her arms, and it was hard to deny that he was grateful and over-whelmed to be in her presence again.

When she finally released him, she looked up and into his eyes. Her voice was so broken she could scarcely speak, but she managed to say, "I can see now why Jeri knew you when she saw you. Your eyes were so beautiful, and they have not changed."

Rusty was without words. These people didn't care what he was now, they only cared that he was their son. There were no reservations. He had never expected that from them. He didn't know what to do next. But his little sister did. "Rusty, I'm Sandy. I was just a baby, but I love you, too," she said, and Rusty found himself locked again in a loving and tearful hug.

Then it was his little brother's turn. They were all strangers to Rusty in a way, but the boy who so resembled himself truly was a stranger. He stepped closer and held out his hand. Rusty took it. "I'm glad to meet you," he said to the boy.

"And I'm glad to meet you," Ryan responded. "I didn't used to know I had a brother. I can't wait to tell Jeremy."

"Who is Jeremy?" Rusty asked.

"He's my best friend. He has a brother on a mission. He always tells me how nice it is to have a big brother. It always made me feel left out, but now I'm not." The boy grinned. "And my brother is bigger than his brother."

The awkward, emotional moments were over. Jeri invited everyone to sit. "I'll bet you are all hungry," she said. "Maybe Kate and I can stir something up." She caught Kate's eye and the two friends moved together toward the kitchen.

Rusty watched Jeri disappear from the room, and the walls began to close in on him. He had met them. They had met him. They had hugged. They had cried. But they were still strangers in a way. There was nothing to talk about. He fought the impulse to flee. His father tried to break the ice that was forming around them by saying, "You sure look good, Rusty. I can see that I'm not the biggest in the family anymore."

Rusty nodded. Mindy smiled and said, "It is just so good to see you. I never thought this day would ever come."

Rusty nodded again. "So tell us, son, what kind of work are you doing?" his father asked.

Son.

The word sent shock waves through him. It was hard to visualize this man as his father. It was hard to visualize having a father, let alone being a son. He had to speak. He had been asked a question, but to be called someone's son was not easy to accept. He had been nobody's anything. It was almost more than he could fathom.

"I do auto body work," he finally managed to stammer.

"Where did you learn to do that?" his mother asked.

"Uncle Bill, I guess. He worked with cars."

"Who is Uncle Bill?" Ryan asked.

Rusty felt his cheeks begin to burn as anger flooded back. "He is the man I hate more than anyone in this whole world," Rusty said with such feeling that his mother and sister both recoiled.

His father understood instantly. "He's the man who took you from us, isn't he?" he asked with a voice that bordered on bitterness.

"That's him, all right."

Suddenly, the conversation was very awkward. Jeri, who had been listening from the kitchen, came to the rescue. "Why don't you all come in here and we can talk while Kate and I fix a meal."

Rusty felt rescued. He was the first to his feet and into the kitchen. "Thank you," he breathed as he brushed past Jeri. She smiled up at him and his heart skipped a beat. She was something special. Never had he met such a girl.

Mindy and her daughter pitched in and helped. Conversation was light as the meal was prepared and consumed. Rusty had very little to say. He did have a few minutes in which he spoke mostly to his father and little brother about such generic things as cars, sports, and the weather. After the kitchen was cleaned up and the dishes washed and put away, they all moved into the living room. Jeri and Kate brought chairs from the kitchen so everyone would have a place to sit, which they hadn't during dinner. Jeri, Rusty, and Kate had eaten standing up next to the counter.

Jeri worried constantly about Rusty, what he was thinking, and what he would do after this night. He was sitting next to her on one of the kitchen chairs. He turned to her and suggested, after another awkward period of stilted conversation, that Jeri might put some soft music on. "Sure," she agreed. "You choose." She took him by the hand and led him to the small stereo and opened her selection of music discs.

He looked through them and finally suggested several which she put in the player. Jeri couldn't help but watch for Mindy's reaction to his choice of music. Every disc he had selected was classical. As the music began to play softly and Jeri and Rusty returned to their chairs, she was pleased with the reaction.

It was sixteen-year-old Sandy who was the first to speak. "Do you like this, Rusty?" she asked in surprise as the music began to play.

As Rusty explained that he did, and how angry that used to make Uncle Bill, a look of pure amazement came over Mindy Egan. She had always played classical music, both on their stereo and on her piano. As young as he had been when he was taken from them, that musical influence had lasted. The evening went a little better after that. Rusty's mentioning the man who had kidnapped him made it a little easier for his family to ask him questions about what had happened to Rusty over the years. A few details of his life came out, but he said nothing about the horrible abuse he had mentioned to Jeri and Kate.

Not once did the subject of crime or prison or stolen money come up. Rusty learned a lot about his family and what they had been doing over the years. He came to understand to a small degree the suffering his kidnapping had caused them. He had never considered that before. His own life had been so miserable that he had never spent time wondering about them. Of course, until Jeri had found him, the memory of them had been repressed. They hadn't existed at all in his mind for most of the seventeen years they had been apart.

It grew late, and Mindy noticed how tired everyone was getting. Patrick offered to give Rusty a ride home. He couldn't think of a way to say no, so he accepted. And around eleven, the Egan family, complete with all its members, left Jeri's apartment. Rusty was the last out the door, and after he was gone, Jeri felt an emptiness that she couldn't explain.

Kate could. "You like him, don't you?" she asked.

"I do, but not in the way you are thinking," Jeri answered.

"Really?" Kate said with a chuckle.

Jeri didn't say anything. He truly had stirred emotions in her that night which were both pleasant and disturbing. She had her goals, and Rusty did not fit, except as a friend or, as she liked to say, as a brother.

Kate changed the subject. "This has been a most interesting evening wouldn't you say?"

"That is an understatement," Jeri agreed. "Rusty seemed a little uncomfortable all night but he behaved marvelously. And his family was great."

"They sure were, and it's natural that he'd be uncomfortable after all that has happened," Kate said.

Jeri was thoughtful for a moment. "I can't help but wonder what he's thinking after meeting them."

***

All night long, cars had pulled in and out of the parking area that served the apartment complex where Jeri lived. Occasionally, one would park along the street, or one would leave from there. At eleven o'clock, a silver Oldsmobile with a rental sticker on the rear bumper pulled into the street from where it had been parked against the curb. The occupants were two men, a woman, a teenage girl and a young boy. They had all come from the same apartment. Moments later, two men in a late model Chevrolet Malibu followed the rental car. That startled the little man who was watching it all from a freshly stolen Honda farther up the street. He too followed, and he was not a happy man. Randy Moore had far too many people in his life for the liking of Charles Chumbian. Some of them had to be cops. He hated cops. And yet it was proof of what he had told Randy. They would never let him get the money. He needed help. And Chum needed to speed his plan up. That brought a smile to the evil little man's ugly face. The cops need not worry; Randy would never spend any of that money. On the other hand, it *would* be spent.

***

From inside the glass doors of the run-down apartment building where he lived, Rusty watched with mixed emotions as his newly found family pulled away from in front. He had promised to see them again the next day and wondered what they would do. He stood there as the car went down the street. He glanced back up the street. He was certain that he had been followed, although it had not been as easy to keep track since Joe and Arnie had been replaced. He was pretty sure he knew which car it was, although it was far enough away to make it impossible to see if it was occupied. Or, he thought, it might be the smaller car that cruised on by and then stopped half a block beyond the apartments.

That car drew Rusty's interest for some unexplainable reason. He watched as it parked, and when no one got out, he decided that it was the car containing his watchers. He glanced back at the first one he had suspected. He thought he had seen that car a few times before, or one that looked an awful lot like it. His anger rising, he put his shoulder against the glass of the door and shoved his way outside. It was one of the two and he intended to find out which one.

He headed for the car parked to the right. It must be the one, because there were two men in it. Both looked down as he approached. He walked right up and tapped on the glass of the driver's door. The man looked up, rolled the window down, and said, "Can we help you?"

"Sure," Rusty said. "You can quit following me. You guys are better at your job than Joe and Arnie, but you are not invisible. You are wasting your time."

The man said, "I don't know what you are talking about."

"Sure you don't. Well, you can tell whomever you are working for that your time is being wasted. There is no money." With that he turned and left the two of them staring at him.

Rusty crossed the street at a trot and hurried toward the other car. He could see it was a Honda and that there was a driver but no passengers. Before he got to it, the engine started and the car pulled away. Rusty stood and watched it until it disappeared. There was almost no question in his mind that the driver of the Honda was interested in him, and it not only made him angry, but for some unexplainable reason, it also made him very uneasy.

As he walked slowly back to his apartment, he realized that he was not sleepy. The events of the evening had his mind in a whirl. He chuckled to himself, knowing that his watchers would wonder what he was doing if he did not go back to his apartment. So he simply walked on by and continued up the street, thinking of the family he had found and their unbelievable reaction to him.

He had thought it would be easy to meet them, satisfy his curiosity, and then simply forget them. But after the evening he had just spent with them, he realized that would be difficult to do. They were easy people to like. They were good people, unpretentious, honest, and forgiving. Not once did any of them ask him about prison or the robbery, and yet he knew they knew about that. It didn't seem to matter to them. They were interested in him as their son and brother. What surprised him the most was how much they loved him. And from deep in his heart, he had to admit that those memories that had returned caused him to feel a warmth toward them that he had never felt for anyone else.

Except one.

He was embarrassed at the way he had hugged Jeri. It was an impulsive thing, as impulsive as the kiss she had planted on his cheek just moments before she opened the door to his family. He touched his cheek where her lips had caressed his skin and felt a tingle all the way to his toes. And as he recalled the feel of her body pulled close to him, it caused him to tremble slightly. They were worlds apart, but she stirred him in a way that no one had ever done before.

He forced himself to quit thinking of Jeri and concentrated on his family again. He remembered his father's embrace. From his experience, that was something men didn't do, and yet it felt right. And his mother. The memory of her familiar scent and sound and touch still lingered. He could now clearly recall that last morning before Uncle Bill had come down the street and shattered his world. After breakfast, his dad had patted his head before going out the door. And then, after he announced that he was going next door to play with Jeri, his mother had laid the baby down. That made his mind wander another direction. Sandy was beautiful, and she was sweet, but how could she be that little baby? Yet there was no doubt she was.

He returned eagerly to the memory of his mother. After laying the baby down, she had knelt on the floor and reached toward him with both her arms. He had stepped into them and she had held him very tightly. She smelled the same now as she had then. And he remembered now that she had said something about how she loved him and what a good little man he was.

It was strange, he thought, how little pieces of his past kept coming back with such clarity. It was hard to believe that the memory had ever left him. He pictured in his mind his parents as they first stepped into the room that evening, and the look on their faces when they recognized him. What they must have suffered, he thought. Yes, they were good people. They were also Mormons, but not once did they mention religion during the entire evening. And just as the case was with Jeri, they were not what Uncle Bill had always told him Mormons were like.

Jeri.

He couldn't keep her out of his mind for long. Everything he thought about brought her into center focus again.

He glanced behind him. Unless his eyes were deceiving him, someone had just faded into the shadow of a large tree. They were always with him. No matter where he went or what he did, he was followed. That brought him back to the money. Getting it was not going to be easy, but get it he must.

Then Rusty experienced the strangest emotion. Guilt. Everything about the money went against what his newly found family stood for. They could never accept his keeping that money. They could forgive him for the things he had done, but they would never condone anything short of him giving all the money back. Not that it mattered; his intention was to forget them now and get on with his life.

Sure, just like it was his intention to forget Jeri. His life was getting too complicated. And yet, something else was happening in his life. There were others who cared about him. That gave him a feeling he hated to lose . . . again. He had been cared for back then, and they cared for him now. How could he throw that away?

How could he throw half a million dollars away?

Another glance to the rear and Rusty saw another shadow move. He needed time to think. He wanted space in which to clear his head. He didn't need to be distracted by his watchers. It was time to ditch them again. He turned and walked between two houses, then he began to run. The man back there was coming. He caught glimpses and heard footsteps. Then as he came onto the next street through the block, the Oldsmobile passed. He cut back into the same block, but only for a moment. Then he came back out and ran across the street. For ten minutes Rusty played his game of hide and seek. But at length, he lost his watchers.

Rusty began to chuckle. He could go for the money now. All he had to do was steal a car and go. The men were not far away, but they also did not know exactly where he was. Totally losing them would be a cinch. He was hiding behind a car and he looked more closely at it. It was parked in a private driveway. He didn't need keys to start this one. He had done it before. It was easy.

But he couldn't bring himself to do it now. This is crazy, he thought, but the idea of stealing the car brought the image of Jeri clearly to mind, and he simply could not do it. It was as if she were watching him. What was the hold this girl had on him? Was he losing his mind?

Rusty got up and started back in the general direction of his apartment, which was now several blocks away. He stayed in the shadows and between buildings as much as he could. Not that it mattered if his watchers found him again. He was only going home. He did think a lot more about his father and mother, and the pretty teenaged girl who was his little sister, and the little boy who was his brother.

He thought about the girl who referred to him as her twin. He tried to examine his feelings, but when he did, he remembered how different they were. He had to forget her, had to get her out of his mind.

Sure.

But he also had to get the money. It was his. He needed it.

The Oldsmobile was back. He didn't care. He'd figure out something about the money. He had lost the men who were assigned to tail him once. He could lose them again. He entered the building and pulled the key to his apartment from his pocket. He inserted it in the lock and hesitated. Something wasn't right. He pulled the key out without unlocking the door and put his hand on the knob. It turned. It was not locked. He was sure he had locked it, but maybe in his hurry to get to Jeri's and talk to her he had forgotten. He continued to turn and shoved the door open. He flipped the light on.

"Hello, cell mate," a smiling Chum said from Rusty's sofa. "Thought you'd be ready for a little help about now."

CHAPTER 23

Rusty had been around the kind of people lately who, even though they were different than he, left him feeling good. Even when there was tension and disagreement, there was no feeling of evil and danger while in their presence. It had been a strange thing to Rusty at first, but as he stood now in his own doorway, he realized how much he had come to like the feeling he had when he was with his family and Jeri.

What he felt as he stared in surprise at his former cell mate was something dark and sinister. He was in the presence of unspeakable evil. He had distrusted and even disliked Chum when they had shared the same small space in prison, but this was worse. Chum had invaded his home, one where the purity and sweetness of Jeri had left its mark. All of that good feeling, that comfortable feeling, had fled at the presence of this horrible little man.

Worse than anything was the way the presence in this room made Rusty want to react. As much as he had resisted change these past few weeks, he had changed, at least a little. If he had not, he would have stolen that car tonight and gone after his money. But he had not done that, and that was evidence of a subtle change in his makeup. But now, as he stood staring at Chum, he wanted to strike out at the man and hurt him, even kill him. He shuddered at his thoughts and tried to shake them off. He succeeded in doing so, and only then did he allow himself to speak.

"What are you doing in my apartment, Chum?" he asked evenly.

"Came to pay my respects," Chum said with a sly grin.

"Well, they're paid, so you can go now," Rusty said.

"Oh, no, not yet. We've got to do some planning. We have money to recover, or did you forget?" His eyes shone with evil mischief.

"I haven't forgotten," Rusty said. "But it may not still be there." That was not true, but a lie to this man only bothered his conscience a little bit. "Anyway, I'm being watched. It would be very dangerous to try to get it now."

"That is why you need my help," Chum said.

"Oh, sure, you'll be a lot of help now," Rusty retorted. "You don't think they'll see you and recognize you and put you under surveillance, too?"

"The men in the Oldsmobile don't know I'm here."

Rusty was taken aback. Chum knew about the Oldsmobile, so he had been watching them, and that meant that he had been watching Rusty as well. But he argued anyway. "They saw you come in, I'm sure."

"Not so, Randy."

"Rusty! My name is Rusty!" he thundered.

Chum smiled and his smile made Rusty shiver. "Okay, Rusty it is. They did not see me come in because they were both busy trying to follow you tonight. I watched. I know. I came in, using my handy little picks on your door, while they were away from here."

Rusty had closed the door as they talked. He was not in the least surprised that Chum had gotten into his apartment so easily. And as the little man waved the picks in the air, it simply explained clearly how he had done it. He advanced into the room as Chum got to his feet, eyeing him warily. Rusty stopped, thinking hard what he ought to do. Finally, he said, "When you leave, they will see you."

Chum shook his head. "No they won't, because they will once again be following you. You will be my decoy. After all, I'm only here to help you. Now let's get down to business. All we need is a plan, and I have one started. You just need to provide a few details."

Rusty was trapped and he knew it. Oh, he could break the man's neck, but then he would have a serious crime to cover up, because no one would ever believe he had a motive unless he admitted he had the money hidden, and he wasn't going to do that. Also, in the back of his mind, another caution arose. Unless he had missed his guess, Chum was a killer. He probably had on his person a knife or a gun or both, and he undoubtably knew how to use them. Rusty had hurt him before, but Chum did not seem the least bit afraid right now.

Rusty came to a decision. He would have to appear to be working with Chum for the time being. Then he would find a way to outsmart him. He had to, for he was quite certain that if Chum ever got his hands on the money, Rusty would lose it all. That was the kind of man he was dealing with. Chum had loyalties to no one but himself.

Slowly, Rusty began to nod his head. "Okay, maybe it will work," he said. "But the split is the same. Twenty-five percent for you, the rest is still mine."

"That was our deal," Chum agreed. "Now, first thing I need to know is where it is."

"Not so fast," Rusty said. "How do I know you won't just take it and run with it all?"

"Randy, Randy . . ." Chum began, shaking his head as if in disbelief. "Rusty."

"Oh, yes, I forget easily," Chum said with a smirk. Then he began shaking his head again. "You can trust me. We were cell mates, and soul mates as well. I am hurt by your lack of trust."

"I risked a lot for that money, and I do not intend to lose it now."

"That's why I'm here," Chum said agreeably, "so that you won't lose it."

Rusty was thinking fast. He had an idea. "Okay, here's what we'll do," he said. "I will give you a location. You go there and you will find a clue. Follow that and you will find another. This will do three things. First, it will help me reestablish my confidence in you. Second, it will make it less likely that you will be discovered and followed to the money. Third, it will give me a chance to find a safe way for us to split the money without being seen together."

"That's silly, Ran . . . Rusty," Chum said.

"It's the only way. I'll give you a location. You go there on Tuesday. There will be a letter for you there. Do as it directs. Within a week or two after that, we will have the money."

At first, from the look on Chum's face, Rusty thought he would argue, but the older man, after a moment of thoughtful silence, said, "All right. Give me the address." Then his face hardened, and he added, "And don't even think of a double cross."

Rusty nodded, rustled around for a piece of paper and wrote a description. It was not an address, but it was a location where Rusty had hidden out for a short time after the robbery. It was inside an abandoned warehouse. After taking the slip of paper from Rusty and looking at it briefly, Chum's face darkened and he said, "The men in the Oldsmobile will see you leave your note there. You don't figure on having someone waiting for me there, do you?"

"I'm not that stupid," Rusty said. "I'll have it there and no one will know." He wasn't sure how he would do it, but he would work something out. Maybe one of the guys at work, or . . . of course. He lost his watchers an hour ago. He could do it again. It would work. And it would buy him some time.

"Okay, we won't be meeting again. At least not for a while," Rusty said. "Now you better be going."

"You first, remember? And keep them occupied for a while. I'll slip out when it's clear."

Rusty did not argue. He was getting very tired, but the horrible feelings he had in the presence of Chum were enough to make him welcome the chance to get out into the fresh air again. He left, heading in the opposite direction of his earlier hike. He couldn't see his watchers this time and made no effort to locate them at first, because he knew they were there. They had just moved, made themselves less visible. He hadn't been walking long before he caught a glimpse of one of the men again trailing him on foot. Later, he saw the green Oldsmobile far up the street. He wandered for an hour, taking in the cool freshness of the night, trying to forget about Chum and the complications he represented. Finally, he returned to his apartment. As expected, Chum was gone. His door was locked. Inside, there was a note on the table.

"Don't double-cross me or even attempt it," was all that was written there. Rusty shuddered. Maybe he would have to let the guy have part of the money. There might not be any other way.

He was ill at ease as he got ready for bed. His apartment felt uncomfortable to him. All of the dark presence did not seem to have gone with Chum. He fell asleep uneasily, thinking not of the good things that had happened to him earlier that evening, but only of the stolen money and of his former cell mate.

***

The pleasant odor of frying bacon wafted into Jeri's bedroom. She bounded from her bed and hurried into the kitchen. Kate smiled as she entered. "You were drained last night. I thought you'd sleep late, so I decided to fix us something to eat. It will be ready in a few minutes. You have time to shower first if you want to."

Kate looked bright and pretty this morning. Her short, blonde hair spilled onto her forehead, and her face was fresh and scrubbed. She had not applied makeup, but she looked good without it. Jeri was glad she was here. "I won't be long," she said brightly as she hurried back into her bedroom.

The girls had barely finished eating when the doorbell rang. Rusty's family were all there. They looked happy and rested as they came in. "We are picking Rusty up at noon. He said he was tired and wanted to sleep late when we left him last night," Mindy said. "We just wanted to come by and thank you for all you have done, Jeri. You'll never know what this means to us. It is like we are living in a dream."

Jeri understood, but she also worried, because Rusty had his mind set on keeping the money. Unless that changed, they would all find themselves out of his life again with aching hearts and painful memories. She did not mention that to his family. She wanted them to enjoy him now and for as long as they could. If they all lost him again, they would just have to deal with that. But for now, why not enjoy his company? she thought.

The next hour was spent in happy chatter. Everyone was relaxed and spirits were high. Only Sandy didn't seem like she was excited and anxious to see Rusty again. Her face had become pale and she had withdrawn from the conversation. It was Jeri who noticed the change first. She ignored it for a while, but finally she had to say something to her. "Sandy, do you feel okay?" she asked in concern.

"I think I must have had something bad to eat this morning. I feel sick," she admitted. "I don't want to ruin our visit with Rusty, but I think I better go back to the motel and go to bed."

"You can stay here," Jeri said brightly. "I'll put fresh sheets on my bed and you can lie down in there. That way, your folks won't be late in picking up Rusty."

"And it will give them a good excuse to swing by here," Kate said with a mischievous grin aimed in Jeri's direction.

Mindy fussed over her daughter and helped settle her in bed before they left. "We'll be back to get you," she promised. "But it may not be until after five." She turned to Kate and Jeri and said, "You two probably have plans, too. Don't let Sandy's illness interfere with them. If you were planning to go somewhere for the afternoon, do so by all means. Sandy will be fine. She gets sick a lot, but she bounces out of it quickly."

They did have plans, and an hour later, they left Sandy resting comfortably in Jeri's bed. "We'll be back in two or three hours," Jeri promised when they left. "We'll bring you something when we return. What sounds good to you?"

Ice cream was her answer, and Jeri smiled. "There is a little left in my freezer. Feel free to help yourself to it, or anything else in the house if you get feeling better. We'll get some more before we come back."

***

Sandy Egan slept soundly for an hour. She awoke to the shrill ringing of Jeri's telephone. For a moment, she was disoriented. Then she finally remembered where she was and located the phone on the night stand beside the bed. She picked it up.

"Jeri," a man's voice said on the other end of the line.

"No, she's not here right now. I'm a friend, could I take a message?"

"Sure, tell her Warren called. Do you know when she'll be back?"

Sandy looked at her watch. "An hour or so. She and Kate went somewhere. They said they wouldn't be too long."

"Kate?" The man on the phone sounded really surprised. "Kate Duffy?"

"I don't know. She didn't ever tell me her last name. She's an old roommate of Jeri's. She's just here from Utah for the weekend," Sandy said.

"Kate Duffy. I can't believe she went to California and didn't even tell me. I wish I were there myself," Warren said.

"Are you calling from Utah?" Sandy asked.

"Yes, I'm Warren Tharp, Jeri's boyfriend. And you are?"

Sandy was stunned. She didn't have any idea that Jeri had a boyfriend. She recalled the hug her newfound brother had given Jeri last night, and she was suddenly jealous for Rusty.

"You are?" Warren sounded a little impatient.

"I'm Sandy Egan. My brother is a friend of Jeri's," she said, feeling a little mean. "My family and I are here for a visit."

"Oh, that's great. So the long lost boy and his family are finally getting together. That's great. Jeri has told me all about Rusty. It was terrible what happened to him. Jeri was so anxious for him to meet his family. Of course, he was resisting the last I knew. That's great. So will he be going to Arizona with you?" Warren asked.

"I don't think so. He's got a good job here." Sandy was puzzled. If Jeri liked this guy so much, why did she seem so friendly with her brother? She found herself not liking this Warren guy very much.

"Oh, that's too bad," Warren was saying. "He needs family or he could end up in trouble again. He has a lot of potential, if someone can just steer him in the right direction," Warren said.

Sandy felt even more mean. "Jeri's helped him a lot. I think if anyone can help him turn his life around, it will be her."

She got the reaction she expected. "He's not for her," Warren said with clear resentment in his voice. "She has been going with me for some time now."

Sandy grinned to herself. "Funny, she didn't ever mention you."

"Well, tell her I called," Warren said. "And tell her I'll call back around four."

"I'll tell her," Sandy said with a frown.

She heard Warren chuckle. Then he said, "So I guess in a way you are Jeri's sister. That's great."

"Sister?" she asked puzzled.

"Yes. You know. She says she and Rusty are like brother and sister. So I guess you and Jeri would be like sister and sister," he explained. "Thanks for taking the message. I can't wait to talk to her. Oh, and tell Kate I said hi."

The idea that Jeri had a boyfriend was upsetting to Sandy. Somehow, in her mind, Jeri and Rusty were just naturally meant for each other. It never occurred to her that he might not change now that he had found his family. It would take time, but it would happen. She was sure of it, and when that happened, this Warren guy would just be a problem.

Despite the upsetting phone call, Sandy was feeling much better. She helped herself to some ice cream and found a book to read. The telephone interrupted her again just as she got really interested.

***

Time got away from Kate and Jeri. They had a great afternoon, and Jeri found herself wishing Kate lived closer. She had made friends here, but none anywhere near as close as Kate. The afternoon together made her realize just how much she had missed her. The hours passed quickly, and before they knew it, it was after four o'clock. "Oh, my, we told Sandy we'd only be gone for a couple of hours, and it's been over three already. We better get some ice cream and hurry back to the apartment," Jeri said.

"I'm sure Sandy's fine," Kate said. "But she is probably wondering what happened to us."

It was another thirty minutes before Jeri and Kate let themselves into the apartment. They were surprised to find no one there. "The Egans must have been here. I thought they were coming around five. I guess Sandy must have felt better and gone with them," Jeri said.

She sounded disappointed. "I'm sure they'll be back," Kate said with a grin. "And don't tell me you don't miss him."

"Who?" Jeri asked.

"Why, Rusty, who else?"

Jeri said nothing. For what Kate said was true. She still felt the strength and the warmth of that hug last night. It was crazy, but she had never felt like that in Warren's arms. But she had her standards and her goals. Nothing, not even the feelings she had experienced when Rusty hugged her, would ever change that.

She noticed that the message light on the phone was blinking. "I better see who's been calling," she told Kate. Her friend was still smiling. Kate was too smart for her own good. Jeri picked up the phone and accessed her messages. "It's Warren," she said to Kate and listened to the recording.

When she put the phone down, she looked puzzled. "He said he called earlier. He asked Sandy to tell me he would call at four. When we weren't here, he said he called back. He tried again before leaving a message. Either no one was here, or Sandy wasn't answering the phone. He will call again at six. Is there a note from Sandy anywhere?"

Both of them looked, but there was not. For some unexplainable reason, Jeri felt a chill come into the room. From the look on Kate's face, she knew her friend felt it, too.

"Surely Sandy would not have left by herself. That makes no sense. She must be with her family," Jeri reasoned.

"But there would have been a note," Kate said. "I don't like this."

"Nor do I, but I don't know what to do about it. Rusty probably wouldn't take his family there; his apartment is so small."

The minutes dragged on, and both girls became increasingly alarmed. "This is crazy," Jeri said at last. "She's with her family. We are worrying ourselves over nothing."

"Let's drive over to Rusty's place," Kate suggested. She looked at her watch. "It's almost five o'clock. At least we could be doing something besides waiting for the Egans. They said they'd be here about five, and maybe they still will, even if Sandy is with them now. We could leave a note for Rusty's folks just in case they come while we are gone."

Jeri nodded her agreement and scribbled a quick note. Then they grabbed their purses and left. They had not even reached their car when they saw Rusty's family drive up. Jeri turned and hurried toward them as the car pulled to the curb. Rusty was driving, and he was the first one out. "Hi, Jeri," he called out. "How's my little sister feeling? Is she any better?"

CHAPTER 24

"Not again," Jeri said and she began to sway slowly. She felt like she was going to pass out. She began to fall forward.

Rusty rushed toward her, catching her just as she fell. He swept her into his strong arms and rushed toward the house. "Someone open the door!" he shouted.

"I've got her purse," Kate said as she pulled Jeri's keys out. "I'll unlock the door." She had to run to beat Rusty there.

Patrick and Mindy Egan were alarmed. They couldn't imagine what had happened to Jeri, but it looked very serious. And the expression of absolute horror on the face of her friend Kate was frightening. "She must have some serious condition she has not mentioned," Mindy said to her husband as they hurried up the walk toward the apartment. "I can't imagine that her mother wouldn't have mentioned it to me."

"Hey, you guys, what's going on?"

Kate had the key in the door when she heard Sandy's voice. She turned the lock, swung the door open and looked back down the walk. Sandy was running up the sidewalk that bordered the street.

Still carrying Jeri, Rusty pushed past Kate. "She'll be okay now," Kate said with a sigh of relief. "She was worried about Sandy."

"Sandy?" Rusty said as he laid Jeri on the couch. "Would you get me a cold, wet cloth?"

"Sandy was not here, and when Jeri saw that she was not with you it frightened her. I'm sure that was why she fainted. We were both very worried. I'll get the cloth."

Kate was back in a minute and handed the cloth to Rusty who immediately began to bathe Jeri's pale face with it. The rest of the family were gathered around. "What happened to her?" Sandy asked breathlessly.

"She fainted," Kate replied.

"Oh. Why?"

"She was scared."

No one said anything for a moment, and Jeri's eyelids began to flutter. Then she came to and they opened. "Rusty," she said. And then she seemed to remember what had caused her to faint and her eyes flew wide. "Sandy!" she cried out in a choked voice.

"I'm right here and I feel a lot better," Sandy said calmly, clearly puzzled over the whole proceeding.

Jeri struggled to sit up. "You're okay?" she asked.

"I'm fine. Why shouldn't I be?" Sandy asked.

"Let me explain," Kate broke in. "When we got home, you weren't here. There was a message on the phone from Warren. He's a friend of Jeri's," Kate said by way of explanation. "He said he had asked Sandy to let Jeri know he had called. When we couldn't find a note from her we got worried."

Jeri was sitting up now and Rusty was still tenderly holding the cold cloth to her face. "Why would she leave a note?" he asked.

"So we wouldn't worry," Kate answered calmly.

"But I did leave a note," Sandy protested. "In fact, I left two of them. One was sitting on the phone and the other one was on the floor just inside the door. It was right where you couldn't miss it," she explained to Kate.

"There wasn't one either place," Jeri said, pushing the rag from her face.

Rusty withdrew his hand and stood up. He walked to the phone. "You left a note right here?" he asked.

"Yes," his sister answered. "And the other one was right there." She pointed toward the door. "They were both written on a full sheet of notebook paper. Here, I tore it from this notebook," she said as she picked one up from the coffee table. "I felt better, and when Kate and Jeri didn't come when I thought they would, I decided to go for a walk."

Rusty paced the room for a moment. His mind was working quickly. He was quite certain Sandy was telling the truth. He was equally certain that Kate and Jeri would have seen the papers if they were there. "Did you lock the door when you left?" Rusty asked.

"Yes. And I'm sure about that, because I knew that if I did I couldn't get back in, but I was sure they wouldn't be much longer, so I decided to risk it. I could have sat outside and waited if I had beaten them back here."

Rusty shivered. He could feel the evil that he had felt last night in his own apartment. Chum had been here. He was certain of it. There was no other explanation. Chum could have picked his way into this apartment as easily as he did his, and he must have taken the notes. But why? That was what did not make any sense. He felt his anger rising and turned and looked out of the window, trying to gain control of himself.

Jeri touched his arm. "Rusty, are you okay?"

"I'm fine."

"And you are angry," she said. "I'm sorry I upset you. I was just so scared. It was like it was all happening all over again. You know, the way you were . . ."

"I know," he interrupted. His voice was louder than he had intended, but he was extremely agitated. "I need to go. I'll call a taxi." He wanted to find Chum and ask him what he thought he was doing. He could strangle the little man with his bare hands. How dare he break into Jeri's apartment?

"You don't need to go. We'll fix dinner together," Jeri offered.

The phone rang before he could respond to her offer. Jeri hurried over and grabbed it. Rusty stiffened when he heard her say, "Oh, hi Warren. Sorry I missed you earlier."

He headed for the door and went out. His father followed. "Rusty," he said as he caught up with his son on the sidewalk.

Rusty did not look up. "I'll be all right. Things like this upset me, that's all."

"Why don't you stay? Jeri would . . ."

"Jeri is talking to Warren," Rusty said coldly. "I need to go home. I don't belong here."

"Then I'll give you a ride," Patrick offered.

Rusty almost declined, but a glance at his father's face changed his mind. There was pain and worry there. He shouldn't care. But for some strange reason, he did. "Thanks, I'd appreciate that," he said.

"Wait here. I'll tell your mother," Patrick said.

The ride back to Rusty's apartment was very quiet. They were almost there when Rusty finally broke the silence. "Would you do something for me?" he asked.

"You can call me Dad, if you'd like, and yes, I'll do anything I can."

"It feels sort of strange. I feel like I hardly know you," Rusty responded.

"But I am your father, and I would be honored if you would call me Dad."

"All right," Rusty said, thinking that he probably wouldn't have many opportunities to do so. After all, he still had no intention of burdening their lives with him. And there was the matter of the money. Even if Chum got part of it, he would still be able to live like other people now.

Or would he? Doubt filled his mind.

"So what can I do for you, son?" Patrick asked.

"It's about Jeri," Rusty said as his mind returned to the thing that was concerning him most. "She shouldn't be alone for a while."

"Oh, she'll be fine. She just had a scare. You know, Rusty, she suffered more than anyone will ever know over what happened to you."

Rusty pulled the car to a stop in front of his apartment building, then he looked over at his father. "Please. She shouldn't be alone," he said again.

"But Kate is with her."

"Can't she . . . can't they stay with you tonight? In the motel?"

"Rusty, there is something you are not telling me. Is something wrong with Jeri?"

Rusty could not explain. All he could do was repeat himself. "She needs to be with someone tonight. Please, talk her into going to the motel with you." Rusty reached into his pocket and pulled out his wallet. He extracted a hundred dollar bill and held it out to his father. "This will pay for a room. Make sure it is next to yours."

"I don't need that," Patrick protested.

Rusty opened the door, leaving the car running. He stepped out and as he did so, he dropped the money on the seat. "I'll be in touch, Dad," he said, savoring the sound of the word. "Take care of Jeri."

He shut the door and left his father sitting on the passenger side, clearly confused and worried. Rusty did not look back as he entered his apartment building. Once in his room, he shut the door and pounded fiercely on the wall. His suppressed anger came boiling out, and in a rage he stormed around the room, tearing the cushions from the sofa, kicking the wall, and stomping the floor. Fortunately, his rage subsided before he did any serious damage.

For the next few minutes he thought about Chum. He had to find him. It was essential. If he did anything to any of the people Rusty had come to love . . . The thought of that word stopped him cold. Was that how he felt about his newfound family?

And Jeri?

Of course not. But he liked them.

Liked Jeri?

"Don't be a fool," he said aloud. "You are in a different world than her."

Then, embarrassed at his outburst, he tried to think rationally. He had never felt like this about anyone in his life. And yet all his plans excluded her, and he was certain hers excluded him. She thought of him as a *brother*.

Brother! That was crazy. But then she did have that jerk Warren. She had been talking to him on the phone when he left. Oh, this was all so crazy. He needed to get control of himself. And he would, but not until he made certain Chum would not do anything stupid, and not until he had his money. Then he would go somewhere and start over. He would live a normal life.

If such a thing were possible for someone like him.

He forced himself to plan, to discover a way to find Chum and put a stop to this madness. Then it hit him. The watchers were out there. Chum probably was, too. And he was probably worried that Rusty would find a way to get the money and leave him out of it. There was a way to keep Chum focused on him and away from his family. That was to lead him on a wild goose chase. He thought of where the money was hidden and he considered his next move. He left the apartment and began to walk. As before, even though it was not yet dark, Rusty led his watchers back and forth over an area of several blocks. He soon had them spotted. He didn't see Chum, but somehow he was certain that the evil little man was nearby.

What he was about to do was risky, but he felt an obligation to protect Jeri. Even if it cost him a little of his hidden hoard. He picked up his pace.

***

It was almost dark, but it was still light enough for Chum to smile smugly at the two men in the car with him. His luck was amazing. The two men's luck was terrible, but they didn't know it yet. They thought they were in for a big fee and part of Rusty's money to boot. Chum had no such end in mind for them. Their fate was sealed, as were Jeri's and Rusty's. They had been enticed and trapped by someone ten times more cunning than they were.

Chum had not been in Jeri's apartment. But he held in his hand the two notes that were addressed to Jeri and signed by Sandy. They were proud of the work they had done for this man. They didn't know anything about him, but he paid well. And, like them, he seemed to have something against Randy Moore or Rusty Egan or whoever he was.

Joe and Arnie were working for Chum. The money they had been given as a retainer had been stolen the day before in San Francisco. They didn't know that, and wouldn't have cared if they did. He had walked into their office that morning and slapped five one-hundred dollar bills down on Joe's desk. "I have a job for you two, and it looks like you need one," he had said.

"Let's talk about it," Joe had suggested.

"No, just do it," Chum had ordered. "There's more where this came from if you do a good job."

He smiled at them now as he thought about how they had both hooted when he had mentioned the name of Randy Moore, alias Rusty Egan. Of all the sleazy private investigators he might have picked out, he had found ones who already knew their subject, and hated him. He had sent them to keep an eye on Jeri's apartment, and, when it was empty, to enter and do something to let her know someone had been there. "Don't do any damage," He had instructed them. I don't want her calling the cops. Just do something that will worry her so she will tell Randy. I want him to think I was there. I want him to worry."

When they had arrived, there was no one home. Jeri's car was gone, and of course, they knew that car, so Joe had entered the apartment while Arnie stood watch. Chum seemed pleased with their report. The missing notes would worry Rusty. They had done well. Dumb luck, that was all, but it served his purpose.

"Do you want us to go back now and keep an eye on the girl, or girls?" Arnie asked.

"No, I want you to watch Rusty. Follow him. And don't let him lose you the way he loses those other fools," he said. "I'll walk from here back to my car. You two keep track of him. If he tries to get the money, take him. And don't let those other guys interfere."

"We'll take care of it, Mr. Jones," Arnie promised. That was the only name the two hapless detectives knew Chum by. "Hey, he's moving again. Better get going, Joe."

Joe stepped out of the car the same time as Chum did. Chum waved a cell phone at them. "Keep in touch," he said. "Anything unusual happens, you let me know."

***

Jeri adamantly refused to stay in a motel that night. It was crazy. She couldn't imagine why Rusty would suggest such a thing. Kate agreed with her. "We'll keep the door locked tight," Jeri promised Patrick.

He continued to try to persuade her, but it was not to be. Finally, he loaded his family in the rental car and left. Rusty was worried, but Jeri had no idea why. She was fine. The whole thing with Sandy was a silly mistake on her part.

Of course, there was the thing about the notes, but she refused to think about them and what might have happened to them.

Kate and Jeri relaxed, but there was an air of tension about them. They talked of Warren's call. "He seemed uptight about Rusty's family," Jeri noted.

"And about Rusty?" Kate asked knowingly.

"I suppose so. But he has nothing to worry about on that count," Jeri said.

Kate was not convinced, but she said nothing of the sort to Jeri.

It was nearly ten o'clock when Jeri said, "I need to run to my car for a minute. I can't find my nail file. I think it's in my console. I'll be right back."

Jeri hurried out, found the file, and started back to the apartment. She did not get there. From the shadows a dark form appeared, and before Jeri knew what was happening, the man was beside her and the gleam of a blade sliced through the air.

She started to scream, but a hand closed tightly over her mouth and sharp steel pricked her neck. "Scream or resist and you'll be dead," a cold, unemotional voice told her. Jeri fainted for the second time that day.

CHAPTER 25

The night was very dark, but by watching and listening closely, Rusty was able to keep track of the shadowy figures of the three men he knew were following him. It was more difficult than it had been before, because there were more of them and they were alert to his quick moves. But at last, he was sure they were no longer with him. He then caught a cab and had it let him off near a location that had been in his mind for many months. It was an old junkyard with literally thousands of decaying car bodies. Only one was of interest to Rusty this night.

He searched for twenty minutes before he found the car he sought. It was a wrecked Chevrolet of ancient vintage with no parts remaining that could possibly be of use to anyone. It was in a huge pile and did not stand out from the others. Beneath the floorboards was a metal box. Rusty felt for it in the darkness. He only used the small flashlight he carried when it was essential. He could not be too careful. There were a lot of people who wanted what he had hidden here.

Rusty's hands found what he searched for and carefully pulled it out. He opened it and felt inside. The money was dry, as he had expected it to be. A thrill went up his spine as he fondled the crisp bills, then he shut the metal cash box and began to work his way out of the junkyard. He walked several blocks before finding a phone booth and calling a taxi. He gave an address a couple of blocks from the phone booth and met it there.

"Where to?" the sleepy cabby asked after Rusty and his box had gotten in.

Rusty gave an address a few blocks from the warehouse where he had promised Chum the first clue would be hidden. He was nervous and kept watching behind him. He was quite sure he was not being followed, but if he was and he was caught with what he now held on his lap, it would be all over. His parole would be revoked and he would find himself in prison again.

Rusty walked several blocks, ducking through alleys, circling around, and stopping for several minutes at a time, his ears alert to every sound. Each time, after hearing nothing that concerned him, he would move on. Finally, he entered the big warehouse. The door squeaked slightly, and he ducked rapidly inside. He had to use the flashlight a little because the interior of the large abandoned building was totally devoid of light.

He moved slowly and carefully to the place where he had told Chum to look for the note. It was already written. He pulled it from his pocket, opened the cash box and clicked on his little light. A quick glance told him the money was all there.

All of it that he had put in this box, that is.

Rusty smiled to himself. Probably no one suspected that all the money was not in one location, but he had not dared to risk that. This box contained only fifty thousand dollars. It was to be sacrificed to Chum. His note told Chum of his intentions and that he would get the rest of his share later if he followed Rusty's instructions to the letter. He shut off his light, stowed the box, and stood to leave.

A sound froze his heart. It could have been a rat, or a bat, or a cat. Or it could have been a shoe scuffing the floor! He listened intently, his heart resting firmly in his throat. A squeak so faint he might have missed it if he had been moving came from the direction of the door. Now he was certain; he was not alone in this building. He crouched low and began to inch his way deeper into the dark interior. There were other ways out. He intended to use one of them. He couldn't get caught now.

He hadn't gone far when a bright light suddenly stung Rusty's eyes, and he froze as a voice from the darkness said, "Game's over, Randy. Move and I'll kill you."

He had no doubt the voice meant what it said, for he recognized it. He had tangled with the man who now stood behind the light, deciding Randy's fate. It was Arnie. What was he doing here? Had he succeeded in losing Chum and the bank's official watchers only to be successfully followed by Arnie? And Joe?

"I've got him, Joe," Arnie called out.

Rusty was right. They were both here. One accounted for the scuff and the other for the squeaking door. Rusty was desperate. He couldn't let these two men ruin everything for him. He spoke softly, "The money. That's what you're after, isn't it?"

"It will help, and so will seeing you suffer. I owe you," Arnie snarled.

"But the money is the most important," Rusty said. He was aware of another flashlight and knew that Joe would be here in a moment. So he waited.

"It's get even time," Joe said with a chuckle as he stepped beside his partner and waved his light at Rusty.

"Or you can be rich," Rusty said.

"Like you have it in here," Joe said.

"I do," Rusty responded. "We'll split it three ways," he suggested after neither man said anything.

"We better just do like Mr. Jones says," Arnie reminded his partner.

A warning note flashed in Rusty's mind. Mr. Jones? He knew no one by that name, but what if that was not the real name of their employer? Who were they working for, anyway? It was not the bank, that he knew.

"Or we can take the money and keep it for ourselves. Randy here ain't going to say nothing," Joe answered.

"That's right. We'll split it and all be happy," Rusty said as he worried about the unknown third person.

The men were weakening. They whispered back and forth for a moment, their lights swaying about. Rusty caught the gleam of a handgun in Arnie's right hand and a moment later he saw the one Joe was holding. He needed to be very careful.

Finally, Joe said, "Show us the money and we'll talk business."

"You have the guns," Rusty reminded them. "Lay them here on the floor and we'll go together to where the money is."

"That don't seem smart. You have one, too."

"I'm not armed."

"And you expect us to believe that?" It was Joe doing the talking.

"No, but one of you is welcome to frisk me," he offered.

They did just that after warning, "Any funny business and you die right here."

Rusty stood silently while hands went over every inch of his body. Finally, Joe stepped back and announced. "He's clean."

"Put your guns on the floor and we'll go to where the money is hidden," he said.

They did as instructed and he retraced his steps to where the cash box was stored. He pulled it out, both men shining their lights expectantly at the box. Rusty palmed the note to Chum as he opened the box. The neatly bundled bills brought a gasp from both men. "A half million," Joe said in awe.

"No, just part of it," Rusty told him.

"Part of it!" Arnie exclaimed angrily.

"Of course. You surely didn't think it would all be in one place?"

"That's stupid—you just increase your chances of getting caught," Joe told him.

"And of staying alive," Rusty countered.

The men were standing close together, and both were intent on the box in Rusty's hand, each shining his light into the box of stolen money. Greed had caused them to become careless. Rusty took advantage. With a sudden swift move he threw the cash box at them. They both threw their hands up and Rusty moved in on them. He snapped his right fist into Joe's face with such force that he felt teeth loosen. Joe's head snapped back and he began to crumple. Arnie tried to grab Rusty, but he was too slow. Rusty moved like a cat, slipped a powerful arm around Arnie's neck and clamped the man in a vise-like grip. Arnie struggled and got off a hard kick to Rusty's shin, but after that he quit struggling and in a moment his body relaxed and he slumped to the ground.

Joe was back on his feet and trying to swing. The only light was from the flashlight of one of the men where it rested, unbroken, on the concrete floor. Joe's punch caught Rusty only a glancing blow on the shoulder, and then Rusty had him in the same kind of hold that had just rendered his partner unconscious. Soon both detectives were lying quietly on the floor. Rusty picked up one flashlight that was not broken and sat it on a large crate where it illuminated the two prone bodies. He took the small flashlight from his pocket and went in search of some rope. He found what he needed, and by the time he came back, Arnie was starting to stir.

Rusty tied him up first and then did the same to Joe. By the time he was finished, both men had regained consciousness. Rusty wrestled them around until they were sitting back to back, and there he tied them securely together. Only when he was done did he finally speak. "Okay, let's talk about Mr. Jones."

"Who is Mr. Jones?" Arnie asked.

"Let's not fool around here. Someone hired you two. I want to know who it was, and Mr. Jones is not good enough."

Both said nothing.

Rusty moved away and came back a moment later with the men's pistols. He shoved one in his waistband and pointed the other one in the direction of his two captives. "You can make this easy or you can make it hard on yourselves," he threatened.

Rusty knew as he spoke that he would never shoot either man. All he wanted to do was get away from here. But if he could bluff them into telling him who had hired them, he might be able to save his money yet.

They remained silent, and Rusty decided to take a chance and heighten the tension. Holding the pistol just over their heads he cranked off a round. Both men jerked. Then he did it again. "Next one is in somebody's foot," he said. Although he knew he would never shoot them, he hoped they thought he might.

Arnie broke first. "He said his name was Mr. Jones. That's all we know."

"And we don't believe that is really who he is, do we?" Rusty said through clenched teeth.

"No, really, he is Mr. Jones."

"Describe him," Rusty said as a terrible suspicion crept into his mind.

"Little guy," Joe said.

"Mousy," Arnie added.

"Chum," Rusty said quietly.

"Who?" Arnie asked.

"You don't want to know. Where is he now?"

"Don't know, but he told us to keep track of you. He gave us this address. Said you might show up here. He was right."

"You men don't know what you have done to yourselves," Rusty said as he felt his own flesh crawl with fear. "Chum is a killer." Rusty had no proof of that, but nonetheless, he was sure it was true. "You messed up. I'd hate to be in your shoes."

He sort of hated to be in his own shoes right now, but what could he do? He had an idea. "You men need someone on your side now. How would you like to work for me? Maybe, just maybe, I can help you save your lives."

"Anything you say, Randy," Joe offered. He was scared. He had looked in the eyes of Mr. Jones and somehow he knew that Rusty had spoken the truth concerning him.

"My name is Rusty," Rusty said sternly. "You will both call me Rusty from now on."

"Yes, sir," Arnie said.

"Whatever you say," Joe agreed. "So we work for you now? What do you pay?"

"Whatever I please," Rusty said. "Beginning, of course, with helping you save your lives. That ought to be enough."

"Oh, yes sir," Arnie said.

Rusty had to think. Chum would be coming here. And when he did there needed to be a note, but the one he had written wasn't good enough now that Chum had double-crossed Rusty. He pulled his pen from his pocket, retrieved the note and proceeded to alter it. That done, he gathered up the money and put it back in the box with the note. All of this he did out of sight of his new employees. Then he dragged the two of them, still tied together, deeper into the warehouse. He left their flashlight on so they could see what he was doing. "I have a little business to attend to," he told them. "You'll just have to be patient with me."

He left them muttering to themselves and returned to the box of money. He brought it back and walked right by the men, making sure they could see him carrying it. Then he circled around, letting his footsteps fall noisily on the cement floor. He climbed a stairway and spent several minutes tromping around on the upper floor. With the box still clutched tightly in his hands and the investigators's guns in his waistband, he removed his shoes and crept silently downstairs again. He left the box and note right where he had originally placed it. Then he crept back up the stairs, put his shoes back on and walked around some more. He stowed the pistols in two different spots, just in case he ever needed them. When he finally returned to Arnie and Joe, his hands were empty. They were quick to notice but neither one said anything.

He cut the rope that held them together and said, "Now we can go. I'll loosen your feet, but remember, if either of you try anything foolish, you will be out of this deal, permanently." Rusty forced them to walk ahead of him. Near a back door he stopped and said. "One of you will be staying with me. The other will be reporting to Mr. Chumbian. Charles Chumbian. And you might let him know that you know who he is when you see him."

Rusty planned to set Arnie free. He was the least intelligent of the two and the least brave. He would keep Joe secured until he was sure that Chum was out of the picture. He now knew what he had already suspected, that Chum would not be satisfied with only part of the money. He had to deal with him firmly, and Joe and Arnie were his tools, he hoped.

He tied Arnie to a steel beam in the warehouse and gagged him. He left him there while he took Joe to the same junkyard where he had earlier retrieved the money. He tied him securely inside an old bus body. Then he returned to the warehouse and took Arnie with him from there. A few blocks from the apartment, Rusty released Arnie and got out of the car. "I can walk from here," he told Arnie. "Joe will be fine if you do as I have told you. And don't let me catch you following me anywhere."

Darkness was fading when Rusty finally approached his apartment. The men who had been hired by the bank to replace Joe and Arnie were there. He purposely walked out of his way to their car. He pounded on the driver's window until he rolled it down. "Have a nice night, fellows?" he asked cheerfully.

He got two angry scowls in return. "You are wasting your time and the bank's money," he told them. "You really should go home and get some sleep. That's what I intend to do."

But it was not what he did. Patrick Egan was waiting at his door, and his father was distraught. "Someone took Jeri," he said.

"What! How? Didn't you take her to a hotel like I asked?" Rusty was alarmed. The someone could only be one person. Chum!

"She wouldn't go. That girl has a mind of her own, son. I'm sorry."

"Have you called the cops?"

"Kate did. Hours ago. I've been here waiting for you since they contacted me."

Never had Rusty felt so devastated as he did right now. His greed had put the most special girl in the world in serious danger. The only way to save her would be to give Chum all the money, and he wondered if even that would be enough. Chum was a ruthless, heartless man. He had no conscience at all.

"Come, the police want to talk to you," his father said, taking Rusty by the arm.

He did not resist. Suddenly, nothing mattered in the whole world but Jeri Satch. It was at that terrible moment that Rusty came to realize that he loved her. He also realized that even if it cost him his money, or his freedom, or his life, he must save her from Chum.

"I'll find you, Jeri," he muttered as he slipped into his father's rental car.

"What's that, son?" his father asked.

"Nothing," he replied.

But to himself he promised that he would do all he could to find Jeri. He would even take Chum's life if he had to. Yes, he would do *anything* necessary in order to rescue her. He would not fail unless he died himself in his attempt to save her. If he did find her and if he came out of it alive, then he would get out of her life, for he was nothing but bad luck to her. He loved her, but she could never love him in return, nor should she, he thought. He was not good enough for her, and he never would be. Anyway, there was Warren.

Lt. Ron Arthur was waiting at Jeri's apartment. There were cops all over the place. Rusty's newfound family was sitting silently in the living room. Mindy hugged Rusty tightly and said, "I'm sorry, Rusty, so very sorry."

"We'll find her," Lieutenant Arthur said to Mindy.

Kate burst into tears as she came into the living room from the kitchen. Like Rusty, she had been awake all night and it showed on her face. Black rings circled her large, round eyes, and mascara stained her cheeks. "She went out for a nail file she had left in her car," she told Rusty. "She never came back."

Rusty nodded. He knew who had been waiting out there instead of following him. Chum had fooled Rusty. And he had taken Jeri.

"Rusty, we need to talk." It was Lieutenant Arthur.

Rusty nodded.

"In my car," he added. "We will be back," he promised the others as he led Rusty outside.

Once in the car, he turned to Rusty and said, "Do you have any idea who might have done this and why? My gut tells me you do."

"Your gut is right," Rusty said in total dejection. "And it is all my fault."

"Who took her?"

"Charles Chumbian. Chum. My old cell mate."

CHAPTER 26

The floor was cold and hard beneath her. Jeri struggled helplessly. The rough ropes held firmly. They would hold for as long as they were needed to serve the purposes of the smelly, evil little man who had brought her to this filthy house. She was alone now that her abductor had left. No one else knew she was here. The place was clearly abandoned. No one could live in the squalor she was surrounded by.

A car passed by on a road that must be quite near, but no one would know to stop and come here to help her. A mouse poked its nose from beneath some rubble near her feet. She was curled on her side, bound hand and foot, and there was nothing she could do but watch as the little rodent examined her. When it had decided she was not a threat, it moved closer and touched her leg. She screamed and the mouse scurried away.

A fly buzzed near her ear and then landed annoyingly on her cheek. She shook her head in an effort to dislodge it, but it was only joined by another. Then more came as light began to seep into the room from the rising sun outside. He would be back. Whoever that man was, he would be back, and she feared for her life when he came. She had never been in the presence of anyone who was as devoid of light and goodness as this man. Had he never spoken a word to her she would have still been convinced that he was totally evil.

However, he had spoken to her, and the words he had uttered had brought terror to her heart. They also brought doubts about Rusty. The man knew Rusty, he hated Rusty, and he felt that Rusty owed him something. What he owed him or why and where the two had met he had not disclosed. But the fact that Rusty had known him well enough to make an enemy of him brought doubts to her mind. Perhaps there was an even darker side to Rusty than what she already knew.

She found her anger shifting from the man who had brought her here to Rusty. Whatever he had done to cause this man to kidnap her, it was clearly very bad. And she had so hoped that he was shedding the bad in his life and becoming good again, as good as he was when they were little friends so many years ago.

Strangely, her anger faded and tears came to her eyes as she remembered that horrible day when Rusty had been so cruelly snatched from her life. The terror she was experiencing now caused her to reflect on the terror he, as a helpless little boy, must have felt. She had known it had been awful, but not until now did she fully realize what he must have gone through. Whatever he had done to put her in this position could surely be excused because of what he had so innocently suffered as a child.

But he was not a child anymore, she thought with frustration. And she was convinced that he should know better by now. Her anger began to build again and she struggled helplessly against the ropes that held her so securely bound. Her wrists and ankles were becoming chafed, and her muscles ached. In desperation she cried out, "Help me! Someone please help me!"

There was no one to hear her calls.

Oh, but there was someone. He knew where she was and he could hear her cries. Jeri's anger faded again as she poured her soul out to God in silent prayer. As she prayed, she recalled the many years she had prayed that Rusty would be found, and though it took so very long, her prayers had been answered. Surely they would be again. A calm settled over her, and in a few moments she fell asleep.

***

Lt. Ron Arthur sat silently and watched as the strong young man in the seat beside him sobbed uncontrollably. During the past half hour, Rusty had told Ron everything. "I will go back to prison for the rest of my life if I must," he had said, "or I will die if that is what it takes. I just want to see Jeri once more, safe and out of the hands of Chum."

There was no doubt in Ron's mind that Rusty was sincere. Never had he seen such a transformation as he had witnessed these past few minutes. With Ron's urging, Rusty had briefly sketched for him his own abduction as a child. Ron found within himself a determination to bring the man Rusty called Uncle Bill to justice. But first, there was the matter of finding and saving the life of Jeri Satch. And that would not be easy.

Rusty wiped his eyes with his sleeve. "I'm sorry," he said. "I just can't believe I let this happen."

Ron nodded. "It's not all your fault."

"I could have prevented it. I knew she was in danger. But I thought I had to have that money!" he exclaimed angrily. "I thought life owed it to me."

"Life owes you something," Ron agreed. "But you must let life give you that something. Your mistake was in trying to take it by force. That never works."

Rusty mumbled his agreement. He had learned that now, but for Jeri it was very possibly too late. "We've got to do something," he said. "We've got to save her."

"Let's go down to the station and we'll see what we can come up with," Ron suggested as he started his car.

"I've got to do it," Rusty said. "I've got to meet Chum and give him the money or we will never see Jeri alive again."

"Possibly," Ron said cautiously.

"Don't play games with Chum!" Rusty exploded. "He will kill her. I know he will."

"We'll get him, and we'll save her," Ron assured Rusty. He just wished he felt the assurance he tried to show the young man at his side.

When they arrived at the Police Station, Rusty was surprised to see Joe and Arnie there ahead of him. He recalled that Lieutenant Arthur had sent officers looking for them, and he knew it wouldn't take long for them to find Joe, but finding Arnie before he reported to Chum had been a long shot. He was glad to learn it had worked. Arnie had been picked up at his office. And he swore he had not yet reported to Chum.

Both men were gloomy and uncooperative at first, but a reminder from Ron that he could charge them both with a number of felonies, including being accomplices to a kidnapping, if they did not cooperate, brought their attitudes into line. "You will still meet Chum," Lieutenant Arthur told Arnie. "Only you will be wired and we will have men close by. We need Chum to lead us to Jeri."

***

"The warehouse," Rusty said. "I'll wait there for him. I know he will go there for the instructions I gave him."

Ron shook his head. "I doubt that, Rusty. He is calling the shots now. He will be the one giving instructions. You need to go home and be near your phone. We'll have someone with you. We are already getting your line tapped."

Rusty shuddered as he thought about Jeri. He wanted to do more than wait by a phone. He had to find her, to rescue her. He owed her that, then he could get out of her life. Ron studied his face. "I know," he said after a moment. "You want to find her yourself. Or at least be there when she is found."

"That's right," he said. "I've got to be there."

Ron thought for a moment, then he lifted his phone. A few minutes later a red-headed, freckle-faced young man with baggy pants and a long tee shirt strolled into the room. Ron said, "Thanks for coming, Sam. This is Rusty."

The two nodded at each other. Then Ron said to Rusty, "Sam is an electronics and computer whiz." He turned to Sam. "Can the phone in Rusty's apartment be forwarded to my car without a caller knowing, and still be recorded?"

"Anything can be done nowadays, Lieutenant. This one, if the phone company is okay with it, is easy. You'll need a court order, but I can get with the company and get started right now if you want."

"Do it," Ron barked and turned to one of the other detectives. "Get the order, and get it fast," he said. Both young officers moved quickly to get their jobs done. Rusty was grateful for how serious everyone was taking Jeri's abduction. But he still was itching to do something himself, something meaningful.

The rest of the officers made plans, and then moved off in pairs to set things in motion. Joe and Arnie were outfitted with concealed microphones and sent to attempt to find Chum. An experienced pair of plainclothes detectives followed them. Two more officers left to set up a surveillance on the warehouse, just in case Chum decided to go there. Two more went to meet with the District Attorney to get a warrant of arrest for Chum, and still another pair left to meet his parole officer.

Officers were also assigned to keep Rusty's apartment under surveillance and still more were with Rusty's family and Kate. Rusty was then taken to his apartment where he sat by the phone while arrangements were being made to forward the number to Ron's car. He entered the apartment alone, just in case Chum was watching.

Rusty paced back and forth in the small confines of his apartment, anxious for the phone work to be done so he could at least be out on the street with the detective. He felt so helpless and cooped up in here. An hour dragged by, and then two. He was so sleepy, he could hardly keep his eyes open, but thoughts of Jeri kept him on his feet and awake.

Finally, the walkie-talkie Lieutenant Arthur had given Rusty crackled, and he was told to leave his apartment and get in the taxi that would be pulling up outside in just a minute or two, watching carefully for anyone who might be following him. He would be taken to Ron's car from there.

The cab was waiting when he got outside. Rusty climbed in and was whisked away. He didn't see anyone following. And he promptly fell asleep.

Ron wakened him a few minutes later and he moved groggily from the taxi to the unmarked police car. From there they went to the police station where Rusty was handed a bullet-proof vest and told to put it on beneath his shirt. When he protested, Detective Arthur said, "You might be glad you have it later. Joe and Arnie should have had them on, too."

"What?" Rusty asked in alarm. "Has something happened since I went to the apartment?"

"I'm afraid so. It appears that Chum shot them both. By the time the officers moved in, Chum was gone. So put it on," he said gruffly.

Rusty did as he was told, although the fit was tight. When they were back in the car, he asked Ron, "Are they dead?"

"Joe and Arnie? I'm afraid so. "

"What happened? I thought they were wired."

"They were. We heard them greeting Chum, calling him Mr. Jones. And then Chum said, 'I won't be needing you two now,' followed by two quick shots. The officers moved fast. All the sounds they heard from the mikes as they approached were a few grunts and a thump or two before Chum said, 'What's this?' Then a second time, 'Wired. Good luck, coppers.' That was it. The wires were jerked loose and smashed. When the officers moved in, both Joe and Arnie were dead and Chum was nowhere to be seen."

Rusty felt sick. He knew Chum was bad and had strongly suspected he was a killer. But this really hit home. And his fear for Jeri intensified. What chance did they have of saving her?

"Where are we going now?" Rusty asked.

"I don't know," he said. "We are just driving, waiting for a call. Remember, when that phone rings, you must pretend you are in your apartment."

"If it rings," Rusty said morosely. He couldn't get the faces of Joe and Arnie out of his mind. He hadn't liked them, and they had been crooks, but now they were dead, and it was his fault. The half million was costing lives.

"The phone will ring, Rusty," Ron Arthur said after a moment.

Rusty looked at him in the semidarkness of the car's interior. "I hope you're right."

Thirty minutes later, it rang. Rusty let it ring twice before picking it up. "Hello," he said.

"Randy, I ain't going to talk long." It was Chum. Rusty nodded to the detective. "I got your girl. She'll be dead like those other two if you don't do exactly as I say."

"Let her go, Chum. She isn't part of this," Rusty said angrily.

"She is now," he said with a snap. "Now listen carefully. Go to the address you gave me. Drop a note with clear instructions on how to find the money in the gutter beside the fence where you drive in. Then you go on inside and wait ten minutes. Not one second less."

"I'll get the money and meet you where you have Jeri," Rusty said. "You aren't getting it all."

"Half now. We'll go halves. I'll take half and leave you the rest. I'll set the girl free and she can find you. I'll be gone. Now do it."

The phone went dead. Chum was gone. Ron was already dialing on his cell phone. "Get a location, Sam?" he asked after one ring.

"Cell phone," Sam said. "He was using a stolen cell phone."

Ron swore and pounded his fist on the dash. Rusty spoke up with determination. "I'll tell you where to drop me off. Where's some paper so I can write the note."

"No, Rusty . . ." Ron began.

"Yes! There isn't another way to do it. Jeri's life is what matters now. Turn south at this intersection."

Ron turned south, and then said, "I can't let you do it, Rusty."

"Why not? I caused the whole problem. I've got to give it my best try. If I die, I don't care. But I've got to try."

"Notebook's in there," Ron said pointing at his briefcase. "And we'll have to put a wire on you."

"No, that won't be necessary. It didn't help Joe or Arnie," Rusty said sadly. "I'll take my chances."

"Rusty, what will you do after he gets the note?" Ron asked.

"I'll follow him, catch him, make him take me to her," Rusty said lamely.

Ron shook his head. "It won't work, Rusty."

"There is nothing else we can do," Rusty protested. "You've got to let me try."

Ron looked sadly at the young man in the car with him. He was desperate. He would do anything at this point. But it all seemed so fruitless. He racked his brain. Not a single good idea came. He doubted that Chum had any intention of ever returning to Jeri, wherever he had taken her. In fact, he would be very surprised if she was even alive. But he could not say that to Rusty. He didn't know what to say to Rusty. Finally, he made up his mind and said, "Okay. You can try, but before I let you out of the car, you must tell me where the money is. You owe that to those you stole it from."

Rusty nodded. "But don't have anyone waiting. Please don't. Let me handle it. After it's over, whether I'm dead or not, you can go get it all."

"Fair enough," Ron said.

"It's not all in one place," Rusty told him as he began to write his note for Chum.

"How many?" Ron asked.

"Five. There was fifty thousand in a wrecked car in a large wrecking lot," he began.

"Was?" Ron asked suspiciously.

"Yes, I moved it. It's in the warehouse where I met Joe and Arnie. The rest is in four other places. Two of them are in the same wrecking lot. The other three are in another one several miles away," he said.

"All right, tell me the names of the yards."

Rusty did. "I'll have to write down how to find each one. Let me finish my note to Chum while you drive, then I'll write down how to find the money." He then gave directions to the warehouse, making Ron promise to stop several blocks away so he could walk from there.

By the time they were where Rusty wanted out, the list was complete. He handed it to the detective and opened the door. He pulled the walkie-talkie from his belt and handed it to Ron as well. "I better not have this on me when Chum and I meet," he said.

Ron took it reluctantly. "I'm not sure we should do this," he said.

"Please, don't follow me. I've got to deal with Chum my way," Rusty said as he slipped from the car, slamming the door behind him and darting into the trees beside the road.

***

Five minutes after Rusty left the car, Lt. Ron Arthur's cell phone rang. He listened for a moment and sighed in relief. Then, before the sigh was complete he swore and pounded his fist on his abused dash again. Rusty was gone, and his life was in serious danger.

Jeri was found.

***

At that moment, Jeri was sitting in a police cruiser, heading for the police station downtown. She was explaining to the two uniformed officers what had happened. Ten minutes later she was in the station, surrounded by cops and telling the amazing story again.

Kate and Rusty's family had been notified and were being shuttled to the station by the police.

Lt. Ron Arthur was directing a swat team and a dozen other officers to the area of the warehouse where Rusty was headed on foot. By some miracle as yet unexplained, Jeri was safe. Rusty, unaware that she was no longer in danger, was walking headlong into a confrontation with one of the most dangerous men the country had ever spawned.

CHAPTER 27

"I'll explain how I got away," Jeri said, "but not until Rusty is here. He has some explaining of his own to do."

The officers Jeri was speaking to were detectives. Both worked regularly with Ron Arthur. The look they gave each other alarmed Jeri. "He is okay, isn't he? Is he locked up or something?" Now that she was safely out of the path of Charles Chumbian, it was easy to get angry again.

"Well, no," one of them said hesitantly.

"No what?" Jeri demanded.

"No, he is not in jail and as far as we know, he's still okay."

Jeri came to her feet, her dark brown eyes flashing. "Where is he? What are you keeping from me?"

So they explained what he was doing, and Jeri said, "Take me there."

"Take you to the warehouse?" one of them asked.

"Yes. I've got to stop him before he gets killed. That man . . . that Chum as you called him, is a killer. He was going to kill me. He told me so. And he will kill Rusty in a heartbeat."

"Lieutenant Arthur is in charge out there. We'll call him."

They did and Ron agreed to let her come, although he made it clear that she would not be allowed to go near the warehouse as long as there was a chance that Chum might show up there. Several minutes later, she was in the car with Ron where he explained why Rusty was doing what he was doing.

"You mean he did it for me?" she asked, her voice much softer than it had been for the past half hour.

"Yes. He said he would do whatever he could to save you from Chum, even if it meant giving his own life," Ron explained.

Jeri felt the sting of tears in her eyes, but she brushed them away. "He would give up his life but not the stolen money," she said bitterly.

Ron smiled at her anger. "He already gave that up," he said.

"You mean the cops have it?"

"No, but he told us where it is hidden. As soon as we have Chum in custody, we'll pick it up. Rusty is seeing things in a different way now." Ron smiled. "It seems that you have a power over that young man that no one else in the world has. I think he'd do anything for you."

Jeri knew better, but she chose not to say so. The one thing she didn't believe he would ever do was search for and accept the truth of the gospel. But if he would turn from his life of crime, that would mean a lot to her. And although she found it hard to admit, she was impressed, even moved, that he would risk his life for her.

"So what do we do now?" she asked Ron a few minutes later.

"We wait," Detective Howard said. "There are officers trying to get close to the warehouse without being seen. So far none of them have spotted either Rusty or Chum. So all we can do is wait."

Jeri sat silently, her emotions running high. She was only free because the Lord wanted her to be free. That she knew. She was alternately angry with Rusty and prayerful for his safety. And she even thought about Warren. She was almost certain Kate had called him. It wouldn't be fair to him not to be told, but she was certain he would be more angry with Rusty than ever. And even though she was upset with him herself, she didn't want anyone else to be, especially Warren.

Jeri worried about Rusty's family. She had left the police station before they arrived, so she didn't know how any of them were taking things. She was sure Kate was okay, for Kate was very strong. She could always seem to cope. She felt bad about leaving the police station before she could talk to any of them, but she needed to be here. She was not sure why. After all, this whole mess was Rusty's fault. But still, she had to be here. Whether he was deserving of it or not, she had invested a lifetime in him.

***

Kate had not been at the police station very long before she was told that there was a call for her from the airport. The pace of her heart quickened. It could only be Warren.

She tried to put her feelings for him aside as she had so often done, but it was getting harder all the time. She had promised Jeri that she would not interfere, and she would not, if she could help it, but she could not make herself not love him. That just was not something a person could do.

Kate had never been able to understand why Jeri had not fallen for him the first day she saw him, the way she had. And yet now, after all this time, she was afraid Jeri was actually falling in love with him. For a time, this thing with Rusty had prevented it. Now, this latest event might very well be the factor that turned her forever from any association with Rusty and firmly into Warren's waiting arms.

Kate shed a tear or two as she moved toward the phone where she was told to take her call. Her hand was trembling slightly as she picked it up. Then she gained control and spoke as if she had no feelings at all for the guy waiting at the other end . . . for news of Jeri.

"Hi, Warren," she said into the phone.

"How did you . . ." he began.

"And who else would it be?" she said with a lighthearted chuckle.

"Of course," Warren said. "You are always there. What a good friend you are."

Kate wondered if he meant she was a great friend to Jeri or to him. Or could he mean both? Not that it mattered, she reminded herself firmly.

"Have they made any progress?" Warren asked anxiously. "Have they heard from Jeri or . . . or . . . the kidnapper?"

The concern in his voice tore at Kate's heartstrings. And it was only because of her strong friendship with Jeri and her hopeless love for him that it gave her pleasure to say, "She's safe, Warren. She got away safely."

There was an audible sigh of relief from the other end of the line. "Oh, Kate. You can't imagine how I've worried."

"I think I can," Kate said. "She is, after all, my best friend. I would do anything for her." *Including letting her have the man of my dreams, even helping her get him,* she told herself.

"Is she there? Can I speak with her now?" Warren asked.

"No, she's not here."

"Where is she? I've got to see her. I am so grateful she is alive. Is she okay? She's not in a hospital or anything, is she?" He was talking himself into a panic.

Soothingly, Kate said, "Warren, Jeri is just fine."

"Then where is she? Why isn't she there with you at the police station?"

She didn't want to tell him that Jeri was out searching for Rusty. That was exactly what he didn't want to hear. And though it might help drive him into her aching, empty arms, it never even occurred to her to betray her friend. She wasn't sure how to respond. Finally, she simply said, "Get a cab, Warren. Come here to the police station, and then you will hear all of it."

He begged her to tell him more, but she was firm. She'd let the cops explain. She didn't want to do it herself. He finally relented and said, "I'll be there in a few minutes."

***

The long night was gone. Daylight filtered through the branches of the trees below which Ron and Jeri were parked. There had been no positive reports from any of the cops who were now positioned where two of them, with the aid of binoculars, could see the note lying in the gutter where Rusty had left it for Chum. Others were watching every entrance and exit to the old building. There was no sign of movement.

A couple of men walked down the street and passed the note without so much as a glance. They were homeless men and moved very slowly to whatever destination they had so early in the morning. Their every move was reported to Ron and Jeri as they sat waiting in the unmarked police car several blocks away.

Fifteen minutes passed. Several cars drove by the place where the note lay. The gust of wind from their passing stirred the note, but it did not blow away. Ten more minutes and an old lady, stooped and limping, shuffled by. Her cane thumped rhythmically on the broken sidewalk. Her head hung low and the officers reported that she appeared to be either intoxicated or very ill. A used and discarded wrapper of some kind was struck by the toe of her worn shoes and she bent and picked it up, examining it like it might hold a hope for food. After a few moments, she dropped it and continued on. She next picked up an empty coke cup. It too got the same prolonged examination before she discarded it and trudged on. Twice more she bent and picked things up only to drop them. Once it was a can, the next time it was part of a paper plate.

Finally, she reached the entrance to the abandoned warehouse. When she spotted the white note paper, she picked it up as she had the other items and looked at it for what seemed like a minute, then she wadded it and dropped it at her feet and moved slowly on.

"Did it land back where it was?" Ron asked the officer on the radio.

"No, she dropped it another ten or fifteen feet farther along her path," he said.

"Will Chum see it, do you think?"

"It's in plain view, but it looks just like another piece of trash thrown from the window of a passing car," the officer told him.

Ron groaned, and said to Jeri, "He has to get that paper if we have any chance at all of catching him. He might be dressed differently than we are expecting, or . . ." he stopped in mid-sentence.

"What's wrong, Lieutenant?" Jeri asked in alarm.

But he already had the mike in his hand. "Can you still see the old lady?" he asked.

"No, she turned and went up the north fence that surrounds the warehouse property and disappeared."

Ron's other hand was turning the ignition of the car. The engine roared to life as he said into the mike. "Get her! It's him!" He turned to Jeri as he put the car in gear. "Fasten your seatbelt and hang on. And whatever happens, stay in this car!"

The tires squealed a protest on the cool pavement, and the car shot away from the curb. Jeri knew exactly what Ron was thinking. The old lady was Chum. He had almost fooled them. And he would probably fool Rusty, too, at least for too long. Her heart almost seized up as panic set in. He wouldn't have a chance.

Ron had the mike to his mouth, speaking with officers at the scene as he drove. And did he drive! Fortunately, it was still early enough in the morning that traffic was light, and they tore safely through each intersection. Jeri could scarcely catch her breath before she found herself holding it again.

"I see the old lady!" an officer reported. "She's approaching the warehouse from a side door."

"How close are you?" Ron asked.

"Not close enough. There's a fence between us."

"Then go over it, but be careful."

"I can see someone," another officer announced.

"Where?" Ron shouted as his car slid sideways around a corner and he fought with one hand to straighten it out.

"He's in a shadow beside the building. He's east of Chum. But he sees him. He's moving that way. He's staying close to the building. As close as he can with all the junk there is around it, that is."

"I'm over the fence," the previous officer reported breathlessly. "She sees me."

There was a pop just as the officer's radio clicked off. The second officer reported in. "The old lady just took a shot at Mike. I can't tell if he's been hit or if he just dropped to get out of her line of fire."

"Close in! All officers close in!" Ron ordered as he skidded to a stop beside the main entrance to the warehouse. "Stay put," he shouted to Jeri as he leaped from the car, a hand-held radio in one hand and his service revolver in the other.

Ron disappeared to the north. Jeri watched as other officers appeared from their hiding places and scrambled rapidly in the same direction Ron had gone. She felt terribly helpless as she listened to the action on the car's police radio. "She's . . . he's spotted Rusty," one of them reported.

"Take Chum out!" she heard Ron's voice order.

"Can't get a shot," one said.

"He's firing," another reported.

"Rusty's down! He took a shot to the chest, it looks like."

Jeri screamed. She fought the urge to faint. She felt herself going, but refused to do so, not this time. Almost in a reflex action, she threw the door open and jumped out, running in the direction where Ron and three other officers had gone. She gulped in the cool morning air as she ran, gaining energy with every breath. Fully revived she charged around the warehouse just as a volley of gunfire erupted.

She continued to run as a deep silence followed the round of shooting. Then a voice called out through the crisp morning air. "He's dead!" she heard someone shout.

"Are you sure?" the voice of Lieutenant Arthur shouted back.

"Positive," was the response.

Who was dead? Jeri wondered as she rounded still another corner and into full view of the scene of the action. "Jeri, get back!" Ron commanded as she skidded to a stop beside Rusty's prone form. He was lying face down in the dirt.

"Rusty!" she screamed and dropped to her knees beside him.

Ron was there before she could turn him over. "I told you to stay," he scolded as he gently rolled Rusty onto his back.

"I couldn't," she sobbed. "Is he dead?"

"No, he's just had the wind knocked out of him," Ron assured her.

Jeri was looking for blood, but there was none. "But that officer, he said . . ."

Ron smiled at her. "I made him wear a vest, a bullet-proof vest."

"Then why is he . . ." she began again, but stopped as Rusty's eyes fluttered and his arms and legs began to tremble.

"I suspect the bullet hit directly over his heart," Ron explained as he placed his fingers over Rusty's carotid artery. Jeri took one of Rusty's hands and watched his face in concern. "The bullet can't get through the material, but the impact is still powerful enough to knock a man down. I think this is what knocked him out," he explained as he touched a dark spot high on Rusty's forehead. Jeri felt the hard knot that was forming there. "He hit his head when he fell. Other than a slight concussion, I'm sure he'll be fine."

Rusty's eyelids fluttered again, and once more a slight tremor shook his body. "Rusty," Jeri said gently. "Can you hear me?"

His eyes popped open, but for a moment he couldn't focus. "Rusty, it's me. It's Jeri," she said.

"Jeri . . ." he mumbled. "But . . . but . . ."

"I got away. I'm fine," she said.

Rusty's eyes finally seemed to focus and he struggled to sit up. "Jeri," he said again, and as Ron and Jeri helped him into a sitting position, he reached out and crushed her to him. "Oh, Jeri, I thought I had killed you," he mumbled.

"I'm fine," she said, gasping for breath in his tight embrace. Her heart raced, and she felt light headed. As his arms loosened their tight grip on her, Jeri's went around him and her head fell against his shoulder and she wept.

She was not sure, but it seemed like Rusty might also be crying. She didn't embarrass him by looking into his eyes; she just continued holding him tightly.

"Chum. That old woman was Chum," Rusty said after a full minute had passed.

"Yes, it was Chum," Ron assured him as Jeri and Rusty finally pulled apart, and Rusty struggled to get to his feet, with Jeri helping him as best she could.

"Where is he now?" he asked when he finally stood on shaky legs.

"Right over there," Ron said. "He won't be hurting anyone again."

"Dead?" Rusty asked.

"Very," Ron assured him as sirens sounded in the distance..

Rusty's full attention then turned to Jeri. "I am so glad you're alive and not hurt. I was so afraid for you."

"And I was afraid for you," Jeri said. "But I was also mad. If it wasn't for that money . . ."

"I know. Stupid of me," he broke in. "But they are getting it back, every dollar of it." He looked at Ron. "I'll help with that right now, Lieutenant."

"In a little bit," Ron said with a grin. "If it's survived this long, it will last a few more minutes."

Rusty nodded and turned again to Jeri. "I'm so sorry. What an idiot I am. How did you ever get Chum to let you go?" he asked.

"He didn't. I got away."

"Impossible," he said.

"I had help," she replied, remembering the feeling of peace that had settled over her as she prayed and the amazing way in which she was delivered from certain death had the Lord not intervened.

"Who? How?" Rusty asked.

"I'll tell you all about it later," she promised. She touched his forehead lightly with one finger. "Are you all right, Rusty?"

"A little dizzy," he admitted, reaching up and placing his hand beside hers, touching the tender spot on his forehead. "I guess I took a hard bump to my head when I fell." He turned to Lieutenant Arthur. "Thanks to you, I'll live, though. This vest saved my life." He unbuttoned his shirt to reveal the vest.

Ron said, "We better have a look below it. I suspect you have some pretty bad bruising."

"Later," he said self-consciously.

"No, now," Jeri said with determination.

There was an angry red spot the size of a silver dollar directly over his heart. "Chum was a pretty good shot," Rusty said, trying to make light of his injury.

Jeri was aware of sirens wailing as they rounded the corner of the huge warehouse. A moment later, several paramedics came running. Two of them began to examine Rusty, while the other one hurried on by. Jeri remembered the officer who had been shot at and asked about him. "Did he get hit, too."

"Right in the chest," Ron confirmed. "He was also saved by a vest. Chum knew how to shoot."

Ron gently escorted Jeri toward his car as the paramedics examined Rusty. "He'll be fine, I'm sure," he told her. "But we are all wondering how you got away from Chum."

"It was a miracle," was all she told him.

CHAPTER 28

Kate waited nervously on the street in front of the police station for Warren. A cab pulled up and he spotted her the moment he climbed out. He smiled weakly as he reached for his wallet and paid the cabby. Then he stepped toward Kate.

"Hi, Warren," she said softly, dropping her eyes for fear they might betray her feelings.

"Hi," he responded, then he reached out and pulled her into his arms, crushing her gently against his chest. "Are you all right?" he asked with concern as she fought her feelings. It felt so good, so right, to be in his arms. For just a moment, a weak moment, she let her head rest against his chest. One of Warren's arms left her waist and brushed her hair. Oh, it felt so good.

But it was not good and it was not right. She pulled away from him and he let her go, all but one hand, and that he held tightly. "Is Jeri here yet?" he asked.

"No."

"Where is she?" he asked.

"I'm . . . I'm not sure. She left with a police officer before you called," Kate told him. She had no intention of saying why, although she knew well enough.

"Then I guess we'll wait," Warren told her. At that point he seemed to realize he was still clinging to Kate's hand and he let it go, smiling at her. "Sorry," he said.

She knew she should be, too, but she wanted so badly to reach out and take his hand again. But she could not . . . would not. "It's all right," she said to him, fighting to keep from crying. What a lucky girl Jeri was.

***

As Ron escorted Jeri into the police station, Kate squealed in delight and ran toward her. Warren stood frozen to the floor. Not until Kate and Jeri were through hugging and crying did Warren step forward. Jeri held out her arms to him, and in a moment he held her in a tight embrace.

"I thought I'd lost you," he said with emotion.

"You almost did," she said as lightly as she could muster.

"I'm glad you're safe."

"Thanks for coming," she said as they stepped back and looked one another in the eye. "It means so much."

"I couldn't stay away. I was sick with fear. You can't imagine how I felt, not knowing, being so helpless," he said earnestly.

"Actually, I understand perfectly," she said.

Warren reddened. "I'm sorry. Of course you do. Well, I can tell you this, Jeri, I have learned something about you through this experience. I went through it for a few hours. You went through it for seventeen years. I'm so sorry for how I acted toward Rusty, and toward you on his account. I think now that I understand."

Jeri stepped close again and kissed him lightly on the lips. "Thank you, Warren," she said. "That means everything to me."

Outwardly calm and collected, Jeri was an emotional whirlwind inwardly. She was truly glad to see Warren, but somehow, this seemed like it was Rusty's time. This had been nothing more than an extension of their already horrible experiences in life. No one else could ever truly understand. Not even Warren.

Rusty's family walked over and hugged Jeri, each in turn. Tears flowed, and old nightmares were once again pushed aside. "How is Rusty?" Mindy Egan asked.

"He was saved by a protective vest," Jeri said. "They said they had to check him at a hospital before coming back here. He got a concussion when he fell after being shot in the chest."

Mindy's face paled. "In the chest?"

"Well, Chum's bullet hit the vest right over his heart. He has a bad bruise there, but that's all. He'll be fine, really."

Lieutenant Arthur joined them and said, "I hate to be a bother, Jeri. I know you folks have a lot to talk about, but we need some information to complete our reports." He turned to Warren, "You are Warren, I assume."

"I'm sorry," Jeri said quickly. "Yes, this is Warren. Warren, Lt. Ron Arthur. He's been great through all of this."

They shook hands and then Ron said to Jeri, "If you would come this way please, we will see if we can piece together all of *this*."

He led her down the hall and into a small office where he was joined by another officer for the interrogation. "We will need as much detail as you can give," Ron instructed her. Then Jeri began telling of her awful experience, and the simple miracle that ended it. And despite her mild protest, it was done without Rusty being present.

***

As Kate and Warren sat down to wait with Rusty's family, a tense silence ensued. Kate could see that Warren was very uneasy around the family of the man who had been the cause of Jeri's kidnapping. It was understandable. They, on the other hand, must be finding it hard to sit with a man who loved the girl who had spent most of her life searching for their son. So after a couple of failed attempts at light conversation, Kate said to Warren, "I could use some exercise. Would you like to join me? I'm going to walk around for a while."

"Thank you," he said as they left the little group. "You always know just what to say." The look he gave her was one of fondness. She smiled at him and he smiled back. As they strolled down the street outside the police station a few minutes later, Kate found it hard not to reach out and grasp the hand of the man at her side. But she felt a burn of shame at the thought. This was Jeri's boyfriend. She had no right to think such things. She had to help Jeri and to help Warren in his relationship with Jeri.

She had watched them hug and was certain that Jeri was not feeling what he was. She was not convinced she ever would. But she had to give them every chance. She could not interfere.

"Will she be able to get over this?" Warren suddenly asked.

"Of course," Kate answered quickly. "Jeri's tough. She'll be just fine."

"Do you think she's angry with Rusty? It was his fault, you know."

"I know, and maybe she is."

"I can't believe he wouldn't just give up the money," he said. "It would have prevented all of the trouble."

"Yes, it would have," Kate agreed. "But you and I have no idea what he has suffered over the years. I sure can't judge him."

"You're right," Warren agreed as they stopped at an intersection and waited for the light to change. He glanced at her and when their eyes met, it was all she could do not to reach out to him, to touch him, to offer comfort . . . and love. "Put yourself in Jeri's shoes—what would you do, Kate?" he asked.

"What do you mean, what would I do?"

"Would you try to get Rusty clear out of your mind? Would you love me and forget him forever?" he asked, shaking her to the core.

That was easy for her to answer, but she had to fight to control her voice and not give her feelings away as she did so. "A person could never forget someone they had gone through such trauma with; but if it were me, yes, I could put him in the past and lo . . . love you," she stammered.

And oh, how she did.

"Really?" he asked, his eyes widening with hope. To her surprise he reached for Kate's hand, held it gently for a moment, and then he released it. "You are so great," he said. "You really would do that if it were you?"

"Yes," was all she dared to say further.

"So maybe Jeri will put her life behind her and she and I can get on with ours," he said with what seemed to be new hope.

Kate said nothing and they began to cross the street. For nearly another block they walked in silence, then Warren said, "Will Rusty go back to prison?"

"I don't know," she answered. "I suppose that's a real possibility."

"I'd say it's almost a surety," Warren said. "How could they not put him back after he tried to keep the money for himself?"

"Yeah, I'm sure you're right."

"So how will Jeri feel about that?"

Kate stopped walking and turned to face Warren. "I don't know," she said. "There is no way that either one of us can know what she feels without asking her. You need to talk to her about this, Warren, not me."

"I can't. You are so much easier to talk to. I'm afraid she'll get mad . . . or that I'll get mad," he said honestly. "I don't want to fight with her again. Can't you talk to her and find out for me what she is feeling? I would be eternally grateful if you would."

"No, Warren," Kate said firmly. "If you and Jeri are going to make it in this relationship, the first thing you must do is talk about your feelings. Both of you must open up to each other. Total honesty is essential or it will never work."

Warren smiled sadly. "It's so hard with her. It's like I'm on edge whenever anything even remotely related to Rusty comes up. I am so afraid he will somehow come between us." He paused and glanced over at Kate who was watching him intently. "I guess I can't get over being rejected by her. She's so hard to talk to sometimes. Why can't she be as easy to talk with as you?" he asked.

Because she doesn't love you and I do, she thought. "Give her time, Warren, and be understanding," was what she said.

"And try to talk to her like I talk to you," he said with a laugh. "Well, I'll give it my best shot, but she is not you."

No, she is not me, Kate thought sadly. And I'm not at all sure she will ever love you as much as I do. She had to turn away to keep Warren from seeing the tears that were forming in her eyes. Then she was jolted as he said, "Sometimes I wonder why it was not you I fell in love with instead of her. We are so much alike."

Her eyes stung. She walked rapidly ahead of him. "Hey wait," he called out, reaching for her hand to slow her down. "Hey, you're crying," he said. "Is it something I said?"

She couldn't speak. He pulled her close. She resisted at first, then she gave in and let her tears stream. After awhile, she was able to quit crying and he gently wiped her face with his handkerchief. "This has not been easy on you," he said.

"No, it hasn't," she agreed. "We'd better get back."

***

Drops of perspiration ran down Jeri's face and she felt hot and sticky all over. As she told her story to the officers, much of the fear and pain she had felt during her ordeal came back. She wondered

how many times in his life Rusty had experienced such things. She
wanted to see him and tell the story to him. She wanted to see what
his reaction would be at the miracle that had brought about her
escape. Ron simply said, "You were one lucky girl."

Luck had nothing to do with it. God had everything to do with
it. She knew that, and yet as she had told her story it really had
seemed so simple, so unlike a miracle. But she had been there, and it
had felt like a miracle, so it was a miracle.

"I guess that's all, Jeri," Ron said as she rubbed the drops of sweat
from her face.

"Good," she responded. "When can I see Rusty? I want to talk to
him."

"I'm not sure," Ron said evasively.

Then a terrible thought occurred to Jeri. She couldn't imagine
why she hadn't thought about it before now. What if he went back to
prison? As mad as she had been at him after being kidnapped,
knowing he could have prevented it simply by giving the money
back, she was still sickened by the thought of him having to go back
to prison. She had to ask and she did.

"Jeri, this is hard to say after all you've been through," Lieutenant
Arthur began. "If I had my way, he'd go free. We have the money
now, or will as soon as Rusty takes us to get it, but it took you almost
losing your life to get it back. Two men did lose their lives. They
weren't honest men, but they didn't deserve to die. Rusty himself had
a close brush with death. He, I am quite certain, has learned more
from this than he could have been taught in any other way, including
more incarceration. And I know his family and you want him to be
through with it. But despite all that, I suspect Rusty will have to do
more time."

Jeri hung her head and fought back the tears. It served Rusty
right, she knew it did, but after the terrible fear she had experienced
and the pain and the humiliation she had endured, and all that in just
a few hours time, she had gained some insight into what he had experienced as a child. He had suffered so much and for so very long.
Shouldn't that count for something?

"I know what you are thinking," Ron said. "He has suffered
enough in his life."

She looked up, wiping her eyes. "Yes. That's right."

"I'm sorry, but under the law, such things don't hold much weight. You need to brace yourself for the worst and hope for the best," he said. "It will be up to the Parole Board to decide. Until then, he will have to go to jail."

Jeri nodded and Ron said, "Go see Warren now. That young man loves you, Jeri. Anybody can see that. It's printed all over his face. He's been suffering, too."

Jeri's head shook slowly. "But I don't love him," she said, surprised that she would say such a personal thing to this rugged police officer. "I want to, I think. I like him a lot. We have fun together. But . . . but . . ." she couldn't go on.

"But Rusty is there," Ron said perceptively.

"Yes," she mumbled.

"Well, you'll just have to sort it all out. Good luck."

Luck wasn't enough. What Jeri needed was another miracle. She needed to fall in love with Warren and forget Rusty for good.

She looked at Ron as she dragged herself to her feet. "I promised Rusty I'd tell him what happened, how I got away. When can I do that?"

"Would you like to go with us to recover the money? You could talk to him then. After that, we have to book him, and then the only way you can talk to him is through glass."

"Please, if it's all right. I'd like to go with you . . . and him."

***

Kate stood up when Jeri appeared in the hallway. She looked drained and sad. Kate's heart ached for her friend. She glanced at Warren as he took a tentative step in Jeri's direction. His look of uncertainty, mixed with longing and love, was almost more than she could stand. Two of the people she loved most in the world were hurting. She was hurting. She wanted to scream.

Kate said softly, "You go to her, Warren. I'll wait here." The smile she gave him was an attempt at courage, and it brought relief and hope to Warren's face. That only served to increase Kate's own pain. She watched as he held Jeri for a moment. They talked quietly as they walked toward her. She wished now that she'd done what Rusty's family had. They had left a few minutes earlier. She felt like an intruder now as her friends approached her

"Let's go to your apartment so you can clean up," Warren was saying to Jeri as they stopped in front of Kate.

"I can't," Jeri said. "Not yet. There is something I have to do first."

"With the cops?" he asked, noticing that Lieutenant Arthur was lingering nearby.

"Yes," she said. "Can you just meet me at my apartment in a couple of hours? Kate has a key, don't you, Kate?"

"I do. We'll wait for you there," she said as she watched the doubt in Warren's eyes.

"What is it they need you to do?" Warren asked, glancing at Kate as he did so.

She shook her head ever so slightly, a warning of sorts. He did not heed it. He forged ahead. "Does it have to do with Rusty?"

Jeri nodded and said, "Yes, but we won't be too long."

"What are you going to do?" he asked. He was getting upset.

Kate stepped over to him and took his arm. "Hey, let's get something fixed for dinner. We can all eat when she is through. Would that be all right with you, Jeri?"

"Great. There's food in the apartment. You two just make your-selves at home."

Kate ushered Warren away before he said something he would regret later. In the taxi on the way back to her apartment, he realized what she had done and the mistake he had nearly made, and he thanked her.

She felt guilty, but for a couple of hours she would have him to herself.

And Rusty would have Jeri. Doing what? she wondered.

"Why do you think she had to go with the cops?" Warren asked. Obviously, he wondered too.

CHAPTER 29

Car bodies were stacked on car bodies for acres. Rusted, dented, windows gone, tires missing, abandoned and sad. What a waste, Jeri thought as they worked their way into the sea of dead and decaying automobiles. She couldn't help but wonder about each one them. Families had driven them. Young men and women had dated in them. Crimes had been committed in them. People had died in them. What a story each car could tell.

Several had for many months held secrets only they and Rusty shared. Now, as they trudged through the dust and the rust and the oil and the odors, each gave up their rich secret, one at a time. With the fifty thousand dollars they had already recovered at the warehouse, they were only one hundred thousand dollars short of the half million Rusty had stolen. Most of it had been here in this vast yard of ancient cars and trucks.

The last of the cash, he told them, was not here. It was across the city in another yard. Lieutenant Arthur ushered Rusty and Jeri to his car and said, "You two can ride in the back. It's time you heard her story, Rusty."

They had spoken very little to each other since they had met at the warehouse over an hour ago. Jeri had tried to get next to him and talk, but he had shied away. Still, as she slid into the police car beside him, he seemed aloof and distant. Once the car was underway, he finally turned to her and said, "I'm so sorry, Jeri. I almost got you killed."

She forced a smile. "I'm fine," she assured him. "You know what? In a way, I'm glad this happened. For seventeen years I thought I knew what you must have gone through. I've tried to imagine myself in your place when that guy took you away. But I really had no idea. Now I know. And I feel even worse about what happened to you than I ever have."

Rusty looked at her in amazement. "Really, Jeri?"

"Really."

Then he scowled. "That doesn't make it any better. I put stolen loot above your life."

"You didn't know you were doing that," she protested.

"I should have known. I knew Chum. He was the worst kind of scum. And I'm not much better."

"Rusty," Jeri said gently as she laid a hand on his arm. "I'm not mad at you. Really, I'm not."

"Come on, Jeri," he protested. "You've got to be angry. It's normal to be angry. You should hate me." He spoke with intensity. His blue eyes were dark and wild. "You should never want to speak to me again."

"Okay, Rusty. I admit it. I was mad. I think I even hated you for a little while. I was scared to death. I blamed you. I wished I had never found you."

He looked at her. Their eyes met. She smiled. "I'm over it now."

He laughed. "Jeri, if you aren't the . . ." He stopped, his face growing serious again.

"What?" she asked. "Finish what you were saying. What am I?"

He shook his head slowly back and forth, then he smiled again. "You are the best person I've ever known. So tell me, how did you get away from Chum? Truth be known, I'd bet he's killed many people, and as bad as he hates women, I'm sure many were . . . you know, girls."

Jeri shuddered. "From the things he said to me, I know you're right."

"I don't mean to eavesdrop," Ron said from the front seat. "But you didn't mention anything like that when I interviewed you this morning. What kind of things did he say?"

"Oh, let's see," she began as she tried to sort out some of Chum's words through the terror the memory brought back to her. "He told me something about how when I died, nobody would ever find me. They never have before. Something like that. And I remember him saying, 'You'll scream just before you die. They always do. Especially the women.'" She shuddered, and so did Lieutenant Arthur and Rusty Egan.

"We'll need to talk again. There are unsolved murders out there that we might be able to connect him to and bring closure to loved ones. I'm sorry, I'm sure Rusty is bursting to hear how you escaped."

Jeri looked over at Rusty again and was surprised to see how ashen his face was. He looked scared. "What's the matter?" she asked.

His voice trembled as he answered. "So he really was a serial killer. And I led him to you." His voice raised a little. "I'm as bad as he is. I'm scum. I'm dirt. I'm . . ."

"You're my friend," Jeri interrupted. "You are the best friend I've ever known. You were hurt, and it was not your fault. Let the past be done, Rusty. There is so much good in you."

At some point while they talked, Jeri had taken Rusty's hand, or he had taken hers—she didn't know which. But they both gently squeezed, and neither tried to pull away. "Do you want to hear how I got away?" she asked.

He looked at her, his eyes moist, and he said, "Yes."

Suddenly an idea occurred to her. "Lieutenant Arthur. I think I can find the place where he took me. Can we go there?"

Ron's response was to grab his mike and bark orders for the others to wait for him at the wrecking yard. "We'll be a little while," was all the explanation he gave.

It took nearly a half hour, but Jeri finally said, "Right there. The old green house." They were beyond the outskirts of the city. Only a few houses dotted the desolate landscape. Not a breathing soul could be seen from where Ron pulled the car to the side of the road and stopped.

Jeri got out. Rusty followed. Lieutenant Arthur said, "This is it?" as he too climbed from the car. The house was old, hadn't been lived in for years. There were weeds where flowers and grass had once grown. Junk of every imaginable kind littered the yard. Rusted beer cans, broken glass, decayed cardboard, twisted lumber, an ancient car body, an old washing machine, and other junk of indecipherable origin littered the yard and the nearby dry fields. Sheds had crumbled, roofs were caved in, fences were knocked down. The nearest neighbor was close to a mile away. The road that led here from the city was full of potholes and ruts, and there had never been pavement or sidewalks in the area. Well outside the limits of the city, this abandoned house was the perfect place for a man like Chum to bring his captive. The chances of her being found here were almost none.

The clatter of iron wheels as a freight train rushed by drew attention to the proximity of the railroad tracks. An opening where a door had once swung offered admittance onto what had once been an open porch. They stepped through.

"Did he blindfold you?" Rusty asked as they worked their way through the clutter of the living room.

"He didn't need to. He'd already told me he was going to kill me, once he got the money."

Rusty's response resembled a growl. They continued into the center of the house. "Did he gag you?" he asked.

"Who could hear me scream?" she asked. "Believe me, I did, but all I accomplished was making myself hoarse."

"Is this where . . ." Ron began to ask, pointing to a pile of coarse white rope.

"This is where he left me," she interrupted. "I was lying right there, on my side with my hands behind my back. My feet were tied together and pulled up and tied to my hands."

She was staring in horror-stricken remembrance at the spot where she had twisted and struggled in the mouse droppings and the dirt and filth that covered the floor, dirt that still soiled her clothes. A stricken, mumbled cry brought her around. Rusty, his hand to his face, looked like he had just seen a ghost. Tears streamed from his eyes. Anguish twisted his handsome face. His broad shoulders were slumped. "Somebody ought to kill me," he groaned. "I don't deserve to live."

"Rusty, no!" Jeri cried.

"I did this to you! For seventeen years you searched for me, and how did I repay you?" he demanded angrily, pointing at the spot where she had suffered. "I did this to you!"

Jeri stepped close to him, wrapped her arms around his waist, leaned her head against his chest and sobbed. "Please, Rusty, don't blame yourself. Chum did this. Uncle Bill did this. You are my best friend. You didn't do this."

Slowly, Jeri felt Rusty's powerful arms as they wrapped her in their strength and pulled her to him. She was conscious of Lieutenant Arthur as he stepped from the room, leaving them alone. Five minutes must have passed as they held each other and cried. "Can you ever forgive me, Jeri?" he finally asked.

"I already have," she said as she looked up at him and smiled. "I already had before I ever left this place."

"What is it about you, Jeri?" he asked. "What makes you so good?"

"I'm not so good. I just don't believe in giving up on my friends."

He chuckled, and it both sounded and felt so good to her. All she wanted in the world at this moment was for Rusty to forgive himself. This was a good sign. She kissed him lightly on the stubble that covered his cheek and said, "Do you still want to know how I got out of here?"

He unwrapped his arms and stooped over, picking up a piece of white rope. "It was cut," he observed.

"That's right. Rusty, will you listen and let me tell you what happened? Don't scoff. Don't laugh. Don't make fun. Just listen. Will you do that?" she asked.

"I will," he said solemnly. "I owe you that and much, much more."

So Jeri explained about the terror, the pain, the hopelessness, even the anger she had felt toward him. Then she said, "Rusty, for seventeen years, I not only looked for you, thought about you, hoped you were okay, but also, during all those years, every single day, I prayed for you."

She was looking directly into those clear blue eyes of his, those troubled eyes, those guilty eyes, as she spoke. He flinched when she told him she had prayed. But she went right on. "What chance did I have? How far did I have to go to find you? What made me come to Sacramento when I could have stayed in Utah, or gone somewhere else for that matter? What were the odds of me getting the prison account? And finally, why would I ever go back into that place where they had you locked up?"

Rusty shook his head, but he made no effort to pull his eyes from her intense gaze. "I thought about all that as I lay here crying and feeling sorry for myself. Then I thought to myself that if God could lead me to you, despite all the terrible odds against it, then surely he could get me out of this mess. So I prayed. I asked God to help me. Oh, Rusty, I begged Him to help me. And suddenly, like someone covered me with a warm blanket, the pain went away. I wasn't cold anymore. I felt peaceful. And I fell asleep."

Rusty said nothing. Tears filled his eyes. She gazed into them, silently trying to assess his real reaction. Doubt was there on his face. But so was something else. She couldn't quite place it. Hope, maybe? She didn't know.

Jeri went on, "I awoke to the sound of voices. My first thought was that Chum had returned and had brought someone with him. Rusty, you probably won't believe this, but I was not scared, not then. There was a light shining somewhere in the house. I twisted around until I could see that door there." She pointed to the one that led into the living room. "I could see two figures. They were just silhouettes and they filled the door. They shined the light around and when it hit me, one of them said, 'My . . .' well I can't say what he said next, but then he said, 'It's a girl!' And the other one said, 'She's tied up.' Then they came over and stooped down beside me.

"They smelled just awful. You know, sweat, smoke, dirt, that kind of smell. But they looked friendly, or sounded friendly. I couldn't really see them very well. They were holding the light on me. I remember saying, 'Help me.' They looked at each other and then without a word, one of them pulled out a knife from somewhere in the rags he wore as clothes. He cut me loose very carefully. Not one time did he nick me with that knife. The other guy held the light while he worked.

"When they had me cut free, the one with the knife said, 'What are you doing here?' I told him and the other guy said, 'I guess you were lucky we got booted off that train. Now you better skedaddle before that guy comes back here. And so had we.'"

"Good grief, Jeri," Rusty said in awe. "Just like that, huh?"

"Yes, just like that. Then they left, and as soon as I could get my legs to work, I left, too. I walked for a long time. I have no idea how long. Then I found a house with a light on inside. I knocked and they called the police for me. I waited outside their house. And that was it. That was my miracle, Rusty. And it really was a miracle."

Rusty kept his promise. He did not scoff. He did not laugh. He did not make fun of what she had told him. All he said was, "Amazing. Simply amazing."

Jeri smiled and then said, "I'd like to leave this horrid place with one more good memory. Maybe it will wipe away all the bad ones."

Rusty started to speak, but she touched a finger to his lips, then she leaned toward him and gently pulled his head down. She kissed him. Not on the cheek or the chin or the stubble that covered both. She kissed him on the lips, and she held him tight. And he held her tight.

"Thank you," she said as they released one another. "I needed that. Now let's get out of here."

The emotion Jeri was feeling now troubled her. She had standards. She had goals. Rusty fit into none of them. Warren fit them all.

Well, all but one. She had promised herself she would never marry someone she didn't love. That one was going to take some time.

***

It had been exactly three hours and twenty-two minutes from the time Kate and Warren left the police station before Jeri walked through the door. Warren had kept track. He was wound tighter than a drum. Dinner was cold and he was angry.

Kate touched his arm and put a finger to her lips as the door began to open. "Remember, Warren, be gentle."

He nodded and Jeri stepped in.

CHAPTER 30

For a moment, Jeri stood just inside the doorway and looked, first at Warren, then at Kate, then at the belongings in her living room, then back at the two of them. A melancholy sadness filled her. This was her home. These were her friends who cared deeply for her. Warren waited expectantly, his arms outstretched. Kate watched him, and the look of love in her eyes could not be masked. Kate loved Warren—Jeri knew it. But *she* did not love him. If only she could, for Warren's sake.

For a moment, all she wanted was to be back in that abandoned, filthy green house, standing on mouse droppings, securely held in Rusty's strong arms.

Stupid thought.

Rusty had told her good-bye at the police station where he was to be taken off to the jail. They had cried. She had held his hand. They had kissed once more, and, Jeri had told herself, this time it really was the last time. She could not allow herself to continue seeing him—if she did, she would fall in love, and that would go against all she had stood for all her life. She and Rusty were in different worlds. And he was almost certainly going back to prison.

Silly girl.

What was this pounding in her chest, this tingling in her spine, this shortness of breath as she thought of Rusty?

Love.

Jeri mentally slapped herself. It could not be. She would not allow it. Warren waited expectantly, hope shining in his eyes. Now *there* was love. He loved her. Finally, reluctantly, shutting out the hurt in Kate's eyes, she held out her arms and he rushed to her, picking her up, swinging her about, and then he kissed her. In front of Kate he kissed her. Passionately, longingly, lovingly, he kissed her. He held her close. She shut her eyes and tried to feel something.

All she could see was Rusty's face. She opened her eyes to look at Kate, but her friend had stepped from the room. Could she blame her?

"Jeri, I've missed you so much," he said. "Come, lunch is cold. We'll warm it up. Kate and I have slaved over it." He chuckled. He was so happy to have her back.

And she was so miserable.

All through their meal, although she tried to be upbeat and happy, she kept picturing Rusty being thrust behind cold, formidable cell doors. Their slamming kept ringing in her head. He didn't belong there. It wasn't fair. He had suffered too much.

"Jeri, there's pie," Kate said.

Jeri looked at Kate. Her friend knew her mind was elsewhere. "Are you really okay, Jeri?" she asked.

Jeri smiled. "I will be."

Warren took her hand. "If you don't feel like pie, that's okay."

"No, I'd love some," she said. "It's cherry. My favorite. You guys shouldn't have."

"Oh, but we should have," Warren said with a chuckle.

After dinner, Jeri once more told her story. Kate and Warren were moved by her miraculous delivery from her evil captor. Warren said, "If you don't mind, I'd kind of like to see the place."

Jeri shook her head. "I'm sorry, Warren," she said, "but I never want to set foot in that place again as long as I live."

"I'm sorry. Of course you don't," he said tenderly. "How terrible the memories must be for you."

They were, but then there was the good memory. There was Rusty standing with her in that horrible place, holding her, kissing her. That was a memory she could never share with Warren, and one she had to put in its proper place before she could ever love him the way he wanted her to.

Rusty's family visited briefly that afternoon. They had been to see Rusty in the jail. "He's a changed man," his father told Jeri. "He is prepared to spend whatever time in prison is required of him. He promised to visit us when he gets out. We will be praying that it's not too long."

"He's gone through so much," Mindy Egan said sadly. "It seems unfair to lock him up again."

Jeri agreed with that, but maybe, she thought, she could get over him while he was back in prison. If things were ever to work out for her with Warren, she had to forget Rusty, or at least think of him as just a brother again.

It seemed so lonely after all her company was gone, and yet Jeri was relieved to have time to herself. Her abduction and the subsequent shootout between Chum and the police had been big news in the area. At work, she was a celebrity of sorts. Everyone had questions for her except Howard. He resigned from the firm following a report from the office receptionist that he had been seen talking with a man who fit the description of Chum not too long before Jeri was kidnapped.

Lt. Ron Arthur talked with Jeri some more about things Chum had said to her that might lead to the solution of several murders around the country. He reported to her that he and several others, including the news media, had testified in Rusty's behalf before the Parole Board had met and reluctantly sent Rusty back to prison. They had agreed to consider his case again in three months.

Jeri even had to endure interviews from radio, television, newspaper, and magazine reporters. But after a week, she was old news, and she slipped back into her regular routine. She worked hard, spent quiet evenings at home, talked regularly with Warren and occasionally with Kate on the phone. They both tried to talk her into quitting her job and coming to Utah. Kate would be graduating and Warren would be busy clerking in a law firm in Provo for the summer. It would be hard for him to get away. But she was firm. She was staying in Sacramento.

She stayed away from the prison just outside of Sacramento.

***

The most faithful man in the prison's weight room and in the prison library was Rusty Egan. He went by that name now. Even inmates he had known before his release called him Rusty. His story was well-known throughout the prison, although he never talked about it, or about the girl they had all heard so much about on the news. A few tried to kid him about her, but that didn't last long. Jeri was not someone Rusty wanted to think about.

But he couldn't help it. Whenever his mind wasn't on something else, he brooded about her. He told himself he had to forget her, but he couldn't seem to do it. He spent more and more time lifting weights. And he enrolled in a correspondence course in accounting. He knew that was crazy, but he wanted to study, and that was the subject that kept coming to his mind. He worked hard on the course. He also read tons of books: fiction, biographies, history, and a lot more. As his body filled out with bulky muscle, his mind became filled with knowledge.

One subject he had avoided studiously was religion, but one day, as he was perusing the books in the library, his hand fell on a copy of the Book of Mormon. He pulled it from the shelf, then he put it back. He pulled it out again and opened it. He read a few words, thumbed past some pages and found what was titled *First Nephi.*

Nephi. That strange name brought back some memories of his mother's lap and a picture book, a Book of Mormon children's book. Quietly, not sure why he was doing it, Rusty took the book to his cell and opened it again. He just wanted to see what it was that made his family click. They were good people, and they wrote to him regularly. Not once did they chastise him, but they expressed love in every page they wrote to him.

Of course, he tried not to think that reading the Book of Mormon might help him understand Jeri better. And he told himself it was not that he was interested in learning about religion. That kind of thing was not for him. No, he would read just a little of it, enough to maybe get some idea about what made his folks the way they were.

He began with the very first verse in the book. "I Nephi, having been born of goodly parents . . ."

He stopped right there, stunned. Those words sank deep into his heart. Goodly parents, it said. Certainly he had also been born of goodly parents. Intrigued, he read on. And he continued to read. He read until lights out, then he began to read again when they came on the next morning. He skipped his daily workout. He ignored his correspondence course. He skipped lunch.

What a strange book, he thought as he read on and on. There was so much he didn't understand, but he could not quit reading. It was like there was a power in the book that held him firmly in its grip. He read all that day and evening. The next day, he came to the last pages. He was brought to an abrupt halt when he read the fourth verse of the Book of Moroni, tenth chapter. "And when ye shall receive these things, I would exhort you that ye would ask God, the Eternal Father, in the name of Christ, if these things are not true; and if ye shall ask with a sincere heart, with real intent, having faith in Christ, he will manifest the truth of it unto you, by the power of the Holy Ghost."

All through the book Rusty had encountered stories of men and their prayers. He recalled Jeri's claim about praying for him, and praying for her own deliverance from Chum, and her absolute belief that God had responded. This Christ that the book talked so much about . . . if Rusty wanted to know whether the things he had read were true, he was told he must ask God in Christ's name.

How did a person do that? He had never prayed.

Or had he?

More memories came back. Almost as if he were hearing his father's voice right now, he recalled being on his knees as a little boy with his mother and father. And his father was talking to God. He remembered that clearly now, and he recalled his mother kneeling beside him at his bed, praying with him. He even remembered praying!

He had always said, "Heavenly Father, please bless Daddy and Mommy, and help me to mind."

Rusty broke out in a cold sweat. Why would these things come to his mind right now? It was crazy. It was surreal. He was not a religious man. Why, he didn't even believe in God.

Did he?

Rusty's cell mate was on the floor of the cell block watching television. It was early evening and he was alone in his room. Almost as if pulled to the floor by an unseen hand, Rusty dropped to his knees beside his bunk. He felt foolish, and yet he also felt compelled.

Bowing his head, he said in a whisper, "Heavenly Father, if you are there . . ." he stopped. He felt a rush of heat flood through him, starting at his head and going to the pit of his stomach. He tried again. "Heavenly Father, if you are there, help me know what to do. Are the things I've been reading true?"

Again he paused. He thought about the story of this Christ, the Son of God, that the Book of Mormon said so much about and how he appeared to the people in the story. He tried to picture Christ as he invited the people to touch him. He really had seemed real as he read. He remembered Jeri's unquestioning faith as she had told him of her experience. Perhaps her faith would help him.

He began to pray again. "Is it too late for me to change?" he asked. "Have I been too terrible? I've hurt so many people. Is it even right for me to know if this book I've been reading is true?"

The feeling that came over him was like none he had ever experienced. It was warm, it was comforting, it brought hot tears to his eyes. It felt good. It was real. "Help me to know," he concluded even as he realized that he did know. He closed his prayer in the way he remembered from when he was a child and moved from his knees to his bunk. When he touched the Book of Mormon again, it was like he was touching something of great worth. He felt like he had to be gentle with it, respect it, and even love it.

Rusty finished the last pages and quietly put the book on his pillow. Then he picked the book up again and opened it. He found himself staring at page 157. He saw the heading to the fifth chapter of the Book of Mosiah. He began to read, starting, he did not know why, at verse two. There he read that the people had undergone a mighty change of heart, that they had no more disposition to do evil, but to always do good.

That sounded like his family. Now he was beginning to understand them. And it sounded like Jeri. Oh how it reminded him of her. He loved her. He just couldn't help himself, but it could never be. Firmly, Rusty thrust her from his mind and turned back to the first page of the Book of Mosiah and began again to read. He loved it. He learned so much from this wise man the book called King Benjamin.

Strangely, Rusty realized that he was undergoing the same change of heart that King Benjamin's people had undergone. And he also realized that this King Benjamin was a real person. He knew it. He felt it in a way he had never, until this day, experienced before. It was too late for him to ever claim Jeri as his closest friend, but despite that, he could change his life. He could become a good and decent person. Perhaps, someday, after he got out of prison, he might talk to his parents about the Mormon Church. It might not be such a bad idea to become a member himself, if he hadn't done things that might prevent it. He recalled the warm feeling that he had experienced, but still he had doubts. What if he could never be worthy to be a Mormon?

Over the next few days, Rusty fell into a new routine. He worked out in the weight room every morning, he studied his accounting course every afternoon, and he read in the Book of Mormon each evening. And at some point every day, he found a private moment in his cell to offer a short prayer. He found himself loving the book and gradually he realized that if some of the people in the book could be forgiven for what they had done, then surely he could be forgiven. He worried less and searched the pages in eagerness. Maybe he could be a Mormon someday and if so, he wanted to be a good one.

Much of the book made a lot of sense to him, but other things were not so clear. As he studied the Book of Mormon, he inserted slips of paper as book marks in places he had questions about. Sometime, somehow, he would like to ask someone to explain those verses that puzzled him.

Who, and when? he wondered. He hated to wait until he got out of prison. He felt the need to know now.

Again, Jeri came to mind. But he could not bother her. She had her life to live. She had Warren. He considered his parents. If he wrote to them, they would come, he knew that, but was that fair to them? He postponed a decision, but he continued to mark pages and specific verses he wanted to learn more about.

Rusty's accounting course was going well, up to a point, and then he became stumped. His instructor was so far away and hard to reach. He couldn't go on until he had some things clarified. Again, unbidden, Jeri came to mind. She was an accountant. She could help him. Just this once, he told himself as he reached for a pencil and paper. And just because he needed help and there was no one else to give it to him.

His letter was brief. He said he was doing fine. He wondered how she was doing. He hated to bother her, but he really needed some help on something. He was taking an accounting course and was stumped. If she possibly could, would she come to the prison just long enough to clarify a few points and he wouldn't bother her again?

Please.

***

Jeri's life was going along quite well. Warren had been down to see her again, and she had enjoyed his visit. She wanted to see him again. Kate called a lot, but she seldom mentioned Warren. It was like it hurt her too much. Jeri's job was going really well. She had asked to be taken from the prison account because it reminded her too much of Rusty.

She thought of him from time to time, but not as much as she had. Spring brought more activities with other young singles, and she enjoyed that. She was now teaching a primary class and loved it. The children were so sweet. They filled a void in her life. Yes, everything was going quite well for her.

Then a letter came in her box.

Her hand trembled and she broke out in a cold sweat as she read the neatly printed name of Rusty Egan in the upper left-hand corner of the envelope. Ironically, it was the only piece of mail in her box on that warm and sunny Saturday morning. She carried it back into the apartment, wondering if she should open it or if it would be better to throw it away. Who knew what kind of trouble might lie ahead if she opened it.

She dropped it into the wastebasket, trying not to think about what Rusty might have written. She sat down on her couch and picked up her scriptures. She was currently reading the Book of Mosiah. Maybe if she read the scriptures for a little while, she could get the discarded envelope out of her mind.

She began to read, beginning with the fifth chapter, right where she had left off the night before. When she came to the words that explained how the people of King Benjamin desired to do evil no more, but to do good continually, she thought of Rusty.

Was *she* doing good if she threw the letter away? What if there was something she could do for him as a friend? But what if the letter led her into something evil again? She read on, only half absorbing what she was reading. She finally closed the book, forgetting to move the book mark from where it had been when she began.

Ignoring the wastebasket, Jeri went into her bedroom, put on a swimming suit, picked up a novel she had been reading, and headed for the backyard of the apartment complex to work on her tan. Warren would be coming as soon as school was out in three more weeks. She wanted to look her best for him.

CHAPTER 31

The scriptures were lying on her bed, ready for her to read a few pages before she went to sleep. Jeri knelt beside her bed and prayed. With the scriptures on her mind, she asked the Lord to help her understand them better and to live by them more fully. She prayed for her family, for Kate, for Warren, and Rusty came to mind. She reluctantly asked the Lord to bless him and help him become the kind of man he could be.

After her prayer, she sat in bed with her scriptures on her lap. She opened the Book of Mormon to where it was marked and began to read the fifth chapter of Mosiah. Not until she read the words about the people of King Benjamin desiring to do good continually, did she realize she hadn't moved the book mark that morning. She started to turn the page, remembered how preoccupied she had been, and decided to read where she was at. She read the same verse she had just finished, thought about if for a minute or two and went on.

Jeri closed her scriptures ten minutes later, then hopped out of bed and headed to the kitchen for a glass of water. Her path took her directly past her wastebasket. She stopped and peered in. The letter was still there. Not that it would have gone anywhere on its own. The scripture about doing good came back to her, and she bent down and retrieved Rusty's letter.

After drinking a glass of water, she carried the letter back to her bed and climbed in. She held the letter for several minutes, deep in thought, before she finally decided it would not hurt to at least hear what he had to say.

She opened the envelope and pulled out the single sheet of lined paper it contained. She slowly began to read. He was doing fine, etc.,

etc. Then she came to where he needed help. He was taking an accounting class, she read, and was stumped. Could she come just this one time and help him?

The letter seemed innocent, but what did he really want? she wondered. But what would it hurt if she went just this once and helped him get going on his course again? It struck her as more than a coincidence that he should be taking an accounting course, but then, it was a good field. She certainly liked it. And when he got out of prison this time, maybe he could go to school and get a degree and really make something of himself. After all, she had prayed for him to become the kind of man he should be.

She decided she would help him, but not in quite the way he might have anticipated. The very thought of seeing Rusty again brought goose bumps to her skin. She just had to stick with her resolve to forget him. She had to be firm. She owed it to Warren. She would send Bob, the accountant who was now doing the work for the prison. If it was help Rusty wanted, then help he would get. If he was not sincere, she would soon know it.

She asked Bob for his help Monday morning. After explaining who needed some tutoring and why she would prefer not to do it herself, he agreed to help. Just this once.

***

Rusty was surprised on Monday evening to hear his name called to go to the visitor's room. Despite himself, he was excited. It could only be Jeri. Well, a surprise visit from his parents was possible, because they had developed a relationship by mail the past few months. But, no, it had to be Jeri. He had been to the prison barber that afternoon. His hair had been getting a little bit long. He combed it carefully before gathering together the books and papers he needed from his accounting course. Smiling, Rusty started the long trek to the visiting area.

To his dismay, it was not Jeri who was seated on the far side of the glass—it was some guy with thick glasses and a long, skinny neck. "Rusty?" the guy asked.

"Yes, that's me, and who are you?" Rusty asked a little sharply.

"I'm sure it wasn't me you wanted to see," the fellow said with a smile. "My name's Bob. I'm an associate of Jeri's. She said you needed a little help. She regretted that she couldn't come herself, but since I do the prison account these days, she asked me if I'd see if I could help you."

Rusty was terribly disappointed. He had wanted so badly to see Jeri. He missed her more than he cared to admit. But he had truly changed, and he graciously accepted Bob's offer of help. It got him going again on his course. Not once did he bring up Jeri's name to Bob. And when they were finished, he simply thanked him. Bob, however, did bring up Jeri. "You seem to have a knack for this sort of work Rusty. I wish you well. I'd be glad to help you again if you need it. Oh, and I'll tell Jeri how well you are doing. She doesn't admit it, but I can tell she cares." With that he parted, leaving Rusty sitting there in that tiny room with his heart fluttering.

She cares. Those two little words lifted Rusty's spirits and sent him back to the cell block with a brighter outlook. Just to have talked with someone who had seen Jeri as recently as that very afternoon gave Rusty a lift. He was whistling when he reached his cell.

***

"Hi, Bob, how did it go yesterday?" Jeri asked when Bob approached her office mid-morning the next day.

"Great. He's a pretty sharp guy," Bob responded with a wink. Jeri felt herself blushing. Bob pretended not to notice. "He was stumped, all right, but I only had to explain once what he was doing wrong, and he got it. I worked with him for a few minutes, but I tell you, the guy will be a good accountant if he ever gets out and goes straight. And you know what, Jeri? I think he will go straight. I was very impressed with him."

"Good," Jeri managed to say.

"And hey, I'd sure hate to ever make him mad. Wow, what a build! That guy must do nothing but pump weights all day, when he's not studying, that is. For the short time he's been taking that accounting course, he is pretty advanced. I was really quite impressed."

"Good," Jeri said again. "And thanks for helping, Bob."

"Glad to. I told him if he got stumped to let me know."

"Really," Jeri said, lifting an eyebrow. "I thought you said just this once."

"I did, but I figured the guy was a flake, thought he was just using this as a ruse to see you. I was wrong. He didn't say a word about you. He really wanted some help. So, I'd be glad to do it again if he needs it. See you around."

Now she felt guilty. It sounded like she had read Rusty all wrong. He really was only interested in getting some help on his course. She also felt strangely wounded. She had secretly hoped he would at least ask about her.

Oh, Rusty! she thought. Why can't I get rid of these feelings that keep cropping up?

She had the same thought that night as she sat talking to Warren on the phone. It was so hard to repress feelings for Rusty while it was so hard to feel them for Warren. Why was that? If she could just fall in love with the guy, life would be much simpler. She had to keep giving herself time. Maybe it would happen when he visited again.

That day soon arrived. School was out and he had one week before he had to report to the law firm for the summer. Jeri picked him up at the airport. Warren had a spring to his step and a smile on his face that was as broad as the Nile. He took Jeri in his arms and kissed her tenderly, right there in front of hundreds of people. His cheerfulness was infectious, and she responded warmly, even eagerly, to him.

The next few days were very good—not great—but better than Jeri had dared to hope. She was not sure what she was feeling, but she found that she genuinely cared for Warren. He had almost succeeded in getting Rusty off her mind without his name having ever come up. It was on Saturday evening, the night before he was to leave for Utah, that he tried for the second time to get a major commitment from Jeri.

It had been an especially good day for them both. They were eating out in one of the nicer restaurants in the city. The table they had was quite private, the lights were dim, and candles glowed warmly between them. The food was excellent, and they had just finished dessert. Jeri thought that at any minute, Warren would reach for her hand to lead her out. To her surprise, he got up from the table and circled around to her side. Then he knelt on one knee and looked up into her eyes. "At the risk of making you angry," he began, "there is something I must say."

"I won't get angry," she promised. She had a feeling what was coming. Maybe it was time. She hadn't seen Rusty in about four months.

Warren smiled. He really was a handsome man. He took her hand in his and gently kissed it. Then he looked into her eyes and said simply, "I love you, Jeri Satch. Will you marry me?"

Despite her intuition, his words took her breath away. For a moment she sat staring at him. He was so hopeful, yet so afraid she'd say no. He reminded her of a little puppy she had been given years ago for her birthday. It used to sit and stare up at her, begging with its big brown eyes for a treat.

The thought made her smile, and she made up her mind. She was not sure if it was deep romantic love that she was feeling, but she cared for this guy. It was time for commitment.

"Yes," she said. "I will marry you, Warren Tharp."

Warren whooped, startling people at nearby tables. But he didn't care. Neither did she. Swept away in the heat of the moment, she jumped to her feet and into his arms. It was several minutes before they had calmed their emotions to the point that he was able to get her to sit again. Then he pulled a small black box from his pocket and extracted a ring. It was almost a perfect fit.

Not quite—but close enough, she thought.

***

Jeri waited until after Warren had left the next day to call her parents. "I'm getting married," she told her mother as soon as she answered the phone.

"To Warren?" her mother asked.

"Yes. He gave me a ring last night."

"When?" she asked.

"We haven't set a firm date, but we're thinking about the Christmas break," Jeri said. "Is Dad there?"

"Yes, just a moment and I'll get him on the other line, dear. I think he's in the backyard."

Jeri waited while her mother went in search of her father. She was puzzled. She had expected her mother to sound surprised but also excited. She was sure that she was surprised, but beyond that, she really didn't know. It didn't make sense. She knew they liked Warren. Maybe it was . . .

"Hi, Jeri," her father said, breaking into her thoughts. "How's my girl?"

"I'm great, Dad. I've got some news."

"So your mother hinted. Let's hear it. No, let me guess. You are coming back to Utah."

"Yes," Jeri said with a chuckle. "How did you know?"

"I didn't," he said. "I just hoped. When are you coming and do you have a job here already?"

"I'll come home in December," she said, grinning to herself. "And I'm going to marry Warren right after Christmas."

"Oh, really?" her father asked.

She felt like a balloon that had just met the point of a needle. She deflated so fast she had to sit down. Not only was her father not surprised, but his tone of voice left no doubt as to the lack of excitement.

"Yes, really," she said with a touch of anger in her voice. "Is there something wrong with that?"

"Oh, no, dear," her mother said.

"Of course not, Jeri," her father responded.

"Then what's the problem?" she demanded.

For a moment it was very silent on the Utah end of the phone line. Then her father asked, "Are you sure this is the right thing, sweetheart?"

"Have you prayed about it?" her mother inquired.

"I'm wearing his ring," was her strange non-answer to both of their questions.

"Does it fit?" her mother asked.

"Almost," she said.

"Just almost?" It was her father asking this time.

"Close enough," she said.

"Jeri," her father said sternly, "is that how it is with Warren? Close enough?"

She didn't answer that question, either, for she was suddenly very uncomfortable with herself. She was angry with her folks, but they had raised doubts she had refused to acknowledge.

"Dad, Mom," she said after a long and strained silence, "I guess I shouldn't have called. I thought you'd be happy for me."

"Jeri, you are a very mature and spiritual young woman," her father said. "We cannot and will not make your decisions for you, but we do care about whether they are the right ones. We love you and only want the best for you. Somehow, from your letters and phone calls we've never got the impression that you were in love with Warren. I guess that this announcement, after what we believed you were feeling, comes as a bit of a surprise."

Her mother began where her father left off. "If you are sure, and if you've prayed about it, and if you love Warren, then we are happy for you. We wish you both the very best."

"Thanks, I guess I better go now. I'll call again."

"Jeri, please don't be angry with us. You have our full support and blessing," her father assured her.

"Thanks, Dad. I love you guys. I'll write or call with more details as soon as I have them. Now, I guess I better let Kate know."

"Jeri." Her mother's voice had that warning note in it again.

"Yes, Mom?"

"Are you sure you want to do that? It is going to break her heart, you know."

Jeri knew. And she was dreading this call, but she had to do it. "She has encouraged me every step of the way," she told her folks.

"With a breaking heart," her mother said. "We have only been around her a couple of times the past few months, but when we mention Warren and you, there is no doubt what she is feeling."

"I'll be gentle," Jeri promised and hung up the phone.

Jeri was more than gentle. She couldn't bring herself to make the call. There was just no way to break this kind of news to Kate. They were just too good of friends. She knew it would break Kate's heart. And here she thought things would get simpler after she finally made a commitment to Warren.

***

Mindy Egan's hands were trembling as she picked up the phone to call her husband. Even though it was a Saturday, he was at work, but the letter she had just received from Rusty couldn't wait for him to get home that evening. When he answered, he said, "I'm quite busy, Mindy, can't this wait?"

Mindy knew the pressure Patrick was under with his job. The overtime was killing him. She also knew how much he worried about Rusty. That was why this letter was so important to both of them. "No, Patrick, it can't wait," she said patiently. "It's from Rusty."

"Oh," he said, his tone brighter. "What does he have to say?"

"He is getting out of prison again."

"Oh, great!" Patrick said, heaving a sigh of relief. "When?"

"Next week, he says. Oh, that's in two days. He's getting released on Monday. And that isn't all," she went on with excitement that was more than she could contain. "His parole is being terminated, also. He will be a totally free man!"

"Parole terminated?" Patrick asked doubtfully. "How can that be?"

"He says the Parole Board and the Judge decided it together. He doesn't say why. It is sort of like when those two hobos cut Jeri Satch loose—it's a miracle."

When her husband spoke it was with more energy than she had felt in him for years. "Mindy, I'll take some time off. Let's head up there. We need to be there to meet him the moment he walks out of those gates," he said.

She could not have agreed more. But there was still one other thing she had to tell him. "Patrick, there is more good news, even better news," she said.

"How could there be better news? This is the greatest," Patrick said with laughter in his voice.

"He says he found a Book of Mormon and he's read it several times. He has met a few times with a member of the Church who comes to the prison. He says that with him being off parole . . ." Mindy could not continue. She was so thrilled, she began to cry.

"What?" Patrick asked. "What else did he say?"

It took awhile, but she finally managed to tell him that their son wanted to be baptized. That he had found the gospel. After her emotions were under control again, Mindy said, "Rusty will be meeting with some full-time missionaries at Brother Gray's home. He's a stake missionary there in Sacramento. He says it will take some time because he needs to put some things more firmly behind him. But he definitely wants to join the Church."

Patrick said simply, "It's too good to be true. I wonder why he hasn't said something sooner. He's been so good to write every few weeks."

"He explains that in his letter. He says that he wanted to be absolutely sure about the Church before he said anything to us, and even though he still hasn't had the lessons, he is apparently sure. He didn't want to be influenced by us, or to get our hopes up."

"What about Jeri?" I wonder what part she's played in this?" Patrick said. "Surely she has been seeing him."

"I don't think so. He doesn't mention her one time in his letter. Not anything about her. Come to think of it, I don't recall him mentioning her at all, in any of his letters. I suppose she and that Warren fellow must have plans or something."

***

Even as they spoke, Jeri sat idly twisting the ring on her finger. It didn't quite fit. It was just a little loose. Suddenly, she threw her hands to her face and began to cry. Like her ring, this whole thing with Warren didn't quite fit. He was a great guy, and she liked him a lot, but she was fooling herself. She did not love him. She was settling for something she didn't really want. Her parents were right. She slipped the ring off her finger and dropped it in the palm of her hand.

CHAPTER 32

There was no call from Warren that night. That was unusual for a Saturday night. He always called on Saturday nights. Not that she was upset by it. Much to the contrary, she was dreading talking to him, for what she had to say would only break his heart again. Her decision to make a clean break with Warren was final this time.

It was not because of Rusty, because they hadn't seen each other since the day he returned the stolen money. Not that she didn't ever think of him, because a day never went by that he didn't enter her mind, but she had been able to control her feelings. The fact that she was going to break up with Warren did not change her firm commitment about never marrying outside of the temple. But she had nearly broken one of her other standards—she had nearly married without it being the true, deep-seated love she had always said would have to be an integral part of her marriage. She would not make that mistake again, nor would she marry the wrong kind of man, or even date one.

That pretty well ruled Rusty out. She wished it didn't. But she couldn't afford to fool herself. Rusty was not for her.

After deciding that Warren was not going to call, she picked up the phone and began to dial as she paced the floor. Her little brother answered. "Is Mom or Dad at home?" she asked.

"Just a minute, Jeri," he said.

"Hi, dear," Katherine said a moment later. "How is everything going?"

"Just fine, I guess," Jeri said, overcome with emotions that made her choke up.

"You don't sound fine, Jeri."

"I am," she said as the tears began to trickle down her face. "I'm just a basket case is all."

Her mother very patiently asked, "What is the matter, Jeri?"

"Nothing, really," Jeri assured her with a broken voice. "I just want you and Dad to know how much I love you. I was rude the other night when I called. I'm sorry."

"No, I'm sorry, dear," Katherine said. "Your father and I had no right to question your decision to marry Warren."

"Mom, that's what I'm calling you about. I need to thank you for what you said. It made me think and it made me pray. I'm breaking off the engagement."

"Oh, Jeri!" her mother exclaimed. "Are you sure?"

"Yes, I'm sure. The ring didn't fit and neither did the idea of marrying a man I like and respect and care for, but don't love."

"Does he know?"

"Not yet. He didn't call tonight. I'll tell him when he does."

Sunday afternoon, Jeri was home, reading her lesson for next week's primary class, when the doorbell rang. She hadn't heard from Warren, and for the briefest moment wondered if she was getting a surprise visit.

She was, but not from him. Rusty's family were all huddled eagerly at the door as she peeked out. She swung it wide and welcomed them in. "What brings you to Sacramento?" she asked after they were all in and seated.

"You don't know?" Mindy asked with a wide smile.

"I guess I don't."

"Well, we are going to pick Rusty up at the prison tomorrow. He's both getting out of prison and off parole," she announced proudly.

"Oh, my," Jeri muttered as she thought she might faint. "I had no idea."

"I guess you two haven't been in touch?" Patrick said.

"No, not at all," she said. "Well, once actually; he wrote me a letter. He needed some help with an accounting class he was taking. An associate of mine, the man who now handles the prison account, met him there and helped him. That's all there was to it. Bob told me he was doing really well and looking great."

Patrick looked quizzically at Jeri, "So you had nothing to do with . . ." he stopped.

"With what?" she asked.

"Well, he has made some rather dramatic changes these past few months. We thought maybe you might have influenced him."

"What kind of changes?" Jeri asked as she felt a flutter in her heart that she was quite helpless to stop.

"Well, I don't know. If he didn't tell you, maybe we shouldn't," Mindy said. Patrick nodded in agreement. "So, how is Warren?" she asked.

"I haven't talked to him for a few days," Jeri said. "He's a law clerk this summer, doing a kind of an internship at a firm in Provo. He says he really likes it."

"Good," Patrick said. "When will he get his degree?"

"He has a year left," she said. Then impulsively, she walked into the kitchen and retrieved Warren's ring from the cupboard where she had put it for safekeeping until she could return it to him.

When she reentered the living room they were all watching her with puzzled expressions on their faces. She held it up. "He gave me this the other day."

There were gasps all around. "Why aren't you wearing it, doesn't it fit?" Rusty's sister, Sandy asked.

"Not quite. It's a little loose. And that's not all. It's not right for me."

"You don't like it?" Rusty's little brother said in awe. "That's a big diamond."

"Oh, the ring's okay, it's just that, well, Warren's not right for me. I'm sending it back to him."

More gasps.

"He's never been right for me. I was fooling myself. I just hope he finds someone who will make him happy."

"Like Kate?" Sandy asked with a grin.

"Yes, like Kate," Jeri agreed in surprise. "But why do you ask that?"

"It was kind of obvious," Sandy said. "Didn't you ever see the way she looked at him?"

"Well, yes, I knew she had feelings for . . ."

"And I'm not so sure he doesn't have feelings for her, too," Sandy broke in. "I could never quite figure out why he was always chasing you but giving her the looks he was. It was kind of strange," she said with a grin.

"Really," Jeri said weakly.

"Yea, really," Sandy quipped. "And if I were Kate, I'd do something about it. Warren's a cute guy, I think."

Jeri just smiled. He was that, but he was not for her. She visited with Rusty's family for the rest of the afternoon and invited them to dinner on the condition that they help her fix it. She felt so relaxed around them, not like last time when Warren was still in the picture. They had a great evening, but when the Egans finally left to go to their hotel, they had not offered to tell her whatever it was about Rusty that they had thought she might already know.

She almost wished she could be with them when they met him at the gates of the prison Monday morning, instead of sitting there in the office with her mind only half on her work. But that would not be right. She had done her part. She had found him; she had reunited him with his family. Now she needed to stay out of the picture.

Oh, how that thought hurt.

***

The sun was so bright that Rusty squinted as he walked into the daylight through the front doors of the prison. It was different this time from the last release. No one from the bank escorted him. No job was waiting, nor an apartment. All he had was a few dollars in his pocket and his freedom. He felt like a new man, and indeed he was. From this point on he would start a new life. He would be an accountant after he got more schooling. He would join the Church and do whatever was asked of him. And he would really get to know his family. He was determined to find a way to get to Arizona if he had to hitchhike. He had so much to talk to them about.

He approached the front gate. The guard there swung it wide for his departure. The sun was still in his eyes and he couldn't see very well, but he was sure someone was waiting a short distance beyond the gate. He looked behind him. Was there another man being released today? But other than the officer who was escorting him and the guard that opened the gate, there was no one around.

Rusty was nearly to the open gate before he realized who was on the other side. His heart swelled and he choked back some tears and ran up the walk, through the gate, and into the waiting arms of his family.

Rusty—stolen away, hated, abused, kicked around, looked down upon—found love in those arms that surrounded him. He found the love of a family to which he really did belong, and in their eyes he now recognized a light that had been a mystery before. They had in their eyes the light of the gospel of Jesus Christ. Soon, he too would have that light.

***

Warren called that night. Jeri had dreaded what she had to tell him, and as they talked, she put it off. She didn't love him in the truly romantic sense, but she did love him . . . like a brother. The same way she had always loved Rusty.

Was that true? The flutter of her heart when she thought of Rusty threw a question mark in that direction.

Anyway, Rusty aside, Warren was a good friend and she was about to break his heart again. She almost hated herself for it, but she had it to do. They talked for a few minutes about his work and hers, and his family and hers, and the weather in Provo and in Sacramento. It dawned on her that something was not ringing true here. He had not once mentioned the wedding. That was not like Warren. He seemed to be hedging as much as she was.

Puzzled, she finally said, "Warren, is there something wrong, something you want to talk about?"

For a moment he said nothing, and she could hear him breathing heavily on the line. Finally, he said, "Jeri, I'm so sorry. I've made a horrible mistake, and it is going to hurt you terribly. I hope somehow, sometime, you can forgive me."

She was alarmed. What had he done that would require her forgiveness? "Warren, talk to me," she said firmly. "What is it that you have done?" Though she spoke firmly, she surely didn't feel firm—she was scared. Something terrible had happened.

"I don't know how to say this," he began.

"Just say it, Warren. Please," she begged.

"I don't think it's such a good idea for us to get married," he blurted.

"What!" she exclaimed as first shock and then unbelievable relief washed over her.

"I'm sorry. I knew it would hurt. It's all my fault," he stammered. "I don't know what I've been thinking."

"Warren Tharp, you listen to me now. It's all right, but why? What made you change your mind? Is there someone else?" she asked.

"I don't know," he said. "It's just that I keep finding myself thinking about this other girl, and, well, I don't even know if she knows I exist, but I think the feelings I had for you sort of transferred themselves to her and I didn't even know it. Oh, I'm so confused," he admitted. "I don't know what I'm doing, I just know that you and I . . ."

"Are not meant for each other," she interrupted.

"Yes, how did you know?" he asked.

"I've known it all along, Warren. Yesterday I took off the ring you gave me. I was going to tell you—I just didn't know how."

"Oh, Jeri, are you okay with this? I really do like you a lot. I really thought I loved you. I never meant to hurt you."

Jeri began to laugh. "Listen to yourself, Warren. You sound just like me. I like you, too. Now get off this phone and go find Kate. She needs you."

"Kate!" Warren exclaimed. "How did you know?"

"It's only obvious," she said with a laugh as she recalled Rusty's little sister's words. "She needs you, Warren. She is the one for you. Go to her."

"Really, Jeri?" the young law student asked in amazement. "She likes me?"

"Warren, take my word for it, she more than likes you. A lot more. Now go. I'll send the ring," she said with a chuckle. It was like a hundred pounds had been lifted from her shoulders. She was free. As free as . . .

Rusty!

"How is Rusty?" Warren asked.

"I don't know; I haven't seen him since the day they put him back in jail." She knew more, but she didn't think it mattered to Warren.

"I can't believe it," he said.

"I was true to you, Warren. Now you go be true to Kate. I mean it—go."

"Will you be okay?" he insisted.

"I'll be fine. I'll be just fine. Now good-bye," she said. Then a thought occurred to her. "Wait, one more thing, Warren. Trade the ring in. Give Kate a different one."

"If she'll have one at all, I will," he agreed.

"Oh, she'll have it all right. You two were meant for each other."

After hanging up, Jeri literally danced around the apartment. She felt so free, so unshackled, that it reminded her a little of that early morning in the old green house when two men she'd never met and would never see again, cut her free. And that reminded her of Rusty again. Why was it that everything reminded her of Rusty?

She stopped her dancing and squealing. Suddenly she was very sober. She had her standards, and she would never, ever depart from them, but would it hurt so much to see the little boy turned handsome man who had been in her thoughts every day for seventeen long years? Almost eighteen now.

Or would he even want to see her? She had cut off all contact with him. He had tried once to get her to come see him, but she had taken care of that. He probably did not want to ever see her again. So much for the euphoria she had experienced for the last few minutes. Surely, though, as a brother, as a twin . . .

***

"Do you think she'd be angry if I went by her house?" Rusty asked his mother. "If it were not for her, I wouldn't be here with you guys. I'd probably be dead or worse. She is the best friend I ever had. Would she see me as a brother, as her twin?"

"I'm sure she would," Mindy said with a subtle smile.

"You're sure she's not married or anything," he said.

"I'm sure. Katherine Satch and I have stayed in touch over the years. Believe me, if Jeri was married to that Warren guy or even engaged to him or anyone else, I'd know it."

"Okay, Mom," he said, relishing the use of a word he had been deprived of most of his life. "I'll maybe drop in on her, but not until you guys go back. As hard as it was for Dad to get a few days off from work, I don't want the time to be wasted. I want to spend every minute I can with my family. Then I'll see what I can do about a job and a place to live, that kind of thing."

"You are always welcome to come to Flagstaff. We have a big house," Patrick told him.

"Maybe sometime. Right now, though, I think I'll just stay here. I'm pretty sure Pink will give me a job."

"And Jeri?" his mother quizzed.

Rusty grinned. "Yeah, I promise, I'll go see her soon. So quit worrying about it."

***

Rusty had his first meeting with the missionaries that week at Brother Gray's home. His family was still there, and he was amazed at how much they knew about the gospel. Even Ryan, as young as he was, had a lot of knowledge. Rusty could see that he had some catching up to do, and he was eager to do it.

As they returned to the hotel that evening, Patrick said to Rusty, "I am amazed at what you have learned about the gospel in the few weeks you've been studying."

He smiled. "I had a lot of time on my hands, Dad."

"Let us know when you are going to be baptized," Patrick said. "We'll be here."

"You don't have to go to all that trouble," Rusty protested.

"Son, we were deprived of you for over seventeen years. No amount of time could possibly fill that void. We'll be here."

"In that case," Rusty said with a grin, "maybe you could baptize me."

***

It was a long week for Jeri. She had hoped that she would hear from Rusty's family after they met him Monday. But there had not been a word. She was disappointed, but she understood. They were certain to be having a great time getting to know Rusty again. She was happy for them. Then she had a thought that made her stomach knot up.

What if he had gone back to Arizona with them?

And why shouldn't he? He was a free man, not even a parole agent to report to. The more she thought about it on Saturday morning, the more she figured he had done just that. She bathed in the sun for thirty minutes just before noon, then hopped in the shower. She could not get Rusty off her mind. She thought about trying to find the Egans, if they were still in Sacramento, but she realized that would be difficult. She didn't even know where they were staying. And Rusty didn't have a home or a job.

Finally, as she dressed and brushed her long, dark hair, she decided that she should just let the whole thing drop. She had found him, he had found his family, and now, if he wanted to see her, even as his sister, she guessed he would find her.

Jeri had brushed her hair until it was shining. She began to apply a little makeup (she didn't use much) when the phone rang. She dropped her things, rinsed her hands, and hurried for the phone.

"Jeri, it's Kate. You won't believe what's happened."

This was the first she had heard from Kate since her talk with Warren on Monday night. "I might. Try me."

"Warren says you guys broke up."

"Mutual agreement," Jeri said.

"I'm sorry."

Jeri chuckled. "No you're not, Kate, and neither am I. Has he asked you out yet?"

"He's coming to pick me up in an hour. I just had to tell you before he got here. He called me a little while ago."

"Kate, I'm glad," Jeri said in such a way that Kate could not possibly doubt her. "Now you be good to Warren. He's a great guy. He'll make *somebody* a great husband someday."

"I hope," Kate said.

"He will. And it better be you or I will be mighty upset."

The doorbell rang. "Oh, oh, somebody's at the door. Call me tomorrow. Tell me how it went."

Kate promised, and then said, "Thank you, Jeri. You're the best."

"I didn't do anything."

"I think you did. Thanks."

Jeri hung up and walked to the door. The bell rang again before she got there. She checked the peephole—a girl couldn't be too careful these days. You never knew who might be standing on the far side of that door.

Jeri squealed. An ex-con was standing out there. The most beautiful ex-con she had ever seen. She opened the door and swung it wide. "Rusty!" she cried, as she impulsively threw herself into his arms.

"That was not quite the greeting I had expected," he said after a breathless embrace and a lingering kiss.

She led him in and closed the door. "It was not what I expected to do, Rusty. I'm sorry, I wasn't expecting to see you, but I'm so glad you came."

"No gladder than me," he quipped.

They stood facing one another, their eyes probing each other. "You've changed, Rusty," she said. "I mean you've really changed."

"In what way?" he asked.

"I don't know, but there's a glow about you. I can't explain it."

"I'm going to be a Mormon," he said with a twinkle in his eye.

"No!" she exclaimed. She had a terrible thought and voiced it. "Not for me, Rusty."

"No, for me first. Then if you approve, for you, and definitely for my family and for God."

Rusty told her of his conversion. "It was a miracle, sort of like the ones you told me about."

It truly was a miracle.

As was the love that blossomed over the weeks that followed.

"I think I always loved you," she told Rusty the night of his baptism.

He smiled and tightened his embrace. "I'm glad, or you might never have rescued me from myself," he said. "You know, that day you walked into the weight room in the prison, I fell in love with you. Yes, I thought I remembered you from somewhere, but even though I knew we were from different worlds and it could never be, I fell hopelessly in love. Chum must have known it, even though I didn't realize it until much later. But it's true."

Jeri smiled. "I think I've always loved you. I tried not to, but I just couldn't help it."

"I'm glad," he said as he leaned close for another kiss.

"Did you see your mother's face when your father lifted you from the water tonight?" she asked a few minutes later.

He smiled. "There was a glow. But hers was not the only face I could see. Yours had a glow even brighter. How thankful I am for you and your unbroken promise and your faith. You found me, Jeri, and I found a love that will endure forever."

"As have I," she agreed. "As have I."

EPILOGUE

Six Years Later

The smell of smoke billowed from the old blue car as it came slowly up the street. A little boy in blue shorts and a yellow shirt was playing on the lawn. His name was Rusty, but his parents called him RJ for Rusty Junior. The car slowed down and Jeri screamed at the top of her lungs, "RJ, run. That's Uncle Bill! Don't let him get you!"

But the bearded man in greasy pants and a ragged shirt snatched the little boy and dragged him screaming into the car. "Rusty! Rusty! Uncle Bill took RJ!" Jeri screamed. "We've got to find him!"

A strong but gentle hand gently shook her. "Jeri, it's okay. You're having another nightmare. RJ is safe in bed."

Jeri sat up, tears streaming down her face, and fell into the strong arms of the man she loved. "Oh, Rusty. I'm sorry. It was so real!"

"It's okay, honey. It'll be all right. Do you want to see him?" Rusty asked gently.

"Please, I know I was dreaming, but I'll be fine if I can just see him."

Together, Rusty and Jeri walked down the hallway and into RJ's bedroom. Jeri leaned over the bed and smiled at the small form of her son as he lay peacefully sleeping. The light from the doorway touched his forehead and illuminated his sandy hair. She leaned down and kissed his little face. "I love you, RJ," she whispered.

The little boy stirred. "I love you, Mommy," he said.

She tucked him in and took Rusty's hand as they returned to their bedroom. Back in bed, she rolled into Rusty's arms. "I am so afraid," she said softly.

"Uncle Bill died in prison. I confirmed that a week ago," Rusty reminded her. "He will never harm our son. He's safe. We'll keep him safe," he soothed.

Jeri rocked slowly back and forth in the strong arms of her husband. Her head was snuggled tightly to his chest. "I love you, Jeri," he whispered.

"I love you, Rusty."

She fell asleep in his arms and he laid her gently back on her pillow, kissed her forehead, and stretched out on the bed. Rusty Egan considered himself the luckiest man in the world.

About the Author

Clair M. Poulson spent many years in his native Duchesne County as a highway patrolman and deputy sheriff. He completed his law-enforcement career with eight years as Duchesne County Sheriff. During that time, he served on numerous boards and committees, including President of the Utah Sheriff's Association, and member of a national advisory board to the FBI.

For the past ten years, Clair has served as a Justice Court Judge in Duchesne County, and currently represents the Justice Court judges of the state as a member of Utah's Judicial Council.

Clair also does a little farming, his main interest being horses. Both Clair and his wife currently help their oldest son run the grocery store in Duchesne.

Clair has always been an avid reader, but his interest in creating fiction began many years ago when he would tell bedtime stories to his small children. They would beg for just one more "make up story" before going to sleep. *I'll Find You* is Clair's sixth published novel.

Service in the Church had always been a priority for Clair. He has served in a variety of stake and ward callings. He and his wife, Ruth, an accomplished piano teacher, are the parents of five children, and they have six grandchildren.